Marcia Muller pioneered the contemporary female private investigator novel, with the first Sharon McCone mystery, *Edwin of the Iron Shoes*, in 1977. The Sharon McCone private eye series has since gained huge critical acclaim, an enormous readership, and dozens of imitators.

Marcia Muller lives in northern California, where she is working on further Sharon McCone novels.

D1048527

Other Marcia Muller titles from The Women's Press:

MARCIA MULLER

A SHARON McCONE MYSTERY

THE BROKEN PROMISE land

Published in Great Britain by The Women's Press Ltd, 1996
A member of the Namara Group
34 Great Sutton Street, London EC1V 0DX

First published in the United States of America by Warner
Books, Inc, 1996

Copyright © Marcia Muller 1996

The right of Marcia Muller to be identified as the author of
this work has been asserted by her in accordance with the
Copyright, Designs and Patents Act 1988.

British Library Cataloguing-in-Publication Data
A catalogue record for this book is available from the British
Library

This book is sold subject to the condition that it shall not, by
way of trade or otherwise, be lent, re-sold, hired out, or
otherwise circulated without the Publisher's prior consent in
any form of binding or cover other than that in which it is
published and without a similar condition including this
condition being imposed on the subsequent purchaser.

ISBN 0 7043 4504 8

Printed and bound in Great Britain by
BPC Paperbacks Ltd

For Marilyn Wallace
with thanks for a wonderful piece of advice

Thanks also to:

Joe Bradley, Bertelsmann Music Group, for his insights into the recording industry

Mary DeYoe, Winterland Productions, for merchandising lore and South Beach companionship

Jan Grape, for use of Jenny Gordon's name and her own persona

Linda Toole, for use of her name, and for her friendship for Sharon McCone

And to Bill, for many reasons, including
for giving me one of the best lines in the book

In the broken promise land
They tell you you're in big demand
But come the brutal light of day
The dreams you have just slip away

They lure you with their talk of fame
They swear you're sure to make a name
The lies you're living take their toll
And in the end they own your soul

In the broken promise land
They make you jump at their command
They use you up, throw you away
And soon your hopes are yesterday

From "The Broken Promise Land" by Ricky Savage

PART ONE

•

July 21–23, 1995

Billboard, June 3, 1995:

Los Angeles—Country recording artist Ricky Savage, attorney Ethan Amory, manager Kurt Girdwood, and former Arista VP of sales and marketing Wil Willis announced this week that they are forming a new label, Zenith Records, with headquarters in Los Angeles and recording facilities at Little Savages Studio in Saguaro Junction, Arizona.

Zenith has received financial backing from Time Warner and will be distributed by WEA.

At a press conference, Savage, whose contract with Transamerica Records was fulfilled upon delivery of his forthcoming *Midnight Train to Nowhere* album, stated that signings with other artists will commence momentarily. He declined to name which acts are being considered.

Savage also stated that Zenith will join in Transamerica's promotional efforts for the new album by organizing a 25-city nationwide tour three weeks in advance of its August 16 debut. Transamerica will release a single of the title song to radio to coincide with the tour kickoff.

Record industry reaction to the news that country star **Ricky Savage** is forming his own label in partnership with his manager, **Kurt Girdwood**, his music attorney, **Ethan Amory**, and former Arista VP **Wil Willis** is mixed at best. Several acts, including **Blue Arkansas**, who will open for Savage on this summer's *Midnight Train to Nowhere* tour, have indicated a willingness to enter into negotiations with Zenith.

Freelance publicist **Andrea Fallaci**, whom Savage fired early this year, commented, "I wish I had a dollar for every artist who's become enamored of his press, gone off to form his own label, and completely disappeared." Rival country star **Crompton Culver** was less restrained: "Ricky must have his head up his butt."

When asked his reaction to losing one of his foremost artists, Transamerica CEO **Sy Ziff** responded, "Ricky Savage, a *loss*? Give me a break! I've seen dozens like him come and go. If there was any way to deliver product without them, I'd eliminate them all." **John Geller**, VP of marketing at the label, told this column that the news was "not necessarily negative. Frankly, Savage's career has peaked to the point where he'd be more good to us dead than alive. A dead superstar is a hell of a lot more marketable than a live one on the way down."

Why such vehement response to a not-unheard-of business decision? Transamerica has poured millions into Savage's career and was hoping to enrich an anemic cash flow with the proceeds from his future releases. The label's financial position is so poor, in fact, that it was unable to finance the singer's summer promotional tour, and his defection could very well sound the death knell for this weakest of industry independents. Also, Savage has never ingratiated himself with the establishment in L.A., New York, or Nashville. He's not a game player, guards his family's privacy, and listens to a drummer that few artists are able to hear—which may explain the innovative quality and wide appeal of his music, which often crosses from the Country to the Pop charts . . .

June 12, 1995:

Whatever happened to my song?

June 19, 1995:

Whatever *happened* to my song?

June 26, 1995:

WHATEVER HAPPENED TO MY SONG???

July 5, 1995:

W H
H A
A P
T P
E E
V N
E E
R D
    TO MY SONG?

July 10, 1995:

WHATEVER

HAPPENED

TO

MY

SONG?

July 17, 1995:

WHATEVER HAPPENED TO MY SONG!!

One

The six notes that were spread out on my desk next to last month's *Billboard* article and the gossip-column item radiated a strange and threatening quality. I studied them longer than was necessary, trying not to betray my alarm. But even if I managed a calm, professional appearance, I wouldn't fool my client: He was my sister Charlene's husband, Ricky Savage, and had been able to see through my pretenses since he first laid eyes on me some eighteen years before.

Besides, the notes were good cause for alarm. They'd been sent to Ricky at his unlisted home address, one a week since the *Billboard* piece appeared. The first was neatly written and centered on a sheet of plain bond paper, but with each subsequent mailing the quality of the penmanship and coherence of presentation deteriorated, as though the writer's personality were disintegrating. Scanning them was like watching a normal person ask a simple question and, after receiving no reply, repeat it over and over while descending into madness.

"Which is probably what's going on here," I said.

"What?"

With difficulty I took my eyes off the notes and looked up at my brother-in-law's handsome face. Frown lines had gathered between his thick dark eyebrows.

"Just thinking aloud."

"Worrying aloud is more like it."

"Look, I'm not all that concerned. They're probably the work of a harmless crank, but they should be checked out."

"Uh-huh."

"What's that supposed to mean?"

"You're doing that thing with the corners of your mouth."

"What thing?"

"The thing you always do when you're worried or upset—or scared."

"I am *not* scared."

He smiled—the crooked, almost pained smile that was a Ricky Savage trademark and only one of his many endearing traits. "Okay, maybe I'm projecting my own feelings onto you. Because I *am* scared. More scared than I've been in a long time. Not so much for me as for your sister and the kids. What if this weirdo goes after one of them?" He spread his hands, smile fragmenting into anxiety and frustration.

At thirty-six Ricky radiated that indefinable star quality and looked as prosperous as anyone I knew. But his admission that he was scared brought vividly to mind the terrified, scruffy eighteen year old who had come calling to tell my parents that he'd knocked up my little sister Charlene on their first date and wanted to marry her.

To ease our mutual tension, I indulged in a long-standing private joke. "You've cleaned up nice, Brother Ricky."

9

At first he looked startled, then said, "So've you, Sister Sharon," and motioned around my new office at the end of Pier 24½.

"Thanks." McCone Investigations and Altman & Zahn, Attorneys-at-law, had occupied the upstairs suite on the north side of the pier for only three weeks; in spite of some obvious flaws, I was entranced by the new location.

"Okay," I said, calm enough now to turn a hard eye on the matter at hand, "you say these notes started arriving at the house the week after the *Billboard* and 'StarWatch' items appeared?"

"A little more than a week, in the case of *Billboard*. And every week after that, except for July third, when it was two days late because of the holiday."

"Then it's probably no coincidence. Did you save the envelopes?"

"No. They were postmarked L.A., though."

"Zip code?"

He thought. "Can't remember. Sorry."

"Obviously you've handled the notes a lot."

"Well, yeah. Why?"

"Makes it more difficult for a lab to pick up on anything useful, like fingerprints. I'll go ahead and have them examined anyway. Why didn't you bring them to me sooner?"

"I wasn't all that concerned at first. In my position you get a lot of strange mail."

"But not at your house; nobody's supposed to know your address."

"Right. I guess my mental alarm should've gone off sooner, but . . . The first one—I shrugged it off, tossed it in a drawer in my office where I keep stuff I plan to look at later. The next I showed to your sister, and she said she didn't think it was anything to worry about. The others . . . I kept hoping the whole thing would go away. But it didn't, and it sounds like whoever's sending them wants a response from me and is more and more upset because they're not getting one. Trouble is, I can't figure out what the question means."

"'Whatever happened to my song?' That doesn't signify?"

"Seems I recall a song with similar lyrics, but I haven't been able to place it."

"Well, it's worth checking into." I made a note on a legal pad. "Now, what about possible senders? You must've given some thought to this. Could it be somebody at Transamerica who's seriously angry with you for leaving?"

"Doesn't fit their corporate image."

"What about another artist or songwriter who's unhappy with the way you've interpreted his or her work?"

"No. I never cover other people's material; all my songs're my own."

"Perhaps somebody's accusing you of plagiarism?"

"Doubtful. The first thing anybody does when they suspect plagiarism is contact their attorney, and nobody's attorney has contacted mine. Besides, people're up-front about things like that; they badmouth you to the media or they file suit. These notes, they're sly and devious—and strange." He glanced at where they lay on my desk and shook his head.

My eyes were drawn to them, too. I gripped the arms of my chair, picturing the five Savage children who still lived at home. I thought of the isolated location of the new house the family had just moved into in the San Diego County hills; the surrounding twenty wooded acres would provide ample cover for someone intent on harming them.

When I looked up, Ricky was watching me closely.

11

Fear had sharpened his features and put a curious sheen on his hazel eyes. Quickly I said, "I'll get right on this, but in the meantime we've got to take steps to insure your safety, as well as Charlene's and the kids'. I don't like the fact that the writer knows where you live."

"We've got security gates, we've got motion sensors, the whole property is wired with a state-of-the-art system. Plus we've got what sometimes seems like half the population working for us. How's anybody going to get past that many people?"

"Did it ever occur to you that the notes might be from one of them?"

"The gardeners? The housekeeper? Come on!" But I could tell I'd given him something else to worry about.

I compounded it. "Besides, what about when you and Charlene are away from home? Or when the kids're on the way to school or at the mall? And then there's the recording studio over in Arizona; it's way out in the middle of nowhere."

"Well, Jesus, what're we all supposed to do! Travel with bodyguards?"

"Actually, I'm surprised you don't employ one for when you're out on the road."

He looked down at the floor. "I tried that for a while, but . . . it didn't work out very well."

"Why not?"

A shrug, still not looking at me. "Cramped my style, I guess."

"How so?"

His lips twitched in annoyance. "I'm a private man, Shar—just read 'StarWatch,' if you don't believe me."

Something there about the bodyguard, and I thought I knew what. Ricky, like many musicians, had been known to play around while out on the road; an indiscreet guard could carry tales that he wouldn't want my

12

sister or the gossip columns to hear. "Well, I wasn't thinking of anything so drastic as round-the-clock armed guards," I said. "Some basic precautions should suffice. What I'd like to do is bring RKI in on this." Renshaw and Kessell International was a corporate security firm in which my lover and best friend, Hy Ripinsky, owned a one-third interest. "I'll ask Hy to handle it personally, if you like."

"God, you must think the situation's pretty dire." He bit his lip and looked toward the window, gaze moving along the silvery span of the San Francisco–Oakland Bay Bridge to where it disappeared among the trees on Treasure Island.

I pushed away from the desk and swiveled slightly. Through the tall arching window I could see a sizeable stretch of water; in the distance the East Bay hills shimmered under July heat haze. Around me tan walls rose to the pier's sloping roofline, broken at the top by multipaned windows that admitted soft northerly light. The furniture I'd brought from my old office at the now-defunct All Souls Legal Cooperative went well with the wall-to-wall Berber carpet. About the only discordant note was a ratty old armchair I'd rescued from the converted closet under the stairs that had been my first working space at the co-op. It sat beneath a potted schefflera by the window—my thinking chair, I called it. Sentimentality had not prevented me from covering its ugly chintz and bleeding stuffing with a hand-woven beige-and-brown throw.

Had it not been for two drawbacks, the eight-room suite at a prime location on the Embarcadero would have been obscenely and prohibitively expensive. But Pier 24½ was right next to the SFFD fireboat station; when the sirens went off they were loud enough to wake the dead. And the span of the bridge hung directly overhead; a cacophony of traffic sounds played continuously above us. In the past three weeks, however, I'd learned that you can get used to anything if the price is right.

I glanced back at Ricky; he was slumped in my visitor's chair, his gaze still on Treasure Island, his thoughts possibly light years away. He barely resembled the down-at-the-heels man I'd known in the early days, when he'd been a backup musician for a seemingly endless series of dreadful bands. During the past few years he'd lost a fair amount of weight, although his shoulders still bulked powerfully under his tan suit jacket. I suspected he'd begun dyeing his thick chestnut hair, but it looked so natural that I couldn't tell for sure. Dye job or not, Ricky Savage was both the image of success and the genuine article, with a minimum performance fee of two hundred thousand dollars, two Grammys, numerous other awards, and four platinum albums to his credit.

But more than Ricky's appearance and tax bracket had changed: At dinner the previous evening, his son Mick, Hy, and I had all noticed an uncharacteristic lack of animation on his part. When he spoke of his industry, his words were larded with cynicism and bitterness; his reactions were detached, as if there were a glass wall between him and the world; and, if anything, he seemed more than a little sad.

After a moment I said, "Do I have your go-ahead to subcontract with RKI?"

"Do what you think is best."

"Okay, Hy's unavailable this afternoon, but we'll talk when we see him tonight. As far as my investigation goes, I'll start by gathering background on your business associates, friends, employees—or anybody else who's recently touched your life. You'll need to pull together a list of them, plus clear some time over the weekend to discuss them with me." As I spoke I realized the enormity of the task ahead. "What about these people who were quoted in 'StarWatch'? They sound like sharks."

"Goes with the territory." Unless you knew country music, you'd have thought his accent didn't go with the territory; instead of a nasal southern twang, it was pure California. But it was pure country as well; Ricky hailed from Bakersfield, the West Coat's equivalent of Nashville.

"Isn't this libelous?" I jabbed my finger at the quote from the CEO of his former label.

"I'm a public figure; it'd be damned hard to prove libel—if I cared to, which I don't. Name-calling doesn't get to me and, besides, Sy Ziff and John Geller apologized a couple of days later. We all made nice, and things're copacetic."

"Sure they are."

"Sure." He winked.

"Okay, while we're on the subject, let's talk about your partners in the new label. Kurt Girdwood's been your manager for years; you've spoken highly of Ethan Amory; and you tell me that Wil Willis is nothing short of brilliant. Do you trust them?"

"No."

"But you're going into business with them."

"Lying down with dogs is more or less an industry tradition." He hesitated, grimacing. "You know, there's another side to this, one that doesn't concern me nearly as much as what might happen to Charly or the kids, but it's got to be taken into consideration."

"What?"

"The effect this situation could have if it was made public on my upcoming tour for the *Midnight Train to Nowhere* album and the new label."

"How so?"

He got up and began to pace around the office, his booted footfalls soft on the carpet. "The recording industry has changed, Shar—at least on the surface. Was a time when I could stagger onto the stage in my jacket and jeans, hair down to my ass, high as a kite, and nobody saw anything wrong with it. That's out now, and it's probably a good thing, because the dope and booze weren't doing it for me anymore, and my doing so much of them sure wasn't doing anything for my family. No, what's in now is credibility."

"Meaning?"

"Personal integrity. You've gotta be worthy of the respect of your audience and peers. You gotta do good works—benefits for this or that cause, like this thing tonight in Sonoma County. You gotta help along the less fortunate—like my opening act tonight, that piss-ant Maxima." He snorted.

"Maxima? Sounds like a Japanese car."

"Stands for maximizing your potential and all that crap. The band's four guys and a girl singer. You read their press, you'll find out they're about all the correct things: antidrug, antibooze, anticrime, anti–premarital sex. They're vegetarians, pro–animal rights, pro–the environment. And they've got a nice ethnic mix: two blacks, two whites, and a Native American."

"So why're they 'piss-ant'?"

"Because that's only their public image. In private they eat meat, do booze and drugs, and the girl singer hops from one guy's bed to another's. For all I know, they litter, pollute, and torture cats. But because of a good publicity campaign, they got cred."

"Then why do they need you to help them?"

"Because their music sucks and their records don't sell."

"And why *are* you helping them?"

"We've got the same booking agent."

"Oh."

Ricky went on, "Anyway, the industry has gotten so faux honorable that I could puke. The music critics buy into it and parcel out praise accordingly. Of course, the business is still rotten to the core, but who the hell cares about anything that's not strictly surface, right?"

He was pacing in a long, angry stride now—more lively than I'd seen him in quite some time. Get mad, Ricky, I silently urged him. Show me some of that spirit that sustained you during those early years of frustration and rejection.

"So are *you* credible?" I asked.

"I sure as hell am. I'm doing the goddamned benefit for victims' rights tonight, aren't I? Not that I'm against victims' rights, but it happens to be Jamie's fifteenth birthday and I would've liked to be home for it. And I'm letting that piss-ant Maxima open for me, aren't I? Don't I give money to save the whales and the rain forests and the spotted owl? Hell, I don't even know what a spotted owl looks like. Where does it all end, I ask you? Given the new political climate in the country, by this time next year my agent'll be signing me up to do benefit concerts *against* the spotted owl!"

Abruptly he stopped pacing and leaned across the desk toward me. "You know, what really pisses me off about acts like Maxima is that I come by my credibility honestly. Part of the cred thing is that the artist's supposed to suffer. Hell, we're supposed to *bleed*. Everybody knows the story of those years I spent playing clubs in places like Needles and Wichita and Saginaw, staring at the ass end of some broken-down, third-rate singer whose road agent'd hired me at less than union scale. I've never been on the receiving end of help from anybody in the industry. No hit act ever let me open for them; nobody ever put on a benefit concert for my hungry wife and kids. But those years're finally worth something: Ricky Savage has paid his dues, big-time. He's got everybody's respect, hot damn!"

He was on a roll now, translating his anxiety about the current situation into anger. Easier for him to cope with, probably.

I said, "So if word of these notes got out to the media, the speculation about what's behind them might harm your credibility. And if something really nasty surfaced, it could blow the *Midnight Train* tour, damage the new label, and possibly wreck your career."

"Yes to all of that."

I moved back to the desk and leaned my forearms on it, toying with my letter opener for a moment. "Okay, then let me ask you this: *Is* there anything nasty that could come out?"

I'd thought the question might further anger him, but instead he sat down and considered. "There's stuff. There's stuff in everybody's life, and more than the average amount in a performer's. But I can't think of anything that would relate to those notes."

I waited to see if he'd elaborate, but he didn't seem so inclined. "Well," I said, "I'll get started on it right away."

"I'm surprised you're willing to take it on."

"Why on earth wouldn't I?"

"Charly wasn't too sure. To quote my wife, 'Sharon might feel there's a problem with working for a family member. Don't pressure her if she says no; she's got very strict professional ethics.' "

My face must have reflected my astonishment; Ricky smiled wryly.

I asked, "Does this mean I've got . . . what do you call it? Cred?"

"You got more than cred. According to Charly, you're practically in line for sainthood."

Oh, little sister, if only you knew! If only you *knew* . . .

Two

Ricky and I settled contractual details and he gave me a retainer that I felt vaguely guilty for taking from a family member. Only vaguely.

Going out on my own the year before had been scary enough, but I'd still been under the umbrella of All Souls, whose partners would have forgiven a late rental payment for the rooms in their Bernal Heights Victorian that my nephew Mick and I occupied. And Mick was working for free in exchange for room and board at my house—sent north by Charlene and Ricky to remove him from the scene of a dreadful transgression involving the Pacific Palisades Board of Education's computer. The overhead was low, the surroundings congenial, and it seemed I had all the time in the world to start generating a profit.

But this spring All Souls had rounded the last curve of a steadily downward spiral: Infighting among the partners became fierce and disruptive; Hank Zahn, the co-op's founder and my oldest friend, decided to leave and form his own firm with his wife, Anne-Marie Altman.

And I, flying high and reckless on the wings of a quarter-million-dollar reward I'd received for services rendered to the federal government, agreed to set up shop next door to them.

Now I had a full suite of offices and an unforgiving landlord. I had new and costly equipment, as well as a nearly new fuel-guzzling company van. Add to that salaries and Social Security and health-plan contributions for two and a half employees, and you had a situation that bore a frightening resemblance to a house of cards. True, most of the reward was tucked away in various conservative and easily liquidated investments, but I'd been poor for far too many of the years I worked at All Souls to let a dollar flow out without fretting.

"Are we all set for this evening?" I asked Ricky as I countersigned our contract.

"Yeah. Do any of your office gang suspect our surprise?"

"I don't think so. They've been working too hard at weaseling it out of me."

"Mick might. He said something about somebody he wants me to meet tonight. You have any idea who that could be?"

I did: Charlotte Keim, one of the data-search specialists with Hy's firm. And that was something else to fret about. Instead of going into it now, I simply said no.

"Then I guess we'll just have to wait and see." He got up and moved toward the door.

"Ricky, one more thing. Do your partners or any of your other people know about the notes?"

"No."

"Why not?"

"Like I said before, I can't really trust anybody in the industry. I learned that early on."

"So who does know?"

20

"Only you and Charly."

I would have liked to ask what my sister thought about them. She was a passionate and possessive woman; throughout their marriage she and Ricky had done some heavy-duty battling over what might or might not go on in the part of his life from which she, by choice, distanced herself. Surely she'd considered the possibility they might be from a woman.

He must have read the question in my eyes. He said softly, "I don't know what Charly thinks about anything these days, Shar."

"Things aren't good?"

He shrugged, pain twisting his lips and melancholy creeping across his face. "We'll talk about it later, okay? Right now I want to go say hello to my son before I head out." At the door he paused. "By the way, I don't want Mick to know about any of this. Don't use him on the investigation, okay?"

I frowned. His son was my computer jock and invaluable in gathering essential background information. If I couldn't use him I'd have to temporarily hire someone else.

"I know you rely on him," Ricky said, "but this is one time when you're going to have to get along without his help."

I nodded and watched him leave, then slouched in my chair and stared moodily at the single blackish-red rose in the bud vase on my desk—a gift from Hy that arrived without fail every Tuesday morning. This week's offering was a little worse for the wear, due to the unseasonable heat we'd been experiencing.

Ricky's insistence that Mick not be used on the investigation bothered me, but not for the inconvenience it would cause. In fact, now that I thought about it I realized it would be unprofessional to turn this job into a family affair; it was bad enough that I had such a personal stake in it. Probably I should have referred my brother-in-law to another investigator, but I hadn't wanted to entrust the Savage family's problem to someone else. And Ricky, with his mania for privacy, might not have gone along with that, anyway. No, I'd been right to take the case, just as he'd been right to ask that his son be excluded.

But his asking had implications I didn't like. Was there some, as he put it, stuff in his life so nasty that he wasn't owning up to it? Would my investigation open a can of worms that would eat away at the family? It already sounded as though all was not paradise in their brand-new twelve-thousand-square-foot home in the hills above La Jolla. Odd that neither Mick nor I had picked up on that when we were down there the month before for their housewarming party. Or maybe it wasn't so odd; like most offspring, Mick tended to view his parents as immutable, and I, in spite of frequent evidence to the contrary, tended to idealize Charlene's and Ricky's union.

He'd spotted her from the bandstand at a high-school dance where the group he'd formed with four Bakersfield buddies was playing: hot, easy Charlene McCone, with her long blond hair and her ripe figure, a sixteen year old with a reputation for giving a good time. That night, after she ditched her date and waited around while the band packed up, he made love to her in the back of their van. She spent two afternoons with him in his cheap motel room, and when he left San Diego he made no promises. He'd be back, Charlene told me. Ricky was the man she'd marry; no more screwing around for her.

Charlene never even accepted another date.

By the time Ricky returned, she was four months pregnant, radiant, and not the least bit worried. She broke the news to him right away, and the next night he appeared at our house wearing a suit jacket that was inches too short at the wrists and carrying a velvet-covered box containing a cheap wedding band. He was pale, a little drunk, and a whole lot determined. And during what had to have been the most harrowing conversation of his young life, he persuaded my staunchly Catholic mother and my irascible ex-military father that he would be a good husband to their little girl.

He had been, in his own way.

The early years of their marriage were rough. Ricky was on the road a lot, and he and Charlene developed a reproductive pattern that would have made the Pope smile in contentment. After Mick was born, Ricky temporarily gave up on his own band and signed on with a Nashville booking agency; the agency sent him off on an extended tour with a group quite appropriately called The Missing Link. Ma and Pa were concerned. Don't be, Charlene told them, he'd be back. And he was—several months later, when he got her pregnant again. He stayed around working with his own band on demo tapes of his songs until Mick's baby sister Chris was several weeks into two o'clock feedings, and then he hit the road again.

He'd be back, Charlene said serenely.

The pattern repeated until there were six of what the family fondly called the Little Savages. By that point even my devout Catholic mother was urging Charlene to get her tubes tied; my sister had to admit it was an idea whose time had come. And the Savage family's lives continued down a marginal track, involving food stamps and substandard housing and generous contributions from relatives, that we all feared would eventually land them on a sewer grating.

And then Ricky Savage suddenly became a household music name.

He managed it with the help of my father, who over the years had observed his struggle toward his dream and come to respect and admire him. Pa didn't know much about music—aside from the dirty ballads he liked to bellow while puttering in his garage workshop—but as a career enlisted man in the navy, he did know something about courage in the face of adversity. So, on the promise that if Ricky didn't succeed this time he'd give it up and go to work for my brother John's house-painting company, Pa loaned him and his band members the money to cut one last high-quality demo tape of four songs, including a catchy new one called "Cobwebs in the Attic of My Mind." Ricky hand-carried the tape to his booking agent in Nashville; the agent listened to it, called a friend in A & R—Artist and Repertoire—at Transamerica Records, and within months both the resultant album and the single of "Cobwebs" had shot to the top of the country charts.

Ricky's success continued. After a number of hits relying on hooks with an architectural theme—"The House Where Love Once Lived," "You Can Get Me Out of Your Bedroom, But You Can't Get Me Out of Your Heart"—he went on to write songs that the critics found as good as anything currently being written. Emotional and frequently profound, they told stories that touched both the mind and the heart. And, more important for his record label, they won award after award and frequently crossed over to the highly desirable pop charts.

Ricky's sudden transformation to superstar wasn't easy on the Savages. With it came too many possessions, too many changes, too little privacy, too little time. The kids became acquisitive and rebellious; Charlene became insecure and depressed; Ricky became bewildered as to how he could possibly be failing them now. But through it all he and Charlene stuck together, drawing on their reserves of good sense to keep the family from going completely haywire. They weathered one son's learning disability, and Ma and Pa's divorce, the tragic deaths of both of Ricky's parents and two of his band members, the destruction of their Pacific Palisades home by wildfire. Oh, there were moments when it looked as though they wouldn't make it. Such as the time she flew to Las Vegas to surprise him and caught him in bed with the singer from his opening act. Such as the time he came home unexpectedly, tracked her down at a restaurant rendezvous with an old flame, and created such a commotion that the cops were called. But through it all they loved each other, and they loved their kids.

So what had gone wrong that could cause such pain and sadness to cross Ricky's face? What could be so bad that my sister hadn't confided the trouble to me?

I reached for the phone. Stopped myself and shook my head.

Not your business, McCone—yet. Let him tell you about it in his own way and time. And then offer aid and comfort to them both.

I made up a case file, stapled the contract we'd just signed inside, and put it in my active investigations drawer. Then I fished out a work request form for a laboratory I often used. After checking boxes that indicated I wanted the notes examined for fingerprints and paper and ink type, as well as analyzed by a graphologist, I enveloped them, grabbed my purse, and went along the catwalk to see Ted Smalley.

Our offices ran along the side of the pier, fronted by a wide railed catwalk with stairways at either end and crossover catwalks to the offices opposite. Below, on the floor where forklifts used to move cargo, we parked our cars. The opposite tenants were a firm of architects for whom I'd done some investigating and a graphic designer. The lower suites contained a similarly diverse group of people whom I was only now getting to know. It was *trés* urban chic to have one's offices in a renovated pier, and the tenants were all quite house proud: The doors to the various establishments were painted in individual colors and styles, and their signs ranged from elaborate to expensively discreet; plants in barrels and redwood tubs flanked the foot of each stairway, straining to grow in the dim light of the cavernous space.

I loved the pier; I loved the southeastern Embarcadero and the lively South Beach district. I hoped we'd be here for a long, long time.

I passed the spacious room next to my office—workplace of Mick and Rae Kelleher, my former assistant at All Souls and the first of what I hoped would be many operatives. Next to that was a somewhat smaller space, temporarily used for storage. The adjoining conference room, which we shared with Altman & Zahn, contained only the old round oak table and chairs that used to sit by the kitchen window at the co-op. Between it and the law offices was the domain of Ted Smalley, our shared manager, whom we'd easily lured away from the corporate shell that remained after Hank left All Souls.

Ted, a fine-featured dark-haired man with a penetrating gaze and neat goatee, presided over our new realm much as a feudal lord over his fiefdom—ruling with an iron hand and providing much-needed guidance to his subjects, who were foolish enough to think themselves his employers. The fact that he displayed a fondness for fancy ruffled shirts and opulent old-fashioned waistcoats—offset somewhat by the accompanying Levi's— did much to further the image.

I tossed the envelope into his out-box and said, "Will you have that messengered over to Richman Labs, please?"

"Sure." He looked up from the papers on his desk and smiled craftily at me. Stood and ceremoniously held out a small gold box that I, from frequent experience, knew contained a single chocolate truffle from Sweet Sins. "For you," he said.

Eagerly I reached for it. "What's the occasion?"

He withdrew the box. "What's tonight's surprise?"

"A bribe? The nerve of you! Where's your integrity?"

"I was corrupted by lawyers." He motioned toward Altman & Zahn.

"What, they can't wait till six o'clock to find out?"

"You know how lawyers are. They hate secrets. They're nosy and sly. Much like investigators."

Thank God my passion for chocolate had tapered off in recent years! There was a time when I would have parted with my darkest secret for one of those truffles. "This investigator," I said, "is incorruptible."

"Too bad. I'll have to eat it myself."

"Enjoy."

"It'll ruin my diet."

"Tough. See you at six."

"And where'll you be in the meantime?"

"With a former lover, I hope."

By my calculations, Don DelBoccio should by now have arrived home from his daily stint as a disc jockey at KSUN, the city's wildest hard-rock station. I drove my red MG—which after a new paint and body job was nearly a classic car—over to his building on Luck Street in the industrial area near China Basin. When I rang the third-story loft, Don buzzed me in and I took the freight elevator that opened directly into his living space.

As the cage rose, his bare feet appeared at eye level, then his blue-jeaned legs, and finally the rest of him. He smiled through the grille at me, eyes dancing with pleasure—a stocky man with a mop of dark hair and an extravagant, bushy mustache. I repressed a giggle, remembering the comment my older brother John had made the first time he saw Don: "My God, he looks as if he's trying to eat a cat!"

Don pulled the grille open and hugged me. "Why is it that you always appear whenever I'm thinking about you?" he asked.

"Don't know. What were you thinking?"

He motioned me into the loft—one enormous space with a galley kitchen and sleeping alcove, crammed with enough books, audio equipment, musical instruments, and aquariums of tropical fish to amuse even the most easily bored individual for eternity. The loft was larger than the one he'd occupied when we were a couple, but during the year or so he'd lived there, he'd nearly managed to fill it. Of course, a set of drums, a baby grand piano, and a trampoline do take up space.

"Wine?" he offered.

"Kind of early, isn't it? What were you thinking about me?"

"Not so early. Besides, this is my evening."

What the hell. "Okay, thanks. What were you thinking?"

"I'll never tell." He went to the kitchen, poured, and brought me a glass of red.

"Hmmm." I sank onto the pile of pillows that served as his couch. "What's with the trampoline?" It was new since the last time I'd visited.

Don sat beside me. "Guy at the station wanted to get rid of it cheap. He used to bounce on it in the mornings, listening to my show and holding onto a pair of weights. God knows why. Anyway, a couple of months ago he got carried away to Pearl Jam and bounced clear off the thing. Weights went through a plate-glass window, he got cut up, plus he broke his leg."

"No wonder he wanted to get rid of it. I guess now you're bouncing with a pair of weights—"

"No way." He grinned wickedly. "But I am bouncing. You'd be surprised how many women've never done it on a trampoline."

"Lecher."

"Wanna try?"

"If I said yes, you'd go into shock."

"I'm not very shockable. But I know I'll never get that lucky again; I hear this thing you've got going with the guy you met up in Mono County is serious." He toasted me, sipped wine. "So what's your reason for stopping by?"

"A trivia question, actually. You know my brother-in-law, Ricky Savage?"

"Of him, yes. I never did have the pleasure."

"Well, he's in town, and we were talking about song lyrics. There's this line that's been running through both our heads, and we can't place it. With your memory of lyrics, I thought you might."

Don regarded me skeptically over the rim of his wine-glass. I looked down, sipped the excellent red.

After a moment he asked, "What's the line?"

"'Whatever happened to my song.'"

"Mmm."

"What does that mean?"

"Strangely enough, I can place it. But before I tell you where it's from, I want to know why you're lying to me."

"Lying?"

"About this being a trivia question."

"It is."

"It's not. I remember altogether too well the tone you use when you lie. Your voice rises, just a little but enough. Don't ever try to fool someone with perfect pitch, Sharon."

Another person who saw clear through me. "Okay," I said after a moment. "Can you keep this in confidence?"

"You know I can."

I studied his face, remembering the good times and all the times I'd trusted him. And then I told him about the notes, Ricky's new label, and the upcoming tour.

Don listened thoughtfully, turning the stem of his glass between his fingertips. "I agree with you," he said. "Savage has good reason to worry about those notes. Let me play you the song the line's from."

"You have a recording of it?"

"Uh-huh." He went over to a bookshelf full of records, CDs, and tapes, and scanned the top shelf. "Lately I've gotten into collecting folk ballads—early stuff, from the southern hill country. There's a woman from Bakersfield who's been doing some interesting versions." He selected a CD and carried it over to his sound system.

Don's range of interests never ceases to amaze me. In spite of a long career as a DJ for some of the most raucous and raunchy stations in existence, he is a classical pianist, trained at the Eastman School of Music; his tastes encompass everything except rap and heavy metal, and he cheerfully admits that spending a good part of his life taking phone-in requests from boorish and possibly brain-dead teenagers is merely a method of subsidizing his true passions.

He slipped the CD into the player and rejoined me. "The song's titled 'My Mendacious Minstrel.' The singer's Arletta James."

A haunting voice filled the loft, accompanied by a simple guitar melody. The woman's tone was pure and soaring, with an aching clarity that put a shiver on my spine. The words intensified it, heartrending in and of themselves—and all the more so because James made the pain behind them sound real. The ballad told a long story—as old as time and chilling as winter's frost.

A woman, walking in the hills, searching for the sweet berries that grow there in summer's sun. A minstrel, wandering also, his homemade fiddle strapped to his back. A chance meeting in a clearing and a passion that ignites as he plays and sings his tunes. And a promise that he will create a song for her alone.

And it will be like none yet heard, the song he'll sing for me.

More clandestine meetings in the clearing. More summer days as hot as the passion that runs in their veins. But still the minstrel fails to fulfill his promise.

When will he sing my song, I ask, the song he promised me?

An autumn day, and the minstrel fails to appear in the clearing. The woman waits in vain. Day after day she returns, until the snow is on the ground and a new life grows within her, then dies.

Whatever happened to my child, the child he gave to me?

Whatever happened to my song, the song he promised me?

The woman leaves the hills and travels to a town where the mansions of the wealthy stand on a bluff. There she finds her mendacious minstrel with his wife and his children, in his fine home. In despair she returns to the hills and wanders throughout the winter and into the spring. When the buds are on the trees and the jonquils in the grass she searches for the Carolina jessamine.

It twines there in its deadly vines, its blooms more deadly still

The woman prepares a potion and leaves the hills forever. By a ruse she gains a position in the minstrel's household and exacts her revenge.

31

> *The touch of the sweet jessamine fast took them by*
> *surprise*
> *And one by one they all died there, and one by one*
> *they died*

As she drinks the last of the potion, the woman remembers the clearing in the hills, the child she lost, and the lies her minstrel told.

> *Whatever happened to my song, the song he*
> *promised me?*

Three

I scarcely noticed when Don got up to turn the CD player off; my attention was riveted on the ballad's message, and horrifying possibilities tumbled in my mind.

He took advantage of my preoccupation to pour us more wine, then sat down beside me. "So," he said, "what do you think?"

"As usual, my imagination's in overdrive. You say the singer, Arletta James, is from Bakersfield?"

"Yes. Why?"

"Ricky's from there, too."

"Then he probably knows James. The music scene out in the valley's pretty inbred. In fact . . ." He got up and fetched the booklet that was slipped inside the CD's plastic cover. "Yeah," he said after thumbing through it, "she mentions him in her liner notes. 'With special thanks to Ricky Savage.'"

"For what, I wonder? What's their relationship?"

"Ah." Don leaned back on his elbows, smiling. "I know how your mind works. You're thinking he had something going with her, knocked her up, and dumped her. And that she's gone off the rails and plans to kill him and his family."

"Sounds pretty far fetched, doesn't it?"

"I don't know. Is that the kind of thing he'd do?"

"Well, it's what he did to my sister—the knocking-up part, I mean. And I know he hasn't lived like a monk all these years on the road. I asked him earlier if there was anything nasty in his past that might have surfaced, but he wasn't very forthcoming, just said that there was stuff in the life of every performer, but he couldn't think of anything that might've provoked a campaign of harassment."

"Stuff, huh?"

I nodded. "He's going to have to be more specific. And I'm going to have to ask him about Arletta James."

Don frowned. "Shar, even if he did have something going there, even if she did get pregnant, this is the nineteen-nineties. People don't go around the bend over something like that."

"People go around the bend over *anything*. If you don't believe me, take a look at my true-crime collection. Better yet, take a look at my case files." I sipped wine, thinking of the investigation that had earned me the reward from the feds; its subject had been about as far around the proverbial bend as you can get, and for a reason that most people would consider insufficient.

Don said, "I'll take your word for it."

I stared down into the burgundy depths of my glass, looking for answers and finding none. "I guess the idea *is* pretty far fetched."

"Maybe not. You read a lot about stalking cases lately."

"Stalking's generally a male crime, though. And stalkers make themselves known to their victims. They come on nice at first—send flowers, ask for dates, whatever—

then lash out when they're rejected. The notes Ricky's been getting don't have that feel."

"What feel do they have?"

"The sender's obviously undergoing a rapid emotional deterioration. And it's clear the person wants something, but unclear what. There's a plaintive note . . . Oh, hell, that's just the hit I'm getting; you could look at them and come up with something completely different. What matters is that the writer knows where Ricky lives and possibly could get at him, my sister, and their kids." I set down my glass and stood.

"You have to go so soon?"

"Yes. Thanks for your help."

"Any time. Let me know how things work out."

From Don's I drove to the Civic Center and spent an hour at the public library trying unsuccessfully to run down something in the trade journals on Arletta James. On the way out I detoured to the science section and checked a detail that was probably irrelevant to the investigation but interesting to me. Then I headed back to the Embarcadero.

The day was unseasonably warm for July, a month which is usually cold and foggy in the city. I had the top down on the MG, but even the rush of breeze didn't do much to clear the wine haze from my head. Near Pier 32, where the World War II memorial *SS Jeremiah O'Brien* is moored, I pulled over, parked, and hurried along the sidewalk to the squat gray clapboard shack that houses Miranda's Diner.

Miranda's, along with Red's Java House and the Boondocks, is a relic of the days when our piers actually catered to ships and cargo, and the longshoreman was king of the waterfront. All that is gone now, along with the seamen's hotels and taverns, the hiring halls and tattoo parlors; condominium complexes and office buildings rise in their place. The Embarcadero, once crowded with freight-laden semis and rail cars, is now a spacious boulevard with a line of handsome new palm trees down its center. Instead of the old Belt Railway, streetcar tracks run along the median strip; when completed they will transport passengers from South Beach to the Muni Metro under Market Street. Only a few operating piers and the small eateries at the water's edge remain to remind us of what our port used to be, and no one knows how much longer they'll be able to hold out against the forces of change.

A while back a client of mine had a grandiose plan to keep a part of our waterfront in maritime use by turning the old Hunters Point Naval Shipyard into a megaterminal for one of the city's venerable shipping lines. As it turned out, his plan was workable and would have changed the course of San Francisco's history. But tragedy shattered his life, his financial backers withdrew, and in the end he decided he valued preserving what remained to him and those he cared about over preserving the port. It was the right decision, but every now and then I remembered his scheme and thought about what its abandonment had cost us.

I pushed through the door of Miranda's, waving to Carmen Lazzarini, the owner. I had no idea of the big bald man's true first name; he'd gone by Carmen ever since his days as a longshoreman offloading South American banana boats. When anyone asked about the nickname, he'd say, "Carmen Miranda—get it?" and do a little dance, hands up, as if supporting a fruit-laden hat. The few things I did know about him were that he made a dreadful chicken-fried steak, a terrific burger, and that his "java" worked like a shot of adrenaline. Those few things, plus that behind the stained apron and gruff mannerisms beat a good and generous heart.

Carmen surveyed me and reached for a coffee pot; I must have looked as though I badly needed a boost. As I headed toward the counter, I spotted Rae Kelleher in one of the booths by the salt-grimed bayside windows and signaled that I'd sit there. By the time I slipped in opposite her, Carmen was sliding a white ceramic mug in front of me.

"Wake-up time?" Rae asked.

"Yes. How you doing?"

"Fair to middling. I wrapped up those two files you gave me this morning; they're on your desk."

"Thanks. You ready for the surprise?"

"What surprise?"

"Aha! You're trying reverse psychology on me." Rae had been a psych major at Berkeley, and she still harbored certain pet theories about human behavior, in spite of strong evidence that they were rules made to be broken.

"Actually, I don't want you to tell me," she said. "My life holds too few surprises as is." Her voice was flat and her round freckled face held none of its usual cheeriness.

"You have seemed down lately."

"Lately? Try six months. Everything's gone stale on me. I haven't even been taping my diary."

Rae was a fervent reader of what she called "shop-and-fucks," and she often joked about quitting the business and trying her hand at writing one. Toward that end, she faithfully recorded her daily activities, complete with dialog, description, and philosophical asides. Her style struck me as not half bad, but her life was going to have to get a good bit more interesting, and her lifestyle a lot richer, in order to provide fodder for a steamy, semipornographic novel. Fortunately for both her and me, she was smart enough to keep her day job.

I said, "Part of this depression could be Coso Street. It must be getting to you." Since the remaining All Souls partners had reincorporated under their own names and put the big Victorian, where Rae still lived, up for sale, I couldn't bring myself to call it by anything other than its address.

"Yeah, it is. I feel like I'm living in a haunted house." She ran her hand through her auburn curls, then nodded to Carmen, who was hovering nearby, to bring her another Coke. "Everybody's gone, now that Ted's moved in with Neal." Neal Osborn was a used-bookstore owner whom Ted had met while browsing at the International Antiquarian Book Fair last winter; they'd taken a wonderful apartment in an Art Deco building on Telegraph Hill.

"Anyway," she went on, "I wish I could get into that condo I've leased, but the owner won't be out till August first. At night I lie in bed in my attic room and I'm all alone. It's kind of spooky—and depressing."

I remembered how the Victorian's creaks and groans could be eerie—even with other people there. "Then for God's sake, why stay on?"

"I don't have a choice. I can't afford a motel, and I don't want to impose on my friends—"

"You wouldn't be imposing on *this* friend."

"Oh, Shar, I can't do that. Hy's staying with you—"

"Only for a couple more days. He's finished the project he was working on at RKI and wants to get back to his ranch. Besides, we've got a full schedule this weekend, so we won't be around much. After the—" Damn! I'd almost given it away. "After the surprise, you're to go back to Coso Street, pack what you need, and move into my guest room."

"Shar—"

"No, it's settled."

Rae looked relieved, a smile crinkling her upturned nose.

I glanced at my watch. "It's almost time. Why don't you ask for a paper cup for that Coke and we'll head back to the pier."

Most of the office gang and their companions were already gathered on the sidewalk by the great arching mouth of the pier when Rae and I pulled in: Ted and Neal; Anne-Marie and Hank and their foster daughter, Habiba; Jessie Coleman, their legal secretary. I let Rae off to join them, then drove inside and parked the MG. As I got out, Mick came down the stairway from the offices, accompanied by Charlotte Keim.

Mick was big like his father, blond like his mother, and in the past year he'd matured into a handsome guy. Keim was a petite curly-haired brunette whose eyes sparkled saucily, hinting at what was a truly bawdy sense of humor. In spite of my reservations about their seeing each other—she was twenty-five to his eighteen, and he was currently living with another woman—I had to admit they made an attractive couple.

Keim waved and came over to me. "Mick claims he knows what the surprise is, but he won't tell me."

"He just thinks he knows."

My nephew smiled smugly.

"Well, maybe he *does* know," I conceded. "Would you excuse us for a minute, Charlotte?"

"Sure." She started toward the mouth of the pier, then called, "Oh, Sharon—Hy said to tell you he's running late and not to leave without him."

"Thanks." I waited till she was out of earshot, then asked Mick, "Where's Maggie?"

His mouth pulled down sullenly. "Working."

"Look, I'm not upset because you brought Charlotte. I just wondered."

"Well, that's where Maggie is, just like last night—working at the damn nursing home. I asked her to try to get off, but she said no. They're depending on her, and she doesn't want to ask for special consideration."

Maggie Bridges, the woman Mick lived with, was a premed student and tended to approach life very seriously. When he first met her I'd been glad of that quality, hoping she would steady him, but now that his life was more or less under control, I could understand how he might find her single-mindedness stifling.

"Well, just have a good time with Charlotte, then," I said.

"I always do. She's easy to be around; she likes to party and she doesn't make any demands. And she doesn't make me feel guilty for wanting to kick back and enjoy myself now and then. I like her a lot."

"So do I. In fact, I'm hoping to hire her away from RKI one of these days."

"You just might succeed." He glanced toward the front of the pier. "Should we be getting out there?"

I nodded and we walked along, waving good-bye to other tenants who were leaving for the weekend. When we stepped onto the sidewalk a white stretch limo was pulling up to the group assembled there. Joggers and other passersby stared.

Rae said, "A limo! I've always wanted to ride in a limo." Hank said, "I think I know what's going on." Anne-Marie said, "Uh-huh." Nine-year-old Habiba forgot she'd decided she was a grown-up and jumped up and down, while Jessie, Ted, and Neal looked puzzled. And Charlotte, bless her, clapped her hands and shouted, "Hoo *boy*!" in the Texas accent she'd labored years to lose.

Mick smiled smugly at me. "I knew."

"Suspected."

"Knew."

Ricky got out of the limo and started across the side-walk toward us.

Rae exclaimed, "My God, it's Ricky Savage!" and dropped her cup of Coke on her foot.

And I, perpetrator of this moment, grinned at all of them. Sometimes the torture of keeping a secret for two weeks is worth it.

While a red-faced Rae—who endures more than the average amount of spills and stains—mopped up, I made introductions and explained that we'd be attending Ricky's benefit concert in Sonoma County's Two Rock Valley as his guests. He shook hands all around—laughing at Rae's sticky one—urged them to make free with the refreshments in the limo's bar, and waved them on board. After much confusion and changing of places, the driver finally was able to shut the door, but before they pulled away Mick lowered a window and stuck his head out.

"Hey, Dad," he called, "aren't you and Shar coming? I mean, she organized this and you're kind of the main event."

Ricky grinned. "I've got another car on the way. Shar, Hy, and I'll ride up together." Then he regarded his son with mock sternness and added, "Don't do anything I wouldn't."

Mick gave him a thumbs-up sign. Before the opaque glass rose a champagne cork popped, followed by another Texas-accented whoop.

My brother-in-law stared moodily at the limo as it edged into traffic. "How come he's not with the one he brought home last Christmas?" he asked. "As far as I know, he was living with her last week."

"And he still is, but I think they may have run their course."

He grunted. "Isn't this one too old for him?"

"She's twenty-five, but your son, as she puts it, plays older than eighteen."

"Yeah, so did I." He turned to me, eyes troubled. "Why's it ending with Maggie? We all liked her."

"She wants him to settle down, but now that he's figured out who he is and what he wants to do, he's looking for a good time. I don't blame him."

"Neither do I." Ricky's gaze moved from me to the massive support of the Bay Bridge on the other side of the boulevard, then scaled it to the heavy span that hung over our heads. "Shar, I want Mick to have all the good times I missed. When I was his age I'd been on the road with my first band for two years. Never even bothered to finish high school. I was driven—*totally* driven. And then all of a sudden I was a husband and a daddy. Wasn't easy."

"You regret it?"

"Not for an instant. Your sister and those kids are the best people who ever came into my life. They were what kept me going. Compared to the look on Charly's face when I told her I'd signed with Transamerica, everything that's happened since is just icing on a beautiful cake." The words were sincere, but the melancholy that underlay them detracted from their import.

I waited, hoping he'd tell me what had gone wrong between the two of them, but he fell silent, his eyes still on the bridge span.

"Ricky," I said after a moment, "I found out where the line in those notes came from."

"Already? Charly told me you were the best in the business, and now I believe it."

"I just have good contacts, that's all. The words're from

a song titled 'My Mendacious Minstrel,' and the artist's Arletta James"

"Letta? I'll be damned. Of course—those ballads she's been resurrecting."

"You've heard the song, then?"

"Sure."

"You recall the story it tells?"

"Only vaguely."

I filled him in. He paled and compressed his lips, making the same leap of logic—or perhaps illogic—that I had.

"I've got to ask you," I added, "have you ever had a relationship with Arletta James?"

"You mean sexual? Not hardly. Letta's a lesbian, in a long-term relationship. She's not interested in me."

"But you do know her well. She acknowledged you in her liner notes."

"Well, yeah. We went to school together in Bakersfield. She's a nice person and a terrific singer. Incredible voice, one of a kind. And she's finally getting the attention she deserves."

I wasn't willing to let go of the idea that there might be some connection between James and the notes, though. "I'd like to talk with her about the ballad. Do you know where I can reach her?"

"Not offhand, but I can find out from her manager. We're negotiating with him to sign one of his other clients." He took a cellular phone from the inner pocket of his suit coat, unfolded it, and punched out a number. Two minutes later he broke the connection and said to me, "You're in luck. Letta's manager says she'll be recording at TriStar Studios in Sausalito tomorrow."

"Great. I'll contact her there."

"I don't understand what you think she can tell you."

43

"You never know what information people might have till you ask them."

"Jesus, it's good to get away from the office," Hy said as we sank onto the backseat of a second limo. "Today was one of those days." His craggy face was so weary that even his mustache drooped; he ran a hand through his shaggy dark-blond hair and yawned widely. "I'm not cut out for a desk job."

"I hear you." Ricky climbed in after us and sat on the facing seat, shrugging off his suit coat and kicking off his boots. "I spent half the afternoon cooped up in my hotel suite with my partners and a team of lawyers from Winterland Productions. Winterland's doing the T-shirts and other stuff for the *Midnight* tour, and my manager came up with the idea of licensing a bunch of other crap with them."

"What kinds of things?" I asked.

"Sweatshirts, hats, mugs, you name it. Fans'll buy anything, and it's a good way to get a quick infusion of cash—which is always nice when you've got six kids and a household that sucks up money as fast as you can make it."

Ricky was not and never had been the stereotypical naive artist who gets taken by everyone from his record label to his manager. He kept a sharp eye on contractual and financial matters, and when he wasn't able to see to them, Charlene did. Between them they had the acumen of a staff of MBAs. In fact, my sister had recently received a degree in finance from USC.

"So anyway," he went on, "we're in this meeting with Winterland's attorneys, and they're all talking, but I'm kind of distracted and not paying real close attention. And then a word makes me sit up and listen, and I realize that what my asshole lawyer really has in mind is to license Ricky Savage condoms."

"What!" Hy and I exclaimed.

"Yeah, can you believe that? Oh, I know a lot of rock groups allow it—personalized condoms with their likenesses or the name of their new release on them. Told you fans'll buy anything. But my God, all I could think of was how I'd feel if one of my kids got hold of a condom with old dad on it!" Ricky's nostrils flared indignantly.

Hy looked aghast. "That's *awful*."

Preposterous images were dancing through my mind. I fought down a giggle and tried to look properly outraged.

"Awful's the word for it." Ricky nodded. "Of course I said no. Said it in no uncertain terms. And then my lawyer's *arguing* with me. Think of the profits, he says. Profits! All I could think of was my face . . . well, you get the picture."

I said, "I don't know. How's this for a slogan? 'You've heard of rough sex? Now try Savage sex!'"

Hy and Ricky stared at me.

I tried to repress a laugh, but it welled up violently. I clapped my hand over my mouth; what came out was a snort—followed by another.

The two of them exchanged looks.

"Listen," I said to Ricky, "if the kids got hold of those condoms, it'd keep them from doing anything. Can you imagine? You're all hot to trot, and suddenly there's your father's face staring at you . . . Oh, God, I'm sorry!" I snorted again.

"You want a beer?" Ricky asked Hy.

"Yeah, thanks."

Ricky pulled a Beck's from the bar, handed it to him, and took one himself. "I had them stock champagne for her," he said, "but I don't know if she should have any. She's behaving peculiar enough as is."

"Ah, go ahead and give her some. Maybe it'll sedate her."

I indulged in a final snort. "I'll be good, I promise. But what is it with you men? Don't you see the humor in this?"

Ricky popped the cork on a bottle of Korbel. "You wouldn't think it so funny if it was *your* face—" Then he seemed to be entertaining some preposterous mental images of his own.

I glanced at Hy; his mustache was twitching.

Ricky started laughing, so hard that after a few seconds he spilled champagne over his fingers.

I took the glass from him. "I assume you . . . er, deflated the idea?"

"Of course I . . . Oh, shit!" Still laughing, he leaned back and closed his eyes. "Lawyers!" he said. "God help me."

I sipped champagne and watched through the tinted glass as we merged with rush-hour traffic on the Golden Gate Bridge. None of us spoke till we reached the Sausalito exit and then I, reminded of Arletta James, got back to business.

"Ricky, now that we know where the wording of those notes most likely came from, do you agree that the situation is potentially dangerous?"

"Yeah. Yeah, I do."

"Then I think we'd best retain Hy's firm to provide security and give you and the family a crash course in preventative measures." To Hy I explained the problem that had brought Ricky to me. "Can you see your way to handling this personally?"

He hesitated. For two weeks he'd been working out of RKI's San Francisco offices on a special project—one that had made it possible for us to spend a good deal of time together—but he'd wrapped it up today and was anxious to get back to his ranch in the high-desert country near Tufa Lake. He planned to fly there Sunday night, spend a few weeks, then meet me at our shared cottage on the Mendocino coast—the place where we were most relaxed and at our best with each other.

I waited, braced for a refusal. Hy was fond of my large and eccentric clan, but he had no family of his own and liked the freedom that a lack of blood or marriage ties afforded. I wouldn't have blamed him for declining; security work was a far cry from the high-risk missions he enjoyed. But at the same time I needed to have him behind me on my own high-risk case.

He seemed to sense that, because he said, "Sure. I'll contact our best domestic security man, have him at the house in San Diego in . . ." He checked his watch. "In less than two hours. Fortunately, he works out of our world headquarters in La Jolla, so he's close by."

Ricky started to protest.

"No," I told him, "let Hy handle it his way."

Hy took another beer from the bar and leaned forward, rolling the bottle between his long fingers. "Rick, every minute that you delay in getting my people there is a potential threat to your family. You've got to place their safety in our hands. My man'll arrive tonight, assess the situation, set some ground rules. Tomorrow morning he'll bring in any additional people he thinks he needs, and I'll fly down and consult with him personally. Then I'll make my recommendations."

"Such as?"

"We'll probably put on a few guards, work with your family and household employees on routine precautions. We're also going to have to take a look at your patterns of travel—where you have to be and when. Two things concern me: the upcoming tour and the recording studio over in Arizona."

"On the tour, security's provided by the concert venues. And I don't have any plans to record for at least two months."

"We won't worry about Arizona, then. But standard security at the concerts may not be enough." Hy reached behind us for the phone that sat on the rear window ledge. In minutes he'd made his arrangements. Handing the receiver to Ricky, he said, "Call Charlene, let her know what's happening."

Ricky looked dazed, as though by wresting control from his hands we'd shaken the foundations of his day-to-day life. Hy had told me of seeing similar reactions from other RKI clients. As my brother-in-law punched in his home number, I felt better about the situation; RKI's people were the best in the business.

To the public, RKI was simply a firm that specialized in high-level corporate and personal security for people who were particularly vulnerable, usually to terrorists. Hy was a partner, but only loosely affiliated with their normal operations, mainly using the company as a resource for the one-man human-rights crusade he'd launched last year, after harrowing circumstances had forced him to reevaluate and restructure his life. But neither he nor I—who had twice worked with them—was a stranger to RKI's methods, and we knew better than anyone that the glossy public image concealed a darker side.

High risk-taking and semilegal practices were commonplace at the firm. The murky pasts of many of its operatives and all of its partners—including my lover—were open knowledge within the company. The clandestine activities directed from its thirty-some offices throughout the world would have been the envy of the CIA. Within the corporate-security industry rumors about

RKI abounded, but no one had proof of the proportion-ately few but tragic instances in which the risk-taking hadn't paid off. I, on the other hand, had heard enough about them to make me want to keep my distance.

Lately, though, I'd had a sense that the distance was shrinking, as if I stood on the edge of a cliff whose ground was eroding beneath my feet, forcing me to re-peatedly step forward. I'd come to rely on their data-search section for information that I myself couldn't access through legal channels; I'd hired one of their op-eratives for an especially sensitive job and not looked too closely at how he accomplished it. On good days I told myself that I could use them and still maintain my integrity. On bad days I wondered. And in the dark hours of the night, when my misdeeds preyed upon my wakeful mind, I became convinced that I'd already evolved into the kind of investigator I detested. It was during those nights that I wanted to scrap it all and flee with Hy to the cottage on the coast that we'd christened Touchstone. There, I would tell myself, we'd find our-selves again, find peace.

Of course, I knew it wasn't that easy. Nobody can slip the reins of the past and run away.

Ricky's voice interrupted what could have turned into a world-class brooding session. "Hi, Jamie . . . Of course it's really me. Happy birthday, honey . . . You already opened it? . . . Well, you're welcome . . . Listen, hon, is your mother there? . . . Let me talk to her, would you? And you have a good one."

He covered the mouthpiece and said, "Jesus, I almost forgot to call her for her birthday! I never thought I'd for-get one of my kids' birthdays." For a moment he waited, then he sat up straighter, his expression becoming wary and defensive. "Yes, Charly . . . Yes, Shar agrees that we have a problem . . . She did, and she's brought Hy in on it, too. He's got one of his people coming to the house in two hours and—"

My sister was speaking now. The set of Ricky's jaw hardened, and he began to drum his fingertips on his thigh.

I frowned, glanced at Hy. He shrugged.

"Well, Charlene," Ricky said in a flat tone, "you'll just have to cancel and stay home."

She spoke some more; spots of red blossomed on Ricky's high cheekbones and his eyes glittered. I tensed, feeling his pent-up anger.

"I don't care about that, Charlene," he said, enunciating clearly and slowly. "What's more important, our kids' safety or your— Yes, that's absolutely correct . . . Well, will you do that for me, Charlene? Will you just the fuck do that?" Abruptly he broke the connection, slapped the receiver into Hy's hand, and reached for another beer.

I said, "Ricky . . ."

"You want to know what's wrong, Shar? You really want to know?"

"Only if you want to talk about it."

"Why shouldn't I? It'll be out in the open soon enough. What's wrong is that your sister's got somebody else. It's all over between us, she tells me."

I stared at him. Impossible. Except that the look on his face told me it was true. "Charlene, somebody else? Who?"

"Why don't you ask her?" He took a big drink of beer and leaned forward, elbows on his knees, all the anger suddenly bleeding out of him. "Why don't you ask *her*?" he repeated, his voice rough with emotion. "Nothing that's going on with Charly has anything to do with me anymore."

50

four

The Two Rock Valley sprawls between the western limits of the small city of Petaluma and the coastal ridge line. Sheep and dairy cattle graze on softly rounded hills dotted with live oak and sculpted rock formations. Ranch buildings nestle in the hollows, protected by windbreaks of cypress and eucalyptus. Winter rains turn the grass a brilliant green; come spring it is dusted gold with wild mustard. But now, in late July, the fields beyond the three-strand barbed-wire fences were sun scorched, the trees dried to tinder.

By tacit consent, we'd quickly dropped the subject of Ricky's marriage. The rest of the way, he and Hy talked about the fans' waning interest in baseball, our governor's political aspirations, and the new record label. I contributed few comments; I was busy trying to reconcile my image of Charlene and Ricky with their reality, but the concept of my sister with another man simply wouldn't fit the picture. Who was he? Why had she turned to him? And if it came to a divorce, how would the children, ranging from eight years to Mick's eighteen, weather it? How would *I* weather it? I loved Ricky as much as I did my blood brothers; how on earth could I take sides?

Change. Recently there had been too much change in my life. The demise of All Souls, the new offices, a deepening commitment to Hy that still held little of the security of a full commitment. How could I cope with yet another of the constants in my world disappearing?

Finally I decided to put the subject aside for a while and sat quietly, watching hawks perform wheeling ballets on the early-evening thermals and listening to Hy and Ricky's conversation.

"The average country singer's career peaks in five years or less," Ricky was saying in answer to a question from Hy. "I've already got that beat, but I'm not fool enough to think I can go on forever, at least not on this level. Besides, I'm not sure I want to. After a while the performing gets to you. Being on the road so much is a pain in the ass, if you want to know the truth."

"So what you're saying is that your interest in the label is a way to keep your hand in the business without the stress of fighting to stay on top."

"Yeah, as well as maintain my income level when my performance fees drop off. From the beginning I looked for ways to do that."

"So what else did you do—make investments?"

"In a way. Retaining all publishing rights to your songs is like having an annuity, so as soon as I could, I set up my own music-publishing company. Lured a top pro in that field to run it by offering a percentage and gambled what extra cash I had on acquiring the rights to other people's promising material. Then there's Little Savages: Initially, building my own studio was an expensive proposition, but it's starting to pay off. For the past three years I've done all my recording there and haven't had to pay for studio time. One of the best sound engineers in the business, Miguel Taylor, lives on the premises and works cheap because he likes the desert. And I rent to other artists who want to work in a private place, get some R and R in as well. The studio has guest houses, a pool, tennis courts. Frankly, I like it a lot better than L.A. or the new house in San Diego."

"You spend much time over there?"

"A fair amount. It's an easy commute by air, and there's a landing strip. Before all this shit with Charly started, I was thinking about taking flying lessons, buying a plane. But now . . . well, till I can get both that situation and the one with these notes sorted out, I won't know what I'm doing."

"McCone or I'll be glad to give you aviation advice, if and when."

"Thanks, I'll take you up on that."

I said, "We won't volunteer any other kind of advice, though. Not unless you ask for it."

Ricky glanced at me, surprised I'd spoken. "Appreciate that, Sister Sharon."

We'd been following a long line of taillights; now directional signals began to blink left. Our driver put his on too, and the car turned off onto a poorly paved secondary road bordered by open cattle graze. The pickup behind us stuck right on our bumper.

I frowned. "This is a lot of traffic for— Oh! Don't tell me all these people are going to the concert?"

Ricky nodded. "My road manager told me the gate was close to twenty-five thousand; they're coming from all over northern California, not just the county. What you're seeing here are the late arrivals."

The driver opened the panel and said, "It's about a mile more, Mr. Savage."

"Thanks. Did I give you that gate pass?"

"I have it right here."

Ricky hunched down, peering out the side window. "Place is a big dairy ranch, belongs to a guy who's head honcho in the victims'-rights movement up this way. His wife and daughter were murdered by a couple of drifters a few years back; they walked on a technicality, returned to the area, and killed a young girl. Got them dead to rights that time, but it didn't bring her or the rancher's family back. Since then he's devoted his life to making sure victims aren't lost in the judicial shuffle."

"Good for him," I said. In spite of certain inequities in implementing our toughened stance on violent criminals—such as across-the-board application of Three Strikes You're Out—I thought it an idea whose time had been far too long in coming.

Ricky leaned closer to the window and whistled softly. "Will you look at that!"

I peered over his shoulder. At the right-hand side of the pavement the land dropped off into a series of rolling hills. A blacktop drive snaked across the terrain from a pair of massive stone pillars to a faraway cluster of white buildings with red roofs. Beyond them a larger hill rose, and on it were parked thousands of vehicles. Late arrivals spilled over into the ranch yard, and people struggled up the hill, laden with coolers and picnic baskets and folding lawn chairs.

"Jesus," Ricky said. He turned to Hy and me, face flushed with shy pleasure. "This probably sounds like false modesty, but I've never gotten over the idea that all those people'll come out to hear me. First time it happened was at this concert at the Hollywood Bowl. I couldn't believe it, thought that somebody like Willie Nelson or Johnny Cash had put in a surprise appearance."

The driver cut to the left, past the line of vehicles that was backed up at the pillars. Curious faces peered at the limo, trying to see who was behind the opaque glass. Two armed guards were stationed at the entrance; one came over, examined the pass the driver presented, then held up the line and let us through. The car glided along the blacktop, detoured past the ranch house and out-buildings, and followed an unpaved lane around the hill. The view on its other side made my breath catch.

"Would you stop here a minute, please?" Ricky asked the driver.

Below us lay a deep bowl with a silver-sheened pond at its bottom. A stage stood on its banks, and the area in front of it and the surrounding slopes were covered with people. They reclined on blankets or sat on folding chairs; most had some kind of picnic, from buckets of KFC to wicker hampers. The stage itself was bathed in garish artificial light that came from platforms to either side; roadies scurried around, and sound equipment screeched and droned. As we held there, a man's ampli-fied voice began making announcements that echoed off the hillsides.

Ricky lowered the window.

". . . extremely fortunate to have with us tonight . . . Ricky Savage!"

Cheers and applause, rising thunderously.

". . . and as opening act . . . Maxima!"

More applause, but not so intense and ebbing quickly.

I narrowed my eyes and studied the distant figures as they moved to the forefront of the stage. Even at this dis-tance, Maxima looked squeaky-clean in plaid shirts and jeans, the men's hair cut conservatively short, the woman's—the Native American—in a long pigtail.

Hy, a western buff, commented, "Roy Rogers's Sons of the Pioneers, plus Pocahontas."

Ricky laughed. The scene below affected him as if he'd just had a triple shot of Carmen's java. He whipped his head around, told the driver, "Let's go." To us he added, "With any luck at all, we won't have to deal with those piss-ants tonight."

The lane dipped down now, behind a eucalyptus windbreak that screened it from the bowl. Ahead stood a group of trailers. The driver pulled the car up to one and hurried around to open the door. Ricky said to him, "You want to go down, enjoy the show, we'll see you back here at midnight."

Outside the pleasantly chilled car the heat was jarring. The air hung perfectly still, perfumed by dusty dead grass and acrid eucalyptus. "What d'you think the temperature is?" I asked Hy, pulling off the cotton shirt I'd worn over a tank top and wishing I had on shorts rather than jeans. "A hundred?"

"Damn near; it was over eighty in the city this afternoon." He stretched his long limbs and glanced toward the darkening hilltops to the west, where the sky was a violent mix of gold and red and magenta. "No fog tonight, no relief for tomorrow." Then he put his hand on my shoulder and we followed Ricky toward the trailer.

As we came closer, a man carrying a clipboard came out to greet us. He was tall and thin, dressed all in black, and his hair fell to his shoulders in the kind of greasy locks that make me want to remind their wearers that the sixties are long over. His eyes were close-set and squinty; below them his nose and mouth protruded at an angle that called to mind an opossum's snout; when he spoke, his small, sharp teeth completed the likeness.

"About time, Savage."

"Hey, Rats. Meet Sharon McCone and Hy Ripinsky. This here's Virgil Rattray, my road manager."

Rattray looked us over, not offering to shake hands. "Oh, yeah, the sister-in-law who's a grown-up Nancy

Drew." To Hy he added, "Don't know who you are, but I don't suppose it matters."

Ricky grinned apologetically at us. "Everybody here?"

"Band's in trailers three and four." Rattray motioned with his head, tresses swaying like dreadlocks. "They want to go over the new arrangement again. And Paul Ciardi, the rancher, wants a word with you; probably gonna make you an honorary member of the Grange for coming out for this thing."

"Okay. Equipment arrived all right?"

"What d'you pay me for?"

"And the stuff I asked for is in the trailer?"

"Christ, Savage." Rattray sighed dramatically and rolled his eyes. "Bottle of Deer Hill Chardonnay, on ice. Six-pack of Beck's, ditto. Two bottles of Pellegrino water. Antipasto tray. Sourdough—Basque variety. Fresh cantaloupe and strawberries. Change of clothes, plus your stage outfit. Maybe you want I should kiss your butt, too?"

"Thanks, Rats, but later," Ricky said mildly.

Rattray scowled down at his clipboard. "Guy from the Santa Rosa paper wants an interview. I told him he could have five minutes while you're on your way down to the stage. You go on at ten sharp; be ready at ten of." Abruptly he turned and sauntered off toward the trees, whistling tunelessly.

Hy asked, "He always that personable?"

"You're seeing him at his best. If Rats isn't being a total shit, we know he's off his feed."

"Why d'you keep him on?"

"He's a great road manager. A genius at bringing schedules together; even better at getting the equipment from place to place in good shape; has it set up and torn down in a flash. Plus he collects what's owed to us and handles it honestly. Besides, Rats is open in his nastiness. In this business, that's kind of refreshing."

"You trust him?" I asked.

"To do his job? Yes. With anything else? No way."

I nodded and made a mental note to have a check run on Virgil Rattray. The road manager was in a position to do Ricky and his band either great good or great harm—and any evidence of tampering on his part might be difficult to spot.

"Look," Ricky said, "are you two planning on joining the others? I had a picnic packed in the car for them, but I've also got food here, in case you want to stick close."

I caught an undertone in his voice that told me he badly wanted us to stay. "We'll stick with you. Any way we can get close while you're on stage?"

"What, you don't think somebody's going to—"

"No, no, nothing like that. But Hy and I ought to observe how things operate during a concert, in case we need to protect you on tour."

Hy added, "I was checking on the way in: security looks good. You've got nothing to worry about. But like McCone says, we ought to be thinking ahead."

Some of the concern faded from Ricky's eyes. "Okay, I'll arrange it. In the meantime, I better see the band. Go on inside, keep cool, get yourselves something to eat."

He and Hy started for the respective trailers, but I remained where I was, scanning the terrain around me. The trees of the windbreak towered overhead, their ragged trunks and silvery leaves backlit by light from the bowl. The last of the sunset was ebbing behind the hills, and the show was well under way. Music boomed up, but I couldn't tell if it was good or bad—only that it was loud enough to mask any nearby noises.

Come on, McCone, I thought. What're you afraid of?

That somebody's going to go after Ricky between here and the other trailers?

All the same, I watched until he was inside number three before I turned and followed Hy.

The trailer was reasonably large, with a seating area to accommodate four or five people. A buffet supper was laid out on a breakfast bar, and Hy had already helped himself. I dumped my bag, took some salami and cheese and sourdough, and joined him on the banquette.

I asked, "Is security really as good as you made it out to be?"

"So-so, but I told him what he wanted to hear."

"The stage layout isn't bad. It's backed by the pond, so we don't have to worry about somebody approaching from behind. The spectators are at a comfortable distance."

Hy opened a bottle of beer. "So all we have to worry about is somebody rushing the stage and making it past the guards. Or a lunatic in a diving suit rising up from the pond like the Creature from the Black Lagoon."

"You can't discount the potential for danger, though. What about one of his own people getting to him? Or somebody on the hill with a high-powered rifle?"

Hy was silent for a moment. "You carrying?"

"No. This was supposed to be a social evening; I didn't bring my gun to the office today." I pushed my plate away, leaving most of the food untouched. "God, I hate this kind of situation!"

"I admit I'd feel better if he were doing this gig after I had my people on the job."

"I don't mean just tonight. The trouble with this kind of situation is that there're too damn many angles of attack, too many possibilities. Whoever's behind those notes could be anybody. Could come from any direction, at any time. Could have any motive. Could be somebody close to him or a complete stranger. Could escalate his or her activities, lay low for a while, or disappear forever. And I can't overlook anything, not when it comes to the lives and safety of people I love."

"You're not saying you're scared, McCone?"

"I am. I'd be a fool if I wasn't. I don't like cases where I'm this personally involved, where there's this much at stake."

He twined the fingers of his right hand through those of my left and leaned forward till his face was close to mine. "Don't let fear get in the way," he said. "And remember—you and I, we make an unbeatable team."

At close to ten the night had gone black and star-shot, but the still air had none of the velvety quality I associated with warm summer evenings. This heat was prickly and rasped against my skin like a dull knife blade. It made me edgy, and I could tell it had the same effect on Hy.

We boarded a golf cart in front of the trailer—Ricky in the seat ahead of us, chatting with the reporter from the local paper—and bumped downhill to the stage area. Maxima had finished; on and around the bandstand an army of roadies had been deployed. I spotted Virgil Rattray in their midst, clipboard in hand, shouting orders. The lights were blinding, making it difficult to see anything more than motion on the hillsides. To our far left, long lines snaked away from a row of portable toilets.

"This is an impossible situation," I told Hy as I took in the scattered activity.

"Well, I can see I'm gonna have to learn a lot fast. But for tonight . . . I'm not all that worried."

Obviously he'd been following a train of thought similar to mine while we'd waited in the trailer. The notes, while escalating in intensity and bizarreness, were still a remote form of harrassment. To move directly from that to violent action was a big step that the sender was not likely to take without a series of smaller steps to bridge the distance. I nodded agreement and began to study the immediate area, blocking it out into manageable segments. After a moment I began to sense a pattern under the chaotic activity: Everyone there had a function; everyone there belonged. The audience was separated from the concert personnel by a phalanx of security guards.

The cart stopped close to the stage, and we got off, Ricky shaking hands with the reporter, who in turn was escorted out by Rattray. When he came up to us, my brother-in-law's eyes glittered with a wired energy that I'd watched build since we'd arrived. He said, "Man, that guy had some strange questions. He asked me how I felt about being Ricky Savage. Why didn't he just ask me how I felt about breathing?"

As Ricky had slipped into his performance mode, I'd noticed that the flat, drawn-out accent of the Central Valley grew more pronounced, as though on some level he was tapping into the roots that had nourished his talent. His reactions were altered, too: quicker, but measured to some inner beat. As he introduced Hy and me to the four members of his band and situated us on a lighting platform at stage right, I sensed he wasn't really seeing any of us; he'd become a tightly controlled, self-contained system that would respond only to the stimuli necessary to give a good performance.

The band members were another story entirely. They clustered together, joking and chatting—buddies out for a good time. Their easygoing manner set them apart from Ricky, made it plain who was support staff and who was the star; their camaraderie accentuated his aloneness. I recalled his comment about playing clubs and looking at the ass end of some broken-down, third-rate singer. Could one of the band members harbor similar sentiments? Did one or perhaps more of them resent my brother-in-law's success?

Throughout the emcee's introduction the four continued to make sotto-voce jokes and comments. But then the crowd's voice swelled and applause thundered; one by one the musicians kicked into the same focused state as Ricky. He glanced at them, gave them a high sign, and ran onto the stage. After a beat they followed.

The crowd noise crested now; floodlights panned across the audience. Most were standing. They clapped their hands, shouted, whistled. A cloud of confetti billowed to one side. Near the front a young woman stood, eyes closed, hands clasped as if in prayer. An elderly woman jumped up and down, face glowing like a teenager's.

A shiver passed along my spine. I shouted to Hy, "I knew he'd made it, but I had no idea how big!"

Hy's eyes were gleaming with vicarious excitement. "Can you imagine standing up there like he is and watching twenty-five thousand people go ballistic over you?"

"I'd rather face down a thug with an Uzi."

The huge number of people and volume of noise didn't daunt Ricky. He stood relaxed in his cream-colored western-cut suit, guitar slung across his chest, then finally held up his hands for quiet. After the roar had died to rustles and whispers, he took hold of his microphone and spoke in a voice that—to one who knew him as well as I—was at once both intimate and at a vast remove.

"Thank you very much. And we also want to thank you for coming out tonight in support of the rights of victims. It's time we're joining hands and saying 'no more of this.' And it's good people like yourselves who help get the word out to the ones who don't want to listen. This song's about them, and it's dedicated to the memory of Tina, Sandy, and Carolyn, the victims whose tragic deaths made us sit up and take a look around."

The crowd grew very still now. The band broke into the opening strains of "The People Who Won't Listen."

Hy tensed.

"What?" I whispered.

"Motion over there on the left."

I kept my eyes on Ricky, ready to move if someone went for him.

"It's a kid . . . wait, security's got him."

"What'd he—"

"He's drunk, that's all."

I let my breath out slowly, still watching my brother-in-law. The intensity and emotion he'd been holding in check was fully unleashed now. He moved to the hard-driving beat, fingers picking quickly over the strings of his guitar, belting out the lyrics of his song. As the sound spiraled and echoed off the hills, the crowd responded with yells and cheers.

Hy spoke close to my ear. "Rattray arranged for me to meet with the head of security in a few minutes. I'll run over to their operations center, warn him that we might have a situation on our hands, then prowl for a bit."

"Okay." I squeezed his arm before he slipped off the platform.

The next number was "Cobwebs in the Attic of My Mind," the song that had started it all. Its opening bars brought forth shrieks of approval. "The Broken Promise Land," last summer's hit, quieted the audience. What up-turned faces I could see grew rapt and serious as Ricky sang of the recording industry.

They lure you with their talk of fame
They swear you're sure to make a name

Marcia Muller

*The lies you're living take their toll
And in the end they own your soul . . .*

What irony, I thought, that a song so bitterly critical of the industry had received a Grammy and a Country Music Award! I was willing to bet, though, that few insiders had recognized its true message.

As Ricky ventilated on stage the same feelings he'd expressed that afternoon in my office, it occurred to me that of late his work had repeatedly dealt with certain elements: melancholy, weariness, disillusionment, alienation, and loss. The price, perhaps, of trying to prevent the industry from claiming *his* soul?

The concert went on: rousing, lighthearted numbers alternating with powerful, moving songs. In the middle of one of my favorites, "Somebody's Waiting Tonight," Hy slipped onto the platform. "Everything okay?" I asked.

"Security's better than I thought. Firm that's handling it specializes in concerts; I picked up some pointers, and they're willing to consult if we have to cover him on tour. Dammit, I wish that wasn't coming up next week."

"You can handle it, though?"

"Sure, but it'll cost him."

"Better I identify the note writer, then. I don't want Ricky dipping into the kids' college funds. And this situation with my sister could get expensive."

"She's never struck me as that kind."

"She never used to be, but who knows? The life they've been living could change anybody."

"What d'you suppose is going on with her? I thought you two were close."

"So did I. Guess I won't know till, as he suggested, I ask her."

The number ended, and the crowd was on its feet

again. Sound surged against us like a tidal wave. Once more Ricky waited, once more he raised his hands for quiet. Then he paused for a long time, blinded by the lights but appearing to survey each face. When he gripped the mike his voice was deeply emotional.

He said, "This next one's for Charly. I guess now it'll always be for Charly."

> *Close the windows, lock the door*
> *You don't love me any more*
> *Stop the paper, give back the keys*
> *Maybe now this pain will ease . . .*

The song's title was "The House Where Love Once Lived."

"Oh, God," I whispered, looking away. "He's always been such a private person. Why's he doing this?"

Hy's arm tightened around my shoulders. "Sometimes opening a vein in public makes it easier to believe that what's happening to you is real. Poor bastard."

When the last strains of the song echoed off the hillsides, the audience went wild—applauding longer and louder than for any number yet. As if, I thought, they felt his pain and hoped to heal him. Ricky's composure failed; he took a step backward and turned as if to speak to the band. His shoulders shuddered and he bowed his head, struggling to regain control. Then he recovered, wiped his face with his hand. Nodded to the band members and returned to the mike.

"Thank you *very* much. You folks have been such a great audience—" Cheers interrupted him. "Yeah! I mean it, you're terrific! So now we want to do something extra special for you. We've got a new album coming out next month; it's called *The Midnight Train to Nowhere*, and we're gonna preview the title song exclusively for you all."

The applause escalated. Over it Ricky added, "We sure do hope you like it." He began to pick out a complicated series of chords, and immediately the noise died down.

> *On the midnight train to nowhere*
> *It's as cold as it can be*
> *In the window I see darkness*
> *And a face that can't be me*
>
> *It's been all too many miles*
> *Since I knew just who I am*
> *And this role that I've been playin'*
> *Is a sham*
>
> *I had no thought when I left home*
> *For the man I'd come to be*
> *Just a thirst I put no name to*
> *And a yearning to break free*
>
> *Now the miles keep on clickin'*
> *It's a lonesome world I see*
> *And the life that I've been leadin'*
> *Troubles me . . .*

I glanced at Hy, saw that his gaze was focused on other places and times. Like the man in the song—like Ricky—he'd left his home in the high-desert country years before, in search of some indefinable thing. And although he'd eventually returned there, what he'd seen and done in the interim had made him a stranger who harbored nightmares and recriminations enough to outlast a long period of reclusiveness, a marriage, and the untimely death of his wife. It was only in the past year that he'd been able to open up and share his secrets with me.

But I also had my secrets. The fresh-faced cheerleader I'd once been had left San Diego looking for . . . what? More. That was all the definition I could put on it. Well, I'd found more, that was certain. Found, too, the demons I'd brought along with me. Now there were emotional doors that I no longer dared to open, and I sometimes wondered what kind of woman I'd become.

The last notes of "Midnight Train" hung on the night air. The crowd was strangely silent. Ricky drew the mike close, spoke again in that oddly intimate-yet-not-intimate voice. "That song's for all of us who can't go home any-more. To Bakersfield." He tapped his chest. "To Missoula." A nod to Norm O'Dell, lead guitarist. "To Austin." Another nod to his bass player, Forrest Curtin. "To Shreveport." The drummer, Jerry Jackson, acknowl-edged with a wave. "And to Oklahoma City." He mo-tioned in the direction of Pete Sherman, on keyboards.

"And now," he added, "would you please give a big hand to these guys behind me? They're the greatest!"

The response was wilder than before. Over it, the band kicked into "Baby, We've Got It All."

It was an early upbeat song written on the first wave of success—for Charlene.

five

By the time we got back to the trailer area I felt drained, both from the heat and the emotional intensity of the performance. Hy himself allowed as how he could use a beer or two. Ricky and his band members, however, were flying high on an enormous rush, even after working for close to two hours in ninety-degree heat. As soon as they climbed off the golf carts they brought out the joints and bottles and passed them around while they rehashed the concert.

"I don't know," Ricky said, "they were awful quiet after 'Midnight Train.'"

"Shit, that's because they *loved* it!"

"You think so, Pete?"

"Yeah. Yeah, I surely do."

"He's right, Rick. 'Midnight Train's' gonna be a blowout."

"I don't know, Jer."

"Hey, Savage, give it a rest."

"Hell, the kind of year I'm having, we'll be lucky if the thing doesn't stiff."

"No way! You get a crowd like that one to shut up—"

"And you're looking at another Grammy and solid platinum—"

"And a *big* bonus for the band—"

"And the doofus prize to Norm for some of the most fumble-fingered gittar I ever heard."

"You had to mention it, Curtin! Christ, did you hear when I . . ."

I turned away, leaving them to their moment. Linked hands with Hy and moved toward the trailer. We mounted its steps and he opened the door.

"What the hell?" he said.

I stared down at a pile of dying weeds lying just inside the threshold.

"Oh, Jesus!"

"McCone, what is it?"

I got down on my knees and grabbed some of the wilted stuff. Held it up to the dim light from inside, calling to mind my seemingly irrelevant research in the library's science section that afternoon.

Shiny green leaves on long streamerlike branches . . . Fragrant tubular yellow flowers . . .

Their scent cloyed. How had someone gotten the plant to flower this late in the year? According to the horticultural guide, it usually did that in early spring.

All parts of the plant are poisonous . . .

"McCone!"

Brings on muscular weakness, convulsions, sweating, and respiratory failure . . .

I said, "This stuff is called Carolina jessamine."

A knowing light came into his eyes. I nodded.

And one by one they all died there, and one by one they died . . .

I rocked back on my heels, staring at the pile of wilting jessamine. The note writer had not only escalated his or her activities but demonstrated an important point: It was possible to get to Ricky. In a crowded place, surrounded by an army of security guards, it was possible to get to him.

"McCone?" Hy squatted beside me.

I glanced over my shoulder. Ricky and his band were still rehashing the concert, oblivious to what was going on here. Quickly I decided on a course of action. "Don't let on to any of them what's happened," I said. "I'll— Dammit, I need a plastic bag."

"Might be one in the trailer." Hy stood, stepped over the jessamine, and went inside. When he came out he handed me a Ziploc. I used it as a glove and bagged a sample of the plant. A lab could probably tell me nothing more than I already knew, but I didn't want it contaminated in case it contained some trace of the person who had left it.

"I'll get rid of the rest of this," I told Hy. "I don't want him to know about it."

"Why? He should be aware—"

"Yes, but not now, not here. I think you'd better put one of your people on him right away; then we'll tell him."

"I'll use the phone in the limo to call in; one of our operatives'll be at his hotel before he gets back there." Hy slipped off the steps and moved toward the car.

I stuffed the Ziploc into my bag, then dumped the remaining jessamine in a trash can inside the trailer. After looking around and deciding its interior hadn't been tampered with, I went back outside and questioned a few of the security people. None had noticed any unauthorized people in the vicinity.

Hy had just returned from making his call and Ricky was seeing the band off when Rae arrived, riding on a golf cart with one of the security men. She was barefoot and had tied the tails of her shirt below her breasts so her midriff was exposed. Her jeans were tight, her smile loose, and in her eyes was the gleam of a groupie.

Ricky took one look at her, and in his eyes appeared the gleam of a man who could become very interested in a groupie.

Rae got off the cart and came toward us; she'd had enough to drink that she put an alluring—and unaccustomed—sway into her walk. "The others," she announced, "decided to go to this shit-kicker bar in Penngrove that somebody told them about."

"What're they going to do with Habiba?" I was fiercely protective of Anne-Marie's and Hank's ward, having recently survived an ordeal with her that few adults could have handled as well.

"The last I saw she was asleep in the back of the limo. The driver'll watch her. Anyway, I didn't want to go along, so Joe offered to bring me here." She waved to the security man, who was watching her wistfully. He waved back, then winked. She blew him a kiss.

I stared at her in astonishment. I'd never before witnessed Rae on the prowl; this was fascinating.

Apparently Ricky thought so, too. He moved closer, smiling.

"So," she added, turning and favoring him with a crinkle-nosed grin, "I hoped you might give me a ride back to the city."

His eyes moved from her face to her well-toned little body. "Ma'am," he drawled, "it'll be my pleasure."

Oh, shit, Savage! Lay it on a little thicker, why don't you?

He'd had just enough adulation and dope and whiskey to be foolish, just enough pain to be rash. But Ricky was a big boy; he could handle whatever came his way. It was Rae who worried me.

She'd been through a lot in the time I'd known her: the collapse of a stifling early marriage; a tempestuous on-and-off-again relationship that she'd eventually torpedoed; a peculiar three-cornered love affair via computer that had ended in New Year's Eve heartache. Since then she'd sworn off men altogether, but now, it seemed, she was ready to fly again. Fly Rae-fashion, with her autopilot set to collision coordinates.

I wanted to grab her and shake some sense into her. I wanted to tell Ricky that he was on the verge of creating all sorts of complications. Rae was not only my employee but my friend; she worked in the same office with his son, and they had become buddies. How on earth would she be able to face us after a one-night stand with my brother-in-law, his father?

But in the end I restrained myself and didn't do or say anything. Both Rae and Ricky were grown-ups—even if they weren't acting the role—and entitled to make their own mistakes.

After Ricky changed into shorts and a T-shirt, we collected our gear and climbed into the limo, and he declared the bar open. Hy drank beer at his usual measured pace, throwing me occasional ironic glances. I sipped wine, cautioning myself against slipping into anxiety-based overindulgence—and then doing so anyway. Ricky knocked back bourbons one after the other, and Rae acted more seductive with every glass of champagne.

Around Novato, Ricky turned off the dim interior lights. I leaned back in the circle of Hy's arms, feeling his warmth and the steady, comforting beat of his heart. He rested his chin on the top of my head, and I felt my tension ebb.

On the facing seat Ricky pulled Rae toward him. In the wash of oncoming headlights I saw them kiss, saw his hand move to her bare midriff. Before it could creep upward I gave them one last steely look—which they were too preoccupied to notice—and closed my eyes. The last thing I wanted to witness was two people I cared about making total asses of themselves.

Suddenly the driver was announcing we'd arrived at Pier 24½. I jerked upright, disoriented.

"Hey, guys," Ricky said, "thanks for coming along."

"Thank *you*." Hy unfolded his lanky frame from the car and extended a hand to me. I yawned, got out, and looked back at Rae. "You coming?"

In the glare from the security lights on the pier her face was pasty white; her curls were disheveled and the top two buttons of her shirt were undone. She saw me looking at them and hastily did them up. "Uh, I didn't drive to work today."

"Hy or I can drop you at Coso Street."

Ricky said, "I'll drop her, Sister Sharon." There was an amused note in his voice that reminded me how the nickname had originated: "Sister Sharon, who is pure, good, and wise in all ways," Charlene used to complain. "She should've been a nun."

But Ricky well knew that subsequent events had proved I was far from pure, good, wise—and the nunnery. I smiled wryly and reached in to hug him. "Okay, Brother Ricky, but one more thing: Hy's put an operative on your suite at the hotel."

"Why?"

I didn't want to go into it in front of Rae; either he'd tell her about the problem or she'd find out if and when I decided to use her on the investigation. "Just a precaution."

"Well, I sure won't be lonesome tonight." He squeezed Rae's knee.

Her eyes clouded, as though she suspected she might

have gotten herself into something she wouldn't be able to handle. I took my spare house key from my bag and tossed it to her. For a few seconds she frowned, apparently having forgotten I'd told her she could move into my guest room. Then she smiled weakly. "Thanks."

"You're welcome." I hoped she'd use it—and soon.

Hy asked Ricky, "When're you going home?"

"We've chartered a flight for three this afternoon."

"See you down there, then."

He shut the limo's door and we stepped back as it edged into the northbound traffic. I watched its taillights, thinking that, in going off with Ricky, Rae had made yet another of her bad choices. But this time it was one that might spell disaster for all of us.

Six

EXCERPT FROM RAE KELLEHER'S DIARY:

Bad choices, the grandmother who raised me used to say, can be costly. What she didn't tell me was that good choices can be costly, too. I knew I'd made the right one in regard to Ricky, but that didn't make me feel any better as I stood with him on the porch at All Souls. And the knowledge sure wasn't going to keep me warm in the few hours that remained of the night.

Why is it that the things you want the most are always wrong?

Since the past New Year's Eve, when my cyberspace love affairs collapsed, I'd avoided men like the plague. But all-night movie bingeing and reading trashy books and then working off your sexual tensions at the Y gets old pretty fast. Late yesterday afternoon at Miranda's I'd been in a classic funk because life held too few surprises. And all I knew about Ricky Savage was that he was Shar's brother-in-law and had a voice that, if I listened closely to it,

*would drive me straight back to the old Nautilus ma-
chine.*

*But a little over six hours later life was full of surprises.
There I was, riding in a limo, half out of my mind on
champagne, necking like a teenager with the man—or at
least the voice—of my dreams. And somewhere between
Pier 24½ and Stanford Court, when I sobered up and told
him to get his hand out of my jeans, he backed off without a protest. I realized then—and continued to realize
during the next two hours when we rode around and
talked—that there was a great deal more to him than the
image. I'd found out just how much more as he revealed
his very private thoughts to me.*

*This was a man I could fall in love with, but I wasn't
going to let that happen.*

*I fit my key into the front-door lock of the Victorian and
turned to him.*

*"Friends?" he asked, brushing my cheek with the back
of his fingers.*

"Good friends."

*"Thank God you put a stop to things, Red. We'd've cre-
ated one hell of a mess for all concerned. Besides, what I
really needed tonight was a sympathetic ear. So did you."*

*He was right about all of that—especially the mess. I
pictured myself walking into the office on Monday and
having Shar look at me like I was some gunk she'd just
scraped off the bottom of her shoe. I imagined the way
Mick would rage at me and then freeze me out if he discovered I'd slept with his father. And Ricky . . . the last
thing he needed on his conscience while he was trying to
save his marriage was a one-night stand with his sister-
in-law's friend and employee.*

*He added, "Look, I don't know what kind of situation
I'm going to run into at home, but I suspect it'll be godawful. Okay to call you if I need to talk some more?"*

"Of course."

"You'll be at Shar's?"

"I'm going to pack up a few things and go over there right away."

"Want me to come inside with you, make sure everything's okay?"

"No. I've never had any trouble here. You're exhausted, and the driver's probably pissed at being kept on the job so long. Go back to the hotel and get some rest."

"I can't say as I don't need it." He kissed my forehead and jogged down the steps, waving when he got to the limo.

I went inside before I could call out to him and ask him to stay.

In my attic room I grabbed a tote bag and stuffed things into it. Tee to sleep in, underwear, fresh jeans, and shirt. Shoes. I needed shoes. I was still barefoot and my tennies were in the other limo. I hoped to God that somebody had noticed and retrieved them, even if they'd cost only twenty bucks at Price Club.

What on earth had I been thinking of, riding off in my bare feet with a security guard on a golf cart? What on earth made me hurl myself at a man I barely knew? The champagne, of course. Blame it on the champagne. And on the pain in Ricky's voice when he dedicated "The House Where Love Once Lived" to Charly. I've always been a pushover for a man in pain.

Anything else to pack? I looked around and saw the voice-activated tape recorder that I use to set down my diary entries, which were really more like stories, with me as the main character. Might as well drag it along. Tonight would make a good tale: "How I Found Romance—and Threw It Away an Hour Later."

Face it, Rae, your life is not material for a shop-and-fuck. The heroine of one of those sagas wouldn't've applied the brakes for an instant. *If fiction is the product of the author's life experience, you should be trying to write soap-opera scripts.*

I dropped the recorder into the bag anyway and started down to the second-floor bathroom for the rest of my junk. The light in the stairwell had burned out. It was always doing that—another thing about this place I wouldn't miss. Nights when I woke up and had to pee, it was an odds-even chance that I'd break my neck on the way down.

I inched along, feeling for the edge of each step with my toes and clutching the wobbly railing. Cool air blew up at me. Strange. There must be a window open somewhere. Then I heard a faint noise down below. I stopped and listened. Nothing. Probably my imagination. Or, if not, one of the remaining partners coming back for something he'd forgotten.

At four in the morning? Come on!

I waited. Still no sound, but the cool air kept blowing. I held my breath, kept very still, straining to hear. I wished I'd let Ricky come inside with me. The temptation it would've presented was nothing compared to the creepiness of this empty old house.

That's it! That noise was just the house settling.

I started down the steps again.

And then it came at me. Up the stairs. A tall shape, blacker than the darkness around me. I yelled—I don't know what. I dropped the tote bag and turned, scrabbling back up.

Attic! The part of the attic where all the castoffs're stored. I could hide there—

A hand grabbed my right foot and I fell hard, banging my chin on the step above. Another hand grabbed the waistband of my jeans. I was being lifted, slammed face *against the wall. I flailed around, screaming, even though there was nobody to hear me.*

Above my screams I heard harsh breathing. The person who held me was strong. Too strong for me to break free. I let my scream trail away into a sob.

The person spoke. Raspy voice that could've been male or female. "Leave him alone," it said. "Do you understand? Leave him be."

"Leave who alone?"

"You know who. Do you understand?" He—or she—slammed me into the wall again.

"Yes," I whispered. The pain made it impossible to speak any louder.

"I didn't hear you."

"Yes! Yes, I understand!"

"Good." Another slam, and the hands let go.

I fell backward, banging into the opposite wall. The breath went out of me, and I fell down the steps to the landing. Downstairs I heard footsteps pounding in the second-floor hallway. Pain flared up all over my body as the front door crashed shut.

Seven

As first light was bleeding around the miniblinds, I woke to a faint rattling sound. I glanced over at Hy, who usually has a hair-trigger personal alarm; he was deeply asleep. The sound came again, from the front of the house.

I slipped from the bed, shrugging into my white terry-cloth robe. The sound was definitely unfamiliar. Not Ralph, my orange tabby, thudding down from a sleeping perch; not Alice, my calico, leaping onto the kitchen counter in search of forbidden treats. Not the *Chronicle* hitting the porch, or an early-rising neighbor—

It came again, louder.

I moved around the bed and took Hy's .44 from where he kept it in the nightstand. My own gun was locked in a U.S. Navy ammo box bolted to the floor of my linen closet, but my lover—conditioned by years of dangerous living—always slept with a weapon within reach. Holding it by my side, I went down the hallway, through the kitchen, and into the sitting room.

The sound came again—from the front door.

Slowly I moved along the hall, both hands on the gun now, stepping carefully to avoid creaky floorboards. Slipped up to the door and put my eye to the peephole. Rae, looking—

"My God!" I stuffed the gun into the robe's pocket, disarmed the security system, turned the deadbolt, and let her in. Her round face was swollen on the right side; she held her arm stiffly and had been fumbling to get the house key into the lock with her left hand.

She said, "I think this key is bent."

I moved her aside so I could lock the door. "What happened to you?"

"Somebody attacked me in the attic stairwell at Coso Street."

"Attacked—"

"No, not raped, nothing like that. Just grabbed me, and I fell."

"Where was Ricky while this was going on?"

"In bed asleep, I guess."

"I thought the two of you were—"

"Well, we didn't." She made a sharp right turn into the guest room and lowered herself stiffly onto the bed. "Shar, do you have any pain killers?"

"Sure, I'll get them. Lie down, cover up." I hurried back to the bedroom and deposited the cumbersome .44 in the nightstand. Hy grunted but slept on. In the bathroom closet I found some codeine my doctor had prescribed after I'd taken a bad fall while pursuing a deadbeat dad last winter. I'd saved some of the pills for this kind of occasion—although I'd assumed, my life being what it is, that I'd be the one who needed them. After shaking out a couple and filling a tumbler with water, I went back to Rae.

She'd slipped under the covers and propped herself against the pillows. I supervised her taking the tablets, then sat down cross-legged on the foot of the bed. "Now tell me exactly what happened."

She pressed her hand to her forehead, looking sick. No wonder—she must have one hell of a hangover as well. "Ricky told the driver to take us back to the hotel, but after about two blocks I realized what a hideous mistake we were making. He backed down right away, and we ended up just riding around. I told him my life story, he told me his." She paused. "He's really hurting over the breakup with your sister."

"He say much about it?"

"A fair amount, but I think you'd better ask one of them if you want to know. Anyway, he also told me about this business with the notes and hiring us. It's . . . creepy. And I think it has something to do with what happened to me later on."

As she recreated the scene in the stairwell at Coso Street, I listened with mounting alarm. By the time she finished her eyelids were growing heavy, and with her bright curls spread out on the pillow, she looked like a small, frightened girl. All my anger over her behavior of the previous night evaporated, and I put my hand on the quilt and squeezed her foot.

"It does sound as though it might have some connection with those notes," I said.

"That's why I didn't call the cops. He told me it could damage him if word got out to the media." She sighed deeply and closed her eyes.

I sat there while she drifted off, still holding her foot. Then I closed the draperies against the morning sun and went to wake Hy.

Hy hung up the phone as I came into the kitchen, toweling my freshly washed hair. "I'm gonna have to get down to San Diego right away," he said. "The situation at your sister's is deteriorating fast."

I poured coffee and motioned at his cup; he held it out for a refill. "How so?"

"Well, the three youngest kids're off at camp. Charlene decided against yanking them out, which is probably a good call. We've alerted the staffs at both camps, and they're exercising precautions. Chris and Jamie are okay with the ground rules our man's laid out for them, but your sister . . ." He shook his head.

"What about Charlene?"

"She had weekend plans that got screwed up, and she's seriously pissed and taking it out on everybody. Plus Ricky's manager—Kurt Girdwood—is due late this afternoon, and his lawyer's been calling and making noises about coming down with him. And there's a cast of thousands working there; no way of controlling them, short of issuing photo I.D. cards. Everybody's aware that something's wrong, and they're all doing their damndest to find out what—which poses a potential threat of it being leaked to the media. My entire team's only been in place two hours, and already they say the situation's out of hand."

"And you think you can do something about it?"

"Yeah. I'll start by laying down the law to the lady of the house."

"Good luck." Like all McCones, Charlene had inherited a long tradition of stubbornness, which she'd diligently practiced until it approximated a minor art form. "So when're you going?"

"I've got a ten-thirty flight from SFO."

"You're not taking the Citabria?" Hy's plane was in the tie-downs at Oakland Airport's north field.

"No, a commercial flight's faster. I'll leave the keys, in case you want to bring her down later."

I looked away from him.

"Come on, McCone. You flew solo to Bakersfield last month. You'll manage."

"I did that to prove a point—and because you shamed me into it."

"And you made your point, didn't you? After a near miss like you had, you get right back on, the same way you would a horse that's thrown you—"

"Yes, okay." I didn't want to think about that near miss; it had almost claimed Hy, Habiba, and myself.

"And once you get back on," he continued as if I hadn't interrupted, "you're fine. So bring the Citabria to San Diego."

"We'll see." But when he tossed me the keys, I caught and hung onto them, my fingers caressing their surface. Quickly I changed the subject. "So what's your take on the incident with Rae?"

"I'd like to believe it had nothing to do with Ricky, but that'd be too much of a coincidence."

"I think so too. Let's suppose the person in the stairwell was the note writer. That means he or she was at the concert, saw Ricky leave with Rae, and followed the limo all the way from there to Coso Street."

"Somebody with access to the trailer area, then. Why warn Rae off him, though?"

"Maybe to remove her as an obstacle, but more likely to drive home the same point that was made by leaving the jessamine in his trailer."

"Escalating the campaign?"

"It would seem that way." I looked down at my hands, realized they were gripping the coffee mug so hard my fingertips had gone white.

Hy came to me, removed the cup, and set it on the counter. He wrapped his arms around me; I nestled my head in the curve of his shoulder, breathing his familiar scent. This should have been a carefree day when we indulged in our favorite city-weekend activities: a trip to the farmers' market and the flower mart; dim sum on Clement Street; a stroll on Baker Beach; an afternoon nap during which we slept little; a movie and late dinner with good friends. And Monday should have been the start of a good period for both of us: He would have winged his way back to his beloved high-desert country; I would have been settling in to three weeks of concentrated, productive work. But now I sensed it could be the start of a bad time—one when the risks would be high, the cost of failure too painful to contemplate.

Hy stepped back, looked deep into my eyes before he kissed me. "I'd better get going."

"Call my pager when you've got something to report."

He smiled wryly. "Two months ago you swore you'd never own one."

"What can I tell you? My office staff are determined to keep me on a short leash."

I got dressed and made a couple of calls to cancel our weekend plans. Then I left a note for Rae—who was sleeping soundly—and headed for Bernal Heights. The old neighborhood slumbered under the morning sun; few residents were up and about. I parked in the driveway of the big Victorian that had housed All Souls and entered by means of the key I'd neglected to give back. A heavy silence permeated the nearly stripped rooms; the air was thick with dust, and musty. I went straight to the stairs, bypassing the parlor where so many scenes of my life had played out, and along the second-floor hall to the enclosed attic staircase. A portion of the rubberized tread on the steps had been pulled loose of its anchoring nails, probably by Rae when she fell, but otherwise there was no evidence of the intrusion.

As I hurried back down I kept my eyes on the floor, telling myself I was searching for anything the intruder might have dropped, but knowing that I was avoiding ghostly memories. For years the Victorian had been my home—more of one in many ways than my own house—and while I was delighted with the new offices, I had yet to sink roots there. Maybe that was why I'd so looked forward to those three weeks of routine work that now, apparently, I wasn't going to have.

On the front porch I shut the door gently behind me, saying a silent good-bye. Then I began walking, canvassing the few neighbors who were out, to see if anyone had noticed anything going on in the early-morning hours. A woman three doors up the hill was airing her house plants on the sidewalk; in spite of our often having chatted in the past, she greeted me with a blank look. Then she did a double take and said, "I thought you moved away." In response to my questions, she told me that she always went to bed at eleven and slept straight through till seven. She didn't ask where I'd moved to or what I was doing back in the neighborhood.

On the other side of the triangular park that bisected the street I found a man washing his car, breakfast beer balanced on its hood. His house was next door to one All Souls had formerly leased for support-staff offices, and we'd often exchanged greetings. Now he also took a moment to recognize me, then regarded me with thinly veiled disapproval. "Thought you all sold out and went downtown," he said. When I asked him about unusual occurrences that morning, he allowed as how he was a poor sleeper and had seen Ricky drop Rae off, but nothing more. "You don't get too many limos in this part of town," he added, "but I guess you've forgotten that by now."

By now. It had only been three weeks, but people had forgotten me and expected I'd forgotten them and the ways of the neighborhood. So much for lasting connections in today's city.

When I drove into Pier 24½ I spotted Ted's little white Dodge Neon parked by the foot of our stairway. He'd taken to coming in on Saturday mornings to tie up the week's loose ends while Neal manned the bookshop; on Mondays when the shop—called Anachronism—was closed, he usually straggled in close to noon. None of us minded; he had the offices so well organized that they practically ran themselves, and besides, we were all so glad to see him genuinely happy for the first time in years that we'd have gladly granted him twice the time off.

I left the MG in its space and climbed the stairway. Ted's door stood open. "Hey," I called, "how was the shit-kicker bar?"

"Don't yell so loud!" his pained voice pleaded. "My head hurts."

"Danced till dawn, huh?"

An unusually pasty goateed face glared at me over a stack of documents. "Watched the straight couples dance till two. Neal and I weren't taking any chances in a crowd like that. Besides"—he grinned sheepishly—"there was this hunky guy in a Bar Ale Feeds cap that I wasn't going to let anywhere near him."

"Gays, in Penngrove?"

"Everywhere. Queer is here." He reached for an envelope in his in-box and handed it to me. "From Richman Labs."

"That was fast. Can you messenger something else over to them for me? They're open till noon today."

"I'll drop it off myself on the way home."

"Thanks." I went to my office and filled out a work-request sheet, hesitating for a moment over which boxes to check. Then under *other* I wrote, "Anything that may identify source of sample," and enveloped the sheet with the plastic bag full of jessamine. When I left it on Ted's desk he was in the copy room, whistling "Mammas, Don't Let Your Babies Grow Up to Be Cowboys."

Paper composition: 25% cotton, 20-lb bond
Manufacturer: Southworth
Ink: black fadeproof & waterproof
Pen type: rolling ball, .22 mm point
Manufacturer: Uni-ball
Fingerprints: smudges only, some containing microscopic steel-alloy fragments

The paper was common, the pen also; I had some of both in the office. No fingerprints, and the smudges probably were made by Ricky, whose hands would contain a residue of steel from his guitar strings. On the whole, not a very interesting report, but the graphologist's analysis held my attention.

All six notes appear to have been written by the same individual, although there is evidence of a marked personality alteration from sample #1 through #6. Gender of writer is indeterminable.

Reference A: Speed. Characteristics indicating clear mental activity alter by sample #3, with indicators of disorganized mental activity predominating by #6.

Reference B: Certainty and flexibility of writing movement. Indicators of mental self-confidence predominate in samples #1–#4, shading to indicators of anxiety in #5 and #6.

Reference C: Regularity of movement. Indicators of self-control in samples #1–#3 altering markedly toward indicators of emotional disturbance thereafter.

Reference D: Expansion of writing movement.
Limited movement throughout, indicating an individual who controls expression, may be reserved or introverted.

Reference E: Firmness and sharpness of writing movement. Characteristics indicating self-assertion, aggression, and competitiveness throughout, but increasing significantly from sample #1 through #6. Strong indications in samples #4–#6 of building anger and frustration.

Summary: Subject appears to have begun writing with a clear sense of purpose which has been thwarted or disrupted by subsequent events, creating the indicated anger and frustration. The rigid, formal structure of sample #4 may represent an attempt to regroup and reassert control. Samples #5 and #6 indicate a marked personality change and loss of control, but it is this analyst's opinion that subject is able to function on a fairly aggressive level and possibly mask his/her true emotional state from others.

At the bottom of the page the analyst, a woman whom I knew personally, had scribbled, "Sharon, I'm not supposed to opine any more than I did above, but I've got to warn you: This person could be *very* dangerous!"

Eight

When I first moved north to UC Berkeley, Sausalito still bore a lingering resemblance to a quiet bayside village. We'd often drive over there on Sunday afternoons, buy fish and chips at a stand that wrapped them in newspaper, and eat on one of the docks, feeding the leftovers to the gulls. Nowadays I avoid the town: It's too tricked-up cute, too congested, too full of tourists. But that afternoon as I viewed the tumble of its rooftops from the high terrace of the festively pink Alta Mira Hotel, I had to acknowledge Sausalito's beauty. From the sweep of its southern seawall to the clutter of its houseboat community, it is a jewel on the band of communities that gird our Bay.

I'd called TriStar Studios from the office, used Ricky's name to get through to Arletta James, and made a lunch date for noon. The studio was easy to locate—a warehouse in an industrial area off the main street to the north of town. A young woman with a diamond stud in her nose and disdain in her eyes sat idly at the reception desk. She took my name, looked over my apparently too-conventional jeans and cotton shirt, and slowly—very slowly—picked up the phone and spoke to someone in the inner sanctum. Then she said, "She'll be out," and went back to contemplating the wall to her right.

I looked at the wall: It was off-white and unadorned; not a crack marred its surface. I looked back at the woman: Her face was as blank as the wall; not a ripple of thought marred its surface.

In less than a minute a door on the other side of the desk swung open, and a woman in a long flowered-challis skirt and pink tee burst through it. Her entrance charged the air in the room; her dark curls radiated energy; her green eyes sparked; even the folds of her skirt and her extravagant silver earrings seemed electrified.

"Sharon," she said, "I'm Letta. Let's get the fuck out of here before I kill somebody."

Half an hour later we were seated at a table on the hotel terrace drinking Ramos fizzes. I'd told Letta about the Great Fizz Hunt that Hank Zahn and I had once undertaken in the company of a dozen kazoo-playing French tourists who were staying there; she'd calmed down enough to explain what was wrong at TriStar.

"First of all, there's that twit on the desk. I think they suctioned out her brain when they pierced her nose. Then there's the interior setup—*gawd!*" She threw back her head, tossing her long curls; her earrings jangled wildly. An elderly couple at the next table stared in frank disapproval.

James turned and looked at them. I braced for a confrontation.

"Sorry," she said. "My mama really did teach me better manners."

They nodded and smiled as they might at a naughty but spirited five year old.

"Anyway," Letta went on to me, "the setup. When I finally convince Ms. No-brains that I'm really who I say I am and get her to pass me through, it's as dark as the devil's fundament. I grope around for a minute, then walk smack into one of the baffles."

I raised an eyebrow.

"Oh, right, you wouldn't know. They're like enormous pillows, designed to suck up sound. They are not there to suck up my *face*. And while I'm trying to escape the embrace of this particular one, the lights come up and a voice booms down from the heavens." She pushed back from the table, half stood, and loomed over me. "'Ms. James,'" she mimicked in an English-accented bass, "'what *seems* to be the trouble?'"

The elderly couple watched her, smiling indulgently.

Letta noticed and sat back down, flushing.

"So," she went on in a low voice, "I look up, but I'm blinded by the lights. I say, 'Who the hell wants to know?' And he goes, 'This is Rodney, your sound engineer.' Then my vision clears and, by God, I see the voice really *is* coming from the heavens. I'm in a goddamned *pit*, like a Christian about to be fed to the lions, and the control booth is maybe twenty feet above me, and there, staring down like Nero and Caligula, are this asshole engineer—who later turns out to have cement blocks for ears—and my goddamned producer."

The waiter arrived with the seafood salads we'd ordered just as I said, "This is not an ideal setup, I assume."

"It's intimidating. It's inhibiting. It *sucks*!" She flung out her arm and caught the waiter on the shoulder. One of the salads teetered, but he made a last-second save.

"Oh *gawd*, I'm sorry!" James exclaimed. "I swear, you can't take me anyplace!"

The waiter also smiled indulgently as he served us.

"So why," I asked after making sure there was no one

else nearby for her to knock over, "are you using that particular studio?"

James signaled for another round of drinks and began eating. "Experiment. Trying out what's available in the Bay Area. My partner—she runs focus groups for ad agencies—got a great offer from a top market-research firm in the city. We're moving up here, but before we sell our L.A. condo I want to check out the recording facilities." Her mouth turned down glumly. "If TriStar's any example, I'll have to keep the condo so I can record down south."

Two fresh fizzes arrived. James set down her fork and seized her glass like a lifeline. "I think I'll sit up here swilling these all afternoon, then go back down there and tell that goddamned Adam exactly what I think of him."

"Adam?"

"My producer. He booked the studio." Her face brightened in anticipation of the scene. "So tell me about Ricky. How's he doing?"

I'd been considering how much of the situation I could entrust to Arletta James. Very little, I decided. Ricky liked her; I liked her; but she liked to hear herself talk. So I gave her an abbreviated version, downplaying its seriousness and making no mention of the more recent developments. "You and he have known each other a long time," I concluded, "so I hoped you might be able to shed some light on who's doing this. For instance, has anybody connected with him shown particular interest in 'My Mendacious Minstrel'?"

If James had anything to hide, she covered extremely well. She grew quiet and thoughtful, leaning back in her chair and twirling the stem of her glass between her thumb and forefinger. "No, nobody has," she finally said, "but it's funny about that song. I associate it with Ricky."

"In what way?"

"Well, I ran into him half an hour after I recorded it, at a place off Burbank Boulevard where a lot of industry people hang out. This would've been around three years ago. It was maybe two in the afternoon, and he was at the bar, downing shots of the hard stuff. That kind of boozing didn't fit with the guy I remembered, so I wandered over to say hello, but mainly to find out if success had changed him that much."

"Had it?"

"No way. We got to talking, and I saw that he was under a lot of stress and really pretty drunk. So I made him sit down in a booth with me while I had something to eat. We chatted—or I guess I did—and after a while I got up the nerve to ask him what was wrong. And he said, " 'Jesus, Letta, I've got this crazy woman after me.'"

"What woman?"

Letta shrugged. "He didn't name names. As I recall, the way it happened, he had three back-to-back performance dates down in Texas, and the first night he met this wannabe. Woman with a nice voice but nothing special, a nicer face and body. He'd been fighting with his wife—I guess that fighting and making up was how they used to get their kicks, but it had grown pretty stale for him and the fighting kept turning serious—" She broke off, shading her eyes from the sun and peering at me. "Sorry, I shouldn't be talking about that. For a minute I forgot you're Charly's sister."

"That's okay, go on." I hadn't thought about it before, but now that she pointed it out, I realized that on some level I'd always known what kind of games Ricky and Charlene were into.

"Well, they'd had a bad fight before he left California, and then this woman came along, and Ricky spent the weekend with her. Wasn't the first time he'd done something like that, although given what followed, it might've been the last." She paused, thoughtful again. "Happens like that, out on the road. People're so damned adoring, you start believing you're wonderful; then you start believing they're wonderful for thinking you are. Next thing you know . . ." She snapped her fingers and grinned impishly. "I myself am the most monogamous of women, but occasionally some sweet young thing can entice me. With most people it's understood that it's just a weekend romance, no strings attached. They keep it loose and get what they want—which is usually to go back to their real lives and tell everybody they slept with so-and-so—and you get what you want, too. And that's the way Ricky thought it was with this woman in Texas."

"But?"

"But after he got home she started bugging him. Somehow she got hold of his unlisted phone numbers, kept calling, sounding disturbed. Got hold of his address and started sending letters after he refused her calls."

"Saying what?"

"Oh, the usual that you hear from fans with overactive imaginations. Claimed he'd promised to leave his wife, write a song for her, make her a star. Happens to a lot of artists, particularly ones on Ricky's level. People they don't even know'll make the most outrageous allegations."

"Then why was he so stressed?"

"Usually the crazies go away if you don't respond to them, but this one wouldn't. And he *had* slept with her. Things were pretty rocky with Charly, and he was afraid if the woman went to her, as she threatened, it might spell the end of his marriage. I sensed there was something else too, something that upset him so much he couldn't talk about it. Anyway, I told him he ought to consult his lawyer."

"Did he?"

"Don't know. The situation must've gotten resolved,

though, because he and Charly are still together and he never mentioned it to me again." Letta frowned. "Of course, I'm not even sure he remembers telling me about it—that's how wasted he was. You don't think that woman is the one who's been writing those notes?"

The parallels between the situation and her folk ballad were obvious, but I said, "Probably not. Three years is a long time to nurse a fantasy—or a grudge."

"I hope you won't let on to Ricky that I told you."

"I'll try to get the story out of him some other way. And I hope you won't tell anyone about those notes."

"My mouth's a whole lot bigger than it ought to be, but I wouldn't do that to Ricky. He stood by me back in Bakersfield when I came out of the closet and, believe me, that took some courage in those days. And he won't own up to it, but I know for a fact that he was the one who brought my work to the attention of the A and R department at my new label. I acknowledged him on the liner notes for *Old-fashioned Lady,* the album that ballad's on."

"I know," I said distractedly.

Again James frowned. "Sharon, I think you *are* worried about that Texas woman."

She'd read me correctly—I was.

By the time I reached the toll plaza on the other side of the Golden Gate I'd come up with something else to worry about—Mick's safety. If I was interpreting the note writer's message correctly, any member of the Savage family was a potential target; yet Mick was on his own here in the city, unaware of the danger because his father had insisted I not tell him about the investigation. True, he was reasonably tough and streetwise, but even the toughest of us are better able to defend ourselves if forewarned. Until I could persuade Ricky to confide in Mick, I needed to take steps to protect him.

I was driving along Motel Row on Lombard Street when an idea came to me, but before I could refine it my pager went off somewhere in the depths of my purse. When I finally retrieved it, the display showed Ricky and Charlene's number; I punched it out on the car phone while making the turn onto Van Ness. Hy answered.

"What's happening?" I asked.

"I've got the situation in hand," he said in a guarded tone that told me he wasn't alone, "but I think you ought to come down here."

"Oh?"

"Hold on, I'm going to switch to another phone."

I held, moving the receiver to my left hand so I could work the gearshift.

"Okay," Hy said after a minute, "I'm in Ricky's home office and can talk."

"I take it Charlene was there."

"Charlene, Kurt Girdwood, the housekeeper, a maid, and the dogs' trainer."

"Dogs?"

"You don't know about them? Two saluki puppies; they've had them a few weeks now."

"But why do they need a trainer? Charlene can't train them herself?"

"Apparently not. Proper obedience training, she tells me, is very important to a dog's development."

"Too bad she didn't apply that concept to her kids' development. How is she?"

"Mean as a snake, but cooperating."

"Ricky there yet?"

"No, but he called earlier to say that Ethan Amory is coming down from L.A. and the band's following tonight. He claims they need to get in a couple of rehearsal sessions before the tour. And Rattray's announced his ETA too. God knows who else'll show before the day's up."

"Ripinsky, you know what I think is going on? I think that having all those people around is Ricky's way of not dealing with the situation—or with Charlene."

"Me too. I reminded him that he didn't want anybody to know why my people are here, but he said he'd put out the word that I'd talked him into increasing security on an experimental basis."

"You sound discouraged."

"I am, sort of. My man's already briefed Charlene, Chris, and Jamie on the usual precautions—varying the routes you normally take, varying your routines, driving with the doors locked and not stopping for anybody—and now he's working with the household staff. But still, having all those visitors here is going to complicate our job."

"I hate to say it, but it's going to simplify mine. I want to take a good close look at all of Ricky's people, and I'll have most of them right there under one roof."

"So when're you coming down?"

"As soon as I can pack and catch a flight."

"You're not bringing the Citabria?"

"Like you said earlier, a commercial flight's faster." When he didn't respond, I added, "Really, that's the only reason." I was telling the truth; any lingering vestiges of near-miss anxiety had vanished when I'd taken possession of the plane's keys.

"Listen," I went on, "I want to use Charlotte Keim to run some checks for me. Who do I clear that with at RKI?"

"Me—and it's cleared."

"Thanks. Do you know if they've got a fax down there?"

"Right here in the office." He recited its number for me.

I told him I'd pick up a rental car at Lindbergh Field and see him at the house, then hung up and dialed Keim at home. Even though tomorrow was Sunday, she was willing to go into the office in the morning. After warning her that Mick was not to know what she was working on, I promised to fax her a list of Ricky's employees and associates. All that was left now was to pack and enlist Rae in my scheme to protect my nephew.

"So Mick is supposed to think he's protecting me from whoever grabbed me at Coso Street, while in actuality I'm protecting him?" Rae was curled up on my bed, watching me pack. The swelling on her face had gone down some, but she still held her right arm gingerly and bruises had formed there and on her legs.

"I know it's kind of lame, but it was the best I could come up with on short notice." I pictured the pool on the hilltop terrace behind the Savages' house and tossed a swimsuit into the bag.

"It's not that bad, and it'll make Mick think he's getting in some fieldwork for a change. But I think Ricky's making a big mistake in not telling him about the investigation." She scowled. "What's he afraid of, anyway?"

"Well, if this involves a woman—"

"So what? Does he really think Mick doesn't know that he screws around?"

I glanced at her.

"No, I'm not putting him down for that. I understand what's been operating there and, besides, I don't think he does anymore. He told me last night was the first time in several years that he'd allowed himself to become interested in anyone. But the point is, Mick must've figured out about his dad ages ago."

"Maybe Ricky's just being overprotective. He has that tendency."

Rae looked down, pleating the hem of her oversized tee between her fingers. "Maybe. Or . . ."

I zipped my travel bag. "Or what?"

"I've got the feeling that there's something else going on with him: guilt. On a subconscious level he's feeling very guilty about something—and I don't think it has to do with your sister or his kids. He may not even be fully aware of it."

A former psychology student embroidering on the situation, or a genuine insight? "What do you base that on?"

"Oh, a combination of little cues, nothing all that specific." Her fingers were pleating faster now. "When you've been . . . fairly intimate with a person, you pick up on stuff like that."

"I thought you said you didn't—"

"I said I came to my senses after we'd driven a couple of blocks. But things can progress very rapidly in two blocks of city traffic, even at that hour. Anyway, guilt struck me as an underlying motif in a lot of what he said to me later. See if you can pick up on it."

I nodded. "In the meantime, you call Mick and ask him if he'll move in here for a few days. And I may need you on the case after I talk with Ricky—if he made his flight and actually turns up at home."

"Oh, he made the flight."

"How d'you know?"

"He called me right before they took off. He wanted to apologize again for coming on so strong last night. I didn't tell him what happened at Coso Street; that's your business."

"Nice of him to call."

"He's a nice man, one of the nicest I know." She hesitated, smiling faintly. "Actually, I was the one who came on strong. I shouldn't have, but there was no way I could resist that great come-fuck-me voice."

"That *what?*"

She gave me a disbelieving look. "You must've noticed."

"He's got a great voice, yes. But he's . . . well, he's married to my kid sister."

"What's that got to do with anything? Just really listen to him sometime."

On the way to SFO I put a tape of *The Broken Promise Land* album into the cassette player and really listened to Ricky.

Rae was right: He *did* have a come-fuck-me voice.

Nine

The home that Charlene and Ricky had built after fire destroyed their Pacific Palisades place was high on a ridge above La Jolla and commanded impressive views of city and sea. In an area of large, heavily wooded properties, theirs was one of the most extensive—some twenty acres covered by eucalyptus and pepper trees and the wind-twisted Torrey pines that are native to the San Diego coast. I approached it on freshly paved blacktop that switchbacked through the hills; after a mile or so, high stucco walls overhung with bright crimson bougainvillea marked the beginning of the estate. A black-iron security gate blocked the drive, and next to it sat a guard wearing RKI's maroon blazer; even at a distance I could detect the bulge of his shoulder holster.

I stopped beside him and lowered the window of my rental car. The early evening heat billowed inside, overcoming the air-conditioned cool. The guard examined my I.D., then opened the gate and waved me through; I drove on toward the red-tiled roof that loomed above the trees on the slope. The land on either side of the driveway fell away into thick vegetation. After about a quarter of a mile I spotted the tennis court and the building that contained Ricky's rehearsal studio. The drive took an upturn, ran under a canopy of arching oaks, and ended in a large circular parking area in front of the house. It was Mediterranean style, cream-colored, two stories at the center with one-story wings extending off at oblique angles—too brashly new and formal for my taste, but I had to acknowledge its beauty.

I pulled the car into the shade of one of the oaks and got out, surveying the other vehicles parked there: Ricky's Porsche, Chris's little Triumph, two maroon-and-gray RKI vans, a BMW, a Cadillac, two newish Ford pickups, and a Geo Prizm that looked to be another rental.

Cast of thousands is right, I thought, shaking my head as I went up to the bleached-wood door.

Hy opened it before I got there; the guard must have called to say I was on my way. I'd thought he looked tired last night before the concert, but now he looked downright haggard. Wordlessly he held out his arms; I went to him and nestled close for a moment. When I stepped back, I said, "What, no salukis rushing to greet me?"

He rolled his eyes. "The boys, as your sister calls them, have been banished to their dog run. Ricky arrived, took one look at the mess they'd made of his favorite moccasins, and ordered them out of the house. Charlene protested, he shouted, and Chris and Jamie fled to their rooms. Then Kurt Girdwood appeared and started yelling at Ricky—"

"At Ricky? Why?"

"No reason. While Girdwood was carrying on, Ricky explained to me that managers always yell because they get yelled at a lot and develop hearing problems. Girdwood finally gave up on getting his attention and headed for the room with the bar with Ethan Amory in tow. And then Charlene and Ricky picked up their argument where they left off, continued with it all the way through the living room and the kitchen and down the hall to their wing, where, if my ears don't deceive me, they're arguing still."

"My God, what a zoo!"

"Oh, that's only part of it. The band members have begun to show up. They've checked into the larger guest house and are now demanding drinks and snacks poolside, like this was some exclusive resort hotel. Keeps the housekeeper—a likeable, overworked woman named Nona—hopping. One of the maids quit this afternoon and had to be paid a fair amount of hush money to keep her from talking about the security situation here. And Rattray's making a pest of himself in the kitchen, so odds are ten-to-one that the housekeeper'll quit, too."

I felt a dreadful sinking sensation, followed by a flutter of panic. "We're not going to stay here, are we?"

"Unfortunately, I think it's best—at least for tonight. We're in the smaller guest house which, mercifully, is at a good remove from the wing where your sister and brother-in-law are currently trying to rip each other's throats out."

I let my body sag against Hy's, my arm circling his waist. "Do you ever get the idea that the good life ain't what it's cracked up to be?"

"Yeah. For all that we've got to tend the fires and cook and clean for ourselves, I'm thinking fondly of Touchstone."

"Me too." I moved away from him and motioned at the open door. "Shall we?"

"Into the fray."

The tiled entryway was chilly after the evening heat. I crossed to the steps that led down to the living room and peered in there. The room was huge, with a hardwood floor and cream area rugs and groupings of tan leather furnishings; a new collection of African masks over the fireplace lent a discordant note, as did the pair of chewed-up moccasins that lay in the middle of one of the rugs. Numerous flower arrangements comprised mostly of sticks sat on the low tables. I went down the steps, crossed to the glass wall at the opposite side, and looked out.

Three men reclined on cushioned lounges around the free-form black-bottomed pool. The setting sun glared over the low terrace wall, dappling the water and bronzing their skin. I recognized red-haired Jerry Jackson, the drummer; big, bearded Norm O'Dell, the lead guitarist; and the blond ponytailed bass player, Forrest Curtin. Curtin was lighting a joint; he took a hit and then offered it to Jackson.

Hy came up behind me. "That should keep them sedated for a while."

"I don't think they're supposed to be doing that where the girls can see them."

"You want to tell them to stop?"

"No, I want Charlene or Ricky to, but apparently they're too busy battling to bother. Maybe it's good they are, though; maybe they'll work things out and make up."

"I don't know. The fighting I heard earlier wasn't the productive type."

"God. What is this going to do to the kids? What is it doing to Chris and Jamie right now? I think I better check on them, see how they're coping."

Hy put a staying hand on my arm. "Before you do, I want you to check out Girdwood and Amory. Something's going on there that I can't get a handle on."

"How so?"

"Well, for one thing, I can't figure out why they're here at all. And I don't like the questions Amory's asking about the security measures; I caught him practically interrogating a couple of our people."

"They tell him anything?"

"No. They're trained to be discreet."

"You say Amory and Girdwood are in the den?"

"Last I saw of them."

I'd been to the house only the one time, for the party after the family moved in. Now I looked around, uncertain of my bearings.

Hy grinned. "A road map would help. Follow me."

He led me back across the entryway and down a corridor where the walls were hung with abstract paintings in bright primary colors—something which, like the African masks and the floral arrangements, I couldn't imagine either Charlene or Ricky selecting. It struck me now that when the fire destroyed their home in Pacific Palisades, it took more than their possessions; it was as though they'd also lost their sense of who they were, and were struggling—with the aid of a bad decorator—to recover their identities. The sudden insight made me even more afraid for them, more frightened yet for their kids.

Noises came from the end of the corridor: the familiar strains of "The Broken Promise Land" overscored by a man's strident voice.

"Now *that* is what makes him great. His *presence*, his *power*. Just watch this!"

I looked into the den, a large room with a bar running along one wall, flanked by a pinball machine and a jukebox. On the perpendicular wall a big-screen TV was playing a video of one of Ricky's concerts. As my brother-in-law picked a complicated guitar sequence, a squarish, bullet-headed man in a lurid Hawaiian shirt paced back and forth in front of the screen, expounding loudly.

"Look at him! All this bullshit about his career having peaked is just so much *bullshit*. Ricky Savage will be turning out chartbusters when we're both in our graves. He is, and will continue to be, a force to be reckoned with in this industry, and I *defy* anyone to tell me otherwise!"

A second man seated in one of the cushioned chairs facing the TV reached for the remote control and muted the sound. He was slender, with wild brown hair and aviator glasses, clad in chinos and a green-and-white rugby shirt. When he spoke his voice was low and gently southern-accented, but it commanded more attention than the other man's ranting.

"You don't have to convince me, Kurt," he said. "Save it for Rick. He'll need it once his wife is done chewing him up and spitting him out."

The bullet-headed man—Kurt Girdwood—whirled on him, pointing his finger. "I've warned you before, Ethan, don't talk to me about Charly! You don't know what's happening with her. You didn't know them in the old days, didn't see what she had to put up with."

Ethan Amory, Ricky's music attorney, made a conciliatory gesture with his long-fingered hand. "Maybe not, but what I see now isn't good. Whatever's going on with her is eating him alive. You want to help the poor bastard, do something about her."

Girdwood's shoulders slumped and he sat down heavily in a second chair, reaching for a drink on the table between them.

"And then there's the other problem," Amory added. "These extreme security precautions—what the hell's the reason for them?"

"He said—"

"I know what he said. But you can't tell me it's the whole story. This RKI is no ordinary outfit; they're international consultants in antiterrorism, based down in La Jolla."

"The sister-in-law's boyfriend is a partner."

"So Rick, out of family loyalty, decided to use people who charge what RKI does to provide routine protection for his family? Bullshit, Kurt. Something's going on here, something serious, and Rick's not leveling. I say we call him on it."

"I wouldn't, if I were you."

"Jesus Christ, what're you afraid of? You act as if he had some hold over you."

Girdwood didn't reply.

"Well," Amory said after a moment, "I'm going to make it my business to get to the bottom of this."

A silence fell. I waited a few beats, then cleared my throat and stepped into the room. "Gentlemen, you must be Mr. Girdwood and Mr. Amory."

They turned their heads toward me, expressions startled. Amory rose from his chair. I went over to them, extending my hand first to him and then to the manager. "I'm Sharon McCone, Charlene's sister. And this is my friend Hy Ripinsky. Or have you met?"

Behind me, Hy said, "We've met."

The two men exchanged glances, probably wondering if we'd overheard their conversation. I took the opportunity to slip onto a bar stool. "Hy's implementing Ricky's new domestic-security program," I told them, "and I came along for the ride. You know, I think I missed both of you at the housewarming. It's a pleasure to meet the people Ricky's spoken so highly of." I paused, smiling at Amory. "Well, he wasn't speaking so highly of *you* after your meeting with Winterland yesterday. Your condom proposal didn't go over very well."

Amory smiled back—thinly. "We've all agreed it was a bad idea, Ms. McCone."

"Please, call me Sharon."

Hy had moved behind the bar. "Drinks, anyone?"

Amory looked down at an empty glass on the table. "Thanks—Glenlivet and water, please."

Girdwood rattled the ice in his glass and took it and Amory's to the bar. Hy dispensed fresh cubes and poured, opened a bottle of Chardonnay and brought a glass of it to me, fetched a beer for himself.

"Ripinsky," I murmured as he took the stool next to mine, "if you ever part company with Renshaw and Kessell, you've got a fallback position as a bartender."

He winked at me.

"So," I said, turning to the manager and attorney, "what brings you down here?"

"Drafts of contracts to go over," Amory said. "Winterland expedited them; that's how eager they are for the additional Savage licensing—minus the condoms, of course."

"And you?" I asked Girdwood.

He shrugged, the flowers on his Hawaiian shirt fluttering. "I'm here in case he needs me."

"Needs you? In what way?"

"Well, for one thing, the single of 'Midnight Train to Nowhere' is being released to radio next week. We'll be monitoring the BDS reports on airplay."

"BDS?"

"Broadcast Data System. It samples airplay on a hundred and forty-three country stations nationwide, twenty-four hours a day, seven days a week. *Billboard*'s charts're compiled from it. If play isn't good, Rick'll need me to hold his stress level down and interface."

"Interface?"

Girdwood stifled a sigh, impatient with my outsider's

ignorance. "That's what managers *do*, Sharon. I interface between him and the label, him and his publicist, him and his booking agent—and anybody else or anything that can come between him and his work. In many ways a manager is a hand-holder."

That still didn't explain why he'd come down here tonight.

Amory tossed back his drink and went to the bar. "Too bad you can't interface between him and his wife," he said softly.

I glanced at him and my eyes met his in the back-bar mirror. He smiled ironically at me and set his glass down. Ethan Amory, I was sure, knew I'd overheard his earlier conversation with Girdwood. I hoped he considered me as naive as I pretended to be.

"Kurt," he said, "drink up. We've got dinner reservations in La Jolla." To Hy and me he added, "If you see Rick, tell him we'll be back around ten and would like him to hold some time open for us."

I nodded and watched them leave the room. "Why," I said to Hy, "do I get the idea that they came down here for other than their stated reasons?"

"Why wouldn't you? Ricky says he doesn't trust either of them; they get my gut-level alarm system going. And your instincts along those lines are finer tuned than either of ours."

"So what *is* going on?"

"Damned if I know."

"Come on, Ripinsky, help me out."

"Well, they're here for reasons of self-interest, that's for sure. And I'd say that their self-interest lies with making sure Ricky stays on top. Girdwood was talking a good fight while they were watching that video, but it's obvious he's worried. Maybe about the same thing that's got

Amory worried—namely, the situation with your sister—but maybe not."

"I don't think Amory likes Charlene."

"No, but Girdwood does." Hy hesitated, frowning. "I wish I didn't feel like everything's caving in here."

"The marriage, you mean?"

"More than that."

"What, specifically?"

"I can't put my finger on it, but—"

A heavyset woman in a plain blue dress that resembled a uniform came into the room; she had a high brow crowned by white braids that twined around her head. Her lips curved into a tentative smile.

"Ah, Nona." Hy got off his stool and motioned for her to join us. "This is Mrs. Savage's sister, Sharon McCone." To me he added, "Mrs. Nona Davidson, the lady who keeps this place functioning."

I shook hands with the housekeeper. She said, "Chris asked me to tell you she'd like to see you in her room, if it's convenient."

That surprised me. Charlene and Ricky's eldest daughter had never related particularly well to her Aunt Sharon; if anything, the cool, blond teenager seemed to find me eccentric and a bit off-putting. "I was about to go up there," I said, "but I'm afraid you'll have to show me the way. The layout of the house confuses me."

Nona Davidson smiled sympathetically. "It's an odd design. I'll be happy to take you to her."

Chris's room matched her cool exterior: a bright, white space with large windows overlooking the pool, dominated at one end by a bed with a black-and-white checkerboard spread and at the other with a desk and computer setup. Everything was spare and high tech, without any of the usual teenage clutter. My niece sat in a director's chair, smoking, her long Spandex-encased legs propped on a second chair. She regarded me narrow-eyed through the smoke and, though it was an activity forbidden by her parents, made no effort to conceal the cigarette. Only the slight tremor of her fingers as she raised it and inhaled told me she was under considerable strain.

"Aunt Shar," she said, motioning at the bed, "please, sit down."

I kicked off my sandals and sat, tucking my feet under me. "So what's happening?"

She smiled faintly. "What's *not* happening? Some crazy person's after Dad. Your boyfriend's ordering us around like we were in the marines. Mom's gone ballistic. Dad lit into Mom the second he walked into the house. And Jamie's in her room puking and crying. Otherwise everything's great."

"And you? How're you holding up?"

"Me? I spent the afternoon on-line to the TechnoWeb's Distressed Teen board. No," she added quickly, "I didn't let anything slip about the Dad situation; Hy cautioned us against that."

"Did the people on the board help any?"

"Some." She hesitated. "The thing is, I know I'll be all right. I know crazies go with Dad's territory. And I know why he and Mom are fighting." To my raised eyebrows she nodded. "Yeah, I do. You can't help but hear things. Their fights, and her whispered phone conversations, and all her stupid attempts to cover up. But *we're* not deaf or blind, Jamie and I. We know she's seeing somebody else, and now that she's told him, it's driving Dad over the edge. What they don't understand is that it's driving *us* over the edge, too."

"But you say you'll be all right?"

She got up, fetched an ashtray, and crushed out her

cigarette; immediately she lighted another. "Yeah, I will be. I'm not like Jamie, all soft inside. And I'm not like either Mom or Dad. Or Mick or Molly or Lisa or Brian. God knows who I take after, but—" And then she broke off and looked into my eyes, cigarette halfway to her lips.

"Uh-huh," I said.

"Well, maybe."

"For sure. Why do you think we've never been the best of buddies? I'm always uncomfortable around people who are too much like me, and I bet it's the same for you."

"Huh." She thought that over. "Well, then you know I'll be okay. But that isn't the reason I wanted to talk to you. I wondered—d'you think you could do something to help Jamie?"

"She's in that bad a state?"

"Yeah, pretty rocky."

I stood up and reached with my toes for my sandals. "I'll try. Point me toward her room, would you?"

When Chris left me at Jamie's door, she gave my hand a tentative squeeze.

Except for its size and general configuration, Jamie's room was the exact opposite of her sister's: a sunny yellow, with bright southwestern rugs. One wall had been turned into a bulletin board covered with layers and layers of pictures, cards, posters, invitations, and drawings. On the back of the bathroom door hung a life-size cutout of Ricky from his *Broken Promise Land* tour; a mustache, beard, and devil's horns had been sketched in, as well as several earrings and a bone through his nose. There was clutter everywhere: books, tapes, clothing, sports equipment, stuffed animals.

Jamie had been lying on her bed listening to rap music

when I knocked, and she called for me to come in. Immediately she muted it, got up, and rushed into the bathroom. Water ran for a moment, and then she came back with a fresh face-wash that did nothing for her red, puffy eyes. Her tiny features were lost and mournful under her mop of outrageously permed brown hair. She perched on the bed again, turning the CD player off with the remote.

"How're you doing?" I asked, removing some sweats from an armchair and sitting.

She shrugged, smiling wanly.

That bothered me; Jamie had always been the outgoing child, the one you could never get to stop talking.

"You have a nice birthday?"

"It was okay. Thanks for the check you sent."

"You have a party?"

"Yeah, but that security guy showed up in the middle of it, and Mom started pitching fits."

"Tough being cooped up like this."

"Yeah—and all because Dad did something stupid."

"Why do you say that?"

"It's what Mom says." She paused. "Of course, Mom says a lot of shit these days, and you never know what's true. Are they still in their room fighting?"

"I don't know."

"I'll bet they are." She balled her fists and pounded them against her blue-jeaned knees. "I *hate* it! I wish they'd just go ahead and get a goddamned divorce!"

I hesitated, unwilling to meddle in what was a private family matter. Then I told myself that my niece badly needed to talk this through and, besides, the Savages were my family too. "You really think divorce is a possibility?"

"About the only one."

"Why?"

114

She was silent, her eyes shifting away from mine.

"Jamie?"

". . . Oh, all right. Mom's seeing somebody else—this guy named Vic who she met last year when he was a guest lecturer in her department at USC. He's head of one of those monster money funds and they're doing something in China and he wants Mom to go on a trip to Beijing with him. I think she's going to do it, and that's going to totally blow the marriage."

"Is she in love with this Vic?"

"I think so. She's been sneaking around for months now, and Dad's been suspicious. She finally told him the truth the other morning before he went up to San Francisco. Now she's scared of what he'll do, and she's making our lives miserable." Jamie paused, out of breath and, I thought, shocked at herself for blurting it all out.

She certainly did know a lot about my sister's affair, but somehow I couldn't imagine Charlene confiding in a fifteen-year-old. "How'd you find this out?" I asked.

She looked down and shrugged.

"I won't tell."

"Promise?"

"Promise."

"Well, I have a bad habit."

"And that is . . . ?"

"I listen in on people's phone calls." She looked up, adding defensively, "Only sometimes. Only when they're talking about things I need to know."

"And you needed to know—"

"Why my mother's ruining all our lives? Yes, Aunt Shar, I *did* need to know that."

I should take her to task, I thought, but she did have a point. Besides, how could I? I'd made a career of snooping into other people's business.

"Jamie . . ." I began.

"I know it's wrong. Even Chris says so, and she's got about a zillion bad habits of her own."

"Chris knows what you did?"

She nodded.

"Who else did you tell?"

"Nobody. Mick's too far away and he'd really kind of disconnected from the family. And I don't think the others're old enough to handle it. I'm not handling it all that well myself; I throw up a lot."

Poor kid! The knowledge of her mother's secret and her guilt over how she'd found it out were eating her up. No wonder Chris had asked me to talk with her.

I asked, "When is this trip to China supposed to take place?"

"In two weeks."

Smack in the middle of the *Midnight* tour; that was going to do wonders for Ricky's performances. Bad, bad timing, Charlene.

But I couldn't muster up any anger toward my sister. Like Kurt Girdwood, I remembered how she'd suffered silently through all the lean years while Ricky relentlessly pursued his dream. I'd witnessed her loneliness and need and desperation. And, I now realized, I hadn't had a clue as to what actually went on inside their marriage.

Jamie was watching me as though she hoped I'd say a few magical words that would make everything all right again. I got up and began to wander around the room, stopping here to study a picture, there to examine a book jacket. There was an entertainment center between the windows, and I ran my eyes over the CDs—

Through the plastic cover of one, Arletta James smiled, sitting on a stool, dressed in lace and satin. A Post-it note had been stuck over the title, and on it the words "Listen to cut 4" were written. Written in the same hand as the notes Ricky had received.

Quickly I picked up the CD and turned it over. Scanned the list of songs. Cut four was "My Mendacious Minstrel."

In an overly casual tone I asked, "You like this album?"

"God, no!"

Of course she wouldn't; the CD she'd been listening to earlier was by Snoop Doggy Dogg. "Where'd you get it?"

"Birthday present. Mom said it just appeared some time in a pile of packages she had put away for me in one of the guest-room closets. The woman who recorded it is an old friend of Dad's."

"Did you listen to it?"

"Uh-uh."

"Then would you mind if I borrowed it?"

"Keep it, it's yours."

"Thanks." I started for the door.

"Aunt Shar? Do you think Mom and Dad'll bust up?"

I wanted to hand her a reassuring lie, but she needed to be prepared. "It's a good possibility."

"What'll happen to the rest of us?"

The question was so forlorn that I went over and hugged her. "Jamie, don't worry. Besides your parents—who love you regardless of what's happening between them—you've got Grandma and Melvin, Grandpa and Nancy, John, Joey, Patsy, and me—as well as our spouses, boyfriends, girlfriends, children, and even pets, if you prefer them. All I can tell you is that you won't be alone in this."

She gave me a tremulous smile and pressed the remote to reactivate Snoop Doggy Dogg's dulcet tones.

On the way down the hall I clutched Arletta James's CD so hard I cracked the plastic cover. My pulse beat was rapid and my mouth had gone dry. Once again the note writer had made his or her point: Ricky and his family could be gotten to—even on their own turf at his daughter's fifteenth birthday party.

When I reached the entryway I heard voices coming from the living room. I skidded slightly on the tiles, hurried over to the archway. The sun had vanished over the distant sea and the sky was layered in glorious reds and oranges, shading to magenta and then deepening to midnight blue.

Irrelevantly I thought, What is that saying about a red sky being a warning?

Outside the glass wall the woodsy vegetation was shrouded in darkness. Light from underwater spots made the black depths of the pool glimmer, but around it the shadows were as thick and warped as the Torrey pines.

Not good for the security lights to be off. I'd have to remind Hy to have his team check them.

In front of the window wall Ricky stood, barefoot and clad in cutoffs and a T-shirt, talking with Virgil Rattray. The road manager was dressed all in black again; his long tresses swayed as he made some point, tapping my brother-in-law's shoulder for emphasis. If it hadn't been for the light from a lamp on a low table, I'd have mistaken him for a tall, thin woman.

I paused at the top of the steps. The wide expanse of glass made me feel vulnerable, naked. I'd seen few blinds or draperies on windows in this house; of course, on twenty wooded acres they wouldn't be necessary for privacy.

Both men heard me and turned. Ricky took a step forward, opening his mouth to speak. Rattray moved around him.

The glass wall shattered.

I saw the bullet hole first. Then cracks began to run

helter-skelter like a slow-motion film of a spring thaw. Shards flew inward as a shot boomed somewhere in the blackness beyond the pool.

Virgil Rattray crumpled to the floor.

Ricky just stood there.

I lunged forward, tackled him, and brought him down.

Ten

People were shouting and running into the room. I could hear Hy on a walkie-talkie, yelling for the guards to search the property, to let no one on or off. There was a heavy weight across my lower body. Ricky. I reached toward him, and my hand touched shards of glass and a thick, slippery liquid.

Blood. I could smell it. Too much blood to have come from superficial cuts.

Panicked, I struggled to move, but Ricky was already rolling off me. People crowded around us now, and someone pulled him to his feet. I moved onto my side, felt glass cut into my forearms, and winced. I couldn't see Rattray.

Ricky said, "Shar—are you okay?"

"McCone?" Hy called.

"I'm all right. What about Rattray?"

Someone stepped back then. I saw the road manager lying in a fetal position and making hoarse, high-pitched sounds that reminded me of a terrified parrot. One of the guards knelt beside him, prying Rats's fingers loose from his right shoulder, where blood seeped through them and ran down onto the floor. He ripped open Rattray's shirt and examined the wound. After a moment he said, "He's lost a lot of blood, but it's not too bad."

"What do you mean, not too bad?" Rattray croaked. "It hurts like hell, you cocksucker!"

Ricky let out a sigh of relief. "Rats is his usual charming self; he'll live." He extended his hands and got me to my feet. He was pale and shaky and had cuts on his forearms, but otherwise seemed okay.

Hy was still on the walkie-talkie. "Nothing? Well, keep searching. And get those security lights on; check the breaker box on the north side of the garage." To the guard kneeling next to Rattray he added, "Call that doctor in Pacific Beach that we use and get him up here. This man's got to be treated, but we can't have a police report on it."

I looked down at the shattered glass on the floor. Arletta James's blood-speckled image stared up from where I'd dropped the CD. For a moment I felt as if I were being sucked into a whirlpool, then Ricky steadied me and the vertigo subsided.

The security lights by the pool flashed on. Hy said into the walkie-talkie, "What was it? . . . Uh-huh, I thought so . . . Nothing? Well, keep at it until you've covered everyplace. Then I want a complete list of everybody who's entered and left the property tonight—times, too. And for God's sake, keep the family out of this part of the house."

Too late. I looked up, saw my nieces in the entryway. Jamie was crying and a white-lipped Chris was restraining her by the shoulders. I started toward them, then stopped when I spotted Charlene at the foot of the steps.

She looked terrible. In the weeks since I'd last seen her she'd grown too thin and hollow-cheeked; her usually sleek cap of short blond hair was dry and unkempt; her skin was pale and papery. But her eyes were the worst: underscored by purplish half moons and, now, black and bottomless with horror.

As I watched her I had the curious sense that time was slowing down. She stood frozen, staring at Ricky. He looked back but remained equally still. Finally she took a tentative step and held out her hands to him.

Ricky turned away.

She blinked, looked down at her outstretched hands, and ran from the room.

Ricky waited till the sound of her footsteps had died away; then he went to his daughters.

I took the last sheet of the batch that I'd been transmitting to RKI's San Francisco office from the fax machine. It was long after midnight, but I wanted the information on Ricky's employees and associates that I'd culled from his files to be on Charlotte Keim's desk first thing in the morning. Behind me the office door opened and shut. Hy.

"Everything under control?" I asked.

"More or less. While I was questioning people about their whereabouts at the time of the shooting I put out the word that it was probably a stray bullet from a deer poacher. Girdwood's not buying that, but he's not challenging it, either. Amory's very curious about both the shooting and the security arrangements; he's asking a lot of questions and pressing hard for answers. I referred him to Ricky."

"He won't get anything there. Ricky doesn't trust him, and I can't say as I blame him. Amory's a manipulator. Reminds me of a blackmailer I once knew: always skulking around collecting information. Never mind whether he needs it; he might be able to use it some day. What about the band members?"

Hy grimaced. "There's some heavy drug use going down tonight. None of them're in a condition to do more than accept the situation at face value."

"Nice house party they've got going here. Great environment for Chris and Jamie."

"Uh, I want to talk to you about them. Your nieces are in Jamie's room—coping, I think, with the aid of some grass they copped off one of the band members."

"Jesus! Their parents don't approve of them doing either drugs or alcohol. I caught Christ smoking a cigarette this afternoon, and she didn't even try to hide it. I can't lay down the law to them, though; they're not my kids."

"Why don't you talk to Charlene?"

"Are you kidding? She's barricaded herself in her room. I tried half an hour ago, and she wouldn't let me inside *or* talk to me through the door. Where's Ricky?"

"Down at the rehearsal studio with the band."

"Now? It's nearly one in the morning."

"Musicians don't operate on normal schedules, any more than you or I. Besides, I think he's acting on the principle that when your life starts going to hell you throw yourself into your work. Anyway, that's where he is. Girdwood and Amory are hitting the bar again. The doctor's come and gone, and Rattray's resting comfortably in one of the guest rooms."

"They've got guest rooms, in addition to the guest houses?"

Hy sat on the edge of the desk and yawned. "I suppose they were anticipating weekends like this."

"No one in his right mind could possibly anticipate a weekend like this. You say the band members are doing drugs. What about Ricky?"

"Well, there's a fine grade of coke being passed around down there, and he offered me some."

I frowned.

"No, McCone, I didn't take him up on it. Do I look like a guy who's running on synthetic energy?"

"Well, if Ricky's coked up, he's not going to be much help as far as the problem with Chris and Jamie. Still, I should tell him about it."

"Why don't you stop in on them first, see if maybe I'm wrong. If I'm not, at least they won't be going anywhere; I alerted the guard in that wing to watch out for them."

That removed some of the urgency from the situation. "So where was everybody when the shot was fired?"

"Unfortunately, what I got out of people is vague and unreliable at best. The band members claim they were in and out of the rehearsal studio, waiting on Ricky to finish with Rattray, but none of them can corroborate the others' stories. None of them admits to hearing the shot, either."

"That's possible; the studio's fully soundproofed and far enough from the house that you might take a shot fired up here for a car backfiring. What about Amory and Girdwood?"

"Had just gotten back from dinner and were talking in the parking area."

"Short dinner."

"Yes, but the gate guard corroborates their arrival."

"None of the staff were on the property?"

"They all live out."

"I hate to ask this, but what about Charlene, Chris, and Jamie?"

He raised an eyebrow.

"Both girls are pretty angry with their parents. And Charlene's completely off the wall. This threat to Ricky may have given one of them an idea."

"Christ, I hope you're wrong there. But whoever fired that shot was familiar with the property. The security lights in back didn't go out by themselves; somebody tripped the circuit breaker. Part of the system—the alarms on the wall by the road—went out, too."

"So where was the family?"

"In their rooms, as far as I know. And Ricky says neither he nor Charlene owns a gun. I had my people search the entire place, including the cars, but of course it's impossible to comb the grounds at night; there're plenty of places out there where somebody who's familiar with the property could hide a rifle."

"A rifle? Then you found the bullet?"

"Yeah, thirty-caliber. Scored Rats's shoulder and embedded itself in a chair."

I was silent, picturing the scene in the living room immediately before the glass wall shattered. "You know, Ripinsky, I don't think that shot was meant to hit anybody."

"No?"

"Uh-uh. Right before it was fired, Rattray and Ricky noticed me standing on the steps. Ricky started toward me. Rattray moved, too—into the space that would've been between them, had they stayed put. My guess is that the shooter was aiming there and already pulling the trigger when Rattray stepped into his line of fire."

"Interesting. Like the CD that was given to Jamie—another teaser or warning." Hy thought about that for a moment, yawned more widely, and motioned at the papers in my hand. "What're those?"

"Information from Ricky's files that I just faxed to Keim's office."

"You go over it?"

"I started to, but I'm too damned tired to focus. Hungry, too. I haven't eaten since lunch."

"Me either, come to think of it. Why don't you and I raid the fridge and call it a night? I noticed a nice deep Jacuzzi in our bungalow."

The idea was tempting, but I shook my head. "I want to check on my nieces and, if you're right about the dope, I'll try once more to get through to Charlene. If I can't, I'll go down to the studio and talk with Ricky. Besides, I want to take a closer look at those band members."

As I followed the flagstone path to the studio, my overactive imagination conjured up a sniper in the shadows. Small spotlights close to the ground illuminated my feet and threw my upper body into outline. I pictured myself as a shooter would: alone, an easy target. I listened for the whine of a bullet, the report of a shot—

Stop it! I warned myself. You're getting off on this game.

This kind of edginess was something I responded to, craved when I didn't feel it often enough. When I was tired while working a long case, it invigorated me. When I was down, it elevated my spirits. The latter was why I was currently indulging in it; the deteriorating scene here threatened to drag me into the depths.

When I'd gone to check on my nieces I'd found them hopelessly zoned out, so stoned they barely made sense. My arrival had turned Chris remote and silent once more; Jamie had lashed out at me, declaring that she didn't give a fuck if I told the whole world including her fucking parents that she was ripped. I left them, feeling hollow and sad.

It was tempting to lay the blame for Chris's and Jamie's condition at the feet of our drug-ridden society, but a great deal of it belonged squarely on Charlene's and Ricky's shoulders—as well as the band member who had supplied them. And tonight my sister seemed bound and determined to shirk her parental duties; the second time I knocked at her door, she didn't respond at all. I was hoping I'd have better luck with Ricky.

God, I thought as I approached the studio, wouldn't it be splendid if we were all hatched from eggs and never had to put up with families? It was an idea that had occurred to me more than once.

The studio was a stucco building in the same style as the house, nestled in a pine grove at the far side of the tennis court. When I stepped through its door a blast of music hit me—"The Midnight Train to Nowhere." Ricky, his lead guitarist Norm O'Dell, and bass player Forrest Curtin stood around the sound system, heads bent, listening intently to a tape. Ricky motioned to me that they'd be through in a few minutes.

"There it is, Norm," he said, stopping and reversing the tape. "That riff, the timing's off."

O'Dell frowned in concentration as Ricky replayed the section. He was a big man with a heavy, graying beard, older than my brother-in-law by a good ten years. "Yeah, now I hear it," he said. "I blew it the same way at the concert. Damn!"

"And here," Ricky told Curtin, "is where the bass is off. Sounds mushy."

"Uh-huh, yeah." Curtin, baby-faced with a ponytail and a single gold earring, nodded in agreement.

Even if Hy hadn't told me they'd been doing coke, I'd have suspected: Ricky's speech was unusually rapid and clipped; O'Dell couldn't keep his hands from moving; Curtin repeatedly tapped his foot and snapped his fingers. Ricky interrupted the play again, reversed the tape, went over the passage two times more. Then he hit the STOP button and switched the system off.

"We'll get an early start tomorrow," he said. "Might be the last good session before we go out on tour."

"Think I'll join the others up at the house," Curtin said, "have a couple of drinks before I turn in." On the way out he smiled shyly at me.

O'Dell seemed reluctant to follow. "Uh, Rick, I've got a question."

"Sure, what?"

"That shooting tonight—"

"Like Hy said, probably a wild shot from a poacher. We've got a lot of deer on the property."

"But all these security people . . . You've never had them around before. I'm wondering if there isn't something going on that we should know about."

"Norm, the increased security is just an experiment—something Shar's boyfriend talked me into. They'll probably be gone in a week." Ricky's speech was more clipped now, as though he were reining in annoyance.

O'Dell looked at him for a moment, then nodded. "Well, I guess I'll go have me a nightcap, too." He shuffled out of the studio, shoulders rounded, big head bent.

Ricky watched with narrowed eyes as he left, sighing as the door closed. "First Ethan, now him."

"Amory's been after you?"

"Buttonholed me up at the house. He'd've made a good trial attorney, the way he goes for the jugular with the questioning."

"You tell him anything?"

"Hell, no."

"That's good. But as far as the band goes—shouldn't they be informed?"

He shook his head.

"What, you don't trust them, either?" It had occurred to me that he might have become overly paranoid.

"It's not a matter of trust, Shar." He began to pace around the sound system, flicking switches on and off.

"What, then?"

"You remember my old band—my Bakersfield buddies?"

I nodded impatiently, anxious to get on to the subject of his daughters, as well as ask questions relevant to my investigation.

"Well, that relationship was totally different. We'd grown up together, we were close. But when I made it, one of them decided to go off on his own, prove he could make it too. Another guy's wife persuaded him to stick with his day job. And when Dan was killed in that accident two years ago, and Benjy OD'd six months later, that ended it. I'll never work with anybody that way again. These guys, they're employees—handpicked because they're the best at what they do. Sure, we share a certain camaraderie, but there're things you *don't* share with the people who work for you."

"Not even if you might be putting them at risk?"

"Shar, whoever's doing this isn't after them. He wants me and my family."

"Speaking of your family, you've got a problem with Chris and Jamie. They're stoned out of their minds on grass, and Hy thinks they got it from one of the band members."

Ricky stiffened. "Who?"

"I don't know."

"Well, dammit, I'll find out! I've already told those guys to stay away from my kids. And I'm gonna read the girls the riot act. Drugs're strictly off limits in this household."

I gave him an ironic look and sat down on a nearby stool.

"All right," he said defensively, "Charly and I do grass,

129

but never in front of them. And when the band's down here, the same rule applies."

"But they haven't been following the rule, at least not since I got here. And you haven't been doing only grass tonight."

"Yeah, so I've done a few lines. It's the first time in years, Sister Sharon, and the way I feel right now, it'll be the last time."

"I hope so."

He picked up a second stool and moved it closer to mine. "Look, I'll talk to Chris and Jamie tomorrow. And I'll lay down the law to the band. I'm sorry about tonight. My judgment's way out of order and I feel like . . . Jesus Christ, when did it get so complicated?"

"You mean this situation? Or the one with Charlene?"

"Both. The business, too. Actually, I know when that happened—to the day, hour, and minute. It happened when Kurt called me up and said 'Cobwebs' was number forty with a bullet—meaning rising fast—on *Billboard*'s country singles chart. Two weeks later it was number one, and nothing about my life was ever simple again."

"Do you regret it?"

"Tonight? Yeah." He paused. "Funny, Red asked me the same question earlier."

"Red?"

"Rae. I called her after the shooting."

"Why?"

"Just to hear her voice. I've been talking with her off and on all evening. She . . . Shar, she likes me for myself, for who I am under all the showbiz trappings. Last night, once she got over being scared of the sex-fiend superstar—and I've got to admit I was doing a damn good imitation of one—we could really talk. I told her things I've never told anybody, and she did the same. Talking with her, I get a sense of peace that I've never found with Charly."

My face must have betrayed my inner conflict, because he added, "I'm not putting Charly down or dismissing what we've had together. And I'm not saying it just because she's hurt me. Jesus, I don't know what to think or feel right now. We've had our problems before, God knows, but this time she's made it clear she's really through with me. Still, I can't tell her the one thing she wants to hear that would get her off the hook as far as guilt is concerned—that I don't love her anymore."

"Then shouldn't you fight for your marriage?"

"I don't know as I can do that. I love Charly in ways that I don't even understand, but there're ragged edges to the relationship, and maybe I'm not willing to rub myself raw and bleeding against them anymore. Maybe it's good that she found this Vic person."

"She told you about him, then."

"In detail. In excruciating detail, as soon as I got home this afternoon. I'll tell you, I preferred it Thursday morning when she wasn't being so specific."

I was silent, thinking about what he'd been through since that Thursday-morning conversation, wondering if now was the time to ask the questions I had in mind. With Ricky, I'd long known that the line defining what he considered an invasion of privacy moved according to his mood. Given his coke high, I suspected that a good many areas were currently off-limits.

He confirmed that by saying, "I'd like to be left alone now."

"Okay, but tomorrow we're going to have to talk about a number of things. And Hy needs to explain some basic security precautions to you."

He nodded.

I got off the stool and gave him a long hug. Wished I

could also hug my sister. But my relationship with Charlene, as is often the case between sisters, had always been complicated, and I wasn't in the mood for further rejection. Until she came to me, I'd have to limit my aid and comfort to her husband.

When I got back to the guest house after a brief stop in the kitchen to forage through the fridge, I found a lamp on in the bedroom, but no Hy. Probably with his team, I thought, and hoped to God there hadn't been another crisis. I crossed the room, stripping off my clothes on the way to the bathroom, but stopped at its door, puzzled by a faint flickering light inside. I peered around the jamb, saw Hy stretched out in the big Jacuzzi tub. A candle burned on a stool, and beside it sat a bottle of wine and two glasses.

"McCone, about time. Come and join me."

I smiled slowly, testing the water temperature with my toes. "Lovely surprise."

"I thought you could use a relaxing soak about now." He poured wine and offered me a glass as I slipped into the tub. The water stung the small cuts that I'd sustained on my arms in the aftermath of the sniping, then soothed them. I took the glass from Hy's outstretched hand and sipped.

"So," he said, "you have any success with anything since I last saw you?"

"None." I filled him in, finishing, "And now I'm afraid Ricky's going to rebound to Rae."

"Would that be so bad?"

I stared at him, astonished. "It'd be horrible! Rae's my friend, Charlene's my sister. How could I deal with either of them?"

"Well, from what you've told me, your sister doesn't want Ricky anymore."

"No, but she's got her pride. If he took up with some-one else right away . . . well, God knows what that would do to her. And I can't imagine what she'd do to me once she found out it was Rae, and that I'd intro-duced them."

"Both of you would weather it."

"But what about the kids? It's bad enough they'll have to deal with their mother having a new man."

"I'm sure Ricky would be discreet about the relation-ship. He's always valued his privacy."

"But Mick would be sure to find out. How would he feel, working in the same office with his father's lover? He's only eighteen, even if, as Keim claims, he does play older."

Hy considered. "I think the first thing Mick'd do is pitch a fit, but in time he'd come around. Besides, guys of his age are a lot more interested in their own love lives than in their parents'."

"Maybe so, but Mick thinks of Rae as a friend. I doubt it's occurred to him that she's closer to his dad's age than his." I shook my head, tears stinging my eyes. "Oh, God, this whole thing is wrong! So many people could get hurt, so many lives could be ruined."

"Charlene's and Ricky's lives could be ruined if they stay together. The kids' lives could be ruined if they con-tinue to be exposed to the kind of vicious fighting I've been hearing today. I've got a feeling it's been going on for a long time; there's a scripted sound to it."

I sank deeper into the water till the ends of my hair trailed out, and let the tears flow. "Jesus, I just want to put things back the way they used to be."

Gently, Hy said, "Maybe they were only that way in your mind."

I sank lower.

He clasped my hands and tried to pull me toward his end of the tub. I resisted.

"Ah, McCone, let it go for a while. Come here, I'll make you feel better."

I let him move me till I was straddling his thighs, put my arms around his neck, pressed my wet cheek against his.

"Just let it go," he whispered, sliding his hand down my backbone. "Just let it go for now."

Eleven

Sunday morning coming down . . .

The title of the old Kris Kristofferson song popped into my head as I walked from the guest house to the terrace, clad in my swimsuit, towel in hand.

Apparently it was coming down hard on nearly everybody at the estate. At ten-thirty Hy and I were up and about, but the grounds and common areas of the house were deserted except for the guards. Even Nona Davidson wasn't due to arrive till noon.

My inner conflict about the breakup of my sister's marriage had still been with me when I woke up, but my depression had lifted and I felt a renewed sense of purpose. I hurried to the house, determined to make my sister talk to me, as well as make Ricky sit down and start going over the information I needed for my investigation. But in the end, closed doors defeated me, so I went back to the guest house, changed, and followed the path to the pool. The water was morning-fresh and cool. I began swimming laps, concentrating on keeping my crawl even and well-timed. The exercise was just what I needed; every time a bad feeling surfaced I was able to push it down.

When I pulled myself up on the side some twenty minutes later, I found Norm O'Dell reclining on the lounge next to the one where I'd left my towel. The big bearded man seemed no worse for his coked-up night, although he was drinking a glass of tomato juice that I suspected was doctored.

"Morning," he said gruffly, nodding.

"Morning. I thought you'd be rehearsing by now."

"Huh?"

"Last night Ricky said you'd get an early start."

"Early start for us means after lunch. We'll hit it maybe about two or three, go at it till we're satisfied."

I sat down on the lounge, running fingers through my wet hair. "Is your schedule always that undisciplined, or is it just because it's kind of a strange weekend?"

"Nothing undisciplined about it. Doesn't matter *when* you work, it's *how*. And don't judge us by last night—the coke and all. That's not normal."

"No?"

"No. Last night wasn't the most productive I've ever spent down here. Usually Rick runs a tight ship; that's what makes us good. You should see some other groups' sessions. I ought to know; I've played with plenty of dogs in my day."

"What're they like—the sessions, I mean?"

He smiled faintly. "Well, it goes like this: Rehearsal's set for a certain time, but then one of the players doesn't show up. So you call around for him and finally get hold of him in bed with his girlfriend. He promises to get right over there. By now everybody's hungry, so one of you

136

goes out for a pizza, and when he gets back the amorous guy still isn't there, so you eat and get into the beer.

"Then one of the wives shows up with a kid or two and gets into a fight with her husband and lets the kids run wild. The missing guy finally gets there with the girl-friend in tow. And the girls suddenly decide they don't like the new song you're working on because somebody at the supermarket told the wife that songs about divorce don't make the charts anymore. The guy who wrote it gets in a snit and stops talking to everybody. And by then you've broken out the dope and everybody's so stoned that they can't stand up. The married couple're well on their way to their *own* divorce, the kids're screaming, the amorous guy's looking amorous again, and you decide to call it a night."

"God."

O'Dell nodded, thoroughly warmed to his subject now. "Nonprofessional behavior like that is exactly what keeps you from making it in this business. We rehearse a minimum of twenty hours a week down here—one of the reasons Rick's got all the guest space. Unlike last night, we don't bring our personal problem or drugs into the rehearsal room. Sessions are closed—no wives, girl-friends, kids. We tape everything on that little system he's got there, play it back, analyze it. When we finally go into the studio over in Arizona, we're prepared and primed to record. We don't waste studio time that could be rented to a paying customer. And we're the same on the road; we're pros."

I took advantage of O'Dell's sudden talkativeness to ask, "You been with Ricky long?"

"Couple of years."

"And you're from Montana?"

"Uh-huh."

"How'd you come to hook up with him?"

137

"I was a friend of his guitarist, Dan—the guy who bought it in the motorcycle accident. I guess you could say I used the connection." An uncomfortable expression had settled on his fleshy face; O'Dell liked to talk about the business, but not about more personal topics. It was with some relief that he looked up and called, "Hey, Jer, Forrest."

Jerry Jackson and Forrest Curtin crossed the terrace toward us. The drummer—short and chubby with wild red-gold curls—grinned cheerfully and inhaled on a joint. The ponytailed bass player looked terrible; I suspected he hadn't slept. He lay facedown on the lounge to my other side and groaned.

Jackson sat on the end of my chair, offering the joint to me. I shook my head, wondering if he was the one who had supplied the grass to the girls. O'Dell frowned pointedly and said, "Rick's not gonna like you smoking; we're supposed to rehearse later on."

"I'll give you fifty-to-one odds that'll never come off. And if it does, we'll be without our keyboards player. Pete's splitting. The situation down here's got him freaked."

"Rick's *really* not gonna like that."

Jackson shrugged. "Tough. Pete's got that pregnant wife of his up in Santa Monica, about to deliver any minute. The last thing he wants to do is sit around here and wait on Rick while he and Charly play games with each other. Rick wants to rehearse, he should set his own house in order first, then arrange it at *our* convenience for a change."

"Come on, Jer, don't talk that way. This lady's Charly's sister."

"I know, and I'm sorry about that," Jackson said to me, "but I've got to call it like I see it. The man's marriage is blowing sky high, yes, but we've all been through it one way or the other, and you can't let it interfere with business. And he's blowing his vibes, too; he screwed up the lyrics on 'Broken Promise Land' Friday night, and when I called him on it, he told me to back off. This place is crawling with guards, and he won't tell us why. And we all know damn well it was no deer poacher that shot Rats."

Curtin said into the cushion, "He's right, Norm. Rick's not being straight with us, and one of the things he's not explaining is why his sister-in-law, who's a well-known private investigator, just happens to be here this weekend."

O'Dell looked at me. "That true?"

"I'm an investigator, yes."

"You working on something for Rick?"

I was silent. Ricky had said there were some things you didn't share with the people who worked for you; on the other hand, a series of threats was something you didn't conceal from people who might be placed at risk. "Listen," I said, "can you persuade Pete to hang around for a little while? I'm going to talk with Ricky, see if I can't get him to level with you guys." I got up and started for the house.

Jackson called after me, "Try one of the guest rooms. Sure as hell he's not with Charly."

But he was—in the beautiful maple-and-cream kitchen. She wore a long white cotton nightdress that made her look childlike and vulnerable; he had on the same cutoffs and tee as last night, and his handsome face was set in angry lines. They stood toe to toe, hurling bitter words at each other.

"None of this is my fault!" he exclaimed as I hesitated in the doorway. "Don't try to blame your bad behavior on me!"

"Bad behavior! You make it sound as if I'd used the wrong fork at one of your awards dinners."

"Shit, you picked up a fork right now, the only thing you'd use it for would be to stab me in the back."

I started out of the room, my stomach roiling. No wonder Jamie threw up a lot!

Charlene said, "At least I wouldn't stab you in the *heart*, like you did me three years ago."

The mention of three years made me pause on the threshold.

"You think you haven't? You think—" He broke off, a strange look coming over his face. "What the hell do you mean, three years ago?"

"Don't pretend you don't remember, you bastard."

"Don't remember what? *What?*"

"Does the name Patricia Terriss ring a bell?"

Ricky recoiled, going pale under his tan.

"I thought it might."

"Charly . . ." He reached out to her.

She slapped his hand away. "You thought I didn't know?"

"Honey, I—"

"Don't you dare try to explain. I don't want any explanations now."

"But it wasn't—"

"Oh, fuck you!" She turned away, moved toward the counter where the coffee maker sat.

Ricky's shoulders slumped in defeat. He watched her bleakly as she filled the pot with water and reached for the beans and grinder. Then he nodded as though he'd come to a decision, moved to the door, and brushed past me as if I weren't there.

Charlene set the grinder down and turned, frowning. In the entryway, the front door slammed. Her eyes met mine, panic seeping into them. Then she ran after him, with me a few steps behind.

Ricky was already halfway down the flagstone path to the parking area, digging in the pocket of his cutoffs and pulling out a set of keys.

Charlene called, "Where the hell do you think you're going?"

He headed for the Porsche.

She ran after him, grabbed his arm as he opened the car door.

He pushed her away. "Leave me alone! I don't belong here anymore."

"Ricky, please, it's not safe for you to—"

What the hell do you care about the safety of the guy who stabbed you in the heart? If I get out of here, at least I won't be jeopardizing the entire family."

I looked around frantically for Hy, one of the guards, anyone capable of restraining him in this fury. Nobody.

"Please don't leave," my sister said. "We won't fight anymore. We'll talk—"

He turned on her, rage twisting his features. "Too little, too late, Charlene. I'm ready to tell you what you want to hear: I don't love you anymore."

She had been reaching out to him; now she drew back. Shock flooded her eyes, followed quickly by a rage that matched his. For a moment they locked eyes. Then she lashed out with her left hand and smacked him across the face; her wedding ring made a thin bloody line on his high cheekbone.

I gasped. Started over there. Stopped. No good would come of interfering—not when they were determined to play out this drama to its last ugly scene.

Ricky's hand went to this face as he stared at Charlene in disbelief. Then, quite deliberately, he smacked her back so hard that she staggered and sank to the ground. Before

I could try to stop him he got into the Porsche, gunned the engine, and sped out of the parking area.

Thoroughly panicked now, I started for the intercom in the entryway, then saw that one of the guards had appeared and was already on his walkie-talkie to the gate. I yelled to him, "Tell them to let him through! He'll crash the car if they don't!"

Tires squealed on the blacktop below. The Porsche accelerated. God, I thought, he'll kill himself if they don't get that gate open in time!

The brakes shrieked once; then the car accelerated again. I listened till the sound of its engine died away. Finally I turned and went over to where my sister sat on the ground, hugging her knees, her face pressed against them. She looked up at me, eyes filling with tears.

"Well, Shar," she said, "what's it like to witness the death of a marriage?"

"So where would he go?" I asked.

Charlene and I sat at the glass-topped table in the pretty cream-and-green breakfast room. My sister had finally stopped crying; crumpled Kleenexes were piled next to her coffee mug, and her eyes were red and swollen. Hy leaned in the doorway, plainly uncomfortable about being privy to the scene.

"Little Savages, over in Arizona. That's where he always runs when we . . . He says it's the only place he feels at home. He wanted this house, but now that it's done he hates it."

I looked at Hy. He asked her, "What kind of airstrip does he have over there? Can it accommodate a jet?"

"A small one, yes."

"Good. I'll have a security team flown in from our Phoenix office; they'll be in place hours before he gets there. He mentioned that his sound engineer lives on the premises."

"Yes—Miguel Taylor. He's kind of a desert rat. He found the land and convinced Ricky to buy it. Now Ricky loves the wide-open spaces as much as Mig does." Her wan face grew even more melancholy.

"If Kurt calls Taylor, will he accept his say-so for my team having access to the property?"

"I'm sure he will, and if Mig's not there, there's also a caretaker. Where is Kurt, anyway?"

"Ricky's office. He's been trying to reach him on his car phone, as well as calling around on the off-chance he contacted someone after he took off."

Charlene watched Hy leave the room, then turned back to me. Tears spilled over again and she swiped angrily at them. "I don't know why I can't stop crying," she said. "I got what I wanted."

"Can we talk about it now?"

She sighed and began picking a damp tissue apart. "No point in not talking about it. You know I'm leaving Ricky?"

"Yes, and I also know there's somebody else involved."

"And you disapprove."

"I didn't say that."

"It shocks you, doesn't it?"

The whole time we were growing up, Charlene had taken perverse delight in being able to shock her older sister. It irked me that she would still think it possible.

Sarcastically I said, "Nothing that you or anybody else in our family could do could possibly shock me." Then, seeing her hurt look, I relented some. "Listen, what you've done is no big deal. Ma was seeing Melvin for months before she told Pa she wanted a divorce. John blew up Karen's car when she left him; it was only blind luck she wasn't in it at the time. Joey's spent his life either behind bars or in them. Patsy's kids all have different fathers—none of whom she bothered to marry. And my own history isn't uncheckered; I'm just sneakier."

"You didn't mention Pa."

"I should mention him, just because he's a manic-depressive who hides out in the garage when he's down, and when he's up scandalizes the neighbors by bellowing dirty ditties?"

Charlene managed a weak grin. "Well, then, whatever problems I have are probably genetic. Speaking of the family, do any of them know you're down here?"

"I haven't even called John. This trip is strictly business."

She sighed. "Good. I'm not looking forward to having to break the news to Ma. She'll either say, 'I told you he was no good when he got you pregnant,' or she'll side with Ricky."

"This doesn't have to be a sides-taking situation."

"Try to tell that to Ma."

It was a task I didn't think I'd ever be up to. I went to the adjacent kitchen for more coffee, came back and said, "I need to ask you something. I overheard you and Ricky fighting before. You mentioned something that happened three years ago, and a woman's name— Patricia Terriss. Who is she?"

Charlene looked away.

"I'm not asking out of idle curiosity," I added. "A woman he . . . saw briefly three years ago may be behind this campaign of harassment." I related the gist of my conversation with Arletta James.

By the time I finished, Charlene had turned very pale; her eyes focused on the distance and she absently fingered a bruise that had formed on her cheek where Ricky hit her. After a moment she said, "I thought a woman was behind it. He was only with this one in Texas for a weekend?"

"That's what he told Letta."

"My God. I went through all of that—put him through it, too—because of a wrong assumption."

"I don't understand."

"A little over a year ago Ricky asked me to go through some old files on Little Savages; he and the others had started to talk about forming the new label, and he wanted cost figures on the studio. Anyway, some of them hadn't been entered into the computer, so I went into his office files looking for them. And I found an attorney's bill."

"For?"

"All it said was, 'IN RE Patricia Terriss.' It was dated two years earlier. It wasn't from Ethan, who's strictly his music attorney, or the man we use for our personal affairs, but I recognized the name. He's a very high-powered guy who specializes in divorce, palimony, things like that. So I made an appointment and went to see him."

"Why didn't you just ask Ricky about it?"

"Things already weren't very good between us. This house was being built and we were in that rented place in Pacific Palisades. It was too small and we'd lost everything in the fire, and the kids resented that we were going to move down here and take them away from their friends and schools. They were acting out something terrible—that was right after the incident with Mick and the board of education's computer, remember? And also I was . . . hearing things."

"Such as?"

"Nothing specific. Just buzzings in our circle of friends and associates. You know how, when people think there's something wrong in your life, they'll give you those sympathetic looks that're more nasty than compassionate? That was happening a lot to me. And people would say things like, 'If you need to talk, I'm here for you,' and then if I asked why, they'd dismiss the question. After a while I decided that something was going on with Ricky that everybody knew but me. So I *couldn't* ask him about an attorney's bill with a woman's name on it, that he'd deliberately concealed from me."

"Did the attorney tell you anything?"

"No. He cited client confidentiality and told me if I wanted to know why my husband had consulted him I should ask *him*. He did, at least, promise not to tell Ricky I'd been to see him."

"So then what did you do?"

"Nothing but brood. Sure, I knew Ricky fooled around out on the road; I even caught him that one time. But the women weren't important to him, and he always came home to me. This was different: If he'd consulted that type of lawyer about the Terriss woman, she had to be more than just a casual lay after a concert. She might've even been somebody who was significant to him. I guess I just didn't want to know. Eventually I got so depressed that I could barely make myself get up and go to my classes at USC."

"Did Ricky notice?"

"Yes, but he attributed it to our living situation and the kids' behavior. And he wasn't home much, anyway; that was when he was touring for *Broken Promise Land*." She laughed bitterly. "Did the title of *that* album ever have significance for me!"

"And you never told anybody what you suspected?"

"Only Vic. Vic Christiansen, a guest lecturer in my department who taught the honors seminar in international finance that I was taking. One day after class he stopped me and asked me out for a drink. I went, and we talked, and finally he said he'd been observing me and was concerned about my emotional state. He's open and easy to confide in, so I told him everything."

"And you fell in love with him."

"Not right away, but over the next few months I did, yes." She hesitated. "Shar, do you know what it's like to live somebody else's dream and never have one of your own?"

"Not really."

"Well, I do. That's the way my life had been since I was sixteen. Our whole marriage was about Ricky and his dream. His drive and talent just plain overwhelmed me, and I ended up placing my wants and needs after his. Enrolling at USC was the first thing I'd ever done for myself. Falling in love with Vic was the second. Now he's convinced me I should go on for my MBA; at last I'm going to have a dream of my own."

"But do you have to break up your marriage to do that?"

"I love Vic," she said gently. "He's part of the dream."

"What about your kids? Don't you love them? Don't they fulfill any of these needs you seem to have?" My voice was rough with anger. Wasn't anybody thinking about my nephews and nieces?

Charlene put her hand on my arm. "Shar, I've never been the sort of mother who tries to live her life through her kids. That's not enough and, besides, it's not healthy for them. A good parent knows that at some point she's going to have to let go and allow her kids to make their own way in the world. If they were all I had, I'd cling, and they'd suffer for it."

"But doesn't a good parent also put her kids' needs ahead of her own?"

"Yes, and I've known for a long time that the one thing my kids need most is a peaceful and loving home.

Ricky's a good man and a wonderful father, but he's also talented and single-minded, and people like that are takers. We had a passionate relationship, but it was also painful and, in the past few years, mutually destructive. Kids shouldn't have to live in that kind of atmosphere, and with Vic and me they won't."

"So you're just going to take them away from their father, whom they love, who loves them?"

She sighed. "I'd never do that to them or to Ricky. He'll be able to have the kids anytime he or they want. But you've got to face reality, Shar: Ricky's on the road a lot; the business takes up most of his time, and with the new label it's going to take up even more of it."

"You've really made up your mind."

"Yes, I have."

I was silent, thinking over all that she'd said. Hadn't Ricky hinted at the same kind of destructive marriage last night, when he'd talked about rubbing himself raw on the ragged edges of the relationship? Maybe it was better it ended before more serious damage was done.

"All right," I finally said, "I understand your reasons, and I'll support you—particularly when Ma comes around to meddle." Then I turned my attention back to the immediate situation. "This Patricia Terriss—Ricky didn't mention her when we were discussing who might be responsible for the harassment. That strikes me as odd."

"Very."

I thought about Rae's contention that my brother-in-law was feeling guilty about something that had nothing to do with Charlene or the kids. Something to do with the Terriss woman, perhaps? "Well," I said, "he's going to have to tell me about her. Let's go to the office and see if Kurt has located him."

She got up and led me through the maze of hallways. At the office door she stopped and said, "You know, I

148

don't like this house any more than Ricky does. I'll be glad to sell it."

When we stepped inside, Ethan Amory, Kurt Girdwood, and Hy were gathered in conversation by a window overlooking a wooded slope. Amory glared at Charlene, blaming her for this latest crisis, but Girdwood came over and held out his arms to her. "Honey, I'm so sorry," he said. She went to him.

"Anything?" I asked Hy.

He shook his head. "Kurt tried Ricky's cell phone and it was busy, so he's in touch with someone. I've already dispatched a team to Little Savages."

"Good. I think you and I should fly over there—"

The office line buzzed. Hy picked up. ". . . Yeah, she's right here, hold on." He handed the receiver to me. "Rae."

I thought of Mick, felt a spark of anxiety. "Yes, Rae. What's up?"

"Can you talk? Privately, I mean?"

"Uh, sure. Let me call you back." I gave the receiver to Hy, excused myself, and hurried out—anxiety at full flame now. Mick would make a natural target, I thought, further proof that the note writer could get to Ricky and his family members at any time and in any place.

In the guest house I sank onto the bed and dialed my home number. Rae picked up after only half a ring. "What's wrong?" I asked. "Is Mick okay?"

"He's fine. I'm in the guest room with the door closed and he's in the kitchen fixing tacos, so he can't hear us. What the hell has happened down there?"

"How'd you know something did?"

"Ricky's been calling me on and off ever since he got home yesterday. The last time was a few minutes ago from his car. He described an awful scene with your sister, said it was all over between them. What precipitated it?"

"A combination of things. But it's over, believe me. I was present at the demise. Where is he?"

"On his way to Arizona."

"Thank God! We've got a security team en route. How did he sound?"

"Angry. Hurt. Relieved, too." she hesitated. "Shar, he wants me to meet him there."

For a moment I was too shocked to speak; then I said sarcastically, "Didn't take him long to bounce back from this anger and hurt you just mentioned, now did it?"

It was Rae's turn to be silent.

"Are you going?" I demanded.

"I think so. He's calling the air-charter company he uses to see if he can get me a flight."

"Jesus, Rae, you can't be serious!"

"Shar, he's my friend. He needs somebody to talk to."

"Just talk?"

More silence.

"You know, you could be getting in way over your head."

"It's *my* head, Shar."

I closed my eyes, gripping the receiver hard. I wasn't handling this well. Confrontation never worked with Rae; reason did.

I said, "What about work? I'm down here, and somebody's got to keep the agency running."

"I wrapped up the last two cases you assigned me on Friday."

"What about Mick? You're supposed to be looking out for him."

"Ricky spoke with him when he called. The news wasn't any surprise to Mick; he heard that song dedication at the concert. Ricky asked him to go home, be there for his mother. He's already booked a flight."

Everything was reeling out of control, out of my hands. "But there'll be nobody left in the office."

"I called Ted. He'll be in touch with you if anything urgent comes up; routine stuff he'll refer to your friend Wolf."

Not only out of my hands, but into the hands of others! "Did it ever occur to you that we need the business?"

"Shar, business has been good lately and, besides, I know how much you'll be making off Ricky's case."

What, had he said I was charging too much? I'd taken a smaller retainer than usual because he was a family member! No, Ricky wouldn't say a thing like that. Rae meant she knew I'd be making a fair amount because it promised to be a major investigation.

Get a grip, McCone!

I took a deep, calming breath and asked, "I can't talk you out of going down there?"

"No, you can't."

And if I kept on trying, I'd end up screaming at her, threatening to fire her. What good would that do? I'd already made my position clear, and so had she.

"Shar," she added, "I'm sorry. I know this upsets you, but it's something I feel I have to do."

Time to tread softly, for the friendship's sake. "Okay, I understand."

"Is there anything I can do to help with the investigation? Any information you need from him?"

After a moment's consideration, I said, "Actually, there is. The note writer's escalated his or her activities."

"You mean the shooting?"

"No, there's more, things I haven't even had the chance to tell Ricky." I filled her in on the Carolina jessamine that had been left in the trailer and the CD that had appeared with Jamie's birthday presents. "You remember I told you about the woman from Texas who was harassing him? Well, now I've got a name. Get him to talk to you about Patricia Terriss. Charlene found a bill from an attorney Ricky consulted about Terriss, and she brought her up while they were arguing this morning; that was one of the things that precipitated the break."

"Patricia Terriss. Spell the last."

"T-e-r-r-i-s-s."

"Got it."

"You know, you were right about his feeling guilty. He's hiding something important from me, and he deliberately put himself at risk by leaving this house alone. It's almost as if he wants to be punished for whatever it is. I think Terriss may be at the root of that—as well as being the person behind the harassment."

"Well, I'll get it out of him. He really needs to talk."

This time I restrained myself from making a sarcastic and pointless comment. Instead I asked, "Rae, are you sure you're going to be okay? Ricky's . . . well, he's been breaking hearts all his life."

"And I've been getting mine broken all my life. Maybe some things never change. Or maybe they do."

Twelve

EXCERPT FROM RAE KELLEHER'S DIARY:

Some people hate the desert. It's too big, too empty, too overwhelming. My old boyfriend, Willie Whelan, is like that. His idea of a trip to the desert is a package weekend in Las Vegas. But me, I love it. There's something comforting in all that vastness. Makes you realize how insignificant your problems are in the grand scheme of things.

Maybe, I thought as the plane began its descent over the reddish-brown landscape south of Tucson, maybe that's why Ricky's running here. Maybe he knows the emptiness will put his anger and pain in perspective. Must be, because he's like me in so many ways.

Through the intercom the pilot said, "We'll be on the ground in five minutes, Ms. Kelleher. Better fasten your seatbelt."

I'd never taken it off, but I checked to make sure it was tight. The whole trip I'd been watching the mountains and the flatlands below and trying to ignore the knot of tension in my stomach, as well as the fact that I really don't like to fly. Shar has explained aerodynamics to me, but I still don't see any reason for planes staying up there; as a result, I expend a lot of psychic energy helping them do so when I'm aboard. And then there was the matter of this hastily undertaken trip. And Ricky. God, I was beginning to wish I was back in San Francisco, eating leftover tacos and staring at the tube with his son! As Shar had suggested on the phone earlier, maybe I'd gotten myself in way over my head this time.

I could see buildings now—reddish-brown brick that blended with the landscape. Most clustered around a swimming pool and tennis courts; a few more backed up to a mesa a fair distance away. Gnarled saguaros that looked like they were shaking fists in the air grew everyplace, as well as weird spiny ocotillos and clumps of sagebrush. A long concrete runway stretched out to our right, its freshly painted markings totally unreassuring. A man leaned on a Jeep beside it. Not Ricky. Our descent got steeper, and I took a deep breath and shut my eyes till I felt the wheels touch down.

When the plane taxied to a stop I grabbed my bag and purse and climbed out, taking the pilot's hand for balance. The heat was ungodly—it had to be over a hundred and ten—and the early evening sun blinded me. At first I saw the man walking over from the Jeep only as a silhouette; then my eyes adjusted to the glare and I noted shaggy black hair and Indian features that reminded me of Shar.

"Ms. Kelleher," he said, "I'm Miguel Taylor, Rick's sound engineer. Welcome to Little Savages."

"Thank you." I shook his hand. "Please, call me Rae."

"And you call me Mig. I'm meeting you because Rick phoned from the road an hour ago. He had some trouble with the Porsche overheating, but it's fixed now and he should be here soon."

154

It probably overheated because Ricky was driving like an asshole, I thought. I don't know why it is, but you put a perfectly normal person behind the wheel of one of those cars, and his absolute worst tendencies come out— especially when he's just broken up with his wife.

Mig took my bag and stowed it in the Jeep. It was, I noted with some satisfaction, as scabrous as the Ramblin' Wreck, my ancient Rambler American. I called a thank-you to the pilot, went around to the passenger's side and climbed aboard, burning my fingers on the hot metal.

Great, Rae. It's bad enough that you'll be greeting Ricky with a sore right arm and scrapes and bruises that'll have to be explained. Let's not try for first-degree burns too.

Mig started the engine and drove quickly toward the nearby cluster of buildings. The largest was low and rectangular with a squarish open-sided tower at either end. Across a courtyard from it were the smaller buildings, also rectangular and forming a U on three sides of the pool and courts. Cactus and smoky trees with fine branches and gray-green leaves screened their entrances. The architecture was as stark and spare as the desert itself.

Mig was chattering on about the studio and bungalows and security arrangements. I tuned most of it out till I heard him say, "No reason you shouldn't feel safe here."

No physical reason, maybe, but emotionally I felt like I was walking a tightrope over an alligator pit.

The bungalow was bigger than the condo I'd leased. Good-sized kitchen and dining area; living room with a stone fireplace and a window overlooking what Mig said was an extinct volcano. Only one bedroom.

Not too subtle about your intentions, are you, Savage?

Mig deposited my bag in the bedroom and left. I stayed in the living room. Normally, even though it's considered bad manners, I like to snoop, but tonight I couldn't bring myself to invade a very private man's closets and cupboards. I did take a look at the framed photographs of his family that sat on an end table. Mick, younger, with braces. The handsome fellow I shared an office with had once been a nerd! Two beautiful teenagers—one with long blond hair, the other with a silly brown perm that reminded me of one I'd inflicted on myself at her age. Two towheaded little girls and a boy with hair the color of Ricky's, ages ranging between maybe seven and twelve; they were sitting on a diving board in bathing suits and looked happy.

It wasn't fair, what they'd have to go through in the time ahead. None of it was their fault.

I picked up the last photograph. A woman with short, stylish blond hair—beautiful like her daughters. Her smile was tentative, though, her eyes questioning.

Charly, he called her.

I took the picture over to the lamp on the other table and studied it. Absolutely no resemblance to her sister. Shar's got what they call a recessive gene, from her Shoshone great-grandmother. The other kids in her family look like California boys and girls, but Shar's dark and exotic. Still, Charlene was a knockout. So why that wary, unsure expression?

She'd been hurt, of course. That's what hurt does to you. Makes you wonder why, and wait for the other shoe to drop. She'd been hurt by the man I'd come here to meet.

The knot in my stomach retied itself. I put Charlene's picture back and went to the window. Sun going down in flames behind purple peaks. Maybe my life going down in flames too. Having few surprises had at least been safe—

Sound of an engine outside, coming closer. The growl and whine of an asshole-creating Porsche as it down-

shifted. It drove up, cut out, and a door slammed. Footsteps on the sandy ground. I turned as he came inside.

He looked like hell—tired, sweaty, rumpled. There was a grease streak on his chin and a line of dried blood on his cheek where, he had told me, Charlene slapped him. And his expression said he'd about given up hope of anything going right.

Come-fuck-me voice, come-bury-me look.

But when he saw me his eyes lit up. "Hey, Red."

All of a sudden I couldn't speak. By some strange biological function the knot in my stomach had traveled upward and was threatening to strangle me. I backed up against the window. The glass was air-conditioned chilly, but I could feel the heat outside.

Ricky smiled in his crooked way and cocked his head quizzically. "What's the matter, Red? You're not gonna get scared of me all over again?"

He was a superstar who'd stepped on plenty of people to get to the top. He was a cheating husband who'd put that look on his wife's face and probably didn't even see it. He was a dad who was about to abandon his family. And he was about to do his damndest to bed me.

But he was also just Ricky: the Bakersfield kid who'd dreamed of stardom and then found out it wasn't all it was cracked up to be. The kid who'd worked his ass off since he was twelve to support his music habit. The only son who'd been all that stood between his mother and his drunken, abusive father. The loner who'd escaped into his lyrics and melodies. The man who right now was toting a heavy load of pain and guilt.

Just Ricky.

I stepped away from the window and put my arms around him. Went up on tiptoe and pressed my cheek to his.

"*Thank God you're here, Red,*" *he whispered.*

I still couldn't speak, so I just held him tight.

"*I don't know what's going to happen with us,*" *he said,* "*but I'll promise you this: I'll never deliberately do anything to hurt you. I'm through with that kind of life.*"

We were lying side by side in bed when I asked him the big question—not the one Shar wanted me to ask, but my own: "*Are you with me tonight because you want to get back at Charly?*"

He put his arms around me and pulled me halfway on top of him so I could look into his eyes. "*No,*" *he said,* "*I am not. If I wanted to get back at her, right now I'd be in some high-visibility nightspot in L.A. or I'd be in San Diego, fucking my brains out with her best friend, who's made the generous offer more than once and would be on the phone to everybody we know before I could get my pants back on.*

"*I'm here in Arizona,*" *he added,* "*because I need the healing power of the desert. And I'm here with you because I care for you, plain and simple.*"

Tears stung my eyes. One slipped over, and he brushed it away. "*You're not gonna cry, are you? Crying women always make me cry, too.*"

"*No, I'm not going to. I hate to cry, except when I want to get my own way.*"

"*Good. I'm not a pretty sight when I weep. So are we settled on that issue?*"

"*. . . That one, yes.*"

"*There's something else?*"

"*Uh-huh.*"

"*Tell me.*"

I rolled off him and looked up into the dusky, filtered light. "*Ricky, do you trust me?*"

"*You know I do.*" *But his tone was now guarded.*

Shar says that when in doubt, take a big risk. I'd always hated that philosophy, but right then I understood the impulse.

I said, "If you trust me, tell me about Patricia Terriss."

The silence seemed to stretch out for hours. Finally he leaned over, took a joint from the nightstand drawer, and lighted it. After a moment he said tightly, "People sure're tossing that name around today."

"Is she the same woman who was hassling you three years ago?"

He passed me the joint. "So you know about that, too. Shar must've found out from my old friend Letta James. Funny, I didn't even remember that I told Letta till I was driving over here. That's how wrecked I was at the time. But I don't remember telling her Patricia's name."

"Shar overheard you and Charlene arguing about her."

"How'd Charly know, I wonder?"

"She found the bill from the lawyer you consulted about Terriss."

"When?"

"About a year ago."

He took the joint from my fingers, drew on it. "So that's what ended it—Charly jumping to conclusions without bothering to ask me about it."

I didn't say anything.

"Actually, it was over before that; we just weren't letting ourselves believe it. You know how some random event can happen and all of a sudden nothing in your life's ever the same? With Charly and me, it was the fire in Pacific Palisades. We'd survived so much down the years, but for some reason that sank us. Afterward, we never could find our way back to each other."

I took the joint and dragged down some smoke. Grass

159

has never affected me very strongly; I guess I'm like a cat that doesn't respond to catnip. But I was feeling a little mellower, mellow enough to ask, "So what about the Terriss woman, Ricky?"

He tensed and shifted away from me. "Is that why you agreed to come down here—so you could pry into my personal affairs? Is that why you went to bed with me?"

"You know it isn't. I'm here because I want to be. I'm in bed with you because I care. And I don't want anything to happen to you—or your family."

"What can happen? We're all surrounded by guards—who're costing me a fast fortune."

"Well, you saw how much the guards could do to prevent that shooting last night. And you can't live this way forever. Besides, there're some other things that Shar didn't get the chance to tell you." I explained about the heap of Carolina jessamine that had been left in his trailer at the concert, as well as the intruder who had grabbed me at Coso Street.

He sat up. "Somebody threatened you?"

"Yes. And then there's the CD of Letta James's Old-fashioned Lady *that turned up with Jamie's other birthday presents. A note in the same handwriting as the others was attached, telling her to listen to 'My Mendacious Minstrel.'"*

"Jesus, and somebody tried to get to my *daughter!*"

"That's how serious the situation is. Whoever's doing this has an in in your household. Can get onto your property. Can follow you. Can breach security at concerts."

He put the joint out in an ashtray and lay back down and took my hand. "Okay, you've convinced me. I'll tell you all of it. But you're not going to like what you hear. I don't want it to change things with us, Red. What's starting here is too important for that."

"We won't let it change anything." But the knot was back in my stomach—tighter than before.

"Okay, here it is. All of it. I was in Austin. Concert date there, another scheduled for Houston the next night, and then on to Dallas. Three years ago, in the springtime. After the show, we went out. Whole bunch of us—my lead guitarist, Dan, and my bass player, Benjy. The concert promoter. My road manager, Rats. The band that opened for us. The place was on a lake north of town; they show-cased up-and-coming local talent. This woman, Patricia Terriss, was singing with the band. She was beautiful, really beautiful, but she had a tiny talent. When they finished they came over to meet us, had some drinks at our table. And I . . .

"Red, that was in the middle of a purely miserable time with Charly. I'm not trying to make excuses for what I did—or maybe I am—but there was this beautiful, willing woman that I didn't have any bad history with, and I ended up back at the hotel with her. The next day I took her along to Houston, and then to Dallas."

I realized I was clutching his hand too hard and eased up some. *"And after Dallas?"*

"I left her there with a first-class plane ticket back to Austin. We parted on what I thought were good terms. Too good, maybe. Two weeks later she called my office line at the house in Pacific Palisades, told me she was in L.A., asked if we could get together. God knows how she got the number. I said it wouldn't be a good idea. But she kept calling. After a couple more weeks she called the house line. As soon as she did that I had both numbers changed. Then the notes started. I don't know how she got my address, either."

"What did they say?"

"More of what she'd said on the phone. That she loved me, wanted to be with me. That I'd promised to leave

161

Charly, write her a song, make her a star. Next, presents started coming. Expensive and personal stuff. Once she even sent flowers. I explained them away as a joke from somebody at the label."

Ricky's hand had tightened on mine now. I ran my thumb over his index finger, trying—and failing—to ease his tension.

"The next thing," he went on, "was threats. She'd tell Charly about us. She'd tell my kids about us. She knew where we lived; she could get at us anytime. God, the thought made my skin crawl! And then . . . then she threatened to hurt the kids. That was what had me so messed up the day I ran into my old friend Letta."

It made my skin crawl, too. "Is that when you went to see the lawyer?"

"Yes. All he could tell me was to get a restraining order. But he also told me that a restraining order probably wouldn't work if she was as crazy as she sounded. And then he . . ."

Something very bad was coming. I could feel it.

"He told me that the only thing somebody like that understands is 'a substantial show of force.'"

Oh, God! "Meaning?"

"Hiring somebody to rough her up and persuade her to leave me alone. He said he could put me in touch with the right man for the job."

"Ricky, you didn't—"

"No. I'd done a lot of things in my life that I wasn't proud of, but hiring some thug—" He broke off. I glanced at him, saw his eyes were bleak. "What I did was worse."

I closed my own eyes, waited.

"Worse, because it was so personal."

I kept waiting.

Finally he said, "I set her up, God help me. Called her at the number she always put at the bottom of her notes.

Told her I was ready to leave Charly. Made a date for a motel up the coast in Ventura; told her to register under her own name and then phone me at Transamerica with the room number. And sent in my place two men she knew from when we were in Texas—my good buddies, Dan and Benjy."

In a weak voice I asked, "To do what?"

"Whatever it took, Red. Whatever it took. And they did."

"Did what?" I was whispering now.

"I don't know. They wouldn't say, and I could tell they didn't feel good about it. No matter how hard I pushed, they never would talk about it. But she stopped bothering me. I didn't hear from or of her again.

"I'll tell you," he added, "since the morning Dan and Benjy came to the house and said everything was taken care of, I haven't had a decent night's sleep. I guess I won't be able to live with myself till I find out what happened in that motel room. And when I do, I may never be able to live with myself again."

Six in the morning, and I was standing at the window watching the now-cool desert turn gold. Ricky stirred in the bed behind me, and after a minute he came over and put his hands on my shoulders. "What're you thinking, Red?"

"That we ought to go back to San Diego. You want to tell Shar in person what you told me."

". . . Yeah, I guess I better. We can leave whenever you're ready."

"You all right to drive?"

"For now. If I start to crash on the way, you can take over."

I'd never driven a Porsche. I wondered if I'd turn into an asshole behind the wheel.

Ricky asked, "You okay?"

163

"Uh-huh."

"*Are* we *okay?*"

I tilted my head and rested my cheek against his right hand. "We're okay."

"Then let's go back to San Diego, turn this whole thing over to Shar, and get on with the rest of our lives."

PART TWO

•

July 24–26, 1995

"StarWatch," *Los Angeles Times,* July 24, 1995:

> Music industry insiders are buzzing about this weekend's sudden appearance of armed guards at country artist **Ricky Savage's** estate in the San Diego hills. Adding fuel to the speculation is the presence of Savage's sister-in-law, San Francisco private eye **Sharon McCone,** and **Hy Ripinsky,** partner in the well-known antiterrorism security firm that supplied the muscle. But where is the two-time Grammy winner and 1994 Country Music Entertainer of the Year, whose double-platinum *Broken Promise Land* album debuted at the top of the charts last season? No one knows. Savage, who was seen departing a benefit concert in Sonoma County Friday night in the company of an attractive redhead, left home Sunday morning after an altercation with his wife and has not yet surfaced . . .

July 24, 1995:

What have you DONE . . . ?

Thirteen

The fax from Kurt Girdwood's L.A. office came in on Ricky's machine at eight-forty Monday morning, only minutes after Rae called to say they were on the road and would be checking into a small hotel in La Jolla around eleven. My brother-in-law, she added, was ready to tell me all about Patricia Terriss, but he wanted to do so in person. I told her to call when they got settled; then the fax buzzed and I hung up and went to see what was coming through.

Underneath the item from the *Times* gossip column, the manager—who had returned to L.A. yesterday afternoon—had scrawled, "McCone—How the fuck did your people let this leak?" And beneath the words in the now-familiar handwriting, he'd added, "And what the fuck does *this* mean?"

I stared at the page, my spirits—which hadn't been any too high to begin with—sinking rapidly. Everything was veering out of control; I was powerless to stop it, and now Ricky's manager was blaming me for the fact that someone who had been at the estate on Sunday had tipped the media. And this latest note . . . How had Girdwood gotten hold of it?

I went to the desk to phone him, but before I could hit the automatic dial the door opened and Mick came in. His jeans and tee looked as though he'd slept in them; his red eyes looked as though he hadn't slept at all. He asked, "Have you heard anything from Dad?"

"Yes."

"Well?"

"He's on his way back from Arizona."

"But not to the house."

"No."

His lips tightened, then he shrugged. "Maybe it's better that way. I don't think anybody here's especially fond of him at the moment."

Charlene and I had agreed it would not be a sides-taking situation. Mick, Chris, and Jamie differed on that point.

"What's this?" Before I could stop him he picked up the fax I'd set on the desk. "Oh, great," he said as he read it. "Way to go, Dad. Now the whole world knows. And this at the bottom—it's another one of those notes, right?"

Charlene and I had also agreed it was time for the three older kids be told exactly what was going on. Knowing how serious the threat was would encourage Chris and Jamie to exercise the security precautions Hy had briefed them on, as well as make Mick more alert and able to defend himself when he returned to San Francisco. "Yes," I told him, reaching for the fax, "I was about to call Kurt to ask where he got it."

But Mick was rereading it, more slowly. His eyes stopped partway down and he said, "This 'attractive red-head'—that's Rae, isn't it?"

Why had I left the fax in plain sight on the desk? I was tempted to say I didn't know who the redhead was, but the lie would do more harm than good. It was obvious to me that Rae had slept with Ricky; she wouldn't be planning to stay in La Jolla with him unless she had. All Mick would have to do was go to see his father and he'd know everything.

"Isn't it?" he repeated.

"Yes."

"She was packing a bag when I left your house for the airport yesterday afternoon. Did she go to Little Savages to be with him?"

"Yes."

"That's all you can say today? Yes, yes, yes?"

"Mick—"

"I should've known." He balled up the fax, tossed it on the desk, and went to stand by the window, his back to me. "The phone at your house kept ringing on Saturday night and Sunday. She'd grab the cordless and take it into the guest room. Afterward she'd come out all distracted and kind of edgy. And she talked to him a long time yesterday before she put me on. Then she made a bunch of calls and seemed to be avoiding me." He laughed bitterly. "Well, no wonder! She was afraid I'd find out she was fucking my father."

"It wasn't quite that way."

"No? You didn't see her during the concert Friday night. She made the most heated-up groupies seem like ice maidens. And when he sang 'The House Where Love Once Lived' and dedicated it to Mom—nice way of letting me know they were splitting up, wasn't it?—when he sang that, she got the old look in her eyes."

"The old look?"

"Come on, Shar—you must've noticed the way women look at him. Even our waitress at dinner Thursday night was doing it. I just never expected something like that

169

from Rae. But when she decided to hitch a ride home in the limo with you all, I should've figured things out."

"She didn't sleep with him, Mick. They just talked."

"Of course that's what she'd tell you."

"I know for a fact." I explained about the incident in the stairwell at Coso Street.

Mick was so fixated on his father's relationship with Rae that he didn't seem to recognize the implications of what had happened. He said, "Okay, so she didn't fuck him on Friday, but you can't tell me she went to Little Savages just to talk."

"It's none of our business why she went—or what they did."

"You don't really believe that. I can tell by your voice that you're as upset about this as I am."

"I'm not happy about it, no." Understatement, McCone.

"Then why didn't you stop her from going down there?"

"How the hell could I have stopped her?"

"I don't know. You're her boss, he's our client. You should've done something!"

I knew he was shocked and hurting, but all of a sudden I was fed up with the Savage family's internal problems. The externals were more than enough to handle. More tartly than I intended, I said, "I didn't know I'd inserted a morals clause in your employment contracts."

Slowly he turned to me. "Don't tell me you approve of what that little home-wrecker's done?"

"Oh, for God's sake! This home was wrecked long before he ever laid eyes on her!"

"You *do* approve!"

"I said I wasn't happy about it. But it's not my place to judge them, any more than it's my place to judge your mother and Vic."

Spots of color appeared on his cheeks. "You can't compare the situations. Mom was driven to Vic."

"Nobody is *driven* to have an affair. Your mother made a choice to have one. So did your father." I paused. "So do you, every time you see Charlotte while Maggie's working."

Mick sucked his breath in sharply and turned back to the window. He was furious with me now, I could tell that much from his posture; it took him a minute to get his anger under control. Finally he said, "Nice shot, Shar."

"Hit home, didn't it?"

Another long silence. "Okay, maybe I'm my father's boy in more ways than one."

"In many ways. You have his generosity and level-headedness and determination and capacity to love. You can't lose sight of all those qualities in him just because he's made mistakes. Any more than he can lose sight of them in you when you make mistakes."

After a moment he turned, mouth twisting wryly. "I've been acting like an asshole, is that what you're saying?"

"You think you're bad? You should've seen me when Ma told me she was leaving Pa. Grown woman in her thirties, and I took it so personally that I shut myself in the bathroom and cried."

"No kidding?" He studied my face, seeing a whole new side of me. "Okay," he said, "I'll try to cut him some slack. But I'm never going to forgive Rae for what she's done. Never."

His reaction was exactly as I'd expected, and I wasn't any too sure about Hy's contention that eventually he'd come around. This was going to create complications at the office—major complications.

"Never," Mick repeated.

I shrugged. "That's up to you, but I hope you won't let it interfere at work."

"Oh, hell, give Rae a week and she'll have quit her job and be living off Dad."

He didn't know Rae, then. She was fiercely independent and always paid her own way. And she loved her work as much as I did.

Mick changed the subject. "What about this note that Kurt faxed?"

It was a relief to get off the personal for a while. "Let me call him." I punched the automatic dial button for Girdwood and put the phone on speaker. When the manager came on the line, his angry voice boomed so loudly that both Mick and I winced.

"Sharon, how could you let a leak like this happen?"

"There was no way I could've prevented it, short of putting everybody who was here yesterday under house arrest and ripping out the phone lines. I believe in this state that's called false imprisonment and punishable by—"

"Don't get smart with me! And what the fuck is this other thing?"

"How'd you get hold of it?"

"Was slipped under the office door before my staff opened up this morning, addressed to Rick."

"So you opened it."

"Of course I opened it! I'm his manager, for Christ's sake!"

I sighed.

"And while we're on the subject of him—is he still sulking at the studio?"

"He's on his way back."

"He and Charly going to patch it up?"

"Doubtful."

"Shit. What's this about a redhead?"

I glanced at Mick. "I don't know."

"Well, when he gets in touch with you, will you for Christ's sake tell him to call me at Zenith headquarters this afternoon? We've got a potential problem with this new single that Transamerica's releasing, and we've been waiting all weekend to talk to him. Time's getting short; we need to decide on a course of action."

"What problem?"

"Nothing for you to worry your pretty head about. You just tell him. And tell him he better come clean with me about why he's got those guards swarming all over the place. I'm his *manager!*"

"Yes, Kurt, I know." I broke the connection. "More problems," I muttered.

"Shar," Mick said, "what can I do to help?"

"With the investigation? Nothing. Your dad doesn't want you working on it and, frankly, I don't think it would be appropriate."

"Because I'm family? You're family, and you're working on it."

I couldn't think of an adequate response for that, but I knew I couldn't involve him. On the phone, Rae had sounded guarded about what Ricky had to tell me—so guarded that I suspected it was extremely bad. I couldn't jeopardize Mick's future relationship with his father for expediency's sake.

"That's different," I said lamely.

My nephew regarded me with narrowed eyes. "There's something you're not telling me."

"You're up to date on what's happened."

"I don't think so. There's something you're afraid I'll find out. I'll bet it's got to do with a woman."

"Why do you say that?"

"Oh, Shar, come on! I've known for years that Dad's no saint. Is that what this is all about—some woman who's stalking him?"

". . . Maybe."

"I can handle that."

"You're not handling his sleeping with Rae too well."

He repeated my earlier statement: "That's different."

I had to agree, but in the interests of fostering at least a surface harmony between Rae and him, I didn't comment. "Your dad doesn't want you on the case, and I have to respect his wishes."

His lips tightened and his color flared. "Fuck his wishes!"

"Mick—"

"You can't just shut me out!"

"If you want to remain employed, you'll have to go along with my decision."

He went rigid, hands balling into fists. "Well, fuck you, too! Fire me. Go ahead—fire me! But you can't stop me from investigating on my own."

"Mick, you're not licensed yet."

"Nobody says you need a license to research by computer. Nobody says you need a license to ask your own father questions. And you can damn well bet he'll answer them, after I tell him exactly how much damage he's done to all of us."

That was not what Ricky needed to hear from his son at this point, and I certainly didn't want Mick lurching off on an out-of-control personal investigation. Maybe if I used him in a limited capacity . . .

"Okay," I said, "you want in on the investigation, you're in. I can use your expertise, anyway. But I'll have to clear it with your dad first."

"If he won't agree, I'll set him straight damn fast."

"He'll agree." I'd see to that.

"So where do I start?"

"At the moment there's really nothing to do. I'm meeting your dad in La Jolla in a couple of hours, and after I talk with him I may have something to go on. In the

174

meantime, why don't you hunt up Hy for me? He's going to have to pull the guards off Little Savages and put others on the hotel where your dad'll be staying."

"Staying there with Rae?"

"Yes."

He compressed his lips and left the room, slamming the door behind him.

I sat down at the desk and rested my head on my arms, unsure whether I wanted to cry or scream.

I'd spent yesterday afternoon helping mop up the aftermath of the morning's explosive events. First the band had to be dealt with. Girdwood called them into the office and explained that Ricky had taken off to think things over. They were understandably angry until the manager told them they'd be paid a bonus for the time they'd spent waiting around. Heartened by that, they made plans: Pete to return to his pregnant wife in Santa Monica; Norm to spend some quiet time on a ranch he owned near Santa Barbara; Forrest and Jerry to stay at Jerry's condo in Palm Springs and play some golf. Girdwood looked at the latter three as if he thought them insane; the manager only felt comfortable in the steel-and-concrete canyons of big cities and had confided to me that the estate unnerved him because of "bugs and whatnot crawling around in that goddamn wilderness outside."

After the band left, Girdwood and Amory took off, too. Rattray was still convalescing in one of the guest rooms and being whiny and demanding enough to put a fierce scowl on Nona Davidson's normally pleasant face. Mrs. Davidson, who had arrived at noon to find a living room full of broken glass and bloodstains and a boarded-up window wall, set to work with quiet efficiency—calling a heavy-cleaning service and a glazier who would come out on a Sunday, and repeating to them with the glibness of a pathological liar Hy's fiction about a stray shot from a deer poacher. In between, she fixed special tidbits to entice us all to eat and even managed to coax a laugh out of Jamie.

Mick arrived mid-afternoon, and Charlene asked me to come to the den and sit in on her conversation with the three older children. Mick was noncommittal at first, and Chris and Jamie seemed relieved that something had finally been settled. But by the time Charlene explained exactly what had prompted the tight security, emotions were running high—and against Ricky. My sister held her ground, refusing to say anything bad about him, and when Mick commented bitterly on her bruised face, she replied with some humor, "You haven't seen the damage I did to *him*, young man."

When the three of them finally drifted off to other parts of the house, Charlene and I sat in silence for a while. Then she got us wine from the bar, curled up in her big chair, and sighed deeply. "I do believe I've accomplished everything on my list."

"What list?"

"I'm a list maker, you know that. After I calmed down this morning, I decided that from now on I was going to handle things properly, so I got out the old legal pad and started one."

"What was on it?"

"Talk to Jamie and Chris about drug use, ground them, and take Chris's car keys. Ask Nona to get the mess in the living room cleaned up and see about new glass. Call Vic and let him know what happened. Explain the truth to all three kids, once Mick got here." She paused. "There's another list, a long-term one: never badmouth

Ricky to the kids; try to eventually be his friend; make the divorce as painless on all of us as possible; have a good life from here on out."

"Well, you checked off everything on the first list, so . . ."

My sister raised her glass to me. "Here's to list-making."

That evening, after a swim and foraging on the cold buffet that Mrs. Davidson had left in the dining room, I curled up in bed with the bios of the band members that I'd taken from Ricky's files the night before. The grounds were quiet; Hy was at RKI headquarters in La Jolla. The bios were short—thumbnail sketches worked up by Ricky's publicist—but still I had trouble concentrating and had to keep rereading.

Curtin, Forrest D. b. Austin, TX, 5/25/69. Educated Austin public schools, grad. 1986. Bass and keyboards player with various bands, notably Texas Rangers and Montana, Austin 1987–90. Session musician, Nashville 1990–93. Member American Federation of Musicians, Academy of Country Music. Unmarried. Interests include golf, sailing, and snorkeling. Hired, 1993.

Jackson, Gerald R. (Jerry) b. Shreveport, LA, 2/12/65. Educated Shreveport and Bossier City public schools, grad. 1983. Enlisted U.S. Army, 1983; honorable discharge, 1985. Drummer for Grass Roots, 1984–86; same for Crompton Culver, 1986–94. Member American Federation of Musicians, Academy of Country Music. M. Tracey Rogers, 1986 (div. 1991), one child. Interests include golf and stock car racing. Hired, 1994.

O'Dell, Norman T. (Norm) b. Missoula, MT, 3/13/48. Educated Powell, MT, public schools, grad. 1965. University of Montana, Missoula, 1965–66. Guitarist and concert promoter, Missoula, 1971–77. Session musician, Nashville, 1977–90. Concert promoter, Albuquerque, NM, 1990–92. Session musician, Los Angeles, 1992–93. Member American Federation of Musicians. M. Jeanne Webster, 1965 (widowed 1970), one child. M. Yolanda Smith, 1972 (widowed 1985), one child. Interests include horticulture and animal husbandry. Hired, 1993.

Sherman, Peter W. (Pete) b. Oklahoma City, OK, 10/5/65. Educated Bartlesville public schools (did not graduate). Session musician, Nashville, 1983–88. Keyboard player for Callie Collins, 1988–90. Member American Federation of Musicians, Academy of Country Music. M. Patty Smith, 1989 (div. 1992), no children. M. Emily Watson, 1993, no children. Interests include songwriting (rights to four have been purchased by Savage Music Publishing) and hunting. Hired, 1990.

All in all, it was pretty dry stuff. My mind kept drifting—to the shooting, to Charlene and Ricky in the kitchen, to the ugly scene in front of the house. In spite of the disturbing quality of my thoughts, my eyes kept closing. In the morning, Hy told me that I'd been so deeply asleep when he returned shortly after ten that he'd been able to watch an entire made-for-TV movie, replete with pyrotechnics and car chases, without waking me.

Toward dawn, though, I awakened myself from a dream in which a couple hurled hateful words and lashed out to strike each other. Only the couple wasn't

Charlene and Ricky, it was Hy and me. I sat up and looked at my sleeping lover. He lay on his side, arms hugging the pillow as he often did.

I sensed Hy had been avoiding me the previous afternoon and evening, and that the trip into La Jolla had been less for business purposes than to get away from this oppressive household and knock back a few drinks with his partners, Dan Kessell and Gage Renshaw. I couldn't blame him; it must not have been easy to cope with the rampaging emotions of people he knew only on a superficial level. And I had to admit that I hadn't been keeping my own feelings under control, especially when alone with him. Still, I missed him, and now it struck me as odd that he hadn't wakened me when he came in.

God, I hoped this job wasn't driving a wedge between us!

Suddenly I felt afraid and reached out to touch his hair. Love was so fragile and often so quickly over.

I lay down again and pressed against his warm back for comfort. I thought of Rae, alone in the Sonoran desert with Ricky. I thought of Charlene, alone in the bedroom she and Ricky had once shared, but secure in her love for Vic. I thought of Chris, Jamie, and Mick, whose lives had been forever altered. And of Brian, Molly, and Lisa, who had no idea that their family had been torn apart.

Everything was changing. Everything.

One of the major changes appeared to have taken place in Rae. At eleven-thirty she greeted me at the door of a suite in the Sorrento, a small, exclusive seaside hotel that was owned by a friend of Ricky's, who had guaranteed him privacy and anonymity. As she led me into a pretty blue living room, she was more self-possessed than I'd ever seen her, although a little tired. Her blue

T-shirt matched the flowers on the fabric of the sofa; the blue of the sea matched her eyes.

"How're you?" I asked.

"Good. Better than I've been in a long time."

The room and the balcony were empty. "Where's Ricky?"

"In the bedroom, talking on the phone with your sister." She motioned toward a closed door.

I raised an eyebrow.

"There're things they've got to settle," she said. "He was kind of nervous about calling, but I told him to bite the bullet and get it over with. He can't just run off and leave his whole family in limbo."

I sat down on the sofa. "Is he okay?"

"He will be. I'm being okay for both of us right now."

"He's not on anything? Coke, for instance?"

She shook her head. "Actually, he got some rest on the way over. I don't think he's slept much since the night before your sister told him about Vic."

I nodded and a silence fell between us. I looked everywhere except at Rae, pretending to study a picture on the wall and the sea view beyond the balcony. Never had I felt such estrangement between us, even during the rocky patches in our long friendship.

"Look," I said.

"Listen," she said.

We both smiled tentatively.

"I know this is hard for you," she went on. "It's hard for me too. But I want you to know I care very much for Ricky; last night wasn't a casual fling for either of us."

"Rae—"

"I know you're going to say what you did yesterday: I'm taking a terrible risk; he's been breaking hearts all his life."

"I wasn't criticizing him when I said that, it's just that

I've known him a long time. He's a performer; they tend to dramatize themselves. He believes what he says or does at a given time, but that doesn't mean it's actually so. What he thinks he wants one minute may not be—"

"You think I don't know that?"

"Then why are you—"

"Because maybe it's time to stop playing it safe and take a big risk. If I go for it, I may end up having it all or having nothing. But if I don't go for it, nothing's all I'll get."

I couldn't dispute that; it was a concept I'd more or less lived by. I put aside my misgivings long enough to say, "Then go for it."

The bedroom door opened and Ricky came out. He did look somewhat rested, but it would take more than a couple of hours in a cramped car to repair the weekend's damage. He nodded to me, his eyes dull, but when they moved to Rae they brightened. She went to him and touched his arm. "I'm gonna take a shower, and maybe a nap. You and Shar talk, okay?"

He caught her hand, holding her back. "Red . . ."

"No, it's better this way."

He let go, but his eyes followed her. Then he turned back to me, folding his arms defensively.

I said, "Sit down and relax. I'm not going to start on you. We've had enough contretemps in this family to last a lifetime. You were talking with Charlene?"

He sat stiffly at the far end of the sofa. "Yeah. It was a little awkward, but we got some things settled—such as not telling the younger kids about the split till I'm back from the tour and we can do it together. And she's decided not to go to China; Chris and Jamie need her right now. Charly's being great about everything, considering all that's happened."

Considering all that's happened . . .

181

"I guess you and Rae got some things settled, too."

I'd meant the comment as a lead-in to what he had to tell me about Patricia Terriss, but he misinterpreted it. "Yeah, and I can practically hear the questions you're dying to ask me. Am I sleeping with her? None of your business, but from the arrangements here that should be obvious. Is what's happening with us important? Damn right. Will it last? I don't know, but I'll give it my best shot. Does she feel the same? Yeah, she does."

"It's happened awfully fast, Brother Ricky."

He grinned wryly. "I seem to recall a tale about a San Francisco woman who'd just busted up with her boyfriend. One morning she got an itch and climbed in her MG and drove all the way up to Tufa Lake, where this guy she'd met a few months back lived on a ranch. I don't know what happened between them when she got there, but it did happen fast. And they're together to this day."

"Point taken. Now, I believe you have something to tell me."

He sobered and leaned forward, elbows on his knees, clasping his hands between them. "Right. I told Red she wasn't going to like what she heard. She didn't. You won't either."

Fourteen

As he told me about Patricia Terriss, Ricky watched me, eyes anxious as he tried to gauge my reaction. I didn't speak after he finished, and it seemed to unnerve him. I wasn't silent out of shock or disgust, though; I was running a progression backward and forward in my mind.

After a bit I said, "I'm glad this is out in the open; now I've got something to go on. And in case you're wondering, I think what you did was pretty damn awful, but what Terriss did was awful, too. I've dealt with far worse, and from people who didn't lose a moment's sleep over it."

He relaxed some.

"I've got a lot of questions," I went on. "First, tell me more about Terriss. Was she from Austin?"

"No, she was there to get a career started; it's a center for country music like Bakersfield. I don't know where she was originally from, but I do recall her saying something about coming from a musical family. Of course, any hillbilly whose daddy could play a fiddle claims that."

"You say hillbilly. From the South, maybe?"

"She had a faint southern accent, but it could've been an affectation. Some of my colleagues lay it on pretty thick to make themselves sound more authentic."

"Was Terriss her real name?"

"I think it was her married name. She mentioned an ex-husband who was working on a Ph.D. dissertation on an obscure area of medieval history. Said he bored her to death, so she took off."

"She mention his first name, or where he was studying?"

"Not that I recall. Tell you the truth, we didn't do all that much talking."

"Okay, describe her."

On that he could be more specific: "Tall, willowy, light-brown hair parted in the middle and falling damn near to her waist. Big, big green eyes. Long, slender hands. She was a pretty fair guitar picker, and I told her she ought to go to Nashville, get herself on as a session musician; they work steady and make good money. But no, that wasn't for her; she *had* to be a star. Why? I asked. It was her daddy's dream for her, she said. Their daddies all have big dreams for them—mainly that they hit it big and buy them Cadillacs."

"Other than the suggestion that she go to Nashville, did you discuss her career?"

"She tried to; I did my best to distract her."

"And you didn't promise her anything?"

"I did *not*. I don't make promises to wannabes— whether they've got talent or not. If I run across somebody who's got it and is willing to work hard, I go away and make arrangements for them to meet the right people. After that, it's up to them."

"Okay, do you remember the phone number where

you called Terriss to make the date for the motel—the one you say she always put on her notes?"

He thought, frowning. "No."

"And I suppose you destroyed the notes."

"God, yes."

"Do you remember what her handwriting looked like? Was it similar to that on the notes you've received recently?"

"She always typed, except for signing with her first initial."

"Well, that's no basis for comparison. Think about that phone number; try to picture it. Was it in the L.A. area code?"

He closed his eyes. "I don't know why I think threeten. Could be because that was my area code in Pacific Palisades."

"And your phone records from Pacific Palisades were lost in the fire?"

"Yeah, but I didn't call her from there. I used a phone in an empty office at Transamerica."

"Well, that's that. No way of accessing their records without stirring up curiosity. Next question—were you having an affair around a year ago, at the time Charlene found the attorney's bill?"

He frowned. "An affair? God, no. After the Terriss thing, I backed off from any kind of entanglement."

"Charlene thought you were having one." I explained what she'd told me about the sympathetic looks and remarks from friends.

"Now that you mention it," he said, "I noticed some of that too, but I put it off to foolish gossip among people with more idle time than good sense. People must've really been talking, though, because Kurt came right out and asked me if I had something going on the side. He

185

never would explain why he wondered. Why couldn't Charly just come out and ask, too?"

"She said she didn't want to know, particularly after she found the attorney's bill."

For a moment he looked regretful, then he shrugged. "Well, if all it took was some gossip and a piece of paper to finish us, we didn't have much left, now did we?"

I had no reply for that, so I went on to my next question. "The house in Pacific Palisades burned six months before that. What started the fire?"

"Well, you remember how that canyon was—chockful of oak and manzanita and eucalyptus. And it'd been a dry year. When that stuff caught, the fire spread so quick there was nothing we could do but get out fast."

"Yes, but what *started* it?"

"The investigators thought it might've been a campfire; a lot of homeless hung out up there."

"Or it might've been deliberately set."

A sick look spread across his face. "Jesus, what're you saying, Shar?"

The scenario was only going to get worse. I hurried on with it. "Benjy died when, in relation to the fire?"

"About three months earlier."

"He overdosed?"

"Yeah. Benjy was a classic abuser—he'd take anything to get high and he mixed his drugs with alcohol. What got him was a combination of downers and booze. It was after a concert in Denver, the last of a series of back-to-backs. Benjy'd been on coke the whole tour, but I guess he decided to come down before he went home. He died in his hotel room early the next morning."

"Your business takes a high toll on its talent."

"It does. You put so much of yourself into the music; you're constantly riding the edges of your emotions, and you're always on display. You're continually upping the pressure to perform well because the rewards are so high; and the label's continually upping the pressure because they've got so much at stake." He paused, thoughtful. "Benjy was a shy man, not comfortable in his own skin. He didn't think he could go on stage without the drugs to help him through."

"You're a private person. You manage."

"I didn't always. But it's true I'm comfortable with myself, and I've got good control. Besides, I decided early on that I didn't want to turn into one of those guys who're in and out of rehab and still end up blowing their lyrics and getting their fingers stuck between their guitar strings in front of fifty thousand people."

I returned to the focus of our discussion. "Okay, before Benjy died, Dan was killed in a motorcycle accident. When?"

"Six months earlier. Dan liked speed, but a different kind than Ben. He lost control of the bike on the Pacific Coast Highway late one rainy night. Sailed right over the cliff."

"There was an investigation?"

"Of course. Kurt kept in touch with the cops; the rest of us were too broken up to deal with it."

"A lot of bad things have happened to you and yours since the Terriss woman entered your life. Too many, maybe."

"What do you . . . oh, no, that can't be!"

"Think about it: It's a large coincidence that the two men you sent to deal with Terriss died so soon afterward. And that your house burned down. And that someone may have started a whispering campaign that eventually led to the end of your marriage. Has anything else happened?"

He considered, then winced as he remembered something. "About six, seven months ago, Chris had an acci-

dent in the Triumph; the brakes failed and she plowed
into the guardrail on the Santa Monica Freeway. She
wasn't badly hurt, thank God, but it shook her up plenty
and she still won't drive the freeways. I talked to the me-
chanic and he said there was a possibility that the brake
line had been tampered with."

"Anything else?"

"Well, about three months ago I had a call from a slea-
zoid music attorney. Said he had a client who claimed I'd
plagiarized one of his songs. Told me that if I didn't settle immediately he'd pursue it in a way that would make
the John Fogerty case look trivial."

"What'd you do?"

"Referred him to Ethan. After that the whole thing
went away; he didn't even bother to call him."

"Didn't you think it strange that this lawyer had your
unlisted phone number?"

"Yeah, I did, but we were about to move, so I didn't
worry about it."

"And now for the latest incident. Have you seen the
L.A. Times today?"

"Catching up on current events wasn't my highest priority."

I took Girdwood's fax—the worse for wear from
Mick's crumpling it—from my bag and passed it to him.
He read, flushing with anger, then balled it up the same
way his son had, and hurled it across the room.
"God*damn* it! Isn't anything off limits to those vultures?"

"I think you'd better be prepared for some bad press."

" 'An attractive redhead.' Well, they got that right.
Thank God they didn't have a name. I don't want her
dragged into this mess. Red's not used to public scrutiny."

"The first time somebody snaps a picture of the two of
you together, her face is going to be in every tabloid in

the supermarket. But she's tougher than you think; for you, she can take the heat."

"Maybe. And now there's been another note. If you find out Terriss is the one behind this shit, I suppose that whole thing'll have to come out, too."

"It might be hard to keep a lid on it."

"There goes my credibility. But then, maybe I don't deserve it. Did I actually have the nerve to tell you I came by it honestly?"

"You did come by it honestly."

"Not too many people see me the way you do. There'll be plenty who'll be happy to watch me take a fall."

"Ricky, this is one of those situations for which you've got a manager; I think you should level with Kurt. He's going to have to do some damage control, maybe hire a consultant who specializes in it—particularly with the tour coming up."

"Jesus Christ, the tour!" He closed his eyes, shaking his head. "We're supposed to kick it off at the Universal Amphitheatre Wednesday night. The single of 'Midnight Train' should start getting airplay today."

"Speaking of that, when I talked with Kurt earlier, he asked that you call him at Zenith. Apparently he and Ethan were waiting around all weekend to discuss some problem about the new release; he wouldn't tell me what."

"Great—he and Ethan were waiting around, sucking up my booze, and didn't even bother to tell me there *was* a problem."

"Well, they didn't get a lot of cooperation from you."

"No, they didn't. Jesus, how much more screwed up can life get?"

"Quite a bit, I'm afraid. And I'm sorry to have to dump something else on you, but you'd better be aware that Mick got hold of that fax and figured out that the redhead was Rae. He also figured out that she went to meet you at Little Savages."

"Jesus!" He clapped his hand to his forehead. "How'd he react?"

"Not well. He was furious with you at first, then said he'd try to cut you some slack. But he says he'll never forgive Rae, and he's demanding to be allowed to work on the investigation."

"You told him no, I hope."

"At first, but then he said he'd investigate on his own. I don't want him going off and making things worse than they already are—or maybe putting himself in danger."

Ricky considered. "So use him in some way, but for God's sake don't let him find out about Terriss."

"That's what I initially intended, but on the way over here I started thinking. Mick takes pride in being an independent adult; he hates for us to act overprotective. What if this whole business came out in the media and he found out we'd been concealing it from him?"

"I just don't want him to realize—"

"He already knows or suspects a fair amount about your extramarital activities."

"Yeah, I guess he does."

"Think, Ricky: The way you handle this could affect your whole future relationship with him."

He thought, long and hard. Finally he said, "Okay, tell him. Don't sugarcoat it, either. And tell him I'll answer any questions he may have."

It was a task I didn't relish.

The bedroom door opened and Rae came out, her curls damp; she was clad in one of her oversized tees and, as far as I could tell, little else. Her eyes darkened when she saw Ricky's agitated expression. Quickly she slipped onto the arm of the sofa and put her hand on his shoulder. I could practically see his stress level decrease.

"How's it going?" she asked.

"As far as Sister Sharon and I, things're copacetic. Everything else is a mess, though." With occasional input from me, he explained what we'd been talking about.

Rae's reaction was calm, simple, and practical: "You'd better call Kurt right away. And Shar and I had better get started on locating this Terriss woman."

"You want to work on the investigation?" he asked with some surprise.

"Of course. I'd love to be the one who finds her. I'd love to get my hands around her neck and strangle her!"

"My fearless defender. I can use one right about now." He actually was smiling when he went to make his call.

Rae turned to me. "So where do we start?"

"There're multiple avenues to pursue. We'll divide them up between you, Mick, and me, plus continue using Charlotte for the data search. I'll take the more sensitive stuff that Mick shouldn't be exposed to and that you probably don't want to deal with."

"Such as?"

"For openers, a motel up the coast in Ventura."

Mick didn't want to come to the hotel suite Rae was sharing with his father, but I needed to outline strategy with both of them present. In the end, we met for a late lunch at the Hard Rock Cafe in central La Jolla. When my nephew arrived he said hello to me and nodded curtly to her. He sat where he wouldn't have to make eye contact with her, and his body language was rigid.

In the interests of harmony between the two members of my team I said to him, "You and Rae were good friends as recently as yesterday afternoon."

He picked up the menu and studied it.

Even though I didn't fully believe it myself, I added, "She's the same person now that she was then."

He set the menu down and looked at her, eyes narrowed as if he were trying to detect some change, however slight.

Rae asked, "How about it, Mick? Can we not let this get in the way of our friendship?"

"By 'this,' you mean the fact that you're fucking my father?"

She winced.

"Isn't pretty when you tell it like it is, huh, Rae?"

"Maybe that's how it looks to you, but I really care for him. And I'm sorry you had to find out about it from a gossip column."

His angry gaze wavered. He looked down at the table, and for a moment his lips trembled like those of a small boy who has been horribly disappointed on Christmas morning.

Rae added, "I know what it's like to have your life torn up in about a dozen different ways."

"Do you?"

"Yes. Please don't hate me, Mick. I couldn't bear that."

He looked up again, face vulnerable and very young. "I don't hate you, exactly. It's more . . . I don't know how to deal with you anymore. And . . . dammit, Rae, why didn't you tell me yesterday, when you knew you'd be going to Arizona?"

"Your dad didn't want you to know."

"Secrets again! Christ, from what Mom and Jamie and Chris tell me, this family's been harboring enough secrets to keep us all tongue-tied for eternity!"

"Not anymore."

"No, not anymore." He hesitated, then held out his hand to her. "Okay, I'll try to deal with you. That's all I can promise."

"That's more than enough." She clasped it and held tight.

Mick added, "Do me one favor, will you? If it lasts and the two of you get married, don't make me call you Mom."

Mick liked Ricky's story even less than Rae and I did. I held nothing back, though, and, per his father's instructions, didn't try to sugarcoat it. He listened without comment, losing his appetite and pushing his food around with his fork. Finally he gave up on it, took out a small spiral notebook, and began jotting things down.

"So that's what happened," I finished. "The leads we should pursue are obvious. I'll take the motel in Ventura, and I'm going to co-opt an investigator I know in Austin to get background on Terriss. Which one of you wants to take what?"

Mick said, "I'll take the motorcycle accident. We'll need the names of the investigating officers from Kurt, and I don't think it's a good idea for Rae to deal with him. He's awfully fond of Mom and bound to be upset about the split and looking for somebody to blame it on. And I'll talk with the fire-department investigators in Pacific Palisades."

Rae said, "That leaves me with the drug overdose. I'll get on to the Denver PD, fly up there if I have to. And I'll talk with the lawyer who called Ricky about the alleged plagiarism. He said Ethan should have the guy's name, since he warned him that he might be calling." She glanced at Mick. "Or should I steer clear of him, too?"

"Hell, no. Ethan hates Mom. I think he hit on her once when she and Dad were going through a bad period, and she blew him off."

"Okay," I said, "we've got our assignments. Mick, why don't you go back to the Sorrento and talk with your dad? He said he'd answer any questions you have, and it would cheer him up to see you."

Mixed emotions crossed his face. I knew how he felt because I still held the same feelings inside myself. Then he shrugged. "Why not? I've declared a truce with the redhead here; might as well do the same with my own flesh and blood."

I'd never been prouder of him.

Another challenge presented itself when I went back to the estate to check in with Hy and make some phone calls before leaving for Ventura. As I passed through the entryway, my sister called to me from the living room. I went in and found her sitting on a sofa beside a tall slender man with a deep saltwater tan and silver-gray hair. Charlene looked rested and at ease; she'd applied makeup to cover the bruise on her cheek and was stylish in green silk pants and a gold sleeveless top.

"Sharon, I want you to meet Vic Christiansen," she said. "Vic, my sister, Sharon McCone."

Christiansen rose and shook my hand. He was not handsome like Ricky, but he had the same confident presence. What had my brother-in-law called it in contrast to his dead friend Benjy? Being comfortable in one's own skin.

He said, "It's good to meet you. Thank you for being here for Charlene this weekend."

I wanted to dislike him on principle, this man whose appearance in my sister's life had dealt the final blow to her marriage. But his presence here meant Charlene was getting on with her life; I'd better accept that, and accept the man she loved. So I unbent and gave Christiansen a real smile. "I didn't do anything," I told him. "She's a strong woman, and she's handling everything well."

He smiled down at her. "You see? Isn't that what I just got through telling you?"

"Two against one; I bow to the majority. Shar—have you made any headway on finding out who's doing these things to us?"

"Some, yes," I said, wondering how much of the story Ricky had told her in their phone conversation.

She sensed the unasked question. "He said he needed to explain some things in person, and that they're pretty ugly. I'm not sure I want or need to know."

"It might be good to be prepared, in case there's media coverage."

"There already has been; that 'StarWatch' column is syndicated in the paper down here."

"Another of those notes arrived too, slipped under Kurt's office door this time."

Charlene shivered. "All the more reason I can't go to China," she said to Christiansen. "I'm not leaving my girls alone with only the housekeeper and a bunch of armed guards when there's a crazy person on the loose."

"Love, believe me, the trip isn't important." He sat beside her again, touched her arm.

I was quickly warming to my sister's new man.

After a moment Charlene said to me, "Curiosity may be in bad form, given the circumstances, but . . . this redhead—do you know her?"

". . . Yes."

"Is he with her now?"

"Yes."

"Is she important to him?"

"I think so."

For a moment my sister looked as though she wanted to ask more. Then she shrugged and smiled at Vic—letting go.

* * *

I found Hy in the office, conferring with one of the guards. A rifle lay on the desk between them.

"Is that the sniper's weapon?" I asked.

They looked around, startled. "Could be," Hy said. "Ironic thing is, it's a Savage model three-forty, thirty-caliber, like the slug we found."

"Savage?"

"Common sporting rifle."

"God, don't tell me this lunatic is making a joke! Where was it?"

"Near the wall that backs up on the north canyon."

Dropped by the shooter as he—or more likely, she—was escaping? No, that couldn't be; the security system on that wall had not gone out. "How come it took so long to locate it? You've been combing the grounds for over twenty-four hours."

The guard said, "It was hidden pretty good—under a pile of leaves with a fallen tree trunk pushed over it. Only reason I noticed, the dirt was disturbed where the trunk was."

I frowned.

Hy said, "Uh-huh." To the guard he added, "Thanks. You can get back to your regular post now."

After he'd left, Hy sat down in the swivel chair. I perched facing him on a corner of the desk. "You're thinking the same thing I am," I said. "The rifle was deliberately concealed by somebody who remained on the property. Somebody who knew he or she couldn't remove it or hide it in the house or a car. And in light of the gun's manufacturer, I think we were supposed to find it. The perpetrator of this nasty game's not only becoming more aggressive, but playful."

"Well, that narrows it down to a family member, Girdwood, Amory, or a band member."

"And that doesn't fit with the new facts in the case." I recapped them for him and added, "If it's Terriss who's behind all this, she's got an accomplice who's close to Ricky. One of the nine people who were here Saturday night. I think we can discount the family—which leaves us Girdwood, Ricky's manager, who has no reason to want to bring him down."

"That we know of."

". . . Okay, that leaves us Girdwood. And Amory. And the band. I'm more inclined to suspect one of them. Keim's checking police records and credit histories on them; maybe she'll come up with something that'll point to one or the other."

Hy was thoughtful, running his fingers over his mustache. "McCone, I can understand a slow progression. Kill the guys who did whatever they did to her; burn down the house; start nasty rumors; tamper with Chris's car; sic a sleazy lawyer on him. But what triggered those notes? What made her—if it is her—all of a sudden step up her campaign?"

I'd been considering that on the drive over here, and I thought I knew the answer. "The first note arrived a week after the *Billboard* item on the new label appeared. It said 'Whatever happened to my song?' A phrase from a ballad performed by an artist who acknowledged Ricky's help with her career in her liner notes."

"So?"

"The logic's skewed and the message is obscure, but it's simple when you know who's probably behind it. Terriss once thought she could blackmail him into leaving Charlene and making her a star. Now she thinks she can terrorize him into signing her to his new label."

Fifteen

Five-thirty on a Monday afternoon. I had picked the absolute worst time to cross L.A.

Or maybe there was no good time, I reflected as I sat at a dead stop under the Rosecrans Avenue overpass on the San Diego Freeway. I'd driven this route countless times since I moved north and had never breezed through the megalopolis; once I'd been stuck in an enormous traffic jam near Culver City at two in the morning.

An hour later I finally reached the intersection with the Ventura Freeway. More dead stopping on the feed-in, but around Thousand Oaks traffic thinned some and I picked up speed. Soon I was out of the L.A. basin, and the air looked clearer. I rolled down the car's window and sniffed it; cleaner, too. At a little before eight I took the California Street exit for Ventura and could smell the sea.

Tourist areas of California beach towns share many characteristics, and Ventura's was no exception: restaurants with oceanview dining; the ubiquitous T-shirt stands; too-cute shops and fast-food outlets; hotels and motels ranging from the luxurious to the shabby. The

Spindrift Inn fit neither category. Tucked on a quiet side street not far from the marina, it consisted of twenty-some tan stucco bungalows set well back from the motel office and screened from one another by latticework overgrown by ivy. The perfect place for a lovers' tryst—or a setup that could turn ugly.

I pulled the rental car into a parking space marked "registration only" and sat for a moment, contemplating the place. Ricky had told me that Dan chose the location—knew the motel from weekends spent there with various women friends. I wondered, not for the first time, if Dan and Benjy had worked out in advance how to handle Patricia Terriss, or if they had come here prepared to let the confrontation play itself out in whatever direction it might take. Wondered, too, about my brother-in-law's uncharacteristically passive role in the scenario and decided he hadn't wanted to know his friends' intentions because he hoped ignorance would somehow make him less culpable.

Didn't work that way, now did it, Ricky?

I got out of the car and went into the office. The motel was clearly a mom-and-pop operation: Behind the counter a door opened into a cozy living room where an older couple were watching a rerun of "Law and Order." I tapped the bell and the man, gaunt and stooped, got slowly up from his chair and hobbled out. His hands were gnarled and swollen with arthritis.

I showed him my I.D., and he looked it over with interest, a gleam of excitement coming into his pale eyes. Then he glanced back at the living room, where the woman sat riveted to the fictional drama. He said nothing to her; the real-life drama was his, and he wasn't about to share.

I asked, "Are you the manager?"

"Owner," he replied with some pride.

"And you owned the inn three years ago?"

"Since the late seventies, when I took an early retirement."

"Three years ago on June twenty-ninth, a young woman registered here. Tall, willowy, waist-length light-brown hair, big green eyes. She may have given her name as Patricia Terriss. Any possibility you recall her?"

"Three years is a long time, miss."

"She was quite beautiful, I'm told. Checked in alone, but someone may have joined her later on."

He glanced toward the living room again; a commercial had come on, and the woman had muted it. When he spoke it was in a whisper. "Well, I could check my records."

I slipped a twenty from my wallet and placed it on the counter. "I'll be glad to pay for your time; I'm keeping you from your TV program."

He made a motion of refusal, but without turning her head the woman said, "Take the money, Harry."

Harry glared at her, took the twenty, and laboriously sat down at the desk below the counter. As he turned on the computer terminal his lips soundlessly formed the words "old bat." He began clumsily tapping the keys to access the old records; after a moment he said, "There it is—June twenty-nine, nineteen ninety-two. Three couples, one family, three single males. No single woman. No Patricia Terriss."

"May I look?"

He swiveled the screen toward me.

I scanned the names, stopped at the listing for Mr. and Mrs. Ricky Savage, at the old address in Pacific Palisades. Ricky had told her to register under her own name. Was this her idea of a joke, or a way of trying to impress the motel owner?

I said, "The Savage couple—did they arrive together or separately?"

Something flickered in his eyes; perhaps he was only now connecting the name with the celebrity. "I really don't recall."

I scanned the screen again, took down the Texas license-plate number of Terriss's Chevy Camaro. "Are you sure you don't remember the woman? She was the one who registered, and she was quite striking."

Harry shook his head, but his eyes shifted away, as though he was remembering something. From the living room, the woman said, "You might as well tell her. Better a private eye than a cop."

He slumped over the desk, both nervous and deflated. Even with the TV going again his wife had managed to follow the real-life drama as well. After a moment he said, "You keep talking about her in the past tense. Is she dead?"

Odd question. "Not that I know of. Why?"

He hesitated, running the tip of his tongue over dry lips.

The woman said, "I told you somebody would come around asking someday."

"Shut up."

"We should've reported—"

"Shut up!"

"Look," I said quickly, "I'm not going to involve the police in this. That's the last thing my client wants."

He frowned, glanced back at his wife for help. She still faced the TV. Finally he sighed. "Okay, the woman came in around six o'clock, paid cash for one night. She said she was meeting her husband. I got the idea she expected some reaction from me, and that struck me as peculiar because a lot of couples come in separately.

201

Maybe she wasn't married to him and was nervous because she thought I'd care."

No, as I'd surmised, she expected him to recognize Ricky's name. Thank God Harry wasn't a country fan! "Go on, please."

"That's all there is."

"Harry, if you don't tell her, she *will* go to the cops, and that kind of attention this place doesn't need."

I took another twenty from my wallet and laid it on the counter. This time Harry pocketed it without hesitation, putting a cautioning finger to his lips. "Okay, the woman was strange. Those big eyes were all jumpy and intense, and she smiled at the wrong times. She went to the bungalow, then called down here asking how to dial long distance. I told her I'd have to place the call and ask for time and charges, since she hadn't put the room on a credit card. She didn't like that, but she made the call anyway and came down right afterward to pay for it."

I looked at the charges listed on the screen; the call had been to the 213 area code—the phone at Transamerica's offices where Ricky said he'd waited to hear from her. "When did her husband join her?" I asked.

Harry shrugged.

"He *did* join her?"

". . . Somebody did, yeah."

I set the publicity stills of Dan and Benjy that I'd gotten from Ricky's files on the counter. "Was it either of these men?"

Harry squinted at them, then pointed to Dan. "That's the guy who came to the door."

"The door?"

"Around ten o'clock the family in the bungalow closest to them called up and complained about loud partying. I went back there, knocked, and that fellow

202

answered. He was polite enough, apologized and said they'd tone it down."

"Did they?"

He didn't reply. His grim expression said that he was finding real-life drama not nearly as pleasurable as what he viewed on TV. "Yeah, they did," he finally said, "and the next morning, early, they were gone."

"And that's it?"

Silence.

"For God's sake, Harry, tell her and get it over with!"

"Okay, *okay!* The wife saw her car was gone and went in to clean. Came and got me. The room was full of bottles and dirty glasses, and it looked like they'd been smoking marijuana, too. The bed had been ripped apart, and the wife . . . well, she claims she can always tell from the sheets. It looked like they'd had a wild night of it."

A chill crept over me; what he'd told me wasn't enough to unnerve seasoned innkeepers. "Anything else?"

". . . Yeah. In the bathroom. There was blood. A lot of it, on the wall by the bathtub and on the towels and bathmat. Some of the towels were missing, too." He shook his head, pale eyes sad and confused. "Can you imagine that? A man having sex with a women and hurting her enough to leave that much blood?"

A man having sex with a woman and hurting her enough to leave that much blood . . .

No, not a man—men.

The innkeeper's words kept rattling through my mind. All the way back to the L.A. basin, all the way through the interminable traffic clogs, all the way down the relatively free-moving straightaway to San Diego.

How the hell was I going to tell Ricky about this?

How do you tell someone that his childhood friends— the buddies who'd stuck with him on the long rise to success, the men to whom he'd entrusted his worst problem, the band members whose untimely deaths he still mourned—how do you tell him that those men were nothing but scum? How do you tell him that by his own self-indulgent actions and terrible judgment he may have caused a young woman to suffer serious injury—perhaps even death?

But no, Terriss couldn't be dead. She had to be the one behind this vengeful campaign. Or did she? Perhaps someone was avenging her death. But that couldn't be right, either. If Dan and Benjy had killed her, they'd covered the crime well; no one knew what had happened.

I was so preoccupied that I almost missed the La Jolla exit, and when I parked in front of the Sorrento I banged the bumper into the high curb. Dreading the conversation that had to follow, I hurried inside and up to Ricky's suite. And found that such a conversation was not an option at the moment.

The living room was full of people. Through the crowd I spotted Kurt Girdwood on the phone, shouting and pacing; he held the base in his left hand, and its cord was in imminent danger of being yanked from the jack. Ethan Amory sat on a chair by the door to the balcony, watching him; the attorney was quietly intense, ready to spring into action if called upon. Several men and women whom I didn't know, as well as Forrest Curtin and Jerry Jackson, stood talking quietly. Linda Toole, Ricky's publicist, whom I'd met at the housewarming, was using a cell phone. Toole was a diminutive woman with spiky dark hair, numerous silver earrings, and an incredibly short shirt worn over patterned tights. Surprisingly enough, her voice competed strongly against Girdwood's.

I finally located Ricky and Rae on the sofa. He sat on its edge, his hand pressing her knee—as wired as if he were about to take the stage. She eyed him watchfully. I hurried over and asked, "What's going on?"

He said, "You remember this afternoon when I asked you how much more screwed up life could get? Well, you're seeing it."

Girdwood shouted, "Goddamn it, you tell that cocksucker to call me back within fifteen minutes or the shit hits the fan bigtime! I'm talking lawsuit, baby, lawsuit in seven figures! Tell him that and see if he keeps ducking my calls!" He slammed the receiver into its base and started toward us, but the cord restrained him. With a disgusted look, he ripped it from the wall, then hurled the instrument to the floor.

Rae flinched, and Ricky said, "So Ziff's still ducking you."

"Yeah, the prick."

"What do we do now?"

"You heard me—we sue! Seven figures—eight, maybe. We'll put Transamerica out of business. Right, Ethan?"

The attorney steepled his fingers and propped his chin on them. "It's not an alternative. Nothing in Rick's last contract specified that Transamerica had to use promotion reps on this single."

"Well, why the hell didn't it?"

"Don't try to hang it on me, Kurt; you vetted the contract. As you may recall, that deal was done over two years ago—the largest to date for a country singer. Transamerica had done a good job of promoting him up to then, and we naturally assumed that with megabucks riding on each of the two albums, they'd continue to do so. At the time, we hadn't begun talking about forming the new label, so we had no reason to anticipate that one day they'd retaliate for his leaving."

Girdwood groaned and collapsed next to Ricky.

I said, "Will somebody please explain the problem?"

The manager looked at me as if I were a mosquito he'd like to squash, but Ricky said, "The single of 'Midnight Train' is blacked out on all the large country stations, both on the West Coast and in the other major markets. It's getting no airplay on them whatsoever."

"That's incredible."

"Damned straight it is!" Girdwood bellowed. "And the hell of it is, we could've headed this off if my client here"—he glared at Ricky—"had been willing to take time out from his personal affairs"—now he transferred the glare to Rae—"long enough to talk with Ethan and me this weekend. We had ample warning."

"What kind of warning?" I asked, thinking of another anonymous note or perhaps something more bizarre.

"What happened was, Friday night at a party I ran into the independent promotion rep Transamerica uses."

"Promotion rep? What's his function?"

The manager sighed impatiently. "The reps are high-powered guys with close connections to the radio stations' program directors—the people who decide which singles get airplay and which don't. They go around, lobby the PDs to put their releases on the play lists. Most labels've got them on staff, but a few years ago Transamerica went into negative cash flow and decided to cure it by letting them go and hiring them only to work on its priority releases—such as my client's."

"Okay, I understand. You say you ran into one of them at a party?"

"Yeah, guy who's always done a good job for Rick in southern California. Right away I ask, 'How does it look for the airplay on Savage's new single?' And he goes, 'What single?' and smirks. I go, 'Transamerica didn't hire you to push it?' And he goes, 'The label's low-balling the promo on your client.' And I ask, 'What is it with them? Do they want the thing to stiff?' And he tells me I better ask Sy Ziff and John Geller. Which I've been trying to do ever since, but neither of those cocksuckers'll take my calls."

I glanced at Ricky. *More of the same?* He shrugged.

The manager went on, "That's not all of it. I call around. The situation's the same with the guys they use in the other major markets. And then I'm talking with a PD I know in New York, and he says Transamerica *is* using the guys—only they're using them to lobby *against* airplay."

"That's ridiculous!"

"Not really. The guys at Transamerica're pissed about Rick leaving. So pissed that we—Zenith—are footing the bill for the *Midnight* tour. This is their way of sending a message to any of their other artists who may be thinking of jumping ship."

I frowned. This didn't fit the pattern of harassment; vindictive as it was, it sounded like a purely internal business decision at the label.

Rae spoke for the first time. "It seems to me that Transamerica's cutting its own throat."

Girdwood gave her a withering look.

Ricky said, "Not really. The point is to sell albums, and I'm in the enviable position where mine practically sell themselves. It's not as if they're trying to break some baby act with this single. They still stand to make back every cent they've paid me—and then some."

I asked, "If nobody stands to lose anything, what's all this commotion about?"

Girdwood rolled his eyes dramatically. "Is there some rare strain of stupidity going around up your way? You ever hear the phrase 'the principle of the thing'? Rick's made them truckloads of money over the years—which they've blown on mediocre acts and bad management.

Now he decides to go out on his own, and they treat him like shit."

"So what're you going to do about it?"

As we'd been talking, the others in the room had begun to pay attention; now they were silent, looking at Girdwood. In turn, he looked at Amory.

The attorney shrugged. "Well, we're not suing. It wouldn't be productive or cost-effective."

Girdwood said, "What I'd really like to do is go over to Sy Ziff's house and break down the door and choke the son of a bitch!"

"You'd be useless to me on death row," Ricky told him.

Forrest Curtin said, "You want, Rick, *I'll* kill Ziff—and John Geller, for good measure."

"This kind of talk isn't getting us anywhere," Amory said. "We've got to come up with a course of action."

Linda Toole moaned. "Between this and that item in 'StarWatch' this morning, it's a publicist's nightmare. Why me, Lord?"

"It's not only *your* nightmare!" Girdwood snapped.

"Well, I'm the one who's going to feel the most heat!"

Rae had taken Ricky's hand and was staring down at where their linked fingers rested on her knee, thoughtful. Now she looked up and said to him, "Why not use it to your advantage?"

Heads turned. Girdwood snorted derisively. Rae flushed.

But Ricky looked at her with interest. "How?"

She took a deep breath, nervous but encouraged. "Well, what Transamerica's done to you makes you the underdog. And this country loves an underdog. We'll forgive most anything if an individual is wronged by a greedy corporation. Especially if the underdog fights back."

He nodded slowly. "If the underdog fights back, people'll forgive him an attractive redhead—or even worse sins. Go on."

"Okay, you fight back. The question is—how? You'll have to finance the offensive yourself. Huge ads in the papers exposing the label for the swine they are come to mind, but that's not only costly but legally tricky." She glanced at Amory, who nodded. "What you need," she added, "is a way to get the word out that's not quite so explicit or costly, and that also turns a buck for you."

"What do you have in mind?"

Buoyed by his prompting, she went on more confidently. "You were talking about the Winterland merchandising earlier. How fast could they get a large order of T-shirts made up?"

Ricky looked at Amory. The attorney said, "Pretty damn fast, since those contracts for the additional Savage merchandising are still only in the draft stage. They want to keep us happy till they're finalized. Besides, orders like that're done all the time."

Rae asked, "Could they deliver in time for Wednesday's kickoff concert? As well as supply other shirts, with a slightly different wording, to the other cities on the tour where the single's blacked out?"

"I'm sure they could."

Everyone was listening closely now, even Girdwood—although the manager's face was set in contemptuous lines. Rae transferred her attention back to Ricky. "You could have a special tee made up. One of a kind. Not a run-of-the-mill concert-tour tee, but one that people'd treasure because of its . . . let's call it 'historical significance.' Everybody on the tour, from you down to the roadies, would wear it. At some point during the concert, you'd explain its significance to the audience, ask them to call the radio stations and request the single. And when reporters asked you about it, you'd do the same. And you'd offer the tees for sale in every city along the route."

Ricky and Linda Toole had started to smile. Girdwood frowned skeptically, but Amory leaned forward in his chair.

"What does it say?" he asked, his southern-accented voice intense.

"Well, something along these lines: 'Blacked Out in Los Angeles: *The Midnight Train to Nowhere.*' "

"Shirt color?"

"Black."

"Lettering?"

"Silver."

"Graphics?"

"A train inside a circle with a slash mark through it."

Jerry Jackson let out a whoop.

"All *right!*" Ricky enveloped her in a hug.

I myself was stunned. Rae had always been bright, quick, and creative, but she often lacked confidence. I'd never seen her so self-assured—or so potentially powerful.

Amory said, "Rick, you better keep this one. She's a genius."

Rae blushed, and Ricky said, "I'll do my damndest." Then he added, "You want to get on to Winterland as fast as possible."

"Yeah. The rep we'll be dealing with on your merchandising is as sharp as they come, and I happen to have her home number. Even at"—he looked at his watch—"one-ten in the morning, Mary'll welcome an order of this size."

It felt as if everyone in the room had let out a collective breath; suddenly they were all talking in light, excited tones. Linda Toole called to Ricky that she'd get started immediately on his statements for audiences and the press, so Ethan could check them for potential legal problems. Amory looked for the phone, spotted it on the floor where Girdwood had hurled it, and headed for the extension in the bedroom.

Ricky had his arm around Rae and was speaking softly into her ear. Whatever he said made her blush again. Girdwood watched them, his expression quizzical. After a moment he said, "Hey, Rae, I thought you were an investigator. How'd you all of a sudden turn into a PR whiz?"

She looked him in the eye. "Both jobs require the same basic problem-solving abilities . . . Kurt." And then she favored him with one of her crinkly-nosed grins.

The manager grunted, pushing his lips out petulantly. Rae grinned some more. He frowned, scratched his head. She winked.

"Oh, hell," he said to Ricky, "I give up. You can keep her. Only treat *this* one good, would you?"

Sixteen

At nine the next morning I was back at Ricky's hotel suite, watching as he, Hy, and Virgil Rattray went over diagrams of the various concert venues along the tour route. Rae drifted in and out of the living room, stopping occasionally to examine one of the plans that were spread out on the floor, but mainly looking cheerful and somewhat distracted. Ricky's gaze followed her, and he seemed to have trouble keeping his attention on the business at hand.

As time went on I became aware of a peculiar nagging feeling. Not the anger I'd directed toward them the day before—I was through with that, anger couldn't alter what was—but more of a prickly discontent. I glanced at Hy to see if he was feeling the same, but he was intent on his security plans, scarcely aware of my presence. The discontent intensified, and I tried to ignore it and concentrate on the discussion.

The diagram that interested me most was of the special Amtrak train that would serve as a publicity vehicle following the kickoff concert at the Universal Amphitheatre. Linda Toole had arranged for the performers and select press representatives to depart from L.A.'s Union Station at midnight, accompanied by much manufactured fanfare. Ricky and his band would mingle with reporters and photographers over drinks and a buffet supper in the lounge car, then detrain a few hours later at Barstow and transfer to a charter flight for Albuquerque. The press would remain on board and be flown from New Mexico to their various home bases, courtesy of Zenith Records.

"Why're the performers flying from Barstow, for God's sake?" I asked Rattray. "Why not just stay on board like the press is?"

He snorted and looked at me as though I'd taken leave of my senses. "Have you ever seen the size of one of those bedroom compartments—even the deluxe ones? Have you ever tried to *sleep* on a train?"

"Uh, no."

"Well, I wouldn't recommend it. There's no way Rick and the guys could endure fifteen miserable hours en route and then perform the same night. Shit, even the crew and equipment're going by air out of LAX! This is a goddamned idiotic scheme dreamed up by that twit of a PR woman, and it only makes my job harder because I can't be in two places at once."

"Where *will* you be?"

"On the stinking train, in case his majesty needs me." The road manager scowled ferociously at Ricky, who merely smiled.

After a while my brother-in-law went into the bedroom to make some calls, and Rae settled down on the balcony with a cup of coffee. I continued to listen to Hy and Rats debate various security options, none of them completely satisfactory. Rats's comments grew more acerbic; his brush with death hadn't improved his disposition, and he complained constantly of pain in his wounded shoulder. Finally I got fed up and said, "Rats, just be thankful you didn't get shot in the ass."

"What the hell's that supposed to mean?"

"I was once, and believe me, it's a thousand times worse than a shoulder wound. More embarrassing, too."

He grunted but ceased complaining.

After half an hour more, Hy began rolling up the diagrams. "Time to take this stuff over to our headquarters," he said. "We're meeting at eleven with an outside consultant that I met at Ricky's Sonoma County concert."

"Why?" Rats asked.

"He specializes in this type of security."

"Uh-huh. I suspected you didn't know what you were doing. Why else would you've let me get shot?"

Hy gave him a forebearing look, but I couldn't control myself any longer. "You know, Rats," I said, "most of what comes out of your mouth must completely bypass your brain. Ripinsky's no ordinary security man; his talents lie in more tricky areas, and you'll be damned glad to have him on the road with you if things get dicey."

"Tricky areas?"

"Try hostage recovery. Counterterrorism. Ransom negotiation. And more sensitive but . . . less easily defined areas."

The road manager turned to Hy. "You *do* that stuff, man?"

Hy just nodded, amused.

I said, "He does that stuff."

"Holy shit." Rattray stared at him with grudging respect.

Rae came in from the balcony after they'd gone. She still looked tired, but her eyes held a soft glow. As she helped herself to more coffee and curled in a corner of the sofa, I said, "Quite a coup you pulled off last night.

You may have found the way to shore up Ricky's credibility. Even Girdwood was impressed."

Her gaze muddied. "Don't count on that. Ricky told me to watch my back where Kurt's concerned. Girdwood likes your sister—for herself, but also because she's stayed out of Ricky's career decisions. At first I was an unknown quantity, but after last night he sees me as a potentially dangerous influence." She smiled faintly. "He called early this morning and in the course of the conversation told Ricky he was thinking with his balls."

"Well, you can hold your own with Kurt. You've already proved that."

"I can, so long as Ricky backs me up—and he will."

"You're very sure of him."

"This is one of a handful of times in my life when I've known something is absolutely right."

I studied her as I had the night before, impressed by her newfound confidence.

"What?" she asked.

"Nothing."

"Uh-huh. I can hear your mind ticking. You want to ask a million questions."

"Why is it that everybody accuses me of wanting to ask questions? Ricky said the same thing yesterday morning."

"Well, we both know from long experience how nosy you are. You pretend not to be, but right now you're dying to ask me how it was."

Over the years we'd played a game, each accusing the other of excessive interest in her romantic life. We'd coaxed and refused, bartered back and forth, and eventually given up single innocuous tidbits. I wasn't sure I could play the game when the man involved was my soon-to-be former brother-in-law, but I gave it a try.

"How what was?"

Rae looked relieved at my stock response. "You know."

"I am certainly not curious about *that!*"

"Just like you weren't curious about my computer love triangle."

I maintained a pseudo-injured silence.

She added, "Back then you plied me with cheap wine."

"I suppose this time I'll have to use the expensive stuff."

"Won't do any good."

"Deer Hill Chardonnay?"

"Not fair!"

"Two bottles."

She sighed. "All right, I'll tell you one detail and let you draw your own conclusions. One detail, and that's all—now or ever."

I wasn't sure I even wanted that much, but I'd gone too far to turn back. "Tell me, if you must."

"Okay, one of the things Ricky said to me last night was, 'Never underestimate a gittar picker; we're great with our hands.' "

No, I hadn't needed to hear that. But I said mechanically, "That's not much of a detail."

"Deer Hill, two bottles."

More prickly feelings. This time I recognized them for what they were: jealousy. Good God, I couldn't be jealous of Rae because of Ricky! Yes, he was attractive, he had that come-fuck-me voice. But for eighteen years he'd been like a brother to me.

No, what I was jealous of was the way his eyes followed her while Hy's didn't seem to see me. I was jealous of the newness of this thing between them. I was jealous of the commitment they seemed to have to each other, even if it probably wasn't real or lasting.

I didn't want what they had; I wanted Hy and me to have more than what we had.

Rae was frowning, afraid she'd upset me.

"Two bottles," I told her, "but you have to share."

"Not to worry," she said. But her eyes were still concerned.

There was a knock at the door. Mick, arriving to confer on the investigation. Rae flushed when he came in—not an unnatural reaction to having the son appear while she was talking about the father's offstage talents. I grinned wickedly at her, then got our meeting underway by asking him for a report on what he'd found out about the fire in Pacific Palisades.

"It was definitely considered to be of suspicious origin," he said, flipping open his notebook. "Point of origin was a quarter-mile up the canyon to the east. It was a box canyon," he explained, glancing at Rae. "Our house was the last on the road, at a fair distance from the neighbors. The fire inspector I talked with said that the wind conditions that night were optimal for the flames to spread toward us. They found no physical evidence like the presence of flammable fluids, but, given how dry the vegetation was, they wouldn't've been necessary to get it going. There was a ring of stones in the area of origin that indicated somebody had built a campfire there, so the investigators theorized that homeless people who'd been seen in the area might've been responsible."

He hesitated, rechecking his notes, then shut the book. "After I talked with the investigator, I drove over to the canyon to see if going back there would make my memory of that night any clearer. The fire started late—after two. Dad was up, working on a song, and he saw the glow and got on to nine-one-one right away. Then he woke us all up. Mom stuffed the little kids in the Porsche; Dad took Chris and Jamie in her car; and I drove that Jeep we used to have. The Jeep was blocking the driveway, so I was out first. When I got to our nearest neighbors I started to turn in to warn them, and this pickup came roaring off their property and I almost broadsided it. Nobody answered their door, so I assumed they'd been the ones in the pickup—until yesterday when I stopped by there."

"They didn't get burned out?" Rae asked.

Mick shook his head. "The fire department got there in time to contain it; only our house went. Anyway, after I'd roamed around where our house used to be—and got myself real depressed—I stopped by the neighbors' and asked them if they'd been the ones in the pickup, and they said no, they hadn't even been home."

"How come you didn't find that out back then?"

"Jesus, Rae, when you've lost everything like that, the last thing on your mind is the whereabouts of the neighbors. None of us kids ever went back to the canyon, and I didn't mention the pickup to Mom or Dad. Didn't really give it a second thought until yesterday afternoon."

I said, "Can you describe it?"

"I was awake half the night trying to call up a clear image. All I remember is light-colored, and muddy above the rear bumper."

"Muddy? The fire happened in October, and that was a dry fall."

He shrugged. "That's what I remember seeing as it roared away down the road. You know how when you're panicked certain small details sear themselves into your brain? You might not remember anything else, but they're as clear as can be. And the mud on the pickup is one of them."

"Above the rear bumper," I said. "Around the license plate."

". . . Uh-huh." He nodded, realizing what I was getting

218

at. "The old time-honored TV-show trick of using mud to conceal the plate number. Mud in a dry season. And ace private eye Mick Savage was too dumb to figure it out."

"Don't fault yourself. The most obvious details are the ones that usually slip right by me. Okay, keep trying to remember anything else about that truck and let me know if you do. Now, what about the motorcycle accident?"

"County sheriff was the investigating agency. Officer there let me go over the file. Dan was heading south from his girlfriend's in Malibu to his place in Santa Monica; she confirmed the time he left. Rainy night, not too much traffic. No witnesses, no skid marks. The bike exploded on the rocks and a trucker saw the fire and reported it. There was evidence that another vehicle had driven onto the shoulder near the scene, but the tire tracks were too washed out by the rain to bother with casts."

"Did you get a look at the autopsy results?"

"Yeah." Mick grimaced. "Blood-alcohol content was over the legal limit but not all that high, and—according to Dad—Dan could handle the bike like a pro, even when he'd had a few."

"Unless something unexpected happened—like a car forcing him off a dark, wet road. Any indication of which direction the vehicle that made the tracks was traveling?"

"They were on the west shoulder, but it could've pulled over there from either lane."

"No drugs, other than alcohol, involved?"

"No."

"He was killed instantly?"

"Thrown clear of the bike and dead when the deputies arrived on the scene. Massive internal injuries, including a ruptured spleen and cerebral hemorrhage . . ." Mick shook his head. "Shar, reading that report . . . Dan was like an uncle to me. The idea that somebody might've deliberately forced him off the road . . ."

"I know." I touched his arm and turned to Rae. "Okay—Denver. What could the PD tell you about Benjy?"

"The investigating officer there was very cooperative and remembered the case well because he's a Savage fan and had been at the concert. Benjy didn't respond to repeated wake-up calls the next morning; the hotel where they were staying has a policy of checking on people who don't. The autopsy report showed that he'd ingested massive quantities of methaqualone—that's Quaaludes— mixed with bourbon. Empty fifth of an off-brand called High Times was on the bedside table." She shuddered. "Remind me never to buy that brand. Overall, it looked to be a simple overdose, but the officer's kept the file flagged."

"Why?"

"A combination of little things, none of which would be important on their own. First, the door of the room wasn't locked. Not unusual for somebody who was stoned to forget, but . . . Second, the maids always stocked the bar with four glasses, but only three were found in the room, as though somebody might've taken one away with him."

"The maids confirmed that they'd actually left four?"

"Yes. The hotel's got a strict inventory policy. And finally there's another thought that the investigator and I kicked around: Why, when you have a fully stocked minibar containing good-quality stuff, would you go to the trouble of buying and bringing in rotgut?"

I considered. "Benjy wanted more than a couple of bourbons? Those minibars don't have more than two or three of any given item."

"But there's always room service; you can order up

whole bottles. I asked Ricky, and he said that Benjy's room-service tabs were always exorbitant. And he always drank good-quality booze. So why the rotgut?"

"It's an interesting question. Let's say somebody came to see him, brought the bottle along. Benjy was trying to come down off his coke high; he'd taken 'ludes, his judgment was warped at best. It wouldn't be difficult for somebody to encourage him to get into the bourbon. Any other signs of a visitor? Evidence of sexual activity, for instance?"

"None."

I glanced at Mick, saw that his eyes were focused on the distance. "You okay?"

"More or less. I didn't like Benjy as well as Dan, but this stuff is still hard to take."

"I understand." To Rae I said, "What about the sleazy attorney?"

"I couldn't even get in to see him. Client confidentiality, he said."

"No way around that, I suppose?"

"Maybe; I'm going to work on it."

"So that's that for now." I shut off the cassette recorder on which I'd been taping our conversation. "I'm waiting to hear from my contact in Austin. Keim's checking further on Ricky's employees and associates, plus making a search of booking agencies, management firms, and professional organizations in case Terriss is working in the industry. And I'm going to see if there isn't some way to find out who leaked that item to 'StarWatch.' By the way," I added to Mick, "Ma saw it and called your mother. She was due to arrive at the house this morning—intent on meddling, no doubt."

Mick rolled his eyes. "I think I'll avoid the place. I love Grandma, but she can be—"

"I know. Why don't you take the day off, go to the beach or something?"

"Nah, I think I'll hang around here in case you need me."

"That's really okay—"

"Hey, what about your report? What'd you find out up in Ventura?"

Damn! I'd planned on withholding that information from both him and Rae, at least till I'd had a chance to talk with Ricky. For a moment I was tempted to lie, say I'd learned nothing. But it had been my experience that a lie found out is worse than a painful truth, and I was fairly certain that by the time the investigation was over, quite a few lies would have been exposed. Why add to their number?

I looked at Rae. "How much more bad news can you take?"

"Whatever it is, I'll handle it."

"Mick, how many more illusions can you stand to have shattered?"

For a moment I thought he'd tell me he didn't want to hear, but then he squared his jaw and shoulders. "If they're illusions, what good are they?"

None, if they're going to be shattered anyway. "Then I'm going to have to tell you a pretty ugly story."

After I'd finished detailing what I'd found out in Ventura, Mick excused himself from our meeting. He said he wanted to revisit Pacific Palisades and canvass other residents of the canyon road to see if anyone else had noticed the pickup on the night of the fire, but I suspected it was an excuse to be alone. Rae waited till he'd left the room, then asked me, "Did you tell Ricky about this?"

"There wasn't an opportunity last night or this morning."

"Don't, then. Not yet."

"Why?"

"He's got to concentrate on the kickoff concert and the tour. They haven't rehearsed well in nearly a week, so he's made arrangements with Charlene to use the studio this afternoon, as well as see her and the girls. Those things're more important than keeping him up to the minute on our investigation."

"You're right. We don't have anything definite, anyway. But can *you* keep it from him?"

"Yes."

"You're being very protective of him."

"I guess so, but it works both ways. He's so concerned about me taking heat from the media that he wants me to go home after the concert tomorrow night."

I'd more or less assumed she would be accompanying him on the tour. "Do you want to?"

"Well, you said Ted sounded frantic when you called in earlier. Things must really be piling up at the office."

"They are, but I've arranged for RKI to loan us Keim for the duration. She can handle the routine work."

"Still, I think it's better if I go. It's looking like the investigation won't be wrapped up before the tour starts, and the last thing you and Hy need is an extra person to worry about."

"True. And I can't say as I won't be glad to have you in charge at the office." I turned my attention to the day's agenda. "Okay, if the investigator I've co-opted in Austin, Jenny Gordon, doesn't call within the hour, I'm going to call her. And Keim should've faxed her report by now; I told her to send it here, so I'd better check with the desk."

"And I have some potential leverage with that music attorney who wouldn't see me yesterday; he owes a friend of Ethan's a favor, and the guy's agreed to lean on him. Ricky's loaning me the Porsche so I can drive up to L.A. He wondered if you'd give him a ride over to the house."

"When does he want to go?"

She looked at her watch. "Right about now."

We collected Ricky, and I picked up Keim's fax from the desk while he and Rae waited for the Porsche to be brought around. When I came outside it had just arrived, and they were walking toward it hand in hand, Ricky cautioning her not to turn into an asshole behind the wheel. She looked up at him, laughing.

And a photographer stepped from behind a van that was parked at the curb. "Smile, Ms. Kelleher, Mr. Savage!"

Ricky let go of Rae and started for him, but he'd already snapped his pictures. The man backpedaled toward the van's open door. Ricky lunged, but Rae grabbed his arm.

"Don't do anything!" she said. "It'll only make it worse."

My brother-in-law was shaking with rage, but he let her restrain him, staring hard at the van. The driver pulled away from the curb, and as he went by Ricky shouted, "What the hell is *wrong* with you people? Why can't you leave us alone?"

Rae rested her forehead against his upper arm. He looked down, touched her curls with an unsteady hand. "Sorry, Red," he said. "This is the last thing I wanted to happen."

She smiled wanly at him. "What's so terrible about getting my picture in the papers with a good-looking guy like you?"

I said, "I'd like to know how he knew Rae's name and where you're staying. Your friend who owns the hotel wouldn't—"

"No." Ricky shook his head. "And the staff is discreet. A lot of celebrities stay here, and I've never heard of one having this kind of trouble." He motioned to the valet standing beside the Porsche, took the keys, and tipped him.

I said, "Well, there were around a dozen people in your suite last night. I suppose any one of them could have tipped off the press."

"Yeah. And I wonder which of those godawful rags is going to print that photo." He grimaced, reviewing the possibilities. "Red, I think we better go up to L.A. tonight instead of in the morning. The Tower at Century Plaza's got good security, and with Hy's people on the job too, we should be okay. I'll have my secretary make the arrangements. Shar, will you and Hy want to come along?"

"Might as well. The situation at your house is under control, and you're our primary responsibility. I'd like to bring Mick, too; he can help me with any leads we pick up."

"I can help," Rae said.

"No. You're off the investigation as of now. Once that picture is printed you'll become as much of a target as Ricky and his family."

"I'm off, but you'll keep Mick on? That doesn't make any sense."

"Mick's expertise is with his computer; he can work in his hotel room. He's probably left for Pacific Palisades, but I'll call his cell phone and tell him to get back here."

"What about that attorney I was going to see?" Rae asked. "Can't I drive up there and meet—"

"No," Ricky said. "I don't want you going to L.A. alone—especially in the Porsche."

"Jeez, I didn't drive that badly on the way back from Arizona!"

"It's got nothing to do with your driving, Red. The Porsche can be recognized by its license plate."

Rae and I looked at it: COBWEBS.

My brother-in-law grinned sheepishly. "What can I tell you? I was younger, a whole lot more foolish, and my older son talked me into it."

"What did I do?" Mick came up behind us.

"Hey," Rae said, "you haven't left yet."

"No, I had to make a phone call, so I sat down in a quiet corner of the lobby." His eyes met his father's and held there; then he corrected himself. "No, I *wanted* to make a phone call. To Charlotte. To tell her I miss her."

Ricky looked back at him for a moment. Mick's expression defied him to comment. Finally he nodded.

Now Mick picked up on our tension. "What's wrong here?"

"A photographer greeted us when we came outside," Ricky told him. "We've decided to move up to L.A. tonight. Shar says she can use your help, if you want to come along."

". . . Sure."

Ricky started to say something else, but hesitated. I sensed he was struggling with the concept that his son was really an adult. Then he shrugged in a way that was characteristic of them both and asked, "Which car're you using?"

"Chris's."

"Also recognizable. Why don't you let Shar have it and take her rental. That way, you can escort the redhead safely to the hotel in L.A. and keep her out of trouble till I get there."

226

Seventeen

The suite Ricky had reserved for Hy and me at the Century Plaza was so opulent that I felt embarrassed. I couldn't for the life of me understand why some people needed so much luxury while others were starving on the streets. But by the time I was relaxing in silky oiled water in the enormous tub, a glass of excellent Chardonnay to hand, I was getting into it.

Where's your liberal guilt, McCone?

On hold till tomorrow, thank you.

Adding more hot water, I decided I might as well enjoy myself while I could; given my budget, this state of affairs wasn't likely to repeat itself in the foreseeable future. Besides, I'd had what Hy would have described as a perfectly hellatious day.

After Mick had collected his things from home and driven away with Rae in my rental car, Ricky packed and checked out of the Sorrento; we then drove in tandem to the estate. Well, in tandem to the freeway, anyway; there he floored the Porsche and left me in its dust. When I got to the house he was leaning on the car in the parking area, a shade anxious, as though he needed my support to enter his own home. And when Charlene greeted us at the door, the San Diego paper in hand, I could feel him bracing for another knock-down-drag-out.

My sister was calm and coolly polite, though. In a low voice she said, "Let's go to the office," and led us there. Once inside with the door shut, she handed Ricky the paper and asked, "Have you seen this?"

It was folded open to the entertainment section and the syndicated gossip column, "StarWatch."

> ... Has anyone noticed that the title single from **Ricky Savage's** upcoming release, *Midnight Train to Nowhere,* is strangely silent on the nation's airwaves? What does this mean for the two-time Grammy winner whose albums and singles routinely debut at the top of the charts? In the meantime, Savage has surfaced at an exclusive La Jolla hotel in the company of the mysterious redhead (see yesterday's column for details), now identified as San Francisco private investigator **Rae Kelleher.** Additional security? Our sources say Kelleher isn't there in a professional capacity. Stay tuned for further details as Savage kicks off his *Midnight Train* tour tomorrow night ...

Ricky was tight-lipped as he read the item. "Jesus," he said. "Charly, I'm sorry."

"Don't be sorry on my account. It's the kids we should worry about. So far, neither Chris nor Jamie has seen this. And there's something else." She went to the desk, took an envelope from the drawer, and extended it to him.

He opened it and stared down at the single sheet of paper. I crowded next to him for a look.

WHAT *HAVE* YOU DONE???

Ricky groaned. Using a tissue, I took the note and envelope from him. The writing was the same as on the others, the postmark Los Angeles. "What's this zip code?" I asked.

He glanced at it. "Substation near the Zenith offices. And Transamerica's. And any number of other companies and people I know."

I said to Charlene, "This came in today's delivery?"

"Yes."

"Who handled it besides you?"

"The guard who brought the mail up."

"Dammit! They were told to watch for something like this and bag it so RKI's lab could go over it. Too late now, I suppose, but I'll pass it on anyway. Ricky, when're the band members arriving?"

"Not till two. I need to talk with Charly and spend some time with my girls first."

"Okay, as far as the band goes, I want to caution you about two things: Do not tell them you're going up to L.A. tonight, or where you'll be staying; and under no circumstances are they to come near the house. They're to be confined to the studio, and I'll make sure the guards know that."

"Come on, Shar! You can't suspect—"

"I can," I said and told him about the rifle being discovered on the grounds. "Somebody close is being used to get at you. From now on, you can't trust anybody but your family, Hy, and me."

"You didn't mention Rae," Charlene said.

Oh God, I thought, here we go! "And Rae."

"I wish one or the other of you had told me she was the redhead when we talked yesterday."

"Why?" Ricky asked bluntly. "Would it have made any difference?"

For the first time since we'd arrived she looked him directly in the eyes. "Yes, it would have. Shar's spoken highly of her for years, and Mick's fond of her. At least I'd've known you weren't involved with another crazy woman. Speaking of whom, I believe you have something to tell me."

"Yeah," he said heavily. "Yeah, I do."

I said, "I'll leave you two alone now."

I took my briefcase out by the pool, planning to go over Keim's fax, but when I got there I found Jamie sprawled on her stomach on a lounge chair, staring morosely at the ground.

"Hey," I said, sitting down beside her.

She grunted.

"What's with you?"

"I feel like shit, that's what."

"You want to talk about it?"

"No."

"Okay." I took out the fax and began reading.

> Forrest Curtin: Arrested, Austin, TX, 1988, D & D—sentence suspended; Nashville, TN, 1991, DWI—license revoked; Los Angeles, 1991, possession (cocaine)—charges dropped. Credit report spotty, showing several accounts past due. Owes balance of $460,000 on home, late payments for past two months.

> Gerald Jackson: One arrest, San Bernardino, 1993, possession (marijuana)—charges dropped. Credit report clean; has extensive real-estate holdings in

Palm Springs (condos) and Orange County (office buildings).

Norman O'Dell: No arrests. Credit report—

Jamie said, "You want to know why I feel like shit?"

I looked up from the fax. "Why?"

"Because my father has run off with your friend Rae and nobody, including you and my mother, seems to care."

"How'd you find out about Rae?"

"Mick told Chris and me. He said the gossip columns have already gotten hold of it, and he thought we should be prepared. He even *likes* this woman."

"She's a nice person."

"You would say that. You probably introduced them."

"Jamie—"

She rolled over and sat up, glaring at me. "You, I'm mad at, but the person I *hate* is Dad! I'd like to smack his face just like Mom did the other day!"

"So why don't you?" I asked, hoping to joke her out of her mood. "He could probably use a little slapping around."

And Ricky chose that inopportune moment to come outside.

Jamie was off the lounge before I could stop her—running at him, her fists flailing. Ricky put up his arms to fend her off, but she evaded them and began pummeling him on the chest. "You bastard!" she yelled. "You rotten bastard!"

One blow caught him on the chin. He grabbed her by the shoulders, pinned her arms. She kicked out, clipping him on the shin, then burst into tears.

He folded her against his chest and let her cry. As he looked at me across her head, I saw tears in his eyes, too. "It's okay, honey," he said. "I understand."

She said something between sobs, but it came out muffled.

"What?"

"I said, it's not okay. You're leaving, and I won't have a father anymore."

"Oh, honey, I'll *always* be your daddy. I'll always be there for you, you know that."

"No, you won't. I know how it works, they all say that and after a while they get married to somebody else and forget their kids."

He closed his eyes, shaking his head. "Look, why don't we go to your room, talk this over?"

"We can't!"

"Why not?"

"Because then you'll see what I did to that poster of you."

"The one where you drew the bone through my nose? I've seen that a hundred times."

"No, you'll see what I did to it last night—something really horrible."

"Nothing you could do could be horrible." He turned her and began walking toward the house. "Come on, we'll talk, and then I'll go see your sister." He looked back at me and added, "Chris is the one who reminds me of you. I hope to God she hasn't taken up kung fu."

His attempt at humor saddened me even more than the scene I'd just witnessed. I sighed and went back to my reading.

> Norman O'Dell: No arrests. Credit report clean.
> Owns 200-acre parcel in Santa Barbara County, free of encumbrance.
>
> Peter Sherman: No arrests. Credit report clean.

Owes $375,000 on home in Santa Monica. Payment record good.

Virgil Rattray: I couldn't find anything on him. Either we've got the wrong SSN, he's going by an assumed name, or he's one of these people who don't believe in property or credit.

There was more, on Nona Davidson, the other employees at the estate, Linda Toole, and Ricky's secretary. None of it was surprising or particularly enlightening. I was about to start on the more lengthy material about Ethan Amory and Kurt Girdwood when Charlene came out of the house, wearing a red swimsuit. She waved to me, slipped into the pool, and paddled over to the side, where she propped her arms on the edge.

"How'd your talk go?" I asked.

"Okay. That's pretty grim stuff, but I wish he'd told me back then."

"Would it have changed anything?"

"Who can say? Is he talking with Chris and Jamie?"

"Jamie, right now. At least, I hope they're talking. She lit into him before—physically."

"Oh, no!"

"I'm afraid I unwittingly provoked her. He handled her well, though."

"He's good with the kids, better than I am, actually." Her gaze turned inward.

I said, "There's something I need to ask. Has Ethan Amory ever hit on you?"

"Oh, sure. For a while there, it was a weekly occurrence."

"You never—"

"Of course not. Ethan's hard to take seriously in the role of seducer." She began drawing patterns on the poolside tiles with her wet fingers. "Ethan's not a very sexual person; what he's into is money and power. For some reason he viewed me as very influential with Ricky, and he wanted to get to me so he could use me to manipulate him."

"To do what?"

"To go on the road more, to make more and more money. The more Ricky makes, the more legal services he requires, and the bigger Ethan's fees. And of course with this new label, he'll get a cut of everything as well. When I refused to play his games, he turned vindictive."

"How so?"

"Nothing I couldn't handle. Remarks, mainly. Once he deliberately screwed things up so I missed an important industry banquet, then badmouthed me to Ricky because of it. I'll tell you, Shar, under that southern-gentleman exterior, Ethan's a nasty piece of work."

I'd have to look closely at the background Keim had come up with on the attorney—as well as warn Rae to watch out for him. I asked Charlene, "What about Kurt?"

She smiled. "Do you mean, has he come on to me? No way. Kurt's got a fatherly streak where I'm concerned. Not that he isn't into the same kind of games as Ethan. He's a top manager, and certain things go with that territory that aren't desirable. But Ricky's been with him for years, and all that time I've never felt he was feeding off him like the other parasites."

"By 'other parasites' you mean Ethan and . . . ?"

"Ricky's booking agent, his producer, his publicist, the people at the label, the concert promoters, the band, Virgil Rattray. They all want their piece of him, and they're all working in different directions. Sometimes it feels like they're tearing him apart."

Her words brought to light yet another facet of my sister's life. I imagined how lonely she must have felt all those years, how much at the mercy of a huge power- and greed-fueled industry that considered her, her children, and even her talented husband objects to be used and thrown away. And I wished I'd understood long ago, so I could have been there for her.

The melancholy, inward look had returned to her eyes. I asked, "What?"

"Hindsight. At a point like this it's so easy to see where you went wrong. Remember when I was pregnant with Lisa? You were down here for a convention and I was visiting Ma and Pa. You noticed I wasn't happy."

I had a vague recollection of that, but at the time I'd been preoccupied with my brother John's divorce, to say nothing of a murder that had happened at the convention. "Go on."

"Well, actually I was miserable. Ricky loves our kids, but after Jamie was born he said maybe we ought to stop at three. I was the one who promoted having more; they were my way of holding onto him. You see, it had worked so well before; he'd go away, but he'd always come back to me. Anyway, after Molly, he *really* didn't want another child. When I told him I was pregnant again, he walked out on me. He came back when Lisa was born, and he loves her as much as the others. But I realized he'd come back because of them, not because of me. And that's when we started drifting apart."

Their youngest had celebrated her eighth birthday in October. Eight years was a long time to drift.

"It's ironic," Charlene added. "For the rest of our lives he'll be coming back—to the kids, but never to me." Then she pushed away from the side and began swimming laps in an unhurried crawl.

I watched her for a moment, my sadness deepening. Then I put the fax sheets into my briefcase and went inside.

* * *

When I came through the office door I saw that the fax machine had spewed out yet another curl of paper. More information from Keim? No, she would have sent it to the hotel. Probably something for Ricky. I went to check.

WHAT *HAVE* YOU DONE???

"Oh, Jesus!" I ripped the sheet from the machine, scanned it for the header that would indicate who had sent it. There wasn't any; all it showed was the number here. Of course—if you didn't program a name and number into the machine, it couldn't transmit them.

The fax did convey one bit of information, though: It confirmed that the sender was relying on an insider who knew the machine's unlisted number.

I put the sheet in my briefcase, took out my address book, and dialed Jenny Gordon's number in Austin. The private investigator—whom I'd met last year at a meeting of our national association—wasn't in, but her gravelly smoker's voice told me to leave a message on the machine. I did, giving both Ricky's number and that of the Century Plaza in L.A.

Then I sat down at the desk, taking deep breaths in an attempt to reduce my stress level. I'd read about the technique in a magazine—something to do with oxygen putting the brain waves in a relaxation mode and reducing the heart rate. All it did was make me feel light-headed, powerless, and frustrated. I needed to take action—

Somewhere in my briefcase I had a file where I stored cards and scraps of paper containing phone numbers and addresses. I found it and took out a paper napkin from the Alta Mira Hotel in Sausalito, on which Letta James had scribbled her home number.

Letta answered my call, her vibrant voice unmistakable. "Sharon!" she exclaimed. "How the hell are you? I've been following the columns and the grapevine chatter about Ricky. Gawd, what's going on down there?"

"Too much, but I can't go into it now. Letta, I called because I need help. Tell me about that syndicated column, 'StarWatch.' "

"It's written by three people, all of them assholes. I know folks who would swap their vocal cords for a mention, but not me. And surely not Ricky, poor guy."

"How closely do they guard their sources?"

"Very. You want to find out who's feeding them the information?"

"Yes."

"I'm thinking . . . hold on, let me call my partner's office and ask her about this."

There was a click. I held, gripping the receiver harder than was necessary.

Another click. "You're in luck," Letta said. "My partner—I think I mentioned she's in market research—she has a client who dates a guy at the *Times* who's tight with one of their staff writers who lives with an underling in the 'StarWatch' office. And this writer is not too happy about being an underling and the treatment that goes with it. Anyway, it might take a while, but there's a good chance we can pry the information loose."

"What a series of connections!"

"Sharon, in L.A. you've got nothing but series of connections—most of which have to do with sex. We'll get working on this, let you know as soon as we find out something. Where'll you be?"

"Either here at Ricky's"—I recited the number of the office line—"or up there at the Tower at Century Plaza."

"Pretty fancy stuff. If I get good at this investigating, will you hire me? It's got to pay better than my royalty account."

At one-thirty I called the head security man into the office and briefed him about keeping the band members confined to the studio. Then I phoned Hy at RKI and told him I'd be over as soon as I was certain the rehearsal was running smoothly. Finally I took out the background information on Ethan Amory and Kurt Girdwood and went over it carefully.

The attorney had been born and raised in Knoxville, Tennessee, and was a graduate of Vanderbilt University in Nashville and Northwestern University's School of Law in Illinois. He'd returned to Nashville and set up a practice whose clients consisted of studio musicians and minor recording artists, but when two of his singers were signed by MCA and had records that went platinum, Amory followed them to L.A. and built up a new and much more lucrative practice there. He was twice divorced, had no children, lived in a three-million-dollar house in Brentwood, and owned a second home in the Bahamas. Keim's research had turned up no arrest record and a sterling credit rating.

Girdwood was a California native, born in Stockton but raised in Pasadena. He'd dropped out of UCLA to work for a concert promoter, then moved on to one of the large booking agencies, and eventually set up on his own as Girdwood Talent Management. Within a few years he represented a good number of top acts, and by the time Ricky walked into his office on the strength of the success of "Cobwebs," GTM was considered one of the major management firms on the West Coast. With Ricky's continued success, Girdwood had parceled out his other clients to his employees and devoted his time exclusively to managing my brother-in-law's career. He was three-times divorced, with a child by each marriage; he lived in a condo in an expensive downtown high rise and owned co-op apartments in New York and London. Like Amory, he had no arrest record and his credit was impeccable.

Keim had dug up and faxed a 1991 article profiling the pair in *Hits* magazine. In essence, it implied that each was cold-blooded and ruthless in his own way, but accorded respect to their abilities. In conclusion, it said, "Any artist would consider himself or herself blessed to be represented by the Machiavellis of music law and management."

I pushed away from the desk and stretched just as the phone rang. The button for the private house line flashed—a call for Charlene or one of the girls. My watch showed two twenty-three; by now the rehearsal was underway, with no apparent breach of security. I wondered if I should pack it in and stop by RKI to drop off the latest note at their lab and see how Hy was doing. Maybe then I'd head up to L.A. in Chris's car and pay a visit to both Amory and Girdwood. A long face-to-face with each man might reveal something that would lead to a break in the investigation.

I got up and began putting files into my briefcase. When I finished I made a brief call to the Century Plaza and found that Rae and Mick had checked in. They were, Rae said, playing double solitaire in a suite of awesome proportions, but later she planned to kick him out and take a nap. Mick still wanted to drive up to Pacific Palisades and canvass his former neighbors, but in light of this latest communication by fax, I vetoed the idea and asked him to get busy trying to trace Patricia Terriss with his laptop.

I'd just hung up when the door opened and Charlene

burst into the room, her face nearly as pale as the white cotton shirt she wore over her swimsuit.

"What's wrong?" I asked.

"That phone call." She gestured at the instrument on the desk, her hand trembling. "It was from the director of Brian's camp. He said that the counselor was helping Brian pack, but since he hadn't personally taken the call, he wanted to verify that I was sending someone to pick my son up."

"What!"

"A woman called there an hour ago and spoke with the secretary, claiming to be me. She said someone would be arriving at five to bring Brian home. I told the director he wasn't to release him to anyone but Ricky or me. And I phoned Molly's and Lisa's camp and left the same instructions with their director. No one has called there—yet."

I reached for the phone and punched out RKI's number. Asked for Hy and put it on the speaker. When he came on I said to Charlene, "Tell him what you just told me."

When she finished, Hy spoke in a voice that would have told nobody but me that he was disturbed. "Okay, nothing to panic about, but the kids're going to have to be moved. You and the girls, too. Is there someplace you can go that's private and that none of Ricky's associates know about?"

She thought. "Well, Vic owns a big place near Lake Tahoe. I'm sure he'd let us use it."

"Get on to him, then get back to me. McCone, I'll be in Dan Kessell's office; he's better at this kind of arrangement than I am."

I took the phone off the speaker and handed the receiver to Charlene. She made her call, spoke at length, jotting down notes, and hung up. "It's all set."

I redialed RKI, asked for Kessell's office, and put the speaker on again.

Hy answered. "Dan and I are both here. Dan, you're talking with McCone and her sister, Mrs. Savage. Charlene, is it okay for the place at Tahoe?"

"Yes. I've got the code for the security system and exact directions."

"Good. Now listen carefully. We have a plan, and Dan's going to tell you about it."

Kessell's deep, rumbling voice came on. "Hello, Mrs. Savage, Sharon. First I want to stress that there's no immediate cause for alarm, but we'll want to move as quickly as possible. Where are the children's camps?"

Charlene said, "The girls are at Mammoth Lakes, and Brian's at Lake Elsinore."

"Give me exact names and locations, please."

While she was reciting them, the fax rang. I stared at it in annoyance, then thought of the earlier communication and backed up so my body shielded it from my sister's line of sight.

"Very good," Kessell said. "Now, here's what you're to do: Call the camps and tell the directors that they'll be receiving further instructions from you late this afternoon. Then get yourself and the older girls packed. Take enough for a long stay. One of our representatives will arrive at your home at four-thirty. He'll identify himself by this code number." He repeated a succession of seven digits twice.

The fax was transmitting. While Charlene wrote down the code, I turned to get a look at the display panel. All it said was "receiving" and there was no header on the page that was emerging. My sister said my name; quickly I turned back and took the sheet on which she'd written the code number.

Kessell went on, "At six-thirty our representative will

take you and the girls to Lindbergh Field and fly with you on one of our jets to Tahoe. I understand there's an older boy."

Charlene looked torn. Finally she said, "My other son is a grown man and has a job to do."

I wished Mick could have heard that.

"Fine. As I said, you'll fly to Tahoe. Guards from our Reno office will already be in place on the property. Give me the exact location and the security code, please."

She repeated them, then asked, "What about my younger children?"

"I'm coming to that. Before you leave the house, at precisely four forty-five, you're to call your boy's camp. Have the director call back so he'll know he's actually dealing with you. Tell him your son will be picked up by helicopter promptly at five. Give him the code number; the pilot will use it to identify himself as your representative. How old is the boy?"

"Thirteen."

"Any problems with having him picked up by a stranger? Or with the chopper?"

A wisp of amusement passed over Charlene's face. "I don't think there'll be a problem with any of the children, Mr. Kessell. In fact, it may be your pilot who suffers."

Hy chuckled, but Kessell didn't respond; the former marine and air-charter operator had absolutely no sense of humor. Behind me the end-transmission tone on the fax went off.

"All right," Kessell went on, "at six you're to follow the same procedure with the director of your girls' camp. They'll be picked up at six-fifteen. You'll have your family together at Lake Tahoe by ten at the latest."

"Why such precise timing, Dan?" I asked. "And why give the camp directors such short notice?"

"Short notice leaves no opportunity for someone at those camps to alert an outsider that the kids are being moved. We don't know who's behind this, so we don't want to trust anyone. And you of all people should know that precision is an RKI policy. Mrs. Savage, are you sure none of your husband's associates know about the place in Tahoe?"

Charlene smiled wryly. "Even my husband doesn't know."

"All right. Why don't you brief your older girls on this and start packing. In the meantime, we'll get the operation rolling."

"Thanks, Dan," I said.

Charlene depressed the speaker button and turned to me, eyes bleak and weary. "I feel like we're going into a witness-protection program."

"Well, it's nowhere near that permanent. Things'll be back to normal soon."

"Will they?" She sighed and started toward the door. "I wonder if our lives will ever be normal again."

I waited till she was out of the room, then turned and ripped the fax from the machine.

YOU *KNOW* WHAT YOU'VE DONE!

Close to five hours later, Ricky met me in the entryway, duffel in hand, garment bag slung over his shoulder. He went to the archway leading to the living room and looked across at the gathering dusk on the terrace beyond. In the distance the sea was midnight blue, streaked with pink and magenta.

He said, "It's really all over here, isn't it?"

"Yes."

"My family's gone into hiding, even the dogs're boarded."

"Hy said to tell you that RKI'll make sure the property's secure."

"The property! Who the hell cares about a place that was built on disappointment and lies?"

"You know that isn't the sum total of your marriage."

"I know," he said. "It's just what I remember most clearly."

A car's engine purred in the parking area and gravel crunched—the limo he'd ordered to take us to L.A. Ricky remained where he was for a moment longer, then turned. Lines of strain made his face look years older.

"Time to go," he said. "I want to get home to Red. I miss her."

Eighteen

So at last I was alone—both in the enormous bathtub and the suite, Hy having decided at the last minute to fly to Tahoe with Charlene and the girls and stay till the entire family was settled. It was after eleven now, and I didn't expect him for hours.

More of the avoidance I'd noticed previously? It certainly seemed so. Once it would have been inconceivable that instead of a quiet evening with me, Hy would prefer a long plane ride with two sullen teenagers, and then a longer settling-in period, complicated by the boisterous presence of the three youngest Little Savages. I felt deeply unsettled, uprooted as well, so I turned, as I usually did, to my work.

I added still more hot water, closed my eyes, and began reviewing the case—both fact and implication. Ricky and I had finally had our in-depth talk on the way up here, and what he'd said about his associates had reinforced my image of him at the center of a circling school of parasitic fish, each eager to attach its suckers and hang on for a fast and profitable ride.

"It's a weird existence," he'd admitted. "Here I am, caught up in the middle of all this cut-throat game playing, but inside I'm still just the kid from Bakersfield who desperately wants to make it, on account of his daddy being one of the town's most accomplished drunks and wife-beaters. And my songs—all they are is stories about my life, both the good and the bad of it. But I lay them down on tape and suddenly they're *product,* and there're hundreds of people trying to cash in on them. And I don't know those people, any more than they know me."

Ricky's take on Ethan Amory and Kurt Girdwood was similar to Charlene's, although considerably more cynical where his manager was concerned.

"He'd rob me blind if he thought he could get away with it, which is one of the reasons I've got a professional money manager—who'd also rob me blind if I didn't keep an eye on him. Kurt and I have an understanding, though. Came to it years ago when I caught him with his fingers in my pocket. I've got the evidence of that in my safe-deposit box in case he ever pulls anything again. And one of the reasons he's been good to Charly—although she isn't aware of it—is that the box has two keys, and one of them's hers."

About Virgil Rattray he could be less specific. "I suppose he is one of those people who don't own property or use credit cards," he said in answer to my comment about the dearth of information Keim had turned up on the road manager. "He's a strange guy. Older than he looks, sort of oozed up out of the muck of the eighties rock scene and presented himself to Kurt one day, said he wanted to work for me. When Kurt asked him why, he told him he was the best and wanted to work with the best, plus country didn't give him migraines like rock did. Who knows what his real reasons were? But he *is* the best, no question about it. He lives in a horrible apartment in Echo Park—I haven't seen it, but Kurt has—and drives a beat-up VW Beetle. So far as I know, nobody's ever heard him mention a woman—or a male friend. Does drugs, booze, you name it, but never lets it get out of control. Strange, strange guy."

The picture of the band members that emerged from our discussion was revealing, fleshing out the dry facts that the bios and Keim's research had provided and putting each in a new and different light.

"Forrest's probably the best musician of the group, but he's also a serious cokehead and he's starting to be unreliable. Was a nice kid when we plucked him out of Nashville to replace Benjy—naive and kind of wide-eyed and grateful to be with a hit band. But the naivete makes him a target for the worst kind of scum in town. You go over to his house and it's all trashed and filthy, and you find the sleaziest hangers-on and pushers waiting around for the chance to take him for a ride. I'm gonna have to replace him once his contract's up this fall.

"On the other hand, Jerry looks like a good ole boy from Shreveport. Likes his dope, his booze, his drums, and his women—in that order. Easygoing, slightly stupid, seldom sober. Right? Wrong. He's no genius, but he's shrewd, and that's a winning quality in this business. With Jer it's all instinct: He senses who to trust and how far, what real-estate investment deal will fly and which won't. He never carries his boozing or doping to extremes; he's careful with his women. Ain't nobody gonna take *that* good ole boy for a ride.

"Now, Norm—he's more complicated, and a loner. When he's not working, he's up on that ranch in Santa Barbara County, growing things. Lives there with a woman named Gina Robinson, who's been his partner for at least five years. They're a private couple; none of us have even met her. Was married twice, both wives died young. Norm doesn't say much, but you look close at him, particularly when we're doing one of the sadder songs, and you'll see the tragedy in his life weighs pretty heavy on him. Too bad, too, because he's disciplined and a damn fine guitar picker; he could've had a big career if his private pain hadn't eaten away at his ambition.

"Of the four, Pete's the most like me: *really* driven, but still torn between getting to the top and having a happy, simple life. He's devoted to his wife, can't wait to be a family man, and worries because the baby's late and will most likely be born while we're on tour. But in the meantime he's staying up all night writing songs, just like I did; my publishing company's already picked up four of them, and one's on hold for a very big star and stands to make Pete a lot of money. He thinks he can take from the business and not let it take from him, but you and I know better. And he admitted to me this afternoon that this situation with Charly and me has opened his eyes some. Maybe that's good, or maybe he's better off not knowing. I can't be sure of that—or much of anything—anymore."

I got out of the tub and toweled off, then put on one of the terry robes the hotel provided. Still thinking about the band members, I went to the living room and sat on the balcony overlooking Century Boulevard and the city's neon-lighted sprawl.

I was more inclined now to believe that one of Ricky's musicians was Terriss's inside contact: They'd been to his home numerous times and, until this afternoon, had had the run of it. They knew the layout well enough to locate the circuit-breaker box, trip the right switch, fire a shot under cover of darkness, and later hide the rifle on the grounds. They also knew the unlisted fax number.

And they were well acquainted with the children: Jerry Jackson, Chris had admitted, was such a good buddy that she'd felt free to ask him for a couple of joints on Saturday night. What was to prevent a buddy from asking her or Jamie for the names and locations of their siblings' camps?

But which band member?

One thing was certain: Whoever the insider was, he'd leave Union Station tomorrow on the Midnight Train.

The phone rang and I went inside to answer. Hy, calling from RKI's Reno office. "Everything's under control," he told me. "The younger kids aren't even upset; they think it's an adventure. Your sister's sworn Chris and Jamie to secrecy about the split."

"How're they doing?"

"Chris is being cool, distant, and somewhat snotty. Jamie's a bundle of emotion, but she's keeping her Walkman on and refusing to talk. McCone, aren't you glad you never had kids?"

"Sometimes I feel as if I might as well have. I've owned a vested interest in each of Charlene's, Patsy's, and John's since the day they were born. How's Charlene holding up?"

"Now, she's amazing. If you'd told me on Saturday that she'd be such a rock, I'd've said you were crazy."

"Crisis brings out the best in us McCones."

"And a good thing, too. I'll tell you—if we pull out of Union Station tomorrow night without you wrapping this thing up, we're in for nothing *but* crisis."

My day began abruptly at seven-sixteen when Jenny Gordon, who had forgotten about the two-hour time difference between Austin and Los Angeles, called. Hy moaned in protest as I fumbled for the phone; gray light had been seeping around the draperies when he'd let himself into the suite, and he'd tossed about for a while before settling into sleep. After Jenny identified herself, I put her on hold and went to the sitting room to talk.

"Sorry to take so long getting back to you," she said, her Texas-accented voice husky from the cigarettes she chain-smoked. "I'm a small operation, and things got kind of jammed up."

"I understand, believe me," I told her, imagining what must be accumulating at my own small operation. "Have you got anything for me?"

There was a breathy pause; I pictured the attractive brunette—whose youthful appearance belied the fact that she was a grandmother five times over—lighting one of her Winstons. "Nothing all that earthshaking," she said, "but I may have come up with a connection between Terriss and Curtin. I'll start with her."

I picked up a note pad and a pen. "Okay, I'm ready."

"According to everybody I talked with, she was kind of a loner. No friends to speak of; one boyfriend, but that cooled off long before she left town. Not sociable with co-workers or neighbors. Lived by herself in a shabby neighborhood of trailers north of town in Pflugerville. Rented a double-wide for a little over four years, from February of eighty-eight to April of ninety-two. Paid her rent in cash, on time. Never even introduced herself to the people next door. Never had any visitors except the boyfriend—the drummer with the band she was with—and he stopped coming around before Christmas of ninety-one. She took off without giving notice late in April, left most of her stuff."

"Were you able to get a look at it?"

"Nope. The landlord stored it for a year, then disposed of it."

"Anybody you spoke with have an idea of where she came from?"

"Uh-uh. She didn't talk about herself—or talk much at all, for that matter."

"What about the band? Were you able to locate them?"

"They broke up a couple of years ago, and the members've scattered. The boyfriend, Tod Dodson, supposedly is up in Nashville, and I'm working on getting a line on him. All told, the band performed around town for five, six years in places like the Broken Spoke, Yellow Rose, and Dallas West, but during the time Terriss sang with them they were mostly at the Sunset Lodge on Lake Travis. Nice place, a lot of local artists get started there and go on to bigger things. The bartender remembers Terriss because he had the hots for her, but she couldn't be bothered."

"Because of the boyfriend?"

"No, this was after that cooled off. He suspects she thought she was too good for him, was waiting for her prince to come—and apparently he did."

"Oh?"

"Uh-huh. One weekend Ricky Savage and his band were in town. They went to the lodge to catch the late show. Afterward she took off with them, didn't bother to give her band any notice. They scrounged up a replacement, and when she came back three days later they fired her. The end of that week she disappeared from her trailer and day job."

"What was the day job?"

"Waitressing at Babe's restaurant near the airport. She wasn't very good at it: made a lot of mistakes and was snooty to the clientele, like she thought the work was beneath her. Nobody was sorry when she took off."

"I don't suppose you were able to get hold of her Social Security number?"

"Nope. Both Babe's and the lodge are solid operations and touchy about giving out that kind of information. I did get a contact at the DMV to run her license-plate number. Registration expired the fall after she left town, and she never renewed it."

"Jenny, did anyone you spoke with give an indication that she might've been unstable?"

"Nobody came right out and said so, but a few people implied they found her strange, and her behavior is a pretty fair indicator."

"Anything else?"

"Well, let me tell you about Forrest Curtin. He's an Austin boy, born and raised. Played with different bands around town from the time he was in high school; folks who know say he's a damned good musician. Went up to Nashville in nineteen ninety, but came back here a fair amount, supposedly on account of a girlfriend, and used to sit in with his old band at the lodge. A number of times they were double-billed with the group Terriss sang with, so there's a better-than-even-odds chance that he knew her."

"Any possibility she was the girlfriend?"

"Well, nobody actually placed them together, but I haven't come up with any evidence to the contrary."

I tapped my pen on the note pad, feeling those prickles of excitement that you get when you think you're on to something. Was it mere coincidence that Forrest Curtin had ended up a member of Ricky's band—or was it part of a complicated scheme?

"Jenny," I said, "can you keep working on this? As a priority job? Reinterview everybody who knew Terriss, and show them that publicity still of Curtin that I faxed you. Maybe someone saw them together. And keep after the old boyfriend in Nashville."

"Will do. Where can I reach you?"

"Here until around seven this evening. Afterward, at this number." I repeated that of Ricky's cellular phone, which he'd agreed to loan me. "And if for some reason you can't reach me there, I'll be at the Hyatt Regency in Albuquerque early tomorrow morning."

"You do get around. Any chance you're coming my way?"

"As a matter of fact, I'll probably be in Austin on Saturday night."

Austin—where it had all started.

At ten o'clock, Hy and I were gathered in our suite with Rats, going over the final schedule and security plan for the tour. Hy had previously told the road manager only minimal details of the campaign of harassment against Ricky, but now we were forced to reveal that we suspected an insider was involved. Rattray seemed to sense he wasn't getting the complete story, but he didn't ask any questions. It would be more his style, I thought, to watch and listen, hoping to pick up information on the sly.

"Okay," Hy said, "the staff at the Amphitheatre has been briefed, and they're coordinating their security measures with ours. Once the concert's over, we'll get Ricky out of there right away, into a limo for Union Station."

"Alone?" I asked.

"No, Rae'll be with him. I wanted to go along, but he insisted on some private time with her before he leaves. Afterward, the limo'll drop her at LAX for her flight to San Francisco."

Rattray snorted and muttered, "Kurt's right—he *is* thinking with his balls."

I glared at him and said, "Go on," to Hy.

"The publicity woman, Toole, tells me they're expecting a big crowd at the station—both press and fans.

Given the recent coverage in the papers, he'll be asked a lot of questions and he's going to have to answer them. We'll try to get him through the station and past the gate to the trains as fast as possible. Nobody gets beyond that point except the performers and people in the press party. Our best bodyguard and I will stick close from the minute he gets out of the limo till he's inside his suite in Albuquerque."

I asked, "We're still transferring to the charter flight at Barstow?"

He nodded.

"How long a trip is it?"

"To Barstow? Three hours and eighteen minutes."

"God, couldn't we have used a closer-in airport?"

Rats said, "Our choices were Fullerton and San Bernardino, which didn't allow enough time for schmoozing with the press, and Victorville, where there was some problem with the airfield. Barstow's the easiest transfer point."

"Okay, what happens there?"

"Cars meet the train and take us to the airport. We've got two planes chartered. You, Rick, Ripinsky, Kurt, and I will go on one; the band and publicity people'll take the other."

"Kurt's going along?"

"Yeah. He decided to at the last minute, after Rick told him about these threats. He thinks his majesty might need his support."

I pursed my lips, wondering if lending support was the manager's real motive.

"What?" Hy asked.

". . . Nothing." Although I hadn't completely ruled out Girdwood as a suspect, I supposed that as long as he was intent on making the trip, he might as well be where

I could keep an eye on him. "So we arrive in Albuquerque at . . . ?"

"The godawful hour of five-forty," Hy said. "We're met by limos, taken to the Hyatt. We've got two floors—one for the road personnel, another for the rest of us. There're two wings on either floor, and we'll divide up like we did for the planes."

I shook my head. "I want Kurt with the band members."

Rats's eyes narrowed, making his face more opossumlike. Another piece had been added to his mental picture puzzle. He said, "Okay, I'll have his room switched."

Hy went on, "People from our Phoenix office're already over there, checking out the hotel and briefing their security staff on our arrangements. After we arrive we'll catch a few hours sleep, then check out the concert venue—it's the Tingley Coliseum at the state fairgrounds. After the show we fly on to Dallas–Fort Worth. The arrangements are fairly standard from city to city. Dallas on Friday, Austin on Saturday—"

I said, "I think Austin might be a trouble spot."

Hy shot me a quick glance, made a note. "We'll talk more about that later. After Austin, we continue across the South—New Orleans, Miami, Atlanta—then up the eastern seaboard and across the Midwest, with a drop down to Nashville, where he puts in an appearance at the Opry. Then back through Denver and Salt Lake City, to the Pacific Northwest, and end up in San Francisco."

No wonder Ricky said that performing got to be a pain in the ass! "God, I hope I can wrap up this investigation fast, so we don't have to go along for the entire tour!"

"Do that, McCone, please. I like his music, but I really don't want to attend the same concert twenty-five times." Hy consulted his notes and said to Rats, "One of my people or I will be close to Rick at all times. McCone will probably be involved in other activities. The RKI people'll be different from city to city—more economical to bring them in from our nearest branch office. I'll want you to meet with them—"

Someone began pounding on the door. Rats heaved a martyred sigh and went to answer it. Kurt Girdwood stood in the hallway, his face nearly apoplectic, brandishing a sheaf of newspapers and faxes. "What I want to know," he roared, "is how they get hold of this shit!"

I went over and took one of the papers from him. It was the *L.A. Insider*—a publication that fell somewhere between a legitimate newspaper and a tabloid. On its front page was a color photo of Ricky and Rae holding hands and laughing in front of the Sorrento. The caption read, "Has Savage marriage reached the Broken Promise Land? Country star only has eyes for his private-eye friend."

"God!" I exclaimed, passing the paper to Hy.

Girdwood thrust a copy of the *Times* at me; it was folded open to "StarWatch."

> Although we have not been able to reach country star **Ricky Savage** for confirmation of the rumors that his eighteen-year marriage to wife **Charly** has collapsed, pals of the very private Grammy winner tell us that he's going very public with his romance with San Francisco private investigator **Rae Kelleher.** In the meantime, the single of "Midnight Train to Nowhere" remains blacked out on major country stations from coast to coast. Will Savage explain this phenomenon at his midnight press conference at Union Station following tonight's tour kickoff at the Universal Amphitheatre? Will Ms. Kelleher be tak-

ing the train to nowhere with him? Again,
stay tuned . . .

I handed the paper to Hy and asked Girdwood, "Has
Ricky seen these?"

"No. The day of the concert he holes up, doesn't read
the papers or talk with anybody—except Ms. Kelleher,
now that he's found her." The manager's mouth turned
down sourly. "And it's a good thing, too, because will
you look at this crap?" He thrust the sheaf of faxes at me.

YOU *K N O W* WHAT YOU'VE DONE!!!

YOU *K N O W*!!!

AND SOON THE WORLD WILL TOO.

Each fax was the same, containing all three lines. I
asked sharply, "Where did these come from?"

"The Sorrento. Manager refaxed them to me. The same
message has been coming in every hour on the hour
since eight o'clock."

I examined the sheets. No header showing the number they'd been transmitted from. They told me two
things: one good, that Ricky's current whereabouts
weren't known; one bad, that Terriss was turning up the
heat with a threat of exposure.

Soon the world will too.

How? When?

I looked at Hy. Our eyes met and held. He asked,
"Austin?"

"I think so."

"We've got to stop her."

"Yes." I reached for my bag where it sat on an end table, then stopped, feeling foolish. Where was I going? I was primed for action, but fresh out of leads—

The phone rang. Hy picked up, spoke, then held it out to me. "Letta James," he said. "She's found out who's been feeding the information to 'StarWatch.' "

258

Nineteen

Guilty as charged," Ethan Amory said.

The attorney sat behind his glass-topped rosewood desk in his spacious office at Zenith Records' new downtown headquarters. He wasn't fully moved in: Boxes sat on the floor, and the desk was clear except for a phone and an antique silver pen-and-inkwell set. And in spite of what I'd just confronted him with, he seemed fully at ease as he leaned back in his leather chair, a faintly contemptuous smile on his thin lips.

I went up to the desk and leaned across it, propping my hands on its edge to keep them from shaking with anger. "Why, for God's sake?" I demanded. "*Why?*"

"Sit down, Sharon. There's no need for such dramatics. Perhaps you'd like a drink?"

"I do not want a drink and I do not want to sit down. I want some answers."

"Suit yourself." He went to a bar cart and served himself.

I strode to the window behind the desk and peered out. The doorman at the hotel had warned me that the smog was at a record level today; it blurred the details of the surrounding spires and made indistinct the figures of people on the sidewalk of Wilshire Boulevard, some forty-eight stories below. After nearly two hundred years of being a city without a distinctly recognizable core, Los Angeles had experienced a renaissance in its central district, and it was there, nearly at the pinnacle of one of its tallest buildings, that Ricky and his associates had chosen to locate their label's headquarters.

Fitting, I thought, for a company called Zenith. An ambitious name for a group of ambitious people, but now I'd found out something that could very well topple the whole enterprise.

Behind me Amory's chair creaked. I turned, saw he was again seated, drink in hand. Cautioning myself against allowing my anger to rule me, I went back around the desk and, in spite of my earlier pronouncement, sat also.

I said, "All right, now answer my question—why?"

Amory sipped his drink and set it down. "It's difficult to explain to someone outside the industry, but I'll try." He steepled his fingers, propping his chin on them and looking introspective. "Your brother-in-law has immense potential, if it's properly channeled. He's a fine performer; in time he could be one of the greats. And his songs, for the most part, are among the best being written today. Already several have crossed over to the pop charts—which doesn't happen all that often with country singers. His popularity has been building, both here and abroad. He's ready for a much larger audience."

"What does this have to do with you leaking—"

"Patience. I'm getting to that. As I said, he has immense potential—if it's directed. But about a year and a half ago I began to sense a serious problem with him. The songs he was writing were either flat and stale, or

260

else they were cynical and bitter. 'The Broken Promise Land' is a good example: With it, he took a big chunk out of the hand that feeds him, and he's fortunate that our industry is so self-involved that very few people recognized what he was saying. In addition, his booking agent was having difficulty getting him to go out on the road. His fees were rising, but his income was leveling off because he'd turn down every third engagement. And it wasn't as if he was doing it so he could spend more time on his songwriting or with his family; he was over at Little Savages a lot, not doing much of anything, according to Mig Taylor. When he was home, I'd visit and find him moping around, as depressed as I'd ever seen him."

Consumed with guilt over the Terriss incident, I thought. "Go on."

"This was a short while after the fire in Pacific Palisades. He and your sister had been drifting apart for some years, and it was as though the fire burned out what little was left between them. And the . . . how do I put it? The sizzle had gone out of Rick—the sexiness that always went over so well on stage. Hell, he wasn't even screwing around out on the road. His marriage was dying, and so was his spirit."

I watched the attorney reach for his drink and sip, as calm and dispassionate as if he were discussing a spell of bad weather. But this was Ricky's life he was talking about—and that of my sister and my nieces and nephews. A dreadful suspicion stole over me, and my mouth went dry. Amory had done something even more monstrous than what I'd previously accused him of.

"So," I said, "you started some rumors to help along the marriage's demise."

He shrugged negligently. "That wasn't exactly my intention. To tell the truth, I didn't care what happened to the marriage. I only wanted to shake him up some. If he and Charly survived it and their relationship grew stronger, that would be good for him; if they couldn't weather the storm, he'd be well off out of there. And it worked, too: As your sister withdrew further from him, he threw himself into his work—and with real emotion. 'Midnight Train to Nowhere' and the other songs on that album are the best he's ever written."

And at such terrible personal cost . . .

Pushing down my anger for now, I said, "Let's get on to you leaking those items to 'StarWatch.' Weren't you concerned about damaging his credibility right before he went out on tour?"

"Ah, he's got you buying into the credibility business, too. I'll admit there's a fair amount of that nonsense going around—particularly with country audiences, who tend to be more conservative than the average. But what really sells—and has always sold—to audiences is sex. We want our idols to be larger than life and a whole lot sexier than we are. And we also want them to be somewhat fallible. Given that combination, we're solidly on their side. Look at his dedication up in Sonoma County of 'The House Where Love Once Lived' to Charly; Rats told me the response was phenomenal. Every single person in that audience had been there at one time or another; every single person was in his corner."

Amory paused to sip his drink. I waited impatiently.

"Rats also told me that Rick left there with a woman," he went on. "A very attractive woman, after two, three years of living like a Boy Scout. It got me to thinking, and I monitored the situation once I went down to his place the next day. It wasn't difficult to figure out that he was making a lot of private calls to San Francisco, both from his office and cell phone, and it was easy to ascertain their nature."

"You eavesdropped on his private conversations with Rae?"

"Only long enough to find out what was going on. I doubt either he or she admitted it even to themselves at the time, but it was apparent to me that the relationship was heating up rapidly. And I saw that as an opportunity to foster the kind of identification the Sonoma County crowd had felt for him—but on a much larger scale. It worked, too: this marital breakup and affair with your employee have already revved up his image."

"Oh, come on, Amory."

"No, I have proof. A couple of days ago we were concerned about filling the Universal Amphitheatre—it's a huge venue, really more suitable for a rock star—but this morning the concert sold out. What with the gossip and the fortuitous fact that the single's been blacked out on radio, we've got a potential monster hit on our hands."

A second suspicion, as horrible as the first, began to turn in my mind. I stared at Amory, unwilling to accept that even such cold-blooded scum as he could have done such a thing.

In response to my look he nodded, eyes calculating. "I see you're figuring out the rest of it."

I said, "Transamerica's people didn't come up with the scheme to black out the single. *You* proposed it."

"Again, guilty as charged."

"You saw it beforehand as Rae did after the fact—as an opportunity to create sympathy and publicity for him."

"Yes."

"What if she hadn't come up with the idea of the T-shirts? Did you have something in mind?"

Amory laughed softly. "Rae surprised me—and fed perfectly into my plans. I was prepared to let a few more minutes go by and then propose the newspaper ads she mentioned. But as it was, out of the mouth of a mere babe came a scheme that not only isn't costly but stands to make us money. The woman's untutored, but very, very bright. As I told him, he'd better keep her."

"She's not a pet, you know!"

Amory blinked, surprised.

My anger had been building, and now it broke the dam I'd placed in front of it and spilled wildly over. "That's what people are to you, isn't it?" I demanded. "Chattel. Things that you wring all use from and then discard. Doesn't matter that they're human and have feelings and talent—or that they have the right to live their lives unmolested. You don't care. You manipulate them, bleed them dry, and destroy them!"

He frowned and reached for his drink. I couldn't tell if he recognized the truth in what I'd said or merely was puzzled because he saw nothing in his actions that should provoke such vehemence.

I took a deep breath, got myself under control. "Was Kurt involved in this?"

Amory took a long, measured drink, then set the glass down with exaggerated care. "Kurt? No. Kurt's all bluster and noise, but underneath he's afraid of Rick. Rick's got something on him, probably evidence of illegal activity. There's no way Kurt would cross him."

I nodded and hesitated before asking my next question. So far, this conversation had been like overturning a series of rocks and finding increasingly hideous creatures under each; I was truly afraid of what I might unearth from beneath the next. "All right," I finally said, "what do you know about Patricia Terriss?"

"Who?"

"The name isn't familiar?"

He shook his head.

I studied him, trying to gauge if he was telling the truth. Not possible to do so, though; Amory was a skilled liar. "Have you done anything other than what you just told me in order to, as you call it, put the sizzle and sexiness back into Ricky's image?"

"I'd say I've done enough in that department, wouldn't you? What kinds of things are you thinking of?"

"Anonymous notes. Anonymous faxes. A . . . floral delivery to his trailer at the Sonoma County concert. A birthday gift to his daughter that had a double-edged meaning."

"Or a wild shot that supposedly came from a deer poacher," he added softly. "Are those the reasons for the tight security?"

"Some of them."

"You want to tell me what's going on?"

"And have it end up in 'StarWatch'? No, I don't think I do." I needed to get out of there; my hatred for the man was making it hard to breathe. I stood and headed for the door.

Amory said, "I suppose now you'll be on your way back to the hotel to tell Ricky about this conversation."

I stopped. "No, I won't do that. He's got a concert tonight; he doesn't need me to unload this on him."

"But you will tell him. It won't make any difference, you know. Business is business, and we have a label to run."

"Amory, I'm not sure of that; I think you underestimate my brother-in-law."

"The fastest way you can bring him down is to encourage divisiveness among us."

"And the best way I can prevent him from being brought down is by wise use of this." I took my cassette recorder from the outside pocket of my bag and held it up so he could see. "You know the evidence Ricky has on Kurt? Well, now he's got some on you. This has been on the whole time we've been talking."

He started to push back from the desk, but I held up my other hand. "I wouldn't. You'd have to rough me up to get hold of it, and I'd yell loud enough to bring your office personnel and building security in here."

Amory's lips went white; he ran his fingers through his wild brown hair.

"So you see," I went on, "eventually Ricky will hear all the specifics, and then this tape will live in my safety-deposit box—just as Ricky's evidence on Kurt lives in his—in case we ever need it."

"You think you can harm me with that?"

"Oh, I'm sure your other clients would be interested in hearing it. *Billboard*? Possibly. 'StarWatch'? Most certainly. And then there's the ABA . . ."

"You've made your point. What would compel you to use it?"

"Any number of things: I'd use it if you ever did anything to hurt my sister or her children again. I'd use it if you did anything more to Ricky. Should you someday find it in your best interests to damage Zenith Records, multiple copies will be distributed. And I'd be especially compelled to use it if you ever, ever did anything to harm Rae."

Amory watched me for a moment, eyes dark and hard behind the lenses of his glasses. After a minute he shrugged, acknowledging defeat. With a bitter twist of his lips he said, "When I first met you I thought you were small-time and naive. I won't make that kind of mistake again."

On the way back to the hotel I tried to analyze the situation, but my anger with Amory made it damn near impossible to focus. My driving wasn't improved by my emotional state, either, and I was relieved to turn the car over to the valet-parking attendant. I hurried inside the pale-marble lobby and immediately spotted Rae, Ricky, and two RKI bodyguards crossing from the elevators. Rae and Ricky were holding hands and looked relaxed and rested. They waved, but as I approached one of the guards stepped forward to block me.

"Hey, she's okay," Ricky told him. "She may look dangerous, but she's family."

The guard smiled faintly and stepped back.

I asked, "You're leaving for Universal City already?"

He nodded. "Sound check at four-thirty, then we'll go have dinner, come back about the time Blue Arkansas opens for us, and start getting ready. You'll be there later with Hy?"

"Probably. If something comes up and I don't make it, I'll see you at Union Station." To Rae I added, "May I speak privately with you for a moment?"

"Sure." She winked at Ricky. "Girl stuff. I won't be long."

I motioned for her to follow me and we began walking toward the elevators, the guard a discreet distance behind us. When we were out of my brother-in-law's hearing, I asked, "Do you still have that Beretta you bought last year?"

"Yeah, it's in the safe at the office."

"And you did get a carry permit?"

"Yes. Why?"

"I want you to keep it with you until this thing's resolved. And keep the alarm system at my house on whenever you're there."

Her face went a little tense. "You're really serious about me being a target."

"I hope you won't become one, but your picture's already been in the *Insider* and it's likely you'll be photographed again tonight, no matter how careful the guards are. You've been identified by name and profession, and so have I. It wouldn't take a rocket scientist to connect the two of us and find out where you are."

She bit her lip, glanced over at where Ricky stood by the doors, chatting with the other guard. "Okay, I'll be careful. What about Mick?"

"He's staying on here overnight, then flying to Tahoe on an RKI jet tomorrow afternoon. Neither Charlene nor Ricky is comfortable with him being on his own until this is resolved, especially since he's not yet firearms qualified."

"Makes sense. Besides . . . I'm not sure I'm supposed to tell anybody, but he broke up with Maggie yesterday. They got into it on the phone, and she told him not to come back except to collect his stuff. So you see, he's got no place to go in San Francisco except your house, and I don't think it's a good idea for the two of us to live under the same roof at this point."

"I thought things were better between the two of you."

"They are, but it's going to take time before he's completely comfortable with me again." She looked at Ricky, who was pointing to his watch, and nodded. "Got to go now."

I hugged her—something I seldom did with Rae—and said, "Take care. If you have any problems, call Dan Kessell at RKI in La Jolla and he'll arrange for somebody from the San Francisco office to help you out."

"Thanks." She hurried across the lobby.

I watched as the guards shepherded them out to a waiting limo, then punched the elevator call button and rode up to Mick's floor. My nephew had his PowerBook set up on the desk, and after he let me in he went back to it, peering at its screen.

Sometimes his intense relationship with what was only a machine made me testy. With an edge to my voice, I asked, "Can you be separated from your alter ego for a moment? I need to talk with you."

"Is it important? Because if not, I'm getting—"

"It's important. I have a tape I want you to hear." I set the cassette recorder next to the computer and pressed the PLAY button. Mick leaned close to listen, and I watched emotions that ranged from astonishment to fury pass over his face.

"So there you have it," I said, clicking the tape off. "Things have happened to your dad that didn't seem like they could've been engineered by Terriss, and now we know who was behind them. I'm not certain he isn't also the insider who'd been aiding her; the man's a talented liar."

"Has Dad heard this?"

"Not yet. I intend to play it for him eventually, but I need your advice on the timing: Should I wait till the tour's over?"

Mick considered. "Well, Mom never used to tell him anything that went wrong at home while he was out on the road. I guess that's the policy you should follow."

"Then I will. And I won't tell Rae about it, either, because I don't know if she could keep something like that from him."

He pushed back from the desk and extended his long legs, crossing his arms on his chest. "It's serious with them, isn't it?"

"Looks like. How does that make you feel?"

"Better than I did a couple of days ago. It's strange, though: All the things that I took as givens in my life have changed in less than a week." He paused, sadness seeping into his eyes. "Maggie and I broke up."

"I'm sorry."

"It was my fault. I hadn't called her since I flew down to San Diego, and when I finally did . . . well, she'd found out that Charlotte and I aren't just friends. A friend of Maggie's was at Dad's concert and saw Charlotte and me; it was pretty obvious what was going on, so she went straight to Maggie with the news. I wish I'd had the guts to tell her first, so she wouldn't've been hurt like that."

"A lot of growing up seems to be going on in our family this week."

"Yeah. And I'll tell you, growing pains're no fun at all."

"Well, ignore them for a while and help me figure out what we've got on this investigation. We really haven't eliminated anybody as the insider except Rats—and that's only because he got shot. But did you catch that about his being the one who told Amory about Rae? He seems to be keeping pretty close tabs on your dad."

"But he *did* get shot."

"Accidentally; he moved at the wrong time. And he could've been the person who tripped the circuit breakers. Terriss could've gotten on and off the property while the security system on the wall by the road was out."

"Why'd she leave the gun behind, then?"

"It was a message—a Savage, remember?"

"I don't know. Would she have had time to hide it and go over the wall, clear on the other side of the property?"

"Maybe, maybe not. I'm still going to have a long talk with Rats as soon as I can catch him alone. And if I can corner Forrest Curtin when he's not hopelessly drunk or drugged, I also want to feel him out about a possible connection to Terriss that my Austin contact's turned up. Otherwise I've got no leads—"

"Yes, you do. I was trying to tell you when you came in, I've come up with something on Terriss's former husband." He motioned at the computer.

"What? How?" I went around and peered at the screen. Nothing but a menu.

"Sit down a minute. I'm almost done."

I sat cross-legged on the bed, watching as he tapped keys, read what came up, moved the mouse, tapped some more. This was one of the times when I loved Mick's symbiotic relationship with the computer—mainly because he made it perform its magic without requiring me to participate. After a bit he pulled a scratch pad over, scribbled on it, and turned away from the desk.

"Well?" I asked.

He smiled, thoroughly pleased with himself. "You remember that Terriss told Dad she had a former husband who was working on a doctoral dissertation in medieval history?"

"Yes."

"Well, I got to thinking about that, so I accessed DIALOG's Dissertation Abstracts Online. It's a guide to every doctoral dissertation accepted by an accredited American institution since eighteen sixty-one. They're indexed by subject, title, and author. And under the name Philip R. Terriss, I came up with—are you ready for this?—'The Decline of the Holy Roman Empire's Spiritual and Political Influence on Europe after the Great Interregnum: A Conceptual/Statistical Approach.' No wonder the woman was bored with him! I guess his profs thought it was hot stuff, though; it was accepted by Texas Christian University in nineteen ninety-one."

"Good work! But how do we find out where Philip Terriss is now?"

Mick grinned more broadly. "Not at TCU. I called there. No Philip R. Terriss on the faculty, and they won't give out information on graduates. So I started thinking about academics: They teach, but what else do they do? And I remembered that thing about publish or perish. Back to the databases I went, and came up with one that indexes scholarly journals, including the *Medieval*

History Quarterly. And there he was—Philip R. Terriss, still going on about the Great Interregnum, whatever that was." He paused dramatically. Mick loved drawing out the suspense when he'd been exceptionally clever.

I rewarded him by demanding, "What? *What?*"

"Ol' Philip R. is currently boring the pants off budding historians at Cal State Long Beach."

"Long Beach! That's practically next door to us!" I jumped off the bed and wrapped my arms around Mick's neck. He pushed me away, flushing, then handed me the scratch pad. "Here's his home address and phone number. Go for it."

Twenty

Philip Terriss lived north of central Long Beach, worlds removed from the busy harbor, the offshore oil rigs, and the hotels and convention center that had sprung up to reclaim much of the waterfront. His was a quiet neighborhood of narrow, palm-lined streets. The homes were mainly California bungalows built in the twenties and thirties: wood-sided, with low-pitched gable roofs and deep front porches designed for sitting on warm summer evenings. They all appeared to be well kept up, but Terriss's was immaculate, its blue-and-white paint fresh, flowering plants hanging in baskets from the wide eaves. As I got out of the car I heard the swish of a lawn sprinkler, smelled newly cut grass.

A light shone behind closed blinds in Terriss's front window; it was after eight—the earliest he'd been able to see me—and the porch was in shadow. I used the shiny brass door-knocker and waited.

The sweatsuit-clad man who answered was thin, somewhat stooped, and prematurely balding; his brown hair stood up in unruly wisps. He wore thick glasses over watery blue eyes and his skin was very pale, as though he spent most of his time indoors. My first reaction was that I must have gotten the wrong house; surely this man couldn't be the former husband of the beautiful young woman Ricky had described. But then he said, "Ms. McCone? Please, come in," and another facet was added to my already contradictory image of Patricia Terriss.

The front room of the bungalow was as lovingly tended as the exterior: Beautifully finished wood beams and window casings stood out against white walls, and the hardwood floor gleamed. Terriss had allowed the architectural features of his classic home to take center stage by choosing simple furnishings and leaving the walls unadorned. The result was a comfortable room, as tranquil as the neighborhood, yet one that caught and held the viewer's interest.

He seated me on a brown leather sofa, offered me coffee or a drink, which I refused, and perched on a chair opposite me. His expression was guarded and slightly apprehensive, as though he were afraid I might be bringing bad news. When he said, "You're looking for my former wife," his tone confirmed it.

"Yes. You said on the phone that you don't know her present whereabouts, but I thought that if we talked in person you might be able to tell me something that would lead to her."

"Why? I mean, why are you interested in her?"

I studied him, debating how much to reveal. If Philip Terriss felt any protective impulse toward Patricia, he might close up if he knew the real reason I was looking for her. On the other hand, they were divorced; she had been the one to do the leaving, and abandoned husbands seldom wish their former spouses well. I decided to ignore his question and probe some.

"I'll get to that, Mr. Terriss, but . . . I wonder, when did you last see Patricia?"

"Over three years ago."

"You were living here at the time?"

"Yes. She came by, wanting something. As she usually did."

"Then you still saw her, in spite of the divorce."

"Not really. Until that spring I hadn't seen her since she left me and moved to Austin in nineteen eighty-eight. But we kept in touch by Christmas card, and when I moved here from Fort Worth, I sent her the new address. When she came out to L.A., she looked me up."

"Why?"

His mouth pulled down bitterly. "She needed money—why else?"

"Did you give it to her?"

"Yes. My ex-wife can be quite persuasive when she puts her mind to it."

"And when was that?"

"Late April of ninety-two."

"And you saw her again. . . ?"

"Three times. Twice she needed a place to stay, once more she needed money."

"And the last time was. . . ?"

He looked away, fingers tensing on the arms of his chair. "Late June. That was the last I saw or heard from her."

Late June. Go slowly, McCone, go carefully.

"You say she needed a place to stay. I take it she didn't have a permanent home, or a job."

Terriss ran his tongue over his lips. "Ms. McCone, I'd appreciate it if you'd tell me why you're looking for Patricia."

I opted for a half truth. "Your former wife had a brief affair with one of my clients. She's been causing him some trouble over it, and he wants me to talk with her and see if I can persuade her to back off."

He nodded, as though he'd expected something of the sort. "Is your client married?"

"Yes. Is that a pattern with her?"

"It would seem so. I was married when I met her. She went after me with amazing persistence. And once she got me, she made sure my wife found out." He laughed harshly. "Of course, I was completely smitten at the time. I couldn't believe that such a lovely woman could want me so much. It wasn't until some months later that I realized she'd found out I'd inherited money and hoped I'd bankroll a singing career for her."

"But you didn't."

"Ms. McCone, it wasn't that much money. I'm good for an occasional loan to a good friend, but I've never had nearly enough to make anybody a star. And Patricia isn't really all that accomplished a singer."

"What can you tell me about her background?"

"Not a great deal. We met at Texas Christian University. She was a freshman, I was a doctoral student. She wanted to be a country singer, but her father had had experience with musicians and insisted she get her degree as something to fall back on. She wasn't happy about that, and as soon as we married she dropped out."

"What was her maiden name?"

"Smith. She liked mine because she said it had star quality."

"And her family lived where?"

"We never talked about them. She hated her father, didn't even tell him we were married. There was a sister, I think, but they weren't close."

"She never talked about her past?"

"Patricia isn't much of a talker, except when it comes to her songs and her desire to become a star. She performed with a few bands around campus, but the response wasn't enthusiastic, and when I suggested her ambitions might be unrealistic, she stopped talking at all. And then she left me."

"What about her friends?"

"She didn't have any. She was a loner, always off someplace inside her own head. The only friend she ever mentioned to me was a fellow she lived with on and off out here—a member of her former band in Austin who had a house in Venice."

"Do you recall his name?"

He thought for a moment. "Tod something."

"Dodson?"

"That's it."

"Do you have his address?"

". . . You know, I may. When Patricia came to the L.A. area, she told the restaurant where she worked in Austin to send her final check in care of me. It still hadn't arrived when she stopped by to ask for a loan, and she wrote down Tod's address so I could forward it." He got up and crossed to a small telephone table, rummaged through its drawer for a moment. "Here it is," he said, adding sheepishly, "Sometimes being a pack rat has its advantages."

I took the paper, glanced at the meaningless street name, and placed it in my bag. Terriss sat down again, but I sensed he was anxious for me to go—and not because he had another engagement or pressing things to do.

I said, "I have a few more questions, if I may."

He hesitated, then nodded.

"You said that seeing a married man would seem to be a pattern with Patricia. Do you know of others she saw?"

". . . I'm not sure."

"There must have been more basis for your remark than the fact that you were married when you met her."

"I . . . Ms. McCone, are you sure you wouldn't like a drink?"

"I'm sure, but if you want one, please feel free."

"I think I will." He excused himself and went to the back of the house. Ice cubes rattled faintly. When he reappeared carrying a glass of what looked to be whiskey, he seemed more at ease. I suspected he'd fortified himself with a shot or two while in the kitchen.

Getting into the hard stuff now—and not just liquor. Getting into the hard facts about his former wife.

"Where were we?" he asked as he sat down.

"We were talking about Patricia and married men."

"Yes." He drank, set the glass on the table next to him. "All right, I'm going to tell you this because . . . because you seem like a decent person, and if you do find her, perhaps you can talk to her, make her see that what she's doing is not only wrong but very self-destructive. Back in ninety-two Patricia became involved with someone in the entertainment industry—a well-known country singer."

"Who?"

"Ricky Savage. She met him in Austin. He's married, has six children, but she claimed he brought her to the coast. She also claimed he was going to make her a star. Now, I'm not a fan of country, but I know Savage's music. He's good, both as a lyricist and a musician. Unless he'd taken complete leave of his senses, he would never have seen star material in Patricia. And he must have quickly tired of her as a lover. Patricia can be sexually intense and very attentive, but eventually everything comes back to her—to her songs, to what she thinks is her due. And finally she becomes strident and demanding. I don't blame Savage for breaking it off." Terriss paused to sip his drink. When he set it on its coaster his hand trembled. The man was plainly nervous about whatever knowledge he held inside—and just as eager to dump it in someone else's lap.

I said, "Nothing you tell me is going to be used against Patricia. This is strictly a private matter, and my client wants it to remain that way."

He let out a long sigh. "All right. It was early in the morning. June thirtieth of ninety-two. Around four-thirty, I guess. Patricia came to the house. She was . . . God!" He closed his eyes, took his glasses off, and pressed the palms of his hands against his lids. "She was wearing a raincoat with nothing under it but a flimsy nightgown. A white one. At least, it had been white. But there was dried blood all over it—a lot of blood. And her wrists were bandaged and wrapped in towels."

I waited, my hands clasped so tightly my fingers hurt.

Terriss went on, more swiftly now. "She was high on something, and drunk too. Her car was parked out front with the keys in it. The seat was pushed way back for a much taller person, so I knew she hadn't driven herself. And there were bloodstains on the passenger's seat. I brought her in and cleaned her up and put her to bed in the spare room, but she couldn't sleep and was afraid to be alone, so I sat with her and she told me what had happened." Terriss took his hands from his eyes and looked bleakly at me. "Jesus, I hope you can do something to keep her from getting into that kind of trouble again."

"I'll try."

He nodded. "All right, I sat with her and she talked to me. She told me Savage had broken up with her and she'd tried to get him back but nothing had worked. She'd threatened to tell his wife about their affair, and he had their phone number changed. Then she threatened

279

to tell his kids. And finally she threatened to do something to them. She told me . . . she told me she was prepared to kill them, if that's what it took."

"Did you believe her?"

"Well, she *was* high, so high it had really messed up her head, but . . . Anyway, she said that after a couple of months of this going back and forth, Savage called her up and capitulated. They arranged a meeting for a motel someplace up the coast, but instead of him, two of his band members showed up to lean on her and persuade her to leave him alone."

"Did they hurt her?"

"Physically? No. Emotionally, it was shattering. Patricia . . . she doesn't respond normally to rejection. She goes straight through disappointment and pain to anger. And she usually acts out anger in ways that are harmful to her. Her reaction to Savage's deception was to get even by seducing the men he'd sent. She suggested they 'party' and took both of them on. And afterward she went into the bathroom, broke a glass, and slashed her wrists. The men stopped her in time, bandaged her, and at her request brought her here."

"Was it a serious suicide attempt?"

"Yes. I saw those cuts."

"Had she ever done anything like that before?"

"She's threatened suicide, but this was the first time I know of that she'd done more than talk."

So there I had it: the ultimate result of Ricky's carelessness and expedient solution to his problem.

I asked Terriss's former husband, "How long did she stay with you?"

"Only till that evening. Once she saw how much her story upset me, she called her friend Tod, and he caught a ride up here and drove her in her car to his place."

"You never checked to see if she was okay?"

"No. To tell you the truth, that episode finished any feeling I had left for her. I never wanted to see her again." His empty eyes met mine, his pain almost palpable now, filling the well-tended room. I'd seen that expression on the faces of people who had lost loved ones, and I supposed in a way he had.

Softly he added, "No matter how badly he treated her, I can't help but empathize with Savage. You see, I was her victim too." He held out the back of his right hand; there was a scar on it that looked like it had been caused by a deep puncture wound.

"She did that to you?"

"Yes—with a letter opener, in one of her black, bloody rages, when she realized I couldn't afford to bankroll her career. Whoever your client is, you'll want to protect him, and if you locate Patricia I suggest you be very careful. You don't want to find yourself on the receiving end of her anger."

By day Venice is the most colorful of California beach towns, with continuous street theater being played out on Ocean Front Walk by rollerbladers, vendors, and eccentric characters of every stripe. But after sunset the actors in this drama disappear and the tourists flee; ordinary people hole up behind locked doors. Then the narrow streets beside the canals belong to the homeless and the gangs, who prowl side by side, an uneasy and unspoken truce between them.

It was close to ten, and the scavengers and predators were out in full force when I arrived at the address Philip Terriss had given me for Patricia's friend Tod Dodson. I locked the rental car and scanned the shadows before I approached the little frame cottage that sagged between two newish architectural mistakes on a side street near the beach. The light from its uncurtained window laid a

swath across the tiny front yard and showed daisies
growing among a tangle of weeds; through the glass I
glimpsed a shabby brown sofa and unframed rock-
concert posters tacked to the walls.

The woman who came to the door had a round,
bloated face under a tangle of blond curls and wore a
soiled white dress and dirt on her bare feet. She looked
at my I.D. with unmasked hostility and shook her head
when I asked for Dodson. "He don't live here anymore."

"Do you know where I can locate him?"

"Why?"

"Personal business."

"What, somebody die and leave him money?"

"Something like that."

Her expression said she only half believed me. "Well,
Tod went back to Nashville, couldn't make it in the pop
scene here. My old man and me, we sublet the place
from him."

"You have an address or phone number for him?"

"Might."

Uh-huh. I reached into my bag for my wallet. The
woman's eyes watched me greedily as I pulled out a
twenty. She snatched it from my fingers, said, "Wait
here," and went inside, shutting the door.

I waited, turning up the collar of my light cotton shirt
and hugging my elbows for warmth. A wind was blowing off the Pacific, funneling up the narrow streets and
canals and rattling the fronds of the tall palms. I glanced
at my watch, realized that Ricky was on stage now,
would be leaving the amphitheatre for Union Station
within the hour.

Hurry up! I thought.

The woman returned and handed me a slip of paper
with a phone number scrawled on it. "No address," she

said. "Me and my old man, we're not much when it comes to writing."

"But you've been in touch with Tod recently?"

"Yeah, sure." Now that money had changed hands she was friendlier, as if it had formed a bond between us. "My guy met Tod when he was playing with this band out in the Valley. The regular drummer quit and the keyboards player knew a waitress whose boyfriend knew Tod and . . . well, you know how that goes. Tod'd come out from Austin thinking to get himself on as a sideman at one of the studios, break into the pop scene—only pop's kind of flat, although everybody says it's gonna rally. Anyway, Tod ended up in my old man's band, and when that fell apart they both got gigs in Marina del Rey at this singles bar, which is where my guy is tonight. Tod hung on till a year ago, but he started to listen to people talking about how country's the big thing now and he decided to get back to his roots and headed for Music City Row."

"What about his girlfriend?"

"Monica? No way. She's an L.A. lady, wouldn't be caught dead living in a town full of hillbillies. She told Tod so, and that blew it."

"I was thinking of Patricia. Patricia Terriss."

The woman's mouth turned down. "That bitch! She split on Tod three years ago. Was in and out of here for a couple of months like this place had revolving doors, and then one day she was gone and so was his emergency stash."

"She robbed him?"

"Took his cash *and* his dope. Can you believe it?"

"When was this, exactly?"

"Well now, I remember him telling us about it at a party. It was . . . yeah, Fourth of July. He was really

283

pissed about the dope, so we gave him some of ours. It had only happened a couple of days before."

"Did Tod ever hear from her again?"

"He never mentioned her again, but we were out of touch for a year and a half after that, when my guy decided to try the scene up in Seattle, so maybe he did."

Another dead end, I thought, looking down at the scrap of paper in my hand. Even though Terriss made a habit of dropping into the lives of her former husband and boyfriend when she needed something, she probably wouldn't have turned to Tod Dodson after she robbed him. Or would she? I'd ask Jenny Gordon to find out.

The woman was leaning in the doorway now, relaxed as if she were chatting over the fence with a neighbor. "You know," she said, "that Patricia was really whacked out."

"In what way?"

"Well, Tod was a fish freak. He had this aquarium with a half dozen of . . . I don't know what you call them, but tropical fish with, like, long traily fins and stuff. Patricia, she named them: Michael, Molly, Brian, Christina, Jamie, and Lisa. I remember, because she used to talk about them in her weird way like they were her kids."

My stomach knotted. "What did she say?"

"Oh, stuff like, 'Michael's off his feed today.' or 'Jamie and Lisa have been fighting again.' Really dumb stuff, and she'd go on and on. It drove Tod up the wall. Anyway, it wasn't her naming them that freaked me. It was what she did to them."

"What she *did?*"

"Yeah. The day she split she poisoned them."

"*What!*"

The woman smiled and nodded, enjoying my reaction. "Yeah. Tod came home and there they were, floating belly-up, every single one of them. And next to the aquarium were two empty cans of fish food. It couldn't've been an accident. The bitch deliberately poisoned Michael, Molly, Brian, Christina, Jamie, and Lisa."

. . . deliberately poisoned Michael, Molly, Brian, Christina, Jamie, and Lisa . . .

. . . I was her victim, too . . . with a letter opener, in one of her black, bloody rages . . .

I'd known the woman was obsessed and dangerous. But I'd had no idea of how obsessed and dangerous.

And now I was stuck in yet another traffic jam, this one on the Santa Monica Freeway, heading for the hub of a system that was dying of slow strangulation. I wished I'd spent enough time in the area to know surface—nonfreeway—routes, but . . .

As I came to a dead halt near Overland Avenue I eased Ricky's cellular phone from my bag and punched out the Nashville number that the woman in Venice had given me. The phone rang twice and a taped male voice told me to leave a message for Tod. I did, stressing that my call was urgent.

Eleven-oh-five. I had to be at Union Station by midnight.

I shifted into first gear and inched along while dialing the number of Hy's cellular unit. No answer. Why not, dammit? When I'd told him I wouldn't be able to make the concert, he'd said for me to call him if there was any problem.

Eleven-oh-six. By now Ricky and Rae should be on their way to the limo. They'd have an interval of security, but then he'd have to brave the crush at the station. Hy and Rats seemed to think that once they got him through the gate to the train he'd be safe enough, but I wasn't at all sure of that—knowing what I did now.

God, I couldn't visualize what horrible thing might happen next. Couldn't imagine what Terriss might be planning.

Eleven-oh-seven. I had to get hold of somebody.

Mick. He had a cell phone—one I'd bought him as a reward for good work last spring. I dredged up its number from memory, dialed. Again, no answer. Had he left it in his room at the hotel tonight, or . . . ?

Had something gone wrong at the concert? Had something happened to Ricky, to Rae, to Mick? Or to *Hy?*

People I loved could be in trouble, and I was stuck in a traffic jam. The lives of people I loved could be on the line, and I was staring at the ass end of a semi trailer.

People I loved: Ricky, Rae, Mick . . . Hy.

Twenty-one

EXCERPT FROM RAE KELLEHER'S DIARY:

Ricky and I collapsed on the backseat of the limo, and the door shut with a solid thump. We'd run the gauntlet of screaming fans and reporters and cameras outside the amphitheatre, RKI's guards bracing us on either side, and still somebody had managed to rip the sleeve of his T-shirt.

He yanked the shirt off and tossed it on the floor. Laughed—as high as I'd seen him since after the concert in Sonoma County. "Red," he said, "that's the way they're supposed to behave for rock stars, not for country boys like me."

I smiled, catching some of his excitement in spite of the lingering scariness of that half minute between the stage exit and the car. I'd always had a touch of agoraphobia, and I could see I was going to have to conquer it if I planned to stick with him. Which I did.

"So," I said, "you gonna board the train half naked?"

"Nah, me half—or wholly—naked is an experience I'm saving just for you. Fortunately, my wardrobe guy fig-

ured I'd be kind of grungy after the performance, so here"—he pulled a bag from the facing seat—"we have another shirt."

I helped him ease it over his head and drew back to admire my brainchild: BLACKED OUT IN LOS ANGELES: THE MIDNIGHT TRAIN TO NOWHERE.

Not bad, if I did say so myself, and the graphics Winterland had supplied were fantastic.

Ricky grinned at me, then pulled me close for a hug. "I'd like to think you're stunned by what a good-looking fellow you've snagged, but I suspect you're more thrilled with the shirt."

"Well, I am proud of it."

"You deserve to be." He pulled a bottle of champagne from the bar and popped the cork. Poured into two glasses, handed one to me, and toasted. "To us."

"Us." I sipped some of the bubbly stuff and thought, I'll never be able to tell the difference between this and the cheapo brands I'm used to, but it doesn't matter, because neither of us cares.

"And to you," I said. "They loved you."

"Thank God." He sobered, shaking his head. "After all this crap in the papers, I was afraid I'd be booed off the stage. You know what I noticed, though? They responded well to 'Midnight Train,' but the song that really got to them was 'The Empty Place.' "

"I noticed that, too."

He took my hand, slouching lower. I moved over and rested my head against his shoulder.

"Funny about the song, Red. When I wrote it I didn't even know you, but it turns out it's about you, me, us."

"I know."

"Listen, what I need to do right now is sit quietly, come down some. The driver'll let us know when we're five min-

utes from the station, and then I'll have to gear up for the crowd."

I'd watched him do the same before the concert, steadily building focus and energy. "How does that work?"

"Well, you know how a producer mixes a song? He raises some sounds, lowers others; some he takes out altogether. That's more or less what I do: raise my concentration, lower my stress level, tune out everything else."

"And how do you come down?"

"Before, it was dope or booze. Now, it's holding your hand."

"Five minutes, Mr. Savage."

"Thanks." He released my hand and sat up straighter. I moved away from him, already feeling shut out.

He noticed and cupped my chin, looking solemnly into my eyes. "Sorry, Red. It's a strange kind of life. You sure you want any part of it?"

"Yes. Yes, I'm sure."

Union Station looked like a Hollywood dream: salmon stucco with turquoise and mosaic-tile trim, its mission-style facade bathed in floodlights, great spindly palms swaying along the approach. The clocktower showed eleven forty-five. And the crowd was enormous.

People jammed the sidewalk between the building and the curb. People with cameras, both still and video. People with recorders and microphones. People who were just plain going out of their minds with excitement. Even with the limo's doors and windows closed I could hear them. This was no Hollywood dream, after all. It was a nightmare straight out of a horror film, and the people reminded me of the villagers swarming around the mill right before they burned Dr. Frankenstein's monster to death.

Panicked, I grabbed Ricky's arm.

"Red, it's okay. They can't get to you. And see who's right there? Hy and the bodyguards. Nothing's going to happen to me, I promise."

"What was the title of your last album?"

"Huh? Oh, no, neither of us is living in the broken promise land anymore." He put his arms around me till the car stopped at the curb. "Look," he added, "I'll call you at Shar's in three hours, exactly. I'll even talk sexy on the phone, if that'll make you feel better."

"Just tell me you're safe. That'll be more than enough."

"That's what you'll hear. You have a good flight; a driver'll meet you, take you to Shar's house. And don't forget—any problem at all, you call Dan Kessell."

I nodded, and then one of the guards opened the door. Ricky kissed me and got out.

The crowd noise was deafening. Most people were just screaming mindlessly, but others—reporters—pressed forward and shouted questions in voices that grated on my already raw nerves. I shrank back into a corner of the seat as Ricky straightened and held up his hands like he would on stage. They quieted down a little.

A woman's voice called, "What about this radio blackout of your single, Ricky?"

He reeled off the prepared publicity spiel that he'd rehearsed for me in our hotel room that afternoon: "... cost-cutting decision on the part of my former label ... very disappointing ... a shame the fans can't get to hear the music before they put down good money for the album ... maybe you could ask your readers to phone in requests to the stations ..."

"Is it true you and your wife are divorcing?"

"Yes, it's true, but it's an amicable split. Charly and I care very much about each other and our children, and we're doing everything we can to make sure we'll all be okay."

"Mr. Savage—what's this about you and a redhead?"

"Yeah, Ricky, where's your new lady?"

I cringed, wishing I could curl up into a little ball and roll under the seat. Or maybe become invisible, even though his body was blocking their view of me, and nobody could see through the tinted glass. Why did they think that Ricky was their property just because he gave of himself on stage? Why did they have to pry? What we had was so new, so private . . .

He was silent. The questions went on, more of the same. The voices grew insistent. Finally he turned, ducked down, and looked questioningly at me.

I couldn't. I just couldn't! Or could I? For his sake?

I took a deep breath and nodded.

He grasped my hand, helped me out of the car. Braced me, arm around my shoulders. The lights were blinding; I couldn't make out anything or anybody. I shaded my eyes with my hand and tried not to look as terrified as I felt.

Ricky said, "Here she is. Can you blame me for falling hard?"

People clapped. Some whistled. Reporters began shouting questions again. My heart was racing like a small frightened creature scrambling for its burrow. I heard Ricky say good-naturedly, "No comment . . . I don't think I'll touch that one . . ." Then he laughed. "Come on, guys, give me a break!"

I looked up at him and our eyes met. He squeezed my shoulders and smiled his wonderful crooked smile. And then he said softly so nobody else could hear, "I love you, Red."

And all of a sudden everything shifted and I was back in the limo with no recollection of how I got there. He was saying, "Three hours, I'll call you. Promise." And by the time I'd fully got my wits together, the car was on a freeway and all I could see were the tops of palm trees back-

lit by a pinkish-gray sky, even though it was the middle of the night.

The driver said, "We'll be at LAX in thirty minutes, Ms. Kelleher."

"Thanks." I realized I was crying and reached into my purse for a Kleenex. There wasn't one, of course, but my fingers found the fax that had come for Shar after she left the hotel—the fax Mick had handed me backstage and asked me to give to Ricky to pass on to her.

Damn! I was so besotted by love that I'd fallen down on the job.

Love.

Ricky had said the L-word. He'd given me the one thing that he knew I needed to get through the bad, scary time ahead.

On Friday night when we swapped life stories, I'd told him about my parents dying in the car wreck when I was only eight—drunk, as they'd been for most of my young life. About my grandmother who had raised me and made no bones about me being a pain-in-the-ass obligation, approximating one of the trials of Job. About how when she died during my freshman year of college I hadn't mourned her for a minute. About how that made me sadder than if I had.

But those were only facts. As the night went on, I'd found myself opening up to him as I never had to anybody. And I'd finally told him about the empty place inside of me.

It was the kind of place that starts out as a bubble in a little girl who knows she's not loved, and gradually expands into a huge vacuum that threatens to turn her inside out and swallow her whole. From the time I was fifteen, my defense against being eaten alive by my own emptiness was to offer myself up, body and soul, to any male I thought might conceivably be lured into loving me. Young Rae Kelleher was God's gift to half the adolescent- and some of the adult-male population of Santa Maria, California, and later to a goodly portion of the student body of UC Berkeley. But easy, superficial affairs and one-night stands are no way to fill a serious, deep, long-term chasm.

And then in my junior year I had a pregnancy scare and realized—with shock and shame—that the father could be any one of three men. Worse luck, it coincided with my meeting Doug Grayson, the first man I'd ever come across who didn't sense my need and immediately take advantage of it. Instead, Doug took me to dinner, to the movies, didn't try to touch me for weeks. And I was so damned grateful that, with the misguided idea that he could somehow save me from myself, I married him.

I've never been too swift on the uptake where interpersonal relationships are concerned, so it was five years before I figured out that Doug hadn't even noticed my neediness because he was more needy yet. Truth was, I'd married a child who was so self-centered that he faked a suicide attempt when my job at All Souls—which was all that stood between us and starvation—conflicted with his demands for my attention.

After my divorce, the empty place took on a cancerous growth rate. What few relationships I had were brief, stormy, and about as deep as a desert stream in July. Finally I stopped trying to fill the void and just let it have its way with me, figuring it would eventually consume me, and so what?

Funny, though: I'd given up, and then there was Ricky. Ricky, who understood because he harbored a similar empty place. And over the past few days both of us had noticed that we felt less hollow. He didn't wake up in the middle of the night and wonder, What's missing in me? *I didn't look at Shar and Hy and wonder,* What makes them worthy of love, when I'm not?

And the strangest thing of all was that song—"The Empty Place." A song about the two of us that he'd written a full year before.

I stared out the windows of the limo at the palm trees and the odd, pale night sky, tears sliding down my cheeks. The empty place was still there. It would always live inside me, just as Ricky's would always live inside him. But if he survived this terrible time ahead, eventually both of our life-threatening vacuums would again be reduced to bubbles.

And, I thought, if anything happens to him, that vacuum'll suck me in and destroy me, and I won't even care.

Finally I told myself I had to stop crying. Like Ricky said of himself when he cried, I wasn't a pretty sight. I sat up straighter and wiped my eyes on the hem of my tee. Totally ridiculous—I was riding in a limo, and I couldn't lay hand to a Kleenex!

I reached into my purse to see if maybe there was a dirty one lurking at its bottom. My fingers touched Shar's fax. Reading material. Something to help me through till we got to the airport. I pulled it out, fumbled for a light switch. It was from Jenny Gordon, the investigator in Austin . . .

"Ms. Kelleher? Your charter flight's ready and we'll be at LAX in two minutes. I'll stay with you till you're safely on board."

"Cancel the flight," I told the driver. "I want to go back to the Century Plaza."

"But Mr. Savage said—"

"Well, Mr. Savage isn't here now, is he?"

". . . No, ma'am."

"Then please take me back to the hotel—as fast as possible."

PART THREE

•

July 27, 1995

AMTRAK WELCOMES *THE MIDNIGHT TRAIN TO NOWHERE* TOUR!

BLACKED OUT IN LOS ANGELES: *THE MIDNIGHT TRAIN TO NOWHERE*

RADIO KZLA TURNS ON THE LIGHTS: *MIDNIGHT TRAIN* A HOTSHOT DEBUT!

SOON THE WORLD WILL KNOW WHAT YOU'VE DONE!!!

Twenty-two

12:01 A.M., Pacific Daylight Time

Even though I was running to make the train, the last banner stretching across Union Station's great arching main concourse slowed me down. Like the others, it hung between two enormous Art Deco chandeliers that looked like flying saucers hovering some thirty feet above the marble floor. But unlike those supplied by Amtrak, Zenith's publicity department, and the FM country station that apparently had ended the blackout, its message was hostile—and unpleasantly familiar.

"Oh, my God," I muttered.

The crowd had dwindled by the time I arrived; only diehard fans and a few stranded travelers remained in the cavernous echoing station. Maintenance people moved around, sweeping up the detritus that any gathering of more than five seems to leave behind. I spotted a security guard leaning on one of the massive old-fashioned leather chairs in the waiting area and hurried up to him. "That banner," I said, pointing, "do you know who supplied it?"

He looked up and shrugged. "Not my department. What does it mean, anyway? Some babe who was with Savage pitched a fit when she saw it, and his security people weren't too happy—"

A chime sounded over the public-address system, and a male voice echoed off the marble-and-wood-paneled walls: "This is your last call for the Midnight Train to Nowhere, eastbound for Albuquerque, Dallas, Austin, New Orleans . . ."

As the announcer continued to reel off all the stops on Ricky's twenty-five-city tour—another of his publicist's clever ideas—I started running toward the bright white-neon sign that said To Trains.

The fit-pitcher, I was sure, had been the publicist, Linda Toole. After months of planning this send-off, she'd been working nonstop for two days at damage control. Although she couldn't have known what the unauthorized banner meant, she'd probably seen that Ricky's reaction wasn't good. And if the star was thrown off balance at the very beginning of the tour, God knew what it would do to Toole's carefully fostered press relations.

God knew what I'd encounter when—and if—I boarded the train!

I shoved my pass at the guard at the gate. He hit the button on his walkie-talkie and said, "Hold it, we've got one more." Then he motioned to his left. "Track nine—and hurry."

The corridor was long and brightly lit. I ran under signs that indicated tracks to both the right and left—one and two, five and six. Nine, of course, was at the very end. An Amtrak employee stood there, pointing the way.

I called thanks as I skidded past him—and was confronted by a long, steep ramp.

"Oh, hell," I panted and started up.

The ramp's slope was graduated, so every now and then it got easier, then got difficult again. The outside air rushed at me—warm and muggy and full of fumes. I tried not to take too much of it into my lungs, but they filled anyway and I coughed. I could hear the train's engine grumbling above, but the ramp seemed to go on forever; reaching level ground was such a shock that I staggered to a halt.

"McCone! This way!"

I pivoted. Hy stood beside the last of four double-level silver cars with a man who—from his dark-blue blazer and cap—looked to be a conductor. The windows of the cars blazed with light, and people milled around upstairs. I hurried over and Hy boosted me up the steps. The conductor waved toward the engine and boarded after us.

We were in a small area with baggage racks to either side and a narrow stairway to the upper level. A hum of conversation and laughter came from above. I leaned against the wall by the stairway, breathing hard; the conductor squeezed around Hy and went through a door toward the front of the train.

"So where the hell were you?" Hy was flushed, stony-faced, and it shocked me. I'd only seen him like that once, years before, when I'd wanted to run into the scene of an imminent explosion to rescue its perpetrator, and he'd accused me of having a death wish.

"Following up on a lead," I said defensively.

"You couldn't call?"

"I tried around five after eleven; you didn't answer."

"That's because I was busy trying to get Ricky and Rae into the limo before his fans dismembered them. You could've tried again, you know." His eyes were narrowed, flashing angry signals I'd never expected to see directed at me. This was about something more than my failure to phone.

"Look," I said, "I'm sorry."

"Sorry doesn't cut it."

I told myself it wasn't worth arguing over. I told myself that we needed to be able to work as a team tonight. But then all the tension and anxiety of the past six days boiled over and I snapped. "What am I, anyway? Your employee?"

He went white around the lips. "No," he said, his voice shaking with restrained rage, "I'm *your* employee on this particular job, and I'll tell you this—you'd better learn to treat the people who work for you with more consideration." Then he turned and started up the staircase.

"Where the hell're you going?"

"Back to my bodyguarding duties. In case you haven't figured it out, we've—you've—got a client who's badly shaken up and doing his best to carry on in spite of it."

"He saw the banner?"

"How could he miss it?" Hy disappeared around the bend of the staircase.

I remained where I was, pressing my hands and body flat against the wall. The train was moving now in a gentle rocking motion. I closed my eyes, thinking, Jesus, what was that *about?*

I knew Hy didn't enjoy security work, had only taken on the job as a favor to me. When I'd contracted with RKI to protect Ricky, I hadn't envisioned my lover in such a hands-on capacity, and I'd also underestimated the magnitude of the threat. Hy had every reason to chafe. But I didn't think that was what had fueled his outburst; this felt like something more fundamental.

Something along the strong-man versus strong-woman

line? Years ago I'd had that problem with a homicide lieutenant I'd been seeing. But Hy liked strong women; he delighted in my independence, just as I delighted in his. When we worked together we worked as a team, each supporting the other when necessary. So where was this anger coming from? And why couldn't I read him, as I almost always did?

As the train picked up speed I wondered if maybe I didn't know my lover as well as I'd thought I did.

Well, I told myself, that wasn't something I could concern myself with now. I had any number of more pressing tasks—the first being to find Ricky and make sure he was okay. I pushed away from the wall, climbed the stairway to the upper level, and went through the door to the lounge car.

It was gray, with modular furnishings facing large windows that were now black mirrors reflecting the festive scene. People in casual clothing—many wearing the *Midnight Train* tee—were talking and drinking and eating; most were standing, but some leaned or sat on the chairs and tables. A bar was set up in the center of the car, flanked by two buffets. The scent of marijuana drifted on the filtered air. I spotted Forrest Curtin chatting with a young woman in western wear; the bass player looked coked-up again. Norm O'Dell and Jerry Jackson sprawled on chairs; both were downing beer at a fast clip. Kurt Girdwood stood at the far end, in intense conversation with Linda Toole; every now and then the manager would run his hand over his bullet head, and the publicist would respond by pushing her fingers through her spiky hair. Pete Sherman leaned alone against a window, his reflected face pale and pensive, his thoughts probably on home. Finally I located Ricky, surrounded by a circle of media people; Hy and a bodyguard stood nearby.

My brother-in-law seemed relaxed and in good spirits. He smiled at something a tall dark-haired woman said to him, tossed back half of a drink that looked to be straight whiskey, burst into laughter at a comment from a pudgy man in shorts. Only someone who knew him as well as I would have noticed the tension in the way he held his head and the set of his shoulders, in the way his fingers played with the glass. His gaze slipped away from the people around him, moved to his reflected image in the opposite window, grew bleak and empty.

On the midnight train to nowhere it's as cold as it can be

In the window I see darkness and a face that can't be me . . . .

The lyrics playing in my head—and most likely in his—put a chill on me. I pushed toward him through the crowd.

"Shar! You made it after all." He introduced me to the people around him and offered me a sip of his drink. Whiskey, all right—bourbon, and straight. On the other side of him Hy turned away, not dealing with me.

"The concert went well?" I asked.

"Fantastic. And we're not blacked out on KZLA anymore."

"I saw the banner. And I like your tee." I plucked at the sleeve of the black shirt with silver lettering and graphics.

"Nice, isn't it?" For a moment his eyes clouded, and I knew he was thinking of Rae, missing her.

The man in shorts, who was from *Country Weekly*, began to ask questions about Ricky's public relations team. I tuned him out and stared at our reflections. They were superimposed upon lights that shone from buildings outside; silver Amtrak cars on a siding flashed past, then vanished, and the night seemed darker and colder.

302

I took Ricky's glass and sipped again to warm up, then excused myself and moved around him toward Hy. The train lurched, throwing me against him.

He steadied me, his eyes cool and overly polite. "Sorry about earlier," he said. "We can't afford to fight. But when this is over, we're going to have to talk."

His last words set off a pang of anxiety under my breastbone, but I only nodded. We *couldn't* afford any disagreements now—nor could we take time to hash things out. I said, "I should brief you—"

A cheer went up at either end of the car. I looked around, saw that TV sets mounted on the walls had been turned on. They were obviously on closed-circuit because a hand-lettered sign had appeared: Radio KMF-LA Ends Blackout! "Midnight Train" Aired at Midnight!

The sign disappeared and immediately a tape of Ricky getting out of the limo in front of Union Station began playing. I watched with interest as he held up his hands for quiet, answered questions, then grew silent, a conflicted expression on his face as the reporters asked about Rae. When he turned and helped her out of the car, I glanced at Hy, raising my eyebrows. He nodded, watching as intensely as if he hadn't already witnessed the scene.

Ricky laughed and joked with the media people, fielding what I considered outrageously personal questions; Rae stood in the circle of his arm, her apparent nervousness and confusion making her vulnerable and appealing. She looked up at him, and he said something that made her flush with pleasure. Then he helped her back into the car, putting a hand on her head so she wouldn't bump it.

Again I glanced at Hy. He had an odd expression on his face—regretful and somewhat melancholy.

"What?" I asked.

303

He shook his head. "Nothing. Watch this."

The scene had shifted inside the station. A crowd surged against the security guards as they shepherded Ricky and the tour party down the main concourse. The camera followed, panned each banner as they passed beneath it, then returned to them. In the final shot, Ricky stopped walking and stared upward. Hy grabbed his arm and forced him on, his jaw set. To one side I spotted Linda Toole, pointing to the banner and yelling at a station security guard. The camera panned the gate to the trains and recorded the party passing through. Almost immediately a second video—of the concert—began playing.

I touched Hy's arm, standing on tiptoe so he could hear me above the music. "Did Toole find out how the banner got there?"

"No, but she's working on it. The last time I talked to her she'd just gotten off the phone with Amtrak's PR director. Got him out of bed and gave him hell. He promised to check on it."

"Listen, can we go someplace quiet so I can brief you on new developments?"

"Maybe later, when things wind down some. I figure most've these party animals'll crash in their sleeping compartments around two, two-thirty. Then I'll feel more comfortable about leaving Ricky with a couple of the guards."

"Just make sure they keep the band members at a distance."

"You still convinced there's an insider?"

"More than ever. By the way, have you seen Rattray?"

"Yeah. The first car's reserved for tour personnel, and he's holed up there, sulking. Toole handed him a bottle as soon as he got on board, told him not to set foot in this car. She doesn't want him stepping on any media toes, and I don't blame her. Rats isn't exactly Mr. Congeniality."

I smiled faintly. "I think I'll wander up there and talk with him. Join me when you get the chance, okay?"

He nodded and turned away.

I weaved through the car, apologizing now and then when the train's motion threw me against someone. In between cars the sway and bounce was more intense, making me feel as if I were walking over earthquake-rippled ground. I passed through two cars containing compartments that looked more like phone booths than sleeping rooms, then reached a third where they were more spacious—if spacious was taken as a relative term. At its far end I could hear Kurt Girdwood bellowing loud enough to raise the dead.

"No, Toole, you do *not* need to know the significance of that banner! Stick to your job and keep the press happy. I'll worry about our star."

Toole raised her own voice—probably in self-defense. "How the hell can I keep the press happy with all this *weirdness* going on? There's one security guard for every five people, and Rick's, like, completely bent out of shape."

"He's doing fine."

"Bull*shit!* That thing he pulled at the station—I work for days to correct his image, and then he drags that bimbo out of the car."

"Dragging that bimbo out of the car may've saved his ass. Did you see her? She looked pretty and innocent—although if she's with Rick, she can't possibly be the latter. But it seemed a genuine love match."

"I thought you were dead set against it. You told him he was thinking with his balls."

"And he is. But he loves her, Toole. Or he thinks he

does, which is damn near the same thing. You can't fight it."

After a moment Linda Toole sighed. "Okay, whatever. I'm gonna call that prick at Amtrak again."

I began walking, checking out the compartments. In the center one, Virgil Rattray slumped spinelessly next to the window. The lights were out, but I could see the bottle in his hand. When I stepped inside, he turned his head and his eyes glittered, reflecting the high beams of a car at a crossing.

I asked, "Can we talk?"

He raised the bottle to his lips, drank, and motioned at the seat opposite him. I sat, my knees so close to his that they touched when the car swayed.

"You been banished, too?" he asked.

"Sort of."

"Story of my life. Not that I mind. I hate big crowds of assholes sucking up to each other."

I glanced out the window. We were passing through a town, but I could make out little of it. "Where d'you suppose we are?"

He looked at the luminous dial of his watch. "Someplace outside of San Berdoo. Pomona, maybe."

"Still a long way to go."

"Yeah."

"Rats, I was talking with Ethan Amory earlier."

"Good for you."

"It occurred to me that you must notice everything that goes on at a concert."

"Damn right I do. Take notes on it, too. That's my job."

"At the one in Sonoma County on Friday—did you arrange for a limo for the band members, or did they provide their own transportation?"

"No limo that night." He frowned, thinking. "Norm and Pete had their own trucks. I think Norm and his lady

306

took a few vacation days beforehand, maybe up the coast. Pete, he just likes to drive. Jer and Forrest flew; they had a rental car, did some wine tasting the day before. Why d'you ask?"

"Just filling in some blanks. Did you actually see any of them leave the concert?"

"Nope. What happens afterward isn't my business."

"But you made what Ricky did afterward your business."

"What the hell does that mean?"

"You told Ethan about Ricky dedicating 'The House Where Love Once Lived' to my sister. And about him leaving with Rae."

"So? There's a law against that?"

"Did you know how he'd use the information?"

"Didn't know, and didn't care. Amory pays me to keep him informed on Rick's activities, and I can use the cash." Rats tipped the bottle and drank.

I asked, "What do you remember about Patricia Terriss?"

Abruptly he lowered the bottle, spilling liquor on his chin. We were at another crossing, one with flashing lights, and his eyes shone red. "Who?"

"Patricia Terriss. Austin, Texas, three years ago this past spring. Ricky did a concert there, and afterward you all went out to a place called the Sunset Lodge, where she was singing. He picked her up and took her along to Houston and Dallas."

"Oh yeah, that one. Hard to keep all of them straight."

"Well?"

He set the bottle between his thighs, fumbled in his shirt pocket and took out a joint. Rattray, I now noticed, was the only member of the tour group who wasn't wearing a *Midnight Train* tee. A match flared, and the pungent smoke drifted toward me.

"Well?" I asked again.

"Well, what? Rick got lucky that night. She was one pretty lady."

"He wasn't so lucky. She followed him to the coast afterward and made his life hell."

Rattray didn't respond.

"Or maybe you knew that," I added. It was a wild shot, but it hit on target; the road manager stiffened, moving his knees away from mine. "You did know," I said.

". . . Okay, so what if I did? And so what if she made his life hell? I'm sick and tired of people like Rick who get all the breaks and screw everybody over and never have to pay the price. That Patricia was a pretty lady and he hurt her bad. He made her promises he had no intention of keeping."

I thought of Terriss's habit of leaning on the men she knew for whatever she needed, and made another guess. "Did she come to you when he wouldn't deal with her?"

Rattray took another hit off the joint. "So what if she did?"

"Did you sleep with her?"

"Me?"

The single syllable was poignant. I waited.

He added, "Nobody like that would ever sleep with me."

"So what did you do?"

"I let her cry on my shoulder. Just let her cry." My face must have reflected my disbelief; Rattray misinterpreted its source, though. "You think I can't comfort a crying woman?"

"I didn't say that."

"You didn't have to; I've got eyes. You think I don't have feelings? That I can't care for somebody? Oh, sure, I'm just Rats—the mean son of a bitch with the foul

308

mouth. Well, maybe I got cause. You think it's easy being me?"

"I guess not."

"Damn right it isn't! Rick, he's always carrying on about how tough he's got it. Well, news flash—other people in this rotten business got it tough, too. Me, I got all these roadies on my hands, and half of them're dumb as posts, and the other half're scrambling for position— *my* position. I got that cocksucker of a manager of his screaming at me so loud I'm like to go deaf one of these days. I got promoters and his booking agent and the security people at the concert venues, and they all want something. The guitar and drum techs're a total pain in the ass, and the lighting guys go artistic on me all the time. Then there's the transportation that never shows up when it's supposed to, and the hotel reservations that disappear right before we get there. I work my butt off twenty hours a day when we're on the road, catch a few z's on the plane, then wake up and do it all over again. And you know what the hell of it is?"

I shook my head, fascinated by this outburst.

"When everything's said and done, the only guy who gives me credit is your fuckin' brother-in-law, and I hate his guts!"

"Why?"

"Why do I hate him? Because of what he does to people."

"People like Patricia Terriss."

"So we're back to her. Okay, you want to know about her and me? I'll tell you. He flat-out rejected her, hurt her bad. So she called me. We talked. She was my *friend*. She even stayed with me once when she had no place else to go. She said I was the first real friend she'd ever had."

Of course she'd told him that. Terriss instinctively

knew how to play others in order to get what she wanted. "And?" I asked.

"Yeah, I know what you're getting at. Okay, I gave her his phone numbers and address. And you know what? I'd do it again."

"Did you know she was planning to harass him? Did you know she was planning to threaten his children?"

"She'd never've done that. She just wanted to get him back."

"She never had him in the first place."

Rattray was silent. "I guess not," he said after a moment. "People like Rick, they can't belong to anybody."

But he was wrong there. In his way, Ricky had belonged to my sister for eighteen years. Belonged to his children, and always would. Belonged to Rae now, with a sureness that had grown swiftly and strongly. People like Ricky had to belong to someone, because there was a piece missing inside of them that only a person who cared could supply. Rattray wouldn't understand that, though, so I pressed on with my questions.

"When did you give her the numbers and address?"

"The office number, about two weeks after we got back from Texas. The house one, a few weeks later. The address, a while after that."

"And when did you last see her?"

"Middle of June, we had lunch. She called once after that, though, toward the end of the month. She said Rick was going to come back to her. She sounded . . . happy." He spoke the last word as if it was foreign to his vocabulary. "It didn't work out, though, and I never heard from her again."

Rattray relighted his joint. I had nothing more to ask or to say to him, so we sat in silence. Around San Bernardino the train began climbing through the mountains. At first the tracks paralleled the freeway, and the lights of night-crawling semis glanced off the window; then we curved away into blackness so total that it seemed we'd left the world behind. I'd resigned myself to seeing nothing till we got to our destination, when the tracks or the freeway—or maybe both—took a different tack and reconnected. Diverged and reconnected again and again as we climbed.

I watched the shifting pattern of light and darkness. Thought how deceptive it was. Thought, too, how much it was like my relationship with Hy. Just when I'd believed we were moving in close parallel lines, I'd found we were actually veering in different directions. Veering off into nothingness, perhaps.

He never came to the compartment as he'd promised. Eventually I fell asleep and didn't wake till Ricky shook me and said that Rae had never arrived at San Francisco Airport.

RAE'S DIARY:
5:07 A.M., PDT

Airports are totally depressing places in the wee hours of the morning, and LAX is even more so than your average. You expect hustle and glitz when in Los Angeles; it's more or less required of the city, if it wants to hang on to its image. But empty baggage carousels, a scattering of bleary-eyed people, and half-asleep employees at the rental-car counters don't do it. At least Hertz was open, though, and more than glad to offload one of their compacts on me.

By now it was after six in New Mexico, and Ricky should be at the hotel. Would have called Shar's house around three like he'd promised and realized I wasn't there. And would be seriously worried.

311

I should have phoned his cellular from the limo as soon as I changed my mind about taking the flight he'd chartered for me, but I knew he'd be boarding the train and caught up in the press party. And later I remembered that he'd loaned the cell phone to Shar, so I couldn't reach him anyway. Shar was the absolute last person I wanted to talk to, because she'd yell at me for continuing to investigate after she'd called me off the case. But I couldn't stop now, not till I knew the truth.

Truth. She and I share this crazy-making obsession with it. It's nearly been the death of her in the past, and the way my life's going, it's likely to be the death of me in the future. Can't help it, though; it's something I was born with, along with freckles and a tendency toward chubby thighs.

Anyway, while I was at the Century Plaza, I should have tried to get hold of somebody—Hy or maybe Kurt Girdwood—to pass along a message to Ricky. But I'd gotten so caught up in my research into Mick's files that I just plain forgot. And then, when I hadn't come up with anything there, I'd been in a hurry to get going. Now the clerk's computer was taking a long time to do its stuff, so I might as well take advantage of the delay.

I excused myself and went over to the phones. I had scrawled the number for the Hyatt Regency in my notebook, and I found the page while shoving my calling card into the phone with my other hand.

The Midnight *tour hadn't checked in yet, the desk told me.*

Damn! I left a voice-mail message for Ricky, just saying I was okay, had had a change of plans, and would get back to him later. Then I hurried to the counter, signed and initialed the rental agreement, and went out to the curb to wait for the shuttle bus

As I stood there I crossed my fingers and tried to cross

*my toes. The information in Jenny Gordon's fax could
lead to the break we needed to put this whole mess behind
us—the break Ricky and I needed so we could get on with
our life together.*

*I closed my eyes, picturing his face when he'd looked
down at me in front of Union Station and said, "I love
you, Red." Opened them and saw the bus was there.*

Twenty-three

7:03 A.M., Mountain Daylight Time

> The City of Albuquerque and Country Radio KRST welcome the *Midnight Train to Nowhere* tour... You're not blacked out in New Mexico!

The words trailed along on a monitor in the center of the nearly deserted ticket lobby at the airport. A couple of the band members cheered and some people clapped, but Ricky barely seemed to notice. Our flight had been late leaving Barstow, and he was both exhausted and preoccupied with worry about Rae.

He'd tried to call her at my house at three, but there had been no answer; he then checked with the service that was supposed to pick her up at SFO and found her flight had never arrived. After he woke me, I got on to the air-charter company; they said the L.A. limo driver had canceled the flight at Rae's request. The limo service had no record of where the driver had dropped her, and refused to give me his home number. I asked if they would check with him and get back to me. They resisted, so I put Ricky on; he reminded them that his label was a major customer and would be forced to find a different service if they didn't cooperate. We were arriving in Barstow by then and, since cellular units can't be used while airborne, he asked them to leave a message at the hotel in Albuquerque. Now he was anxious to get there and check his voice mail.

Fortunately, the transportation worked smoothly on this end, and we were soon at the Hyatt Regency—some twenty stories of pebbled granite and marble, with a palm-filled atrium in the center of its lobby. As we waited for our room keys, I studied the palms, wondering if they actually were alive; ever since a friend told me that the very lifelike palms in Orange County's John Wayne Airport are embalmed, I've viewed all indoor trees with suspicion. My contemplation gave me a good excuse to avoid dealing with Hy, who had acted increasingly distant on the plane.

Ricky came away from the desk looking semi-relieved. "The clerk says I've got a number of voice-mail messages; I'm hoping one's from Red."

"I'll come to your suite while you check them out."

Hy joined us, handing me my key card. "I'd better come too, make sure the room's secure."

We went to the elevators and rode in silence to the top floor with Forrest Curtin, Pete Sherman, and Kurt Girdwood. The party was long over; everyone was tired and looking forward to getting some sleep. We separated in the hallway, the three of them going to the left, the three of us to the right. Guards from RKI's nearest office, in Phoenix, were already in place at the entrances to the wings.

Ricky went straight to the phone in his sitting room, while I collapsed on a chair and Hy checked out the adjoining bedroom. My brother-in-law accessed his voice mail and began jotting things down on a note pad. A couple of times he grimaced and shook his head, then his face softened and an expression of longing stole over it. He replayed the last message and replaced the receiver.

"Well, she called at a little after six—five, California time. She says she's okay, has had a change of plans, and will get back to me later."

"Not terribly forthcoming."

"No, but at least she's all right."

"Anything from the limo service?"

"The driver's home number; he's willing to talk with us anytime. You want to call him?"

I nodded and picked up an extension phone on the table beside me. As I dialed the number he'd circled on the pad, Hy came out of the bedroom, gave us a thumbs-up sign, and sat on the sofa. Ricky paced while I spoke with the driver.

"Lady asked me to cancel her flight to SFO," he said. "I dropped her at the Tower at Century Plaza around one o'clock."

"Did she make any calls from the car?"

"None."

"How did she seem?"

"You mean, was she all right? I guess so. She was kind of upset when we left Union Station, cried a little. Then she got real quiet. But when I dropped her at the hotel she acted more cheerful."

I thanked him and placed a call to Mick.

"Yeah," his sleepy voice said, "she showed up asking to access my files on the investigation."

"Let me talk to her."

"She's not here."

"When did she leave?"

316

"Damned if I know. I went back to bed and didn't even realize she was gone till now."

"Did she mention what information she was after?"

"No. She said she wanted to go over all the files. I asked her why, when you'd taken her off the case, and she gave me that look. You know the one."

I knew. When crossed, Rae would wither her opponent with a fiery glare.

My next call was to the desk of the Century Plaza. The clerk told me Rae had ordered a taxi to take her to LAX around four-thirty.

"Where the hell would she go?" Ricky asked when I relayed the information.

"I haven't a clue."

He sat on the sofa and began pulling off his boots. "What in God's name d'you suppose she's up to?"

"I suspect she's working some lead."

"Dammit! You took her off the investigation."

"I think you'd better get used to the fact that when she wants to do something, nobody—including you—can stop her."

"We'll see about that." But he didn't look too sanguine about his prospects.

I glanced at Hy. He was watching me, his gaze coldly analytical. I'd seen that look most recently when he was trying to determine the cause of a power loss in the starboard engine of a Beechcraft we'd rented; I didn't like him applying it to me.

Ricky said, "Where would she have gotten a lead, anyway? The driver said she didn't use the phone."

I shrugged. "Maybe she remembered something, made some connection. I'll call Mick back, ask him to find out what flights left LAX within an hour of the time she arrived. There couldn't have been many. Then he can check with the airlines to see if she was listed on any of the passenger manifests; if they won't give out the information, he can contact a friend of mine on the SFPD and have her go through official channels to get it."

Ricky nodded, his face falling into weary lines. "The desk is holding all my calls, but I'll ask them to put Red through if she phones again."

Hy said, "You going to be able to sleep?"

"I've got to, so I will. I developed this shut-down mechanism back when I toured by bus. I'd hit the bunk in one of those customized diesels and I'd be out right quick." He shook his head. "I'll tell you, I'm glad I don't have to travel that way anymore. It's a young man's game—a young man who's hungry and on the way up. Even this kind of tour's no picnic."

"You sound like you're thinking of cutting back on the travel."

"Maybe, if I can get the redhead safely home and keep her there. Something about that woman makes me look fondly upon evenings in front of the fireplace, without the noise and neon lights."

Hy and I exchanged glances. While Rae didn't share our addiction to dangerous situations, there was a restlessness in her that couldn't be tamed. And as for getting her home safely—we couldn't hope to accomplish that till we knew where she was.

Hy yawned widely as we walked down the hall to our room. I, on the other hand, felt alert and edgy about being alone with him. His moods were unpredictable at best, and the last thing I needed at this point was a confrontation.

He fit the key card into the slot and silently motioned me inside. Our bags had been delivered; I took my toiletry kit out, went into the bathroom, and shut the door. Through it I could hear him prowling around the room as he always did when arriving at a hotel: the closet door opened; the draperies closed; the TV came on and went off. When I emerged he was removing his shaving kit from his duffel.

He said, "I left a wake-up call for two; at three I'll go over to the fairgrounds and check out the coliseum."

I sat down on the bed and untied my athletic shoes. "Okay if I tag along?"

"Whatever." He disappeared into the bathroom.

His curtness stung me. I shrugged, shed my clothes, and slipped under the covers. When Hy joined me a few minutes later, he simply said, "Sleep well," and turned his back to me, hugging his pillow. Soon his breathing became deep and regular.

Well, I thought with some irritation, whatever's bothering him may be keeping me on edge, but it certainly isn't interfering with *his* ability to sleep.

RAE'S DIARY:
8:06 A.M., PDT

Sleep.

By the time I passed Santa Maria, where I'd been born and raised, I was wishing I'd gotten some. I should've curled up on the couch in Mick's hotel room, but I'd been so anxious to get started for Paso Robles that I hadn't even considered it. If I'd been able to fly I could've napped on the plane, but by the time anything was leaving LAX for anyplace near the little town at the southern tip of the Salinas Valley, I could have already arrived there by car. Besides, flying was impractical; this spiffy little rental would take me anyplace I needed to get to. No way I was going to leave myself to the mercy of airline schedules.

Basically, I'm a car person—that type the environmen-

319

talists despair of. I'm always poking along in the jammed-up part of the freeway while the civic-minded zoom down the car-pool lane. I love the freedom a car gives me, and I love to drive—although you'd never know it if you saw the Ramblin' Wreck, my ancient and ailing Rambler American. And although I pretended otherwise, secretly I loved Ricky's Porsche, even if it had turned me into an asshole driver on the way back from Arizona.

Ricky . . .

I'd be in Paso Robles by nine-thirty. I'd call him then.

"I couldn't have been going that fast, officer!"

"I clocked you at eighty-six."

"Trucks were passing me."

He kept on writing out the ticket.

"Those trucks're the real menace, you know. Why don't you guys pick on them for a change?"

Stern look.

"I didn't mean . . . Look, this is a rental car. At home I drive an old Rambler that would fall apart if I went over fifty. I thought I was going the speed limit."

"Sign here, please."

I considered pouting—prettily, of course—or maybe letting a tiny tear fall. Then I decided it was a cheap trick, signed the ticket, and pulled into traffic at a sedate fifty-five.

God, that Porsche had ruined me! I'd been driving like an asshole in a Ford Probe!

Paso Robles is one of those little towns that make you wonder why they're there. At least you do until you grasp the fact that it serves the surrounding agricultural community, as well as sits at the intersection of north-south Highway 101 and 166 from Bakersfield. Its main street roughly parallels 101 and is loaded with motels, my fa-

vorite being the Marianna because the first time I saw it I misinterpreted its sign to read "Motel Marijuana."

My destination was a pink-stucco house on a western side street, the third in a long row of identical bungalows that made me think of a lumber-company town I'd once driven through south of Eureka. It was the address that Patricia Terriss had listed five years ago on her Austin gynecologist's records, for her nearest relative—a sister, Veronica Keel. How Jenny Gordon had pried that information loose was a mystery to me, doctors being the most closemouthed of individuals. Terriss hadn't provided a phone number, and when I called Information there was none listed, so a personal visit seemed in order.

Besides, one of the first things Shar taught me was the axiom that if you don't know what sort of situation you might encounter, it's best to just show up and let the element of surprise work in your favor.

The man who came to the door was old and frail. He peered myopically at me through the screen. No, he said, Mrs. Keel didn't live there anymore. He'd bought the house in a foreclosure sale four years ago.

"Do you know her current address?"

He cupped his hand to his ear. I repeated the question more loudly.

"Oh, address. No. She might've gone to live with relatives after the accident."

"What accident?"

"Bad smashup out on the highway. She and her husband, they owned a big rig, were almost home from a long haul. He fell asleep, was killed. She ended up paralyzed."

I'd told the highway-patrol guy that truckers were the real menace. Too damn many of them are either hopped up on speed and driving like lunatics or coming down and falling asleep. "D'you know anybody who might've kept in touch with Mrs. Keel?"

"Sorry, I don't."

So what now? Canvass the neighbors. No—first find a phone, call Ricky, then get a cup of coffee. No—breakfast. I was starving.

The Hyatt Regency wouldn't put me through to Mr. Savage. He'd given strict orders to hold all calls, but I could leave a voice-mail message, if I liked. I thought about raising hell, but what good would that do? Besides, he needed his sleep if he was to perform well tonight. I left basically the same message as before: I was okay, was following up on a promising lead, and would get back to him. Then I went to the coffee-shop booth where the waitress was just delivering my breakfast and tore into a stack of pancakes drowned in butter and maple syrup.

When Shar is frustrated or upset she loses her appetite— which has always struck me as grossly unfair, since she never gains an ounce, no matter what gastronomic atrocities she commits. I, on the other hand, stuff my face and then pay for it by extra poundage and long workouts at the gym. I'd surely pay for today, because not only was I frustrated but—now—upset and a little hurt.

I understood why Ricky had his calls held before a concert. He'd done the same yesterday in L.A. But couldn't he have asked them to put mine through? Didn't he want to hear my voice, as he'd said he did every time he called during the desperately unhappy weekend when he realized his marriage had come unraveled?

Well, maybe he had faith in my ability to take care of myself. Maybe he knew that when I said I was okay, I really was.

No, I thought, adding more syrup to what was left of the stack, blasé wasn't his style when it came to the people he *cared for. And he'd admitted to a protective feeling toward me, which I didn't mind, because nobody had ever wanted to look out for me before, not even when I was a little girl. When you feel that way about the woman you love, you don't have her calls held and just go to sleep.*

The woman he loved . . .

I'd phone him again before he had to go to the coliseum to run his sound checks.

Twenty-four

The phone was ringing. Loudly.

Hy mumbled something, grabbed for it, knocked it off the nightstand.

"Goddamn it to hell!"

I winced. It was going to be a long afternoon and evening.

"Hello! . . . Yes, she's right here."

With the heavy draperies closed I could barely see his hand as he extended the receiver. Our fingers collided and the ring he wore grazed me.

"Ow! Dammit!"

He sighed. "Sorry." He must've also thought it was going to be a long afternoon and evening.

"Hello?"

"Shar, what's going on there?" Mick.

"Don't ask. What have you got?"

"She didn't fly anyplace. She rented a car at LAX. Hertz."

"What did she give as her contact address?"

"Here at the hotel."

"Damn. Look, Mick, she didn't by any chance make any notes while she was using your computer?"

"I already checked—no."

"Well, thanks." I peered at the digital clock on the nightstand. "You heading up to Tahoe soon?"

"I'm packed and about to leave."

"Give my love to the family. I'll see you when . . . when this is all over."

Hy had gone into the bathroom. He came out, got back in bed. "We could've slept nearly another hour," he said wistfully.

"I know." I told him what Mick had found out.

"You know," he said, "sometimes Rae can be a pain in the ass."

I restrained myself from saying that sometimes he could too, and went into the bathroom myself. When I came back he had the bedside lamp on and was talking on the phone. He held out the receiver. "Ricky."

"Hi, what's happening?"

"She called again, but the desk screwed up and didn't put her through. Same message—except this time she said she was following up on a promising lead."

"I suspected as much. What time did the message come in?"

"Eleven-twenty—ten-twenty at home, if that's where she is."

"Well, wherever she is, at least she's okay."

"She better be." His voice grew ragged with emotion. "I don't think I could take it if anything happened to her. A person can stand only so much loss."

"You're not going to lose her."

325

We talked a moment more, then I gave the receiver back to Hy and propped myself against the pillows. He hung it up and did the same. For a while we lay there without speaking.

Always before we'd had such a strong, close connection that we often didn't have to speak to know what was on the other's mind. But today I couldn't fathom his thoughts—only sensed that he was disturbed and a little sad, turning inward in a way that he hadn't for quite some time. Finally I took his long-fingered hand. He didn't pull away.

The phone rang again.

He sighed and disentangled his fingers, leaned over and picked up. "Yes? . . . Yes, she is." He handed the receiver to me. "Jenny Gordon, in Austin."

"Hi, Jenny."

"Hi, did ya'll get my fax?"

"What fax?"

"About Terriss's sister. I sent it to your hotel in L.A. late yesterday afternoon."

"It must not've gotten delivered."

"Well, Terriss gave her doctor here the name of a sister as next of kin not living with her, lady in Paso Robles, California." She gave me the details and I wrote them down.

"How'd you get a doctor to give you information about a patient?"

In a sultry voice she replied, "I've got my ways." Then she added, "Actually, he's a poker buddy."

"Well, thanks. Did you come up with any connection between Terriss and Curtin?"

"Nothing more than them both performing at the lodge. They knew each other, but people I talked with said it was no big thing."

"Listen, I've got a Nashville phone number for that Tod Dodson, but he hasn't returned my call."

"I'll see what I can do." She took down the number and hung up.

Hy had placed the phone on the bed between us. I put the receiver into its cradle and told him what Jenny had said.

When I finished, he stroked his mustache thoughtfully. "That hotel's pretty good about delivering faxes. Wonder if Jenny's found its way to somebody else."

"Rae?"

He nodded.

"Would she withhold it from me?"

"Who knows what she'd do these days? A week ago I wouldn't've expected to see her holding hands with your brother-in-law on the front page of the *Insider*."

"Or facing down that crowd at Union Station. You know—"

The phone rang again. Charlotte Keim. "Hey, there. I've dug up a report from Richman Labs from the pile that's burying your desk; it's about some kind of plant, and the case number is for Savage."

The analysis on the Carolina jessamine. "What does it say?"

" 'Sample is *Gelsemium sempervirens,* commonly known as Carolina jessamine. Due to flowering cycle (late winter to early spring), it can be assumed to have been hothouse grown. Evidence of frost damage throughout.' That's it."

"*Frost* damage?"

"Yeah. Weird, huh?"

Not so weird, if you considered that the heat in the Two Rock Valley had been intense the night of the concert. Whoever had placed the jessamine in Ricky's trailer had probably kept it fresh in a cooler.

Keim and I discussed a few more of the items on my desk, and she agreed to take care of them. I'd just hung up when the phone rang yet another time.

"Jesus!" Hy exclaimed. "I feel like we're running a bookmaking joint here!"

I answered. Linda Toole. "I'm getting to the bottom of this thing with the banner, and I don't like it one bit. The Amtrak representative who received it swears up and down that it was in the package with *our* banner."

"Interesting. Who packaged yours?"

"Well, I picked it up at the printer's; it was a rush job, and I was worried it wouldn't get delivered on time. I took it to the office, gave it to the receptionist, and told her to have it messengered over to Amtrak."

From yesterday's visit to Ethan Amory, I could picture that reception area: large and open, with easy access from both the hallway and the inside offices. "Who was around there at the time?"

"Well, Ethan. Kurt. Pete, Norm, and Forrest. Rats."

"What were Rats and the band members doing there?"

"Picking up cash for incidentals while on tour."

"Anybody else?"

"My assistant. Rick's secretary. Ethan's secretary. Other office support staff."

"You ask the receptionist about this?"

"Uh-uh. She's taking a couple of vacation days, and I can't reach her."

"Damn! Well, keep trying."

As I hung up, Hy gave the phone an evil look. "We might as well get up," he said. "That thing isn't going to quit."

"No, wait a few minutes. I want to tell you what Toole found out—as well as what I found out yesterday. You never did give me the chance to brief you."

"Sorry about that. I wasn't in a very good mood last night."

I waited, but he didn't elaborate, so I launched into my lengthy account. When I finished he was silent for a moment.

"Terriss's killing the boyfriend's fish was a nasty symbolic act," he finally said.

"A nasty indicator of her mental state then—and a nastier indicator of what it might be now."

"And of what she might do. You know, McCone, I think you were right in what you said yesterday morning—we'd better be prepared for something very, very grim on Saturday night in Austin."

RAE'S DIARY:
1:18 P.M., PDT

"Austin?" the records clerk at Sierra Vista Medical Center said. "No, she didn't go there after she was discharged."

"But you won't tell me where she did go?"

"Our patient records are confidential, Ms. Kelleher. I've already told you more than I should."

"If I were a police officer, would you tell me?"

"I'd have to check with my supervisor on that, but he's out of town, and since you're not an officer anyway—"

"I know." I left the office, followed the arrows on the floor to the lobby, and went out into the early-afternoon sunlight. The heat was godawful here, and even though I'd changed into a sleeveless shirt in the rest room of the coffee shop, I was about to melt into a tired little puddle.

And I was fresh out of leads.

One of Veronica Keel's former neighbors had told me that after the accident she'd been taken to the trauma unit at Sierra Vista, so I'd zoomed down here, sure I could get the address I needed. But I'd forgotten how prickly hospital administrators can be, and now I was at a dead end. Or was I?

I went back into the air-conditioned chill of the hospital and found a phone booth. In my address book I located the SFPD number for Adah Joslyn, Shar's friend on Homicide. But Adah wasn't there; she'd gone to Mexico on vacation.

Did I wish to speak to anyone else? Immediately Greg Marcus, Shar's former boyfriend and a captain on Narcotics, came to mind. I asked for him, the Homicide guy transferred me, and I was told Greg was off duty. I had his home number, but I couldn't bring myself to call him. Greg thinks I'm a ditz, and his condescending manner always sets me off; the last time had been two weeks ago, when I called him a chauvinist porker. You don't ask somebody you're barely speaking to to use his official status to extract information from a hospital-records clerk— especially on his day off.

Another dead end.

Think, Rae. Think about what you know about Veronica Keel.

Okay, she and her husband owned their big rig. They were independent truckers, probably a driving team. Not an easy life: You've got no union, no benefits; you've got big payments on the truck, lots of repair and mainte- nance bills.

Repairs and maintenance . . .

I opened the Yellow Pages. The listing under "Truck" in the index was nearly a column long. In addition to buy- ing trucks and their various components, you could have them lettered, painted, pooled (whatever that was), steam cleaned, washed, weighed, and wrecked (which was what eventually happened to the Keels's).

I took a look at the long listing under "Truck Equipment, Parts, and Accessories," said, "Damn!" and shut the directory. It would take me a week to contact all of them and ask if they knew anything about Veronica Keel's present whereabouts.

Now, wait a minute, Rae. What else do you know about truckers?

They eat at truck stops. They probably take a lot of Rolaids. They talk on CB radios. They drink too much coffee. Some of them take uppers. They have hemorrhoids. They probably listen to Ricky Savage songs.

Ricky . . .

Concentrate, Rae. Okay, a trucker's life is rough. You're out there on the road alone all the time. If you're an independent, you're really alone. Nobody to fall back on but yourself. Sort of like independent private investigators, come to think of it, or even small-agency owners like Shar and Jenny Gordon.

So what do they do?

They join organizations and bitch a lot about how they get stuck paying for their own health insurance.

I opened the directory again and looked up "Organizations." Turned to "Business and Trade."

Central Coast Independent Truckers Association, on Higuera Street.

It was worth a try.

Twenty-five

2:27 P.M., MDT

Can you blame me for being worried?" Ricky asked.

He sat in one of the big leather chairs in the dark-paneled bar off the lobby, wearing shorts and a *Midnight Train* tee, his fingers toying nervously with a glass of beer on the low table between us. Driven from his suite, I thought, by sheer stir-craziness and not even noticing the sidelong glances of the pretty cocktail waitress, who had recognized him. His bodyguards were drinking Cokes at a nearby table.

Hy and I had tracked him down before heading over to the fairgrounds, and I'd taken a few minutes to brief him on what Rae was probably doing. I'd thought it might reassure him some, but instead it made him even more edgy.

"What if this sister is as whacked out as Patricia?" he asked. "What if Patricia's there, for God's sake?"

"Hy and I think she's in Austin, and I doubt Rae'll find

the sister, anyway. I checked, and there's no phone listing for her in Paso Robles; she's probably moved."

"If that's the case, why'd Red go up there? And why hasn't she called again?"

"I don't know. If she does, will the desk remember to put her through?"

His eyes narrowed. "They will now—and they know exactly where to find me."

"Shouldn't you be upstairs getting some rest?"

"Sister Sharon, I couldn't rest if I drank two six-packs of this." He motioned with his glass, sipped.

"Well, try to go easy. When're you supposed to run your sound checks?"

"Five, but maybe I'll go over early."

"See you later, then."

Hy and I went out into the dry, blistering heat; the sky was milky blue and a heat haze blanketed the Sandia Mountains. As we climbed into the RKI van that was waiting in front, he asked, "Is he going to blow his performance tonight?"

"I don't think so; he's always had good control on stage. Of course, he's never been this stressed before. It sure would help if Rae surfaced."

"Especially if she surfaced with a solid lead."

The Tingley Coliseum, where Ricky would be performing, was next to the racetrack on the New Mexico State Fairgrounds. Hy steered the van past an iron-gated main entrance that reminded me of a military base's, explaining, "I want to go in the way the limos will, follow the route they'll take to the east end of the building."

I glanced at him, trying for perhaps the dozenth time that day to assess his mood. He seemed more laid back, but I still felt a remoteness—a tension, too. But why shouldn't he be tense? He'd told me that from the diagrams he'd studied, the coliseum looked to be something of a security risk.

We turned in at a second gate, drove past livestock barns, made a right onto a tree-shaded street lined with low, salmon-colored buildings trimmed in turquoise. The coliseum appeared ahead of us: also salmon, and domed. Numerous wide pipe-railed staircases descended from exit doors on the upper tier, and the bowed-out canopy over the lobby entrance was garnished with chromium trim and bold block letters that spelled its name. Straight out of the fifties, I thought, and proud of it.

Hy parked in a lot across the street and we walked toward the building. When we reached the curb I tugged at his arm and pointed to an oil-pumping rig that stood like a penned dinosaur in a fenced enclosure on the sidewalk. He looked at it and shrugged but didn't display his usual curiosity about incongruous phenomena. His face was set in lines of concentration as we skirted the ticket windows.

Tonight—8:00
RICKY SAVAGE
and
Blue Arkansas

Hy motioned at the sign above the windows, then put his hand on my shoulder and steered me around a couple of pickups and a truck loaded with sound equipment to a wide side entrance. The interior was cool and dim, the arena's floor easily the size of a football field. Tier upon tier of white seats rose behind walls topped with turquoise railings. There was a press box up to our left, and signs advertised Bud, Coors, and 92.3 KRST, New

Mexico Country Radio. I turned, saw bleacher seats on the second tier behind us, as well as at the far end.

Now I knew why Hy was concerned about this venue.

A raised stage had been erected in the center of the floor, and roadies moved about, laying electrical cable. Others were rigging lights on the overhead grid, their voices echoing off the domed ceiling. My gaze moved from them to the stands and swept the oval perimeter. I pictured someone in the topmost row, with a high-powered rifle.

I asked Hy, "What's the seating capacity here?"

"Close to ten thousand, and it's sold out."

"Are they checking for weapons at the door?"

"Uh-huh. It'll slow things down, maybe make for a late start, but it can't be helped."

We started walking toward the stage, stepping over taped-down cables. I motioned at the openings in the walls where stairways descended from the seating area and raised my eyebrows questioningly.

He said, "Two guards on each, with others stationed in between."

Suddenly Virgil Rattray loped down the nearest stairway, clipboard in hand, long locks swaying violently. "That's not right, you idiot!" he yelled, shaking his fist at one of the men on the lighting grid. "Can't you assholes at least *try* to get it right?"

Hy muttered, "Why must Rats always charm the hell out of everybody?"

"He tells me it's not easy being him."

"Being *around* him, maybe."

We went past the stage toward open doors at the far end of the arena. I eyed the bleacher seats there and said, "Better make sure that weapons check is thorough. Where'll you be during the concert?"

"With Ricky all the way from his dressing room to the stage, and there throughout."

"And me?"

"Out of harm's way."

"Ripinsky—"

"I mean it." His tone didn't invite debate. I let it go—for now.

Immediately before the exit, he motioned to our right, and we went into a dim yellow corridor that curved with the shape of the building. A number of doors opened off it; I poked my head through one and saw a dressing room with shabby gray armchairs and brown carpeting.

Hy said, "The band'll be in here and the next room. Blue Arkansas has the smaller ones across the hall. We'll put Ricky farther down where we can control who gets in to see him."

"And that is?"

"You, me, and my people."

"Girdwood, Toole, and Rats aren't going to like that."

"Tough." He stopped walking, looked along the curve of the corridor. "It's not a bad setup, and we're ready for damn near anything. I'll tell you, though: It'd go a hell of a lot easier on everybody if Rae would show up tonight."

RAE'S DIARY:
3:09 P.M., PDT

"Tonight? I can't wait that long. I need to charter a flight to Albuquerque right away!"

The woman behind the desk at SLO Flight Service at San Luis Obispo County Airport shrugged and scratched her bare arm. No sympathy for my predicament there. "Sorry. All our people're gone till then."

I closed my eyes and refigured the driving time to LAX.

It came out the same as before: nearly three hours if traf-fic cooperated, and you knew damn sure it wouldn't. And even if a miracle happened, I'd arrive hours after the next Albuquerque-bound flight left, and hours before the one after that was due to depart.

I must've looked pretty pathetic because the woman said, "I've got an idea. My boyfriend, he just bought this Cessna One-fifty-two, and—"

"No way!" I pictured something tiny with wings, falling fast over the Santa Monica Mountains. Besides, a plane like that would take forever and a day to get to New Mexico.

"Suit yourself." The woman turned her back on me.

She'd given me an idea of my own, though. I went out-side and made for the pay phone I'd spotted on the way in. Dug out my calling card and punched in RKI's La Jolla number. Asked the operator for Dan Kessell.

"Sorry, he's not available at the moment. Can someone else help you?"

Not likely. "This is an emergency."

"Who's calling, please?"

I told him and as an afterthought gave him the security code Ricky had jotted down in my notebook in case I needed help from RKI.

"One minute, please."

In half that time a deep, growly voice came on the line. "This is Kessell. How may I help you, Ms. Kelleher?"

"I'm in San Luis Obispo working a lead on the Savage investigation. Turns out I need to get to Albuquerque as soon as possible, but there's nothing direct from here, and I can't charter a flight till tonight. Is it possible you could have one of your planes fly me down there?"

"Let me check on availability." He put me on hold, came back a few minutes later. "You're in luck, Ms. Kelleher. One of our jets is about to drop a passenger at

Santa Barbara. It can pick you up in less than thirty minutes. Pilot says the flight time to Albuquerque will be around two hours and ten minutes. Does that suit you?"

Two hours and forty minutes, give or take a few. Half an hour at most to get a rental car. Say, another half to find Parkview Convalescent Home, where the Central Coast Independent Truckers Association sent Veronica Keel a small monthly check from their disability fund. And if I was lucky, another hour or so to interview her and learn her sister's present whereabouts. Four hours and forty minutes—maybe less. By then it would be a little after nine, given the hour's time difference, and Ricky wouldn't yet have taken the stage. If Patricia Terriss was anywhere near Albuquerque, I'd be able to alert Hy and his security people in time.

"That suits me fine, Mr. Kessell," I said. "Thank you."

Funny about Keel having been in Albuquerque since shortly after her accident. The woman I'd talked with at the truckers' association hadn't known her, didn't know why she'd chosen a convalescent home there. Not that it mattered to me. The poor woman had done me a favor; tonight I'd be with Ricky again.

Less than thirty minutes, Kessell had said. I needed to tell Hertz where they could find their car. Screw Hertz. I'd notify them later, if there was time. Right now I wanted to talk to Ricky.

Mr. Savage had already left for the fairgrounds, the desk at the Hyatt told me. Did I wish to leave a voice-mail message?

I did—even though he probably wouldn't hear it till we were together. All I said was, "I love you." I'd never told him so, and if I was going to fly I wanted it on record, just in case.

I suppose I should've bitten the bullet and called his cell phone, but sure as hell Shar still had it, and I didn't want to fight with her or—worse yet—have her order me home to San Francisco. When this was all over I was going to take up a collection around the office—or maybe pilfer from petty cash—and buy her her own cellular unit. That way she wouldn't always be borrowing other people's toys. The woman had caved in and bought a car phone and a pager. Why, for God's sake, wouldn't she—

But I knew the answer. Any more gadgets would tie her down, take away a chunk of her independence. Shar pretends to be technologically incompetent, but she's actually as adept as the rest of us—and twice as stubborn.

For a moment I toyed with the idea of calling Hy's cellular, but decided against it since, with my luck, Shar would probably be standing right next to him. I could try Kurt at the hotel, but I wasn't sure I could trust him to pass on a message. But what about the fairgrounds office? They could page Ricky.

No, that would be a mistake. He was running his sound checks, totally focused on the concert. No one was allowed to interrupt him then—not even me.

In the end I did the noble thing and called Hertz. Then I sat down on a bench in the shade and prepared to risk my life in the unfriendly skies.

Twenty-six

6:03 P.M., MDT

What the hell?" Virgil Rattray demanded. "His majesty can't go back to the hotel and have room service like the rest of us?"

"Just send somebody out for the food and have it here by seven," I said through tight lips.

"Jee-sus! This kid-glove treatment makes me want to puke."

"Just do it, Rats."

"Yeah, yeah. But I'll tell you . . . First he shows up early for his sound checks and throws everybody else's schedule off. Then he sulks around in his dressing room and won't let anybody in to see him. Now he wants a catered supper. That woman of his better show soon and take up some of the slack for me."

I frowned.

"What, now I'm not supposed to mention her? Hell, everybody knows he's misplaced her and is all bent out of shape. If I could get the kind of women Rick does, I'd sure as shit keep better track of them."

Rattray started down the curving corridor, away from Ricky's dressing room, but I went after him and grabbed his arm. He yanked it free, fury honing his features. "What the hell do you want now?"

"To talk some more about Patricia Terriss."

His little eyes darted nervously over my shoulder and he licked his lips. "You tell Rick about me giving her those numbers?"

"No."

"You going to?"

"That depends."

"On what?"

I ignored the question. "Did Patricia ever mention a sister named Veronica Keel, who lives in Paso Robles?"

". . . Uh, she mentioned a stepsister. She was older, and they weren't close."

"What did she say about her?"

"Well, the sister'd had a bad accident before I got to know Patricia. Was in a nursing home, paralyzed. Patricia felt guilty about not going to see her—I guess the sister had helped her out when she was having a hard time with her dad—but she couldn't deal with seeing her like that and, besides, she was afraid she might run into their father."

"What was the problem with the father?"

Rattray shrugged. "He was an asshole, I guess."

Typical Rats-style assessment. "Do you know his name or where he lives?"

"Uh-uh."

"Or anything else about him? Or the stepsister? Or their mother?"

"Nope."

"Anything else at all?"

341

"I told you everything about Patricia that I remember. Now, are you gonna keep quiet about what I did?"

"For now."

"Jee-sus!" He whirled and strode angrily down the corridor. When he reached its end, he turned and pointed his finger at me. "You tell his majesty anything, it better be that I'm ordering his goddamn supper!"

With Rats's departure, the corridor suddenly became very quiet. The band had gone back to the Hyatt, and Blue Arkansas were having dinner at a nearby restaurant. They were a friendly, shaggy bunch—high-spirited when they'd stumbled off their big customized bus earlier, after an all-night breakneck ride across the desert. They'd be hard pressed to make Dallas in time for tomorrow night's concert, their lead singer had confided, but when you were traveling on a near maxed-out credit card, you learned to make sacrifices. Ricky had shown up right then, getting out of a limo, and as the band greeted him with shy deference, I couldn't help but contrast the weary cynicism my brother-in-law often displayed with his younger colleagues' seemingly boundless enthusiasm. I'd begun to suspect that, in the music business, the becoming was a lot more fun than the being.

Now I stepped back to the wall and leaned against its cool concrete, listening to the silence. All I heard was the hum of a distant generator and the whine of the neon tubes above my head. The coliseum was in readiness; everyone had taken a break except security.

Calm before the storm? Maybe.

After a few minutes I took Ricky's cellular unit from my bag and dialed Jenny Gordon's number in Austin. Her answering machine gave a pager number this time, so I redialed. Within five minutes Jenny got back to me.

"I'm in Nashville," she said, "staking out that Tod Dodson's apartment house. Got a good description of him and his car from the manager. So far he's a no-show."

"The manager tell you anything about him?"

"He's a good tenant, pays his rent on time, works as a session musician around town. Has a couple of women friends, one that might or might not be Terriss."

And if she was, what were the chances that Dodson was with her—either in Austin, Dallas, or here in Albuquerque?

"Well, thanks, Jenny. Let me know when you've got something."

I hung up and contemplated the silence once more. Then I went past the guards near Ricky's dressing room and stuck my head through the door. He sat in an arm-chair, his feet propped on a low table, holding this week's issue of *Billboard* on his lap and staring into space.

"Rats is ordering your dinner," I said.

"You didn't have to ask him to do that."

"You've got to eat."

"I'm not all that hungry. Can I have my cellular for a minute? I want to check my voice mail."

I handed it to him, sat on the table while he called the hotel. As he listened, his eyes grew brighter and his lips curved in surprised pleasure. He pressed a button to re-play the message, then hung up and silently handed the unit back to me.

"She called?"

"Uh-huh."

"What did she say?"

"That's private, Sister Sharon."

"Well, when did she call? Where is she?"

"Four twenty-five. And I don't know."

"But you think she's all right?"

"She sounded all right, and she wouldn't've said what she did if she wasn't."

Mystified and somewhat relieved, I nodded and left him to contemplate whatever Rae had put on the tape that so pleased him.

The corridor was still silent. Calm before the storm, I thought again. And seconds later the thought proved true. Loud voices came from the entrance—Kurt Girdwood's familiar bellow and the softer, southern-accented tones of Ethan Amory.

"I tell you, Ethan, they're not letting anybody in to see him—even me. Christ knows what he's doing for hand-holding; the redhead's disappeared and the sister-in-law doesn't strike me as having much on the ball in the TLC department."

"The sister-in-law is a pain in the ass and a dangerous influence—" Amory stopped both talking and walking when he spotted me.

I started toward them. "Speak of the devil," I said with a smile. "You come here to cover your ass, Amory?"

Girdwood frowned and shot the attorney a puzzled look.

Amory ran his fingers through his hair. "Ms. McCone, I need to see my client. Something important's come up—"

"I'll be glad to relay a message."

"Sorry, it's confidential." He attempted to brush past me.

I grabbed his arm, pushed him back. "I wouldn't do that. There're two guards outside his door—armed guards."

Amory flushed angrily. "Who gave the orders that nobody gets in to see him?"

"Ricky himself."

"I don't believe that. He wouldn't turn on his own team."

"Why not? His own team sees nothing wrong with turning on him."

Girdwood asked, "What's that supposed to mean?"

"I think you know. And I'm sure Ethan does."

Again the manager gave Amory a puzzled look.

I added, "I suggest you two leave now. Go someplace and swap stories about the different ways you've tried to screw my brother-in-law. Just don't bother him—or me."

They exchanged wary looks, each wondering what dirt I'd dug up on the other. Without further comment or protest, they went out the way they'd come in. I watched their retreating backs thoughtfully. While Amory's sudden appearance here didn't necessarily add to the risk factor, he was one more person to contend with. Why hadn't he stayed put in Los Angeles—

"Son of a bitch!"

Rattray's outraged voice came from the second dressing room. I went down there, looked inside, and found him kneeling over a metal suitcase crammed full of diagrams, notebooks, tools, and clothing. "Goddamned son of a bitch!" he yelled again.

"What now?"

He twisted around violently, almost falling over. "Somebody's been in my case!"

"You mean that suitcase?"

"What the hell else would I mean, you fool? Yes, my case, where I keep all the shit I need to get through these fuckin' tours! Somebody's been in it."

"Well, was anything taken?"

". . . Not that I noticed." He glanced at it, then slammed its lid and snapped the catches. "But that's not the point. Everybody knows that case is off limits. And it's the second time this has happened."

"When was the first?"

"This afternoon before I left the hotel. I set it down in the lobby and went over to the desk to deal with some screw-up about the drum tech's room. When I went back the seal was broken."

"What seal?"

"I always stick a piece of tape on it so I'll know if any-body's messed with it. The tape was laying on the floor."

I'd begun to wonder if the members of our group—myself included—might have cornered the market on paranoia. This more or less proved it. "Maybe the tape just fell off, Rats."

"No way."

"Did you ask around to see if anybody saw someone tampering with it?"

"What, do you think I'm crazy?"

"I don't understand."

"I sure as shit don't want to call attention to this case!"

"Why not?"

He rolled his eyes. "Because," he said, enunciating as if he were speaking to a retarded person, "it is where I keep all the stuff I need to get me through."

Oh. The case was where he kept his drug stash. "Rats, why don't you lock it, then?"

"Lock's broken and I haven't gotten it together to have it fixed. Besides, the case is kind of a symbol."

"Of what?"

He drew himself up with as much dignity as one who resembles an opossum can muster. "It's a symbol of my trust in my fellow man. So long as nobody tampered with it, I had some hope for humanity. Now . . ." He looked down, gave the case a vicious kick, and slouched out of the room.

I stared after him. He had to be putting me on! Virgil Rattray, clinging to vestiges of hope for humanity?

The mere concept rendered me speechless.

RAE'S DIARY:
8:59 P.M., MDT

346

Speechless. That was how the news about Veronica Keel's condition left me. The accident had made her a vegetable: completely paralyzed and brain-damaged.

I felt so awful for her, when the woman on the desk at Parkview Convalescent Home told me, that for a minute I didn't even consider how Keel's disability would affect my investigation. Then it sunk in and I let my breath out in a long, disappointed sigh.

The woman said, "You're not a relative?"

"No. Just a . . . friend of her sister, Patricia Terriss. Has she come to visit lately?"

"No one ever visits. I thought Mrs. Keel had no family."

"Oh, yes, she has a sister." I hesitated, then began embroidering upon my story like the great little liar I can sometimes be. "You see, Pat was my roommate in Texas, and when she moved out she left behind these paintings— for safekeeping, you know? And my new boyfriend, he's an art dealer. He looked at them and it turns out they're quite valuable. He's got this client who wants to buy them, but I haven't been able to locate Pat, but I know she could use the money because she hasn't gotten her singing career off the ground yet, so—"

I noticed the woman's expression and stopped talking. She was looking at me as though she found me fascinating—the way she'd find a freak in a sideshow fascinating, that is. Shar has warned me time and again not to get carried away with my cover stories, but I can't help myself. Maybe someday I'll become a writer, after all.

Lamely, I added, "So I was wondering if your records would show a current address for her. As next of kin, maybe."

"The records office is closed for the evening, and I wouldn't know how to access the information."

"Is there someone else on the staff who could help me?"

The woman tapped the eraser end of her pencil on the

desk—eager to get rid of me, no doubt. "Well," she said, "you might try Nurse Finch. She's been here for years, and Mrs. Keel is one of her patients."

"Where can I find her?"

"Follow the blue line to the nurses' station in the south wing."

I followed the blue line, trying not to take too much notice of my surroundings. The benches along the hallway were empty, but a pair of old men in pajamas and bathrobes slumbered in wheelchairs, their pale ankles bare and vulnerable between their cuffs and slippers—people the world and, apparently, the nursing staff had forgotten. From open doors to either side came coughs and groans and wheezes and the mutterings of TVs. A medicinal odor overlay the more subtle smells of sickness and decay.

I don't want to end my days like this, I thought. And then I remembered my parents, drunk and dying in a fiery crash on the coast road near Pismo Beach. That wasn't such a great way to go, either. Of course, there was my grandmother—dropping over of a massive heart attack at seventy-seven while attempting to murder a perfectly good blackberry bush that had invaded her garden. Of the alternatives, I'd opt for the latter. At least Grandma had been active, cold sober, and doing something she loved—even if it did involve the slaughter of innocent and harmless vegetation.

The woman at the nurses' station was short and plump, with wide-set dark eyes and Native American features. Her name tag said "R. Finch," and she was crocheting a sweater in a wild shade of pink. When I explained what I was after, her eyes got darker and somber. She set her work aside and said, "Come with me."

The room behind the counter was a cozy lounge with a

coffee urn and a plate of tired-looking doughnuts. The woman motioned at a chair and then at the urn.

"No coffee, thanks," I said, sitting.

She poured herself a cup and sat also. "You do not know Mrs. Keel?" she asked.

"We've never met."

"She is a sad case, the same today as when she came here. The ones like her are not living, yet they refuse to die. Sometimes I wonder what it is that makes it impossible for them to let go."

She seemed to be talking around my earlier question about Terriss. I said, "The woman on the desk says no one ever visits. I'm surprised Patricia doesn't make the effort."

"She did come once. How long has it been since you heard from your friend?"

". . . Years. Three, at least."

She nodded. "And you have not seen her father, either?"

"I don't know him. Do you?"

"He also came once, when he had Mrs. Keel admitted, but never again."

"What's his name?"

She thought. "I can't recall. Records could tell you, since he pays her bills, but you'll have to come back tomorrow during business hours."

"There's no way of getting a look at the records now?"

"I'm sorry, no."

I put on a disappointed face. "I really do need to locate Patricia tonight."

Nurse Finch laid her hand on my arm and looked into my eyes. Hers were full of a scary kind of wisdom—the kind a person who deals with sickness and death on a daily basis develops.

She said, "There is something you ought to know."

Twenty-seven

9:42 P.M.

Soon the world will know what you did three years ago tonight

Jesus!" Hy exclaimed. "Give me that card. What florist did these weeds come from, anyway?"

I examined the floral arrangement that had just been delivered for Ricky. The yellow lilies resembled Carolina jessamine somewhat and were badly wilted from the heat. The plastic stake that held the card was imprinted with the flower shop's name. "Someplace called Dixie's Blossoms."

"I'll get on to them. In the meantime"—he motioned to the guard who stood outside Ricky's door—"dispose of this, would you?"

I said, "This afternoon I was nervous because things seemed too calm. Now . . ."

"I know." He took out his cellular and went into one

of Blue Arkansas's dressing rooms. The band had been on stage since eight; judging from the sounds echoing in the arena, they were good, damned good.

Sounds also came from the forward dressing rooms—Ricky's band, kicking back before they took the stage in fifteen minutes. I glanced in there: Forrest Curtin looked coked-up yet again; Jerry Jackson was smoking a joint; Norm O'Dell was picking out the melody of "The Empty Place" on his guitar. Only Pete Sherman stood aside, pensive—worried about his long-overdue child. As I watched them, I wondered what had happened to the disciplined approach to performing that O'Dell had boasted of. More evidence of the chaos into which we all seemed to be spinning.

In the next dressing room Virgil Rattray sat in an armchair, his feet propped on his metal suitcase, calmly going over notes on his clipboard—a far cry from the man who had pitched a fit hours before. Probably he'd fortified himself with some substance from his stash. He didn't notice me watching him; after a moment my eyes were drawn downward to the infamous case, and an idea that I didn't like one bit began forming. I turned and hurried toward the dressing room across the corridor where Hy had gone.

He was on the phone and motioned for me to come in. "She did, huh? . . . Well, of course I told her to call you if she needed anything. Did she tell the pilot what she was doing in San Luis? . . . And nothing about what she planned to do here? . . . Figures. Well, at least she's all right. Got to go, Dan. I'll keep you posted."

He folded the unit and slipped it into his pocket. "That was Kessell. Rae's here in Albuquerque."

"What!"

351

"Uh-huh. She called him this afternoon from San Luis Obispo, asked if he could have one of our planes fly her down. They arrived at seven-oh-nine."

"That's nearly three hours ago. Where the hell is she?"

"Damned if I know."

I took out Ricky's phone, dialed the Hyatt. No, Ms. Kelleher hadn't called either Mr. Savage's voice mail or mine. "She can't be here at the coliseum," I said to Hy. "The first thing she'd've done is come backstage to see him."

"Shit, she drives me crazy sometimes!"

"Me too. Now the question is—should we tell him?"

He considered, shook his head. "He's into his performance mode. And since that last voice-mail message, he doesn't seem as worried about her."

"Not as worried, and terribly pleased with whatever she left on the tape."

"Then I opt for not telling him. The idea that she's in town might throw him, and then we'll have a situation on our hands."

I nodded in agreement. "Anything from the florist?"

"Closed. You know, McCone, I think those lilies are probably just another warning. Terriss is building up to doing something big in Austin."

"Then why did the card say 'three years ago tonight'? And Rae's in town for a reason even more compelling than a sudden yen to see Ricky. Besides, I think somebody's smuggled a weapon into the arena."

"Who?"

"I don't know."

"What kind of weapon?"

"Probably a handgun."

"How'd they bring it in?"

"Rats's metal suitcase." I explained about the case having been tampered with both at the hotel and in the dressing room.

"Okay," Hy said, "where is this gun?"

"I don't know that, either. But we need to find out."

RAE'S DIARY:
10:51 P.M.

"I need to find out about this tonight, sir."

"Ms. Kelleher, will you go over your story once more?"

I closed my eyes and took a deep breath. Patience is something I've always had in short supply, but it was clearly a requirement for dealing with the night shift at the Albuquerque PD. Not that I'd've had smooth sailing at any other police department, coming in with the bizarre story I'd offered up.

"The woman, Patricia Terriss, had a brief affair with my agency's client, Ricky Savage, who's performing at Tingley Coliseum right now," I began, and went over it slowly and in as much detail as I thought the department was entitled to. I had to walk a fine line between giving the cops enough to persuade them to open their files, and withholding enough in the interest of damage control, so I left out the really bad stuff—such as Ricky's sending his former band members to deal with Terriss, and their subsequent deaths.

I also didn't mention that I was in love with him and would die if anything happened to him.

The plainclothesman who sat across the desk from me listened quietly. He had intelligent brown eyes and so far hadn't displayed any of the attitude a lot of cops have toward private investigators—unlike the first officer I'd talked with. He had been downright obnoxious, and I'd had to start writing down his badge number before he would pass me along to his superior. The superior, whose name was Sergeant Boyd, heard me out, then verified my California investigator's license. As a reference, I gave him Greg Marcus's name and home number. Fortunately, Greg was there and not in one of his flippant moods. He'd come through for me and, dammit, one of these days I was going to have to apologize for calling him a chauvinist porker.

By that time it was ten-forty. Ricky had been on stage for over half an hour. The thought of what might happen any minute had me bouncing back and forth between panic and anger.

"Okay," Sergeant Boyd said, "I understand what you're telling me, but I don't see that there's any significant threat to your client."

Was he stupid, or just one of those people who want everything graven in stone before they take action?

He added, "I'm afraid I'll have to pass this on to my lieutenant. If you come back in the morning, we can discuss it further."

Neither stupid nor graven in stone. He was a cover-your-ass type.

"Tomorrow morning may be too late for my client."

"Ms. Kelleher, I think you're making too much of this."

Right then I lost it. I stood up and leaned across the desk, my palms pressed flat on its surface. And I re-minded myself of yet another McCone axiom: Don't ever raise your voice and go screechy. Keep it low when you let somebody have it.

I pitched it low. "Tomorrow morning a lot of people may be making much *too much out of your failure to help me."*

"What does that mean?"

"Tomorrow morning my client's blood may be splat-tered all over Tingley Coliseum. Tomorrow morning the

*press may find out that the Albuquerque PD refused me
information that could've saved him. Run that one by
your lieutenant—and your city's chamber of commerce."*

*Sergeant Boyd stiffened. He began to tap his fingertips
on the edge of the desk.*

I held my pose, waiting him out.

*After a moment he shrugged, turned to his computer,
and began accessing the file.*

Twenty-eight

11:24 P.M.

W ell, we've searched all the backstage areas, and no weapon's turned up," Hy said.

"Then whoever brought it in has it on him."

"There's no proof of your theory."

"Don't you think it strange that nobody's ever broken into Rats's case before, when today it happened twice? Did any of the guards search the case before he brought it into the coliseum?"

"He's been in on the security planning the whole time; they didn't see any reason to."

From the arena came wild applause. Ricky had just sung "The Broken Promise Land," and the audience loved it.

I, on the other hand, was beginning to hate that song. For me it symbolized all the careless and stupid and vile things people did and then tried to justify. Symbolized how we hurt and destroyed one another and then refused to take responsibility for our own actions. Did any of those nearly ten thousand people out there understand that? Did they even *care?*

Hy saw the frustration and fear on my face; he put a hand on my shoulder and started to speak. And Ricky's phone buzzed inside my bag. I fumbled it out and answered. Jenny Gordon.

"I'm here in Nashville with Tod Dodson on the extension," she said. "He's got something to tell you."

The voice that spoke next sounded young and nervous. "Ms. McCone? This is Tod Dodson. I was Patricia Terriss's friend—"

"I know, Mr. Dodson. Where can we find her?"

A pause.

Jenny said, "Tell her, Tod."

"Ms. McCone, Patricia . . . she's dead. She killed herself; I've got a letter she wrote telling me she was going to do it."

Oh no, this couldn't be! "Are you sure she went through with it?"

"Yes. A mutual friend saw the story in the paper. She killed herself in Albuquerque three years ago tonight."

RAE'S DIARY:
11:34 P.M.

"Three years ago tonight? My God!"
"Are you okay, Ms. Kelleher?"
"This information—are you sure it's all correct?"
"That's the responding officer's report, and the follow-up confirms it."
I pushed away from the desk and headed for the door.
"Ms. Kelleher! Just one minute!"

I stopped. Where did I think I was going? It was close to the end of Ricky's performance, and I didn't even know how to get to the fairgrounds, much less Tingley Coliseum.

"*May I use your phone?*"

Boyd motioned toward it.

I dialed Ricky's cellular unit. Busy. What was the number of Hy's? I couldn't remember, and by now the coliseum offices would be closed.

Okay, ask Boyd to send squad cars over there. No, that would create a panic situation, could trigger a tragedy. Besides, the sergeant still didn't fully believe my story.

"*Sergeant Boyd,*" *I said,* "*how would you like to do something that your department, your chamber of commerce, and the powers-that-be in this city will commend you for?*"

It wasn't going to work. He stared at me as though he thought me quite demented. Which I might very well be.

Okay, Rae—last resort.

"*Please,*" *I said tremulously, allowing tears to leak into my eyes.*

Quickly he stood up. "*What can I do?*"

At last—a man who truly appreciated a damsel in distress.

"*Get me to the fairgrounds as fast as you can.*"

11:37 P.M.

"As fast as you can," I said in reply to Hy's question. "Just get him off that stage."

"He's not going to like it."

"No, but that's the way it's got to be."

"Okay—logistics. We can't rely on fairgrounds security for something this tricky. Frankly, I don't even want to entrust it to my own people."

"And that leaves—"

"You and me, McCone. You and me."

RAE'S DIARY:
11:40 P.M.

"You and me, we make a pretty good team."

Once he'd seen that I wasn't going to cry all the way across town, Sergeant Boyd had begun to enjoy our mission.

I clung to the dashboard of his unmarked car as it weaved from lane to lane on the straight, flat streets, the pulsar light he'd clapped onto its roof flashing off the surrounding vehicles. My stomach was queasy and my skin tingled. In spite of the late-lingering heat I felt very cold.

"How much farther?" I asked.

"You see that wall? That's the fairgrounds."

God, I felt cold . . .

11:45 P.M.

I felt cold and focused as we laid our plans.

"I'll take this side of the stage," I told Hy. "You circle around to the other."

"Okay. Ricky's more likely to respond to you than to me, so you pull him off of there. But you're also gonna have to cover O'Dell and Jackson."

"I can handle it. You'll cover Curtin and Sherman."

"Where're the others? Rats?"

"Front row of the seats, section, three, taking notes on the performance."

"Girdwood?"

"I haven't seen him or Amory since I ran them off earlier, but that doesn't mean they're not in the arena."

"Jesus." Hy shook his head grimly. "Okay, take away the ones we can locate, and who's left to watch out for?"

"Anybody."

He picked up a duffel bag that sat under a table in the room reserved for security personnel. Took out a .38 and placed it in my hand. Took out a .44 for himself.

"Luck," he said, squeezing my shoulder.

"Luck."

RAE'S DIARY:
11:50 P.M.

"Luck—we're in it tonight," I said to Boyd. "The concert's still going on, and nothing's happened yet. Pull in here."

He turned left and stopped the car at the coliseum entrance that I knew—from the diagrams that Hy and Rats had gone over with Ricky when we were in San Diego—was closest to the dressing rooms and security station. I jumped out and ran toward it.

"Hey!" Boyd called.

I flashed my I.D. at the guard on the door. She must've been told to look out for me, because she said, "Ms. Kelleher! Go on."

I left Boyd to fend for himself and rushed inside, drawn by the sound of Ricky's voice.

11:51 P.M.

Ricky's voice filled my ears, but it didn't drown out Rae's when she called from behind us, "Get him off that stage, for God's sake!"

I turned around. She was out of breath, sweaty, and quite plainly terrified. She recoiled when she saw my gun.

No time for questions; I let her go on.

"The next song he's supposed to sing is 'The Empty Place,' followed by 'Midnight Train' on the stroke of twelve. We've got to stop him."

"We'll get him off of there. But the song—what about it?"

"Terriss killed herself at her stepfather's house here in Albuquerque three years ago. She left a suicide note— the cops let me see its text. Some of the lyrics of 'The Empty Place' are a dead steal from the note—probably planted in Ricky's mind by her stepfather."

"Who?"

She pointed toward the arena and said his name.

RAE'S DIARY:
11:54 P.M.

His name had surprised Shar, but she recovered right away and drew me into the plan. Now thunderous applause filled the arena as I started moving as inconspicuously as I could along its left-hand wall. Shar was already halfway to the stage. Hy was circling along the opposite wall, alerting the guards with his walkie-talkie to what was going on. We'd left Sergeant Boyd at the security station, calling for backup; he'd agreed to let the three of us get Ricky offstage before taking over.

The applause died down. Ricky picked out the opening chords of "The Empty Place."

My pulse went crazy and I felt cold all over again. I picked up the pace.

He stopped playing, looked over the stands for a long moment, and said, "This one's for Red, wherever she is tonight."

Oh, God! Totally wrong thing to do! But how could he know that?

Shar and Hy were in place now.

My smile hides the empty place
That lives inside of me
It turns away with all good grace
The prying inquiry . . .

Faster, Rae. Any one of those words could set the guy off!

My laughter covers up the fears
That lie within so deep
It turns aside the healing tears
That then would give release . . .

The guards had stepped back into the stairwells so I could pass, but dead ahead one still stood at his post. When I tried to slip around him, he grabbed my arm.

"Let go of me, you idiot!"

His walkie-talkie crackled and Hy's voice said, "This is Ripinsky. Let her through."

The man gave me a puzzled look and took his hand away.

Ricky was deep into his song—our song—now. I moved faster.

You stand before me offering hope
So fresh, so wild, so free
But I'm captive to my sadness
And the empty place in me . . .

I stood directly opposite him now. Shar and Hy were moving onto the rear of the stage.

Your smile hides the empty place
That lives inside you too
It turns away with all good grace
What I might ask of you . . .

Shar motioned for me to walk forward.

Your laughter covers up the fears
That lie in you so deep
It turns aside the healing tears
That then would give release . . .

*Nobody in the audience was paying attention to me—
their eyes were riveted on the performers. Nobody on stage
noticed me—their eyes were blinded by the lights.*

Between us we have come to terms
With who and what we are
But now and then one of us yearns
To take it much too far . . .

*I walked straight toward the man I loved, praying that
I'd get to him in time.*

You lie beside me offering love
So fresh, so wild, so free
And I slip the chains of sadness
And the empty place in me . . .

*I reached the stage's edge just as he sang the final
words. The guitar strains hung in the air, drifted off into
silence. Then the crowd was on its feet, just like
in L.A. the night before—clapping, yelling, whistling,
stomping.*

Ricky seemed stunned by the extreme reaction. He re-

moved his guitar, set it aside. Turned back to the audi-
ence, dropped his arms, bowed his head.

And saw me.

I held out my hands, urging him to come forward.

His lips formed the word "Red" and he took a step to-
ward me.

Over the crowd sounds a microphone squealed vio-
lently, and Patricia Terriss's stepfather began to shout.

11:58 P.M.

Norm O'Dell shouted, "The song's right on, but the
dedication's wrong!"

I'd been crouched on the stage and ready to go for
him when he grabbed the microphone. Now I motioned
for Hy, covering on the other side, to move in closer.
Ricky had taken a step toward Rae. Now he stopped.

Abruptly the crowd grew silent. Then a confused mur-
mur rose.

Everything seemed to slow down, as it had at the San
Diego house in the aftermath of the sniping. I saw it all
so clearly: O'Dell ingratiating himself with Ricky's lead
guitarist Dan, one of the men who had accelerated his
stepdaughter's downward spiral into self-destruction;
O'Dell engineering the motorcycle accident on the
coast highway; O'Dell using the false friendship he'd
fostered to get on with the band; O'Dell perpetrating
his other crimes and mounting his campaign of
harassment.

O'Dell stepping up that campaign when he learned
that the second concert on the *Midnight* tour had been
booked for Albuquerque, on the anniversary of Patricia's
suicide at his former home in that city.

It was all so clear in this one slow moment.

I eased forward, gun held low and shielded by my body, so as not to panic the audience.

O'Dell said, "The dedication should've been to my stepdaughter, Patricia Terriss. She wrote most of those words. And she died here in Albuquerque three years ago tonight."

The crowd's murmuring stopped. Ricky turned toward him, bewildered and disbelieving. Rae scrambled onto the stage.

O'Dell looked Ricky straight in the eye. "Yeah, she's dead, you bastard. And you killed her."

Ricky took a step toward him. "Norm . . ." he began.

"You *know* what you did!"

O'Dell reached under his *Midnight Train* tee and yanked a short-barreled revolver from his waistband.

Shocked cries and gasps rose from the crowd.

Hy or I would have shot O'Dell then. I almost did, as Ricky stood frozen, his eyes on the gun. But it wasn't necessary.

It wasn't necessary because, in that second, O'Dell said, "Live with it, asshole," and did what he must have been planning all along.

He jammed the revolver into his mouth and pulled the trigger.

RAE'S DIARY:
11:59 P.M.

As the shot boomed off the arena's dome I leaped forward, grabbed Ricky around the waist, and dragged him over the stage's edge. We landed hard in a tangle on the floor. Then people were screaming and footsteps thundered and Hy shouted something about crowd control. Shar's voice called down, "Are you two okay?"

"Yeah." Ricky moved off me and looked up. Flinched and rolled back as though he was trying to shield me. His breath came short and hard, and he whispered, "Oh, Jesus!" into my hair.

Panicked, I tried to sit up, but he pushed me flat. He looked into my eyes with a wealth of misery in his and said, "You don't want to see."

"He really did it, didn't he?"

"Yeah, he did it, poor bastard."

It felt like something tore in my chest. I pulled him close and shut my eyes. Tears leaked from their corners and slid across my temples and into my hair.

I said, "I hate to cry, except when I want to get my own way."

Ricky touched my cheek. I opened my eyes, saw his were wet.

"That's okay, Red," he told me. "You go ahead and cry."

PART FOUR

•

July 29–August 25, 1995

Los Angeles Times, July 29, 1995:

SAVAGE GUITARIST LEFT SUICIDE NOTE
ALBUQUERQUE, NM—A spokeswoman
for the Albuquerque Police Department revealed today that country star Ricky
Savage's lead guitarist, who shot himself in
front of a sellout crowd of 9,775 at Tingley
Coliseum Thursday night, left a suicide
note in the possession of a woman friend.

The note written by Norman O'Dell, 47,
was surrendered to the authorities by his
longtime companion, Gina Robinson, 39,
after she learned of his death on Friday
morning. Robinson stated that O'Dell left
the note in her possession with instructions to mail copies of it to the media on
Friday. She denied knowledge of O'Dell's
intentions, but admitted to making a
phone call to the camp of one of Savage's
children and transmitting threatening fax
messages to the singer at O'Dell's request
earlier in the week.

The contents of the note were undis-
closed, but sources close to the investigation indicated that O'Dell blamed Savage
and two of his former band members, both
deceased, for the suicide of his stepdaughter, Patricia Terriss, in Albuquerque, three
years prior to the date of the concert.

Savage, who has so far canceled four
stops on his promotional tour for his forthcoming *Midnight Train to Nowhere* album,
could not be reached for comment. His
publicist, Linda Toole, stated that a press
conference will be scheduled for early next
week.

Letter from Patricia Terriss to Tod Dodson, July 27, 1992:

Dear Tod:

I'm sorry. Sorry I stole all your cash and dope. Sorry
about the fish. Those were horrible things to do. I was
just so out of control. I'm better now, though. Quite
clear on everything. I'm at my stepfather's house in
Albuquerque. We've made up. I've forgiven him for
being such a control freak after Mom died, and he's
forgiven me for disappearing on him. I was even able to
tell him about Ricky—all of it, even the stuff with Dan
and Benjy. He said I should forget it, get on with my
life. And I am, in a way. I even went to see Veronica at
the nursing home, to say good-bye.

Yes, good-bye. Because, Tod, I can't take it anymore. All
my life I've known that there's this empty place in me.
My smile hides it, my laughter covers it up, but I'm
chained by it and it sets me apart from everybody. For a
while I thought Ricky was offering me hope and maybe I
could slip those chains, but like all the others, he didn't
love me. And every day now I lose more of my control.

Hey, that's good stuff. I've been looking for a way to
explain to Daddy why I did what I'm going to do. Maybe
telling him about the empty place will make him
understand.

I don't blame Ricky, not really. He never made any
promises—I lied about that. And there's a lot else you
don't know, about things I did to him. No, I don't blame
anybody, just this damn empty place. Sorry, Tod, I'm
stoned and tired, and I've got one more letter to write—
to Daddy. And then, finally, I'm going to get some rest.

Love,

P.

Twenty-nine

We were back in Los Angeles and gathered in the conference room at Zenith Records. It was Saturday night. Ricky, Kurt Girdwood, Ethan Amory, Virgil Rattray, Linda Toole, Pete Sherman, and Jerry Jackson were there. Wil Willis, the fourth partner in the label, was in Nashville on business, and they had him on the speaker phone. Hy was there because Zenith had made the decision to hire RKI on a permanent basis for corporate security. Rae was there because it was unlikely she and Ricky would ever again be more than a phone call apart.

And I was there because Brother Ricky—he would always be my brother, in spite of the impending divorce—had promised me satisfying closure to my investigation.

"So," Willis's voice said through the speaker, "what's the damage?"

Toole replied, "Hard to tell yet. We've scheduled a press conference for Monday, and I'm already at work on Rick's statement."

"Forget it," Ricky said. "I'll write it myself."

"Are you sure that's—"

"A good idea? Yes." He glanced at Rae, who sat beside him, and nodded emphatically. They both looked better than they had at any time since Thursday night, but the dark smudges that underscored her eyes told me she was still waking from nightmares, and his face was set in lines of strain that might be permanent.

Girdwood looked skeptical about Ricky's pronouncement but only said, "We canceled Dallas, Austin, New Orleans, and Miami. The rest of the dates're still up in the air."

Willis asked, "What about replacing O'Dell?"

Girdwood motioned to Ricky.

"It's gonna take time to find somebody of his caliber," he said. "And I fired Forrest this afternoon, so we'll need a new bass player as well."

Amory had been standing by the window behind the conference table, contemplating the view, but now he turned. "You *what?* He has a contract, you know."

"Screw the contract; it's up in the fall and I'm buying out the remainder. I'm sick and tired of watching him get coked to his eyebrows before every performance."

Toole said, "But the *tour,* Rick. We can't carry it off with two replacement players."

"I know. I'm canceling."

Toole sucked in air so hard that she started to cough. As the others muttered protests, Ricky took Rae's hand and twined his fingers through hers; supportive energy seemed to flow between them, and he repeated, "I'm canceling."

"Not smart, Rick," Girdwood said. "Not smart."

"Maybe not, but that's how it's gonna be."

"Think about the money we'll lose."

"I don't care about the money."

"Think, then, about what this could do to the album sales. Both 'Midnight Train' and 'The Empty Place' are getting enormous airplay. We could have a monster hit on our hands."

"My canceling the tour isn't going to stop that. And, frankly, I wouldn't care if it did."

Girdwood's eyes narrowed and he glared at Rae. *"She* tell you to cancel?"

Rae's fingertips went white against Ricky's.

"No," he said, "but she agrees that it's the only decent thing to do."

Girdwood snorted. "Decent!"

"You ever hear of paying respect to the dead, Kurt?"

"Respect! The asshole would've killed you—"

"The police said his note made it clear he never intended to do that."

"So he took a different kind of revenge. You can't tell me it's going to be easy to live with what happened."

"No, but maybe that's what I deserve. Anyway, when I said respect to the dead, I was talking about others, too—Dan, Benjy . . . and Patricia."

Amory was frowning thoughtfully. He stepped away from the window and came over to the conference table. "I think we're missing a promotional gold mine here."

Girdwood, Toole, and the remaining band members turned to him with interest. Wil Willis asked, "What, Ethan?" Rats rolled his eyes and stared up at the ceiling.

Ricky, Rae, Hy, and I exchanged glances that said, *What now?*

"Okay," Amory said, "I'll run the game plan by all of you. And, Rick, once you hear it, I think you'll agree to go on with the remainder of the tour. Norm said 'Empty Place' should've been dedicated to his stepdaughter, right? Because a lot of the lyrics were suggested to you by him, right? And he lifted them from her suicide note, right?"

Ricky nodded, regarding the attorney intently.

"So what you do in concert is dedicate it to her memory."

Rats's lip curled. Jerry Jackson made a disgusted sound. Rae glanced nervously at Ricky.

Amory paused for a few beats, then added, "Better yet, you dedicate it to *both* their memories."

I looked at Toole and Girdwood. They were frowning.

Again Amory paused, fingertips pressed to his forehead. "No!" he exclaimed, his hand swooping into the air as if he'd just experienced an epiphany. "You take it a step further. You dedicate it to both of them, and *then* . . . you read the part of that letter her boyfriend gave us where she talks about the empty place!"

Pete Sherman groaned and covered his eyes with his hand. Through the speaker phone Wil Willis made a peculiar sound, as though he'd choked on something. I glanced at Hy; he wore a faint, knowing smile.

Amory said into the silence, "Too bad we can't get hold of Norm's suicide note. The bit would be perfect if you could read from it, too."

Silence continued to fill the room. Girdwood and Rae were staring at the attorney as they would at a worm crawling around in a salad.

Calmly Ricky took his hand from hers and stood. He walked around the table and looked down at Linda Toole. Her mouth was twisted as if she'd just bitten into the worm.

"You," he said to her, "are still on the team. And you"—he turned and pointed at Amory—"are off!"

Amory blinked and stared around the room, bewildered as to what had gone wrong.

Before he could speak, Ricky was moving toward him. Amory registered the scowl on his face and put up his hands in self-defense. Then he backpedaled and started the other way around the table. Ricky moved faster, re-

versed, and collared the attorney next to his empty chair.
With his other hand he grabbed him firmly by the seat of
his pants and, as Amory yowled in protest, he propelled
him toward the door.

Rats was on his feet. "Allow me," he said, and opened
it ceremoniously.

"Thanks." Ricky heaved Amory unceremoniously onto
the floor outside. To Rats he added, "Get this piece of
garbage out of here, would you?"

"My pleasure."

After he had slammed the door on Amory's protracted
yowls, Ricky turned back to the rest of us. He looked
first at Girdwood and then at the speaker phone. "I
know we've got a partnership agreement with Ethan," he
said, "but Shar's given me some pretty damning taped
evidence on him that we can use as leverage. And if that
doesn't persuade him to bow out gracefully, I swear I'll
mortgage my soul to buy him out."

Rae said softly but in a tone that commanded everyone's attention, "You may have just *bought back* your
soul."

Billboard, August 6, 1995:

Los Angeles—At a press conference on July 31, country artist Ricky Savage announced the dissolution of the Zenith Records partnership among himself, former Arista VP Wil Willis, manager Kurt Girdwood, and attorney Ethan Amory. The partnership will be reconstituted with Savage, Willis, and Girdwood as principals. Savage declined to elaborate on the reasons for the dissolution, stating only that it stemmed from "a fundamental difference in management philosophy" between Amory and the remaining partners.

Savage also alluded to the onstage suicide of his lead guitarist, Norman O'Dell, last week: "I won't go into detail, because I strongly believe that private matters should remain private. However, I will say that Norm O'Dell was a basically good man who experienced more than his fair share of tragedy, and I contributed to his problems by my failure to take responsibility for my actions in regard to his stepdaughter, Patricia Terriss. His death has taught me a tough personal lesson."

The singer added that, "We in the recording industry should all be looking at how we're handling responsibility for the messages we're sending—both in the music we're making and in our public and private lives. This past week has been one of major change in both areas of mine, and

I hope to use those changes as a spring-board for positive growth and action."

Savage went on to state that although he has canceled his *Midnight Train to Nowhere* tour, he expects to reschedule for spring, after he has replaced O'Dell and bass player Forrest Curtin, whose contract is up in October.

"StarWatch," *Los Angeles Times,* August 7, 1995:

While much has been reported in the press about the suicide of **Ricky Savage's** lead guitarist **Norm O'Dell** and Savage's role in it, as well as the recent shake-ups in the country star's professional and personal lives, little has been said about his integrity. While others would have gone public with the guitarist's rumored crimes against himself and his family and friends, Savage has remained silent. While others would have covered up the lack of responsibility that led to the suicide of O'Dell's stepdaughter, Savage has admitted to it. While others would have capitalized on the glut of publicity surrounding the *Midnight Train to Nowhere* tour, Savage canceled. And, in a manner consistent with his previous behavior, he has maintained his privacy in the face of intense media curiosity about his impending divorce and new relationship with San Francisco private investigator **Rae Kelleher.** In this column's opinion, the entertainment industry could use more stars with Savage's credibility. Of course, were that to come to pass, we'd soon find ourselves out of a job . . .

Thirty

Rae and I sat on the low concrete blocks—part of a dubious city-funded sculpture—in front of Red's Java House, drinking Cokes and eating cheeseburgers. Normally I would have felt guilty for such disloyalty to Carmen, our favorite waterfront restaurateur, but again it was one of those unseasonably hot days that are so rare in San Francisco, and neither of us had felt like walking that far for lunch.

Rae had just finished reading me a report on Ricky's press conference from *Billboard,* as well as an item that had appeared yesterday in "StarWatch." Now she finished her burger and crumpled the wrappings.

"Not bad, the way he handled the situation," she commented. "The best part is, he really meant what he said."

If you knew Ricky as well as she and I did, you couldn't doubt his sincerity. But I was willing to bet that plenty of the cynics in his very cynical industry viewed his actions and subsequent statement as a bald-faced whitewash. I didn't voice the comment, though, only asked, "You say he's driving up today?"

"Like a maniac in the Porsche, and if he survives the journey, tomorrow afternoon we're off to Bakersfield." She paused, serious. "Are you sure you don't mind me taking off in the middle of the week like that?"

"I'm sure." To tell the truth, I'd resigned myself to losing her as an operative—so much so that I'd made Charlotte Keim an employment offer she couldn't refuse.

"I'd feel more secure if you told me I'd be sorely missed."

"Well, with Keim coming on board . . ."

"About that, Shar—you didn't hire her because you think I'm going to quit, did you?"

". . . Not exactly."

"Because I have no such intention."

"Oh?"

"I may have to ask for a leave of absence, just till things're more settled for Ricky. He's still pretty shaken up about all that's gone on and, frankly, so am I. We need some quiet time together."

"I understand." And after the quiet time, then what? It was hard to believe that out of last month's shattering events such tidy, happy endings could be forged: Ricky and Rae in a lasting relationship; Charlene and Vic an equally stable couple; the Savage children healing and accepting the changes with the help of both their parents. Yet, at least on the surface, that was taking place.

Hy and I seemed to be the only people who weren't in harmony; during the past two weeks the distance between us had widened.

I watched a man in a business suit come out of Red's, a box in his hands piled dangerously high with take-out. A breeze off the Bay caught a bunch of paper napkins tucked down the side and wafted them away. Rae seemed to sense my low feelings; she got up and took the wrappings from our lunch to a trash bin. By the time she came back, I'd put on a falsely cheerful face.

"So," I said, "what do the two of you plan to do—make the airlines rich by flying back and forth between here and the southland?"

"For a while, anyway. He's already given me his account number with the air-charter outfit he uses."

"I can tell you're going to adapt splendidly to his lifestyle."

"Actually, I find it weird—him having so much money, I mean. If he wasn't so casual about it, I'm not sure I could keep up with him." Again her freckled face grew somber. "You aren't still mad at us, are you?"

"No. I've adopted a wait-and-see attitude toward all concerned."

"Well, we can't ask for more than that. Mick seems to feel the same, although he's still kind of stiff with me, and every now and then I catch him looking at me like . . . well, like he's speculating on our sex life."

I smiled. "That's what eighteen-year-old men *do*, Rae. Besides, when Charlotte comes on board, he'll be too busy thinking about his own sex life to worry about yours." My nephew had been staying with me since he'd returned to work, but he saw a great deal of Keim. I'd hesitated about offering her a job for that reason, until the three of us had hashed it out and decided they were both mature enough to maintain professional behavior in the workplace.

I looked at my watch: almost time to head back to the office. But not yet; it was too nice a day to rush inside. "So the two of you haven't any definite future plans?" I asked.

"We're going to talk over our options on the way to Bakersfield."

"Bakersfield in an August heat wave. You must be insane."

"Shar, this is an important trip."

"How so?"

"Well, he's going to introduce me to his aunt, uncle, and cousins. He's going to show me the house he grew up in, the schools he went to. He's going to take me to the bars and clubs where he and his band got their first gigs. He even wants to show me the parking lot behind the supermarket where he first got laid."

"Now *that's* impressive. I hardly know what to say."

"Come on, didn't Hy ever give you a tour of his old haunts?"

I thought, then smiled. "You know, he did. He even showed me his streetlight in Bridgeport."

"He has a *streetlight?*"

"Well, sort of. He had to pay to replace one after he lassoed it from the bed of a pickup and drove off dragging it behind him, one drunk and disorderly night."

When she got done laughing, Rae said, "God, aren't you and I in love with a couple of romantic souls? Trips to view streetlights and parking lots—what will they come up with next?"

"StarWatch," *Los Angeles Times,* August 14, 1995:

> Our San Francisco sources confirm that country star **Ricky Savage** has contacted a prominent real-estate broker about locating a home in that city for himself and his lady friend, private investigator **Rae Kelleher.** Savage specified that it be large enough to accommodate a rehearsal studio and his half-dozen children when they visit. Does this count as one of those positive actions he talked about at his July 31 press conference? We suspect so . . .

Thirty-one

I stepped out of the seaside cottage we called Touchstone just as Hy's Citabria set down on our newly graded airstrip. It sped along the clifftop, then slowed and taxied to a stop at the tie-down chains. I walked toward it, nervous about our reunion. It was Friday, August twenty-fifth, and we hadn't seen each other since we parted in Los Angeles on July thirtieth.

The prop feathered and after a moment Hy stepped down and waved. I waved back, hurried over, and helped him secure the plane. Then he grabbed his duffel bag from the backseat, put his hand on my shoulder, and steered me toward the cottage.

"How's everything at the ranch?" I asked. We hadn't been talking much on the phone lately, and what few conversations we'd had were brief and impersonal. The discussion we'd promised ourselves had never happened, and emotional distance still spread between us.

In answer to my question, he said, "Everything's good. You dig out from under all that paperwork?"

"Finally. Rae took some time off, but Keim picked up the slack."

"Ricky and Rae bought a house yet?"

"Yes—Seacliff, right on the bluff near China Beach. She's subletting the condo to Mick."

"That was fast."

"Uh-huh. She and Ricky are so in agreement about everything that it's a little spooky." Like we used to be, I added to myself.

Hy seemed to sense the thought. He stopped at the door of the cottage and set down his bag. "Let's sit out on the deck for a while, wait for the sunset."

The deck was a platform with built-in benches and a stairway that scaled the cliff to Bootleggers Cove, hundreds of feet below. I dusted off a couple of the weatherproof cushions and curled up in a corner. Hy sat next to me, but a little apart. The sun was already low on the horizon, staining the water and sky.

After a moment he said, "We never did have that talk."

"No."

"We should. This being together but not being together—that's not us."

"We were completely together when things got rough in Albuquerque."

"Yeah, but it's a hell of a situation when you only relate when things get down and dangerous."

"Ripinsky, we've always been at our best under those conditions."

"I know. But we used to be at our best other times as well."

The sun had sunk quickly. It colored the water in shadings from flamboyant red to delicate pink; closer in, the waves shimmered purple at their crests, gray-blue in their troughs. Flocks of seabirds skimmed north in orderly formation. I watched them, afraid of what he might be trying to tell me.

I loved this land, which could alternately be beautiful and welcoming, weather-torn and inhospitable. The thought of losing our piece of it because Hy and I no longer connected was saddening. I loved this man, whose many sides were perfectly suited to our north coast. The thought of losing him was unbearable.

I said, "That night on the train—where was all that anger coming from?"

His eyes remained fixed on the horizon, fine lines deepening at their corners as he squinted against the glare. "The day that had just ended was July twenty-sixth, the anniversary of Julie's death."

His wife, Julie Spaulding, had died of multiple sclerosis a number of years before. I'd never known her, had in fact only seen one photograph. She'd been a dedicated and active environmentalist in spite of her illness, and a lifeline to Hy after he returned from a grim period as an air-charter pilot in war-torn, corruption-ridden Southeast Asia. I knew he'd loved her very much, but now it seemed—

"No, McCone. I wasn't angry because I was missing Julie. I loved her a lot, but that was years ago and, sad to say, there're times now when I can barely conjure up her image."

"What was going on with you, then?"

"You'd disappeared on me. You hadn't told me where you were going and you were late for the train. You're never late for anything unless something's gone wrong. All I could think was, 'I'm going to lose *her* today, too.'"

"Oh, God. And when I showed up and you realized it was only my carelessness that had caused all that worry—"

"I got pissed and took it out on you."

Okay, that explained his angry outburst, but not the remoteness that had enveloped him since. "There's more," I said.

He compressed his lips for a moment. "Yes."

I watched him, waiting. In the dying light, the planes of his craggy features were sharp, the expression in his eyes dark and unreadable. For a few seconds I felt as if I were sitting beside a stranger.

"Yes," he repeated, "there *is* something else. You'll probably think it trivial, but it's been eating at me."

"Tell me."

"Do you remember when we were in the lounge car on the train and they played that video of Ricky and Rae in front of Union Station?"

"Yes."

"Right before she got back into the limo, he said something to her."

"He did? Oh, right. I don't know what it was, but it really pleased her, the same way whatever she said on his voice mail in Albuquerque pleased him."

"Well, I do know. I can read lips—comes from spending all those years around noisy aircraft."

"So what did he say?"

"He told her he loved her."

"And that *upset* you?"

He got up, moved to the railing, and braced his hands on it, his back to me.

"McCone," he said, "when was the last time you told me you love me?"

I thought. Shook my head. "I don't know."

"Yeah."

"Ripinsky, what're you getting at here?"

He turned, sad lines bracketing his mouth. "You've never told me—not once, the whole time we've been together."

"That can't be." But as I spoke I realized he was right.

"Not once," he repeated, his voice rough with feeling.

An incredible lapse, considering how much I did love him. But there was a reason for it: I'd grown up in a household where a lot of lip service had been paid to love, but there was a falseness and coldness deep at the core of our family. When I'd left home I'd put all that aside, vowed there would be no place for similar dishonesty in my adult relationships. Sometimes when you make such decisions, you unwittingly go overboard in the opposite direction.

Hy was watching me in that analytical manner I remembered from Albuquerque. Waiting for an explanation.

But how to present it? How to convince him that I'd only kept my silence because love wasn't a word I easily used? I thought back over the time we'd been together: the mutual understanding that had existed between us from the first; the closeness that transcended the greatest of distances; the friendship and the laughter and the shared danger and the lovemaking; the—

"Wait a damn minute!" I exclaimed.

He frowned.

I stood up. "Okay, Ripinsky, let me ask you this: When was the last time *you* told *me* you love me?"

"Well . . ." He shrugged and spread his hands. "I must've."

"When?"

"Your birthday? Christmas? Last New Year's Eve? Hell, a man doesn't keep track of stuff like that."

"Right—you only keep track of what's said or not said *to* you."

"All right, maybe I'm not free with words—"

"And neither am I."

We faced each other, scowling fiercely in the day's last light. Then, slowly, he smiled, and I smiled too.

"McCone, we better do something about this sorry state of affairs."

I nodded and walked into his outstretched arms. "We better."

Still, we both hesitated. The silence spun out. I understood the fear inside him, because it was inside me, too.

I said, "I love you, Ripinsky."

At the same time, he said, "I love you, McCone."

Fax received at Touchstone, 11:32 P.M., August 25, 1995:

ZENITH RECORDS
INTEROFFICE MEMORANDUM

Date: August 25, 1995
To: All concerned
From: Wil Willis, Marketing & Sales

"Empty Place" tops the singles charts for third straight
  week.
"Midnight Train" holding at #2 for second week.
Midnight Train album at #1/Hot Shot Debut.

LET'S *PARTY,* FOLKS!!!

Shar and Hy:
    Did I ever tell you you're
    #1 on <u>my</u> personal charts?
        Love,
        Ricky